Stories
from the
Transatlantic
Review

Stories
from the
Transatlantic
Review

edited by
Joseph F. McCrindle

LONDON
VICTOR GOLLANCZ LTD
1970

ISBN 0 575 00554 8

Printed in Great Britain by
Lowe & Brydone (Printers) Ltd., London

Grateful acknowledgment is made to the authors of all the selections included in this volume and to the following agents and publishers:

Joseph McCrindle for permission to reprint: "A Different Thing" by Walter Clemons copyright © 1959; "The Ice Cream Eat" by William Goldman copyright © 1959; "A Game of Catch" by George Garrett copyright © 1960; "Johnny Dio and the Sugar Plum Burglars" by Harry D. Miller copyright © 1960; "The Fair of San Gennaro" by John McPhee copyright © 1961; "The Enemy" by Bruce J. Friedman copyright © 1963; "Girl in a White Dress" by Edward Franklin copyright © 1964; "Changed" by Norma Meacock copyright © 1964; "Acme Rooms and Sweet Marjorie Russell" by Hugh Allyn Hunt copyright © 1966; "Black Barbecue" by Daniel Spicehandler copyright © 1966; "My Sister and Me" by Asa Baber, Jr. copyright © 1967; "Before the Operation" by Paul Breslow copyright © 1967; "The Road" by Alan Sillitoe copyright © 1968; "Home Is" by Morris Lurie copyright © 1968; "Music to Lay Eggs By" by Thomas Bridges copyright © 1968; "Summer Voices" by John Banville copyright © 1968.

John Cushman Associates, Inc. for: "The Adult Education Class" by Malcolm Bradbury copyright © 1966 by Malcolm Bradbury.

Farrar, Straus & Giroux, Inc. for: "Making Changes" by Leonard Michaels from *Going Places* by Leonard Michaels copyright © 1969 by Leonard Michaels and "The Zodiacs" by Jay Neugeboren from *Corky's Brother* by Jay Neugeboren copyright © 1969 by Jay Neugeboren.

Harper & Row, Publishers for: "The Siege" by Sol Yurick from *Someone Just Like You* copyright © 1963 by Sol Yurick and "Sing, Shaindele, Sing" by Jerome Charyn from *The Man Who Grew Younger* by Jerome Charyn copyright © 1966 by Jerome Charyn.

Holt, Rinehart and Winston, Inc. for: "The Hyena" by Paul Bowles from *The Time of Friendship* by Paul Bowles copyright © 1962 by Paul Bowles.

John Johnson for: "A Meeting in Middle Age" by William Trevor copyright © 1964 by Joseph McCrindle and "The Collector" by Austin C. Clarke copyright © 1967 by Joseph McCrindle.

Alfred A. Knopf, Inc. for: "During the Jurassic" by John Updike copyright © 1966 by John Updike.

Harold Matson Company, Inc. for "The Educated Girl" by V. S. Pritchett copyright © 1960 by V. S. Pritchett.

Virginia Moriconi for: "Simple Arithmetic" copyright © 1964 by Virginia Moriconi.

Joyce Carol Oates for: "Dying" copyright © 1966 by Joyce Carol Oates.

Random House, Inc. for: "Ismael" by Alfred Chester from *Behold Goliath* by Alfred Chester copyright © 1961 by Alfred Chester and "The World's Fastest Human" by Irvin Faust from *Roar, Lion, Roar* by Irvin Faust copyright © 1964 by Irvin Faust.

Random House, Inc. and Secker & Warburg for: "The Redhead" by Penelope Gilliatt from *Come Back If It Doesn't Get Better* (English edition, *What's It Like Out?*) by Penelope Gilliatt copyright © 1965 by Penelope Gilliatt.

"At Home with the Colonel" is reprinted with the permission of Charles Scribner's Sons and Harold Matson Company, Inc. from *The Admiral and the Nuns* by Frank Tuohy, copyright © 1962 by Frank Tuohy.

The Sterling Lord Agency for: "The Star Blanket" by Shirley Schoonover copyright © 1961 by Joseph McCrindle.

Jean-Claude van Itallie for "François Yattend" copyright © 1961 by Jean-Claude van Itallie.

Contents

Introduction

In the first issue of the original *Transatlantic Review,* whose very apt name we borrowed, T. S. Eliot wrote: "Good literature is produced by a few queer people in odd corners; the use of a review is not to force talent, but to create a favorable atmosphere. And you will serve this purpose if you publish, as I hope you will find and publish, work of writers of whatever age who are too good and too independent to have found other publishers." This, almost fifty years later, is what we are trying to do.

The first issue of our *Transatlantic Review* was printed in the summer of 1959 in an edition of only 500 copies by an amateur printer near Rome. The contents consisted largely of work which I, then a literary agent in New York, had been unable to sell. George Garrett, who was at the time at the American Academy in Rome, provided the remainder and saw to the printing. The second issue appeared in Rome in a larger edition a few months later. Subsequently we changed to a printer in London, a printer in Holland, and finally to the Lavenham Press in Suffolk. In the process we came to realize that finding good short stories and poetry was less time-consuming and probably less difficult than our problems with printers, distribution, advertising, and misplaced manuscripts. These are worries that have continued and which we share with all other literary magazines, particularly those not sheltered by universities or foundations.

We have tried to strike a balance between new and often unpublished writers and those already well known, and between American and British writers, with occasional contributions from Europe and South America and from India and the African nations.

There are many stories we should have wished to add to this volume were there space to do so. We believe, however, that this is a collection which shows the range of stories we have published and, hopefully, the quality of writing we have tried to encourage in our first ten years.

J. F. McCrindle

A*

Stories
from the
Transatlantic
Review

Thomas Bridges

Music to Lay Eggs By

Thick pine sap bubbled on bark from the heat. Saplings were dead. Only the tall pines—hundreds of years old, whose roots searched a hundred feet below the ground for water, remained, but the woods were still thick with heavy trunks till maybe fifty miles away the underbrush started again and there was water. There was water far into these fifty miles—almost a circle—swamp water, and there were cypress trees dying as the water receded. Gar and catfish dying in puddles. Alligators and other walking and crawling things following the water deeper into the woods, with the mud sucking up those that followed too quickly. There was a road that wound through the pine, and along it the earth was red and hard, and a wind blew, along the road edge, red dust that choked snakes and toads looking for moisture. The colors of decay blended yellow with gray and red like a dream color wheel spun by the wind.

A town ended the road with a dirt street and dry houses cracked with poverty. No one was on the street or broken boardwalks by stores. The stores—empty and windowless, some boards crisscrossed over the windows and empty store fixtures inside. Above a few of the stores, there were windows, and clotheslines stretched across an alleyway from the window above one store to the window above another. The street ended at the end of the last store. A cleared field of dead grass that turned to the right of the last store, still turning to the old auction stand. A crowd of people were assembled, fidgeting in groups on the field. The crowd had started to gather in lines like a procession with rag festive garments when they heard about the stranger.

It was Bobby Lee who had first seen the stranger. He had been looking out of the window above the old drugstore, Bess Ann with him, who had run downstairs and out the back door, so she wouldn't be caught with Bobby Lee after he had seen the car making the last turn before it came into town. He had shouted and Bess Ann had run downstairs. People had heard his shout, and when he had claimed his right, it was given to him. Sam's boy, Harold, had seen the stranger too, but it was Bobby Lee who was first, the people agreed. A few of the old people spoke out that it was good that there were only two of them claiming the right. When there were more, the ones that remembered said, there was too much arguing and confusion, and when it was finally decided and done with, there was only more trouble later on. So it was better that there were only two, Fred Conley had repeated.

The crowd had formed patterns on the field in front of the auction stand. Thin people with long hair were prominent. Tongues chattered quietly, and cracked lips split more with the soft chant of giggles and sneers were held firm on burnt faces. A car was parked by the crowd, with a thin film of red dust on it, and curious children found the metal too hot to touch. On its side was black lettering:

MUSIC TO LAY EGGS BY, SOUND EFFECTS CORP., BEAUMONT, TEXAS

Bobby Lee walked around through the crowd, looking for Peter Hinges. He had been told that Hinges would arrange things as he had been the last to have the right. He would tell Bobby Lee what had to be done. Bobby Lee could still remember, though barely, that there had been preparations or something, but he had been just six when his father led him out to the auction stand. He could remember that the stranger had been a man and that his father had put him high on his shoulders so that he could see. And he could remember Peter Hinges being a hero from then on. Bobby Lee stopped to light a cigarette. He was tall and thin like the others. His hair curled around his ears and over his shirt collar. But he stood out today. He could hear his name in the crowd as he passed by people. This was the best day that he could remember. And he'd be remembered like Gowry, and Waters and Wyatt and the others dating back to the start of the town and even before when the original thirty came out of the mountains and settled in the thicket. Peter Hinges would be a legend, and now he was going to tell Bobby Lee what to do, exactly; then there would be just two of them who knew how. And maybe soon, Peter Hinges was getting old, he'd be the only one. The only one, Bobby Lee thought to himself.

Back around the last store, about half way down the row of stores and across from them, near a clump of cyprus trees was Peter Hinges' house. Peter had heard about Bobby Lee having the right from Fred Conley who had come around to tell him. He had said to Conley "Is that so?" and had closed the door in his face. Peter lay on his couch stretched out. He repeated to himself . . . So finally it happened and by the son of Jesse Lee. It was disgusting to him. The son of Jesse Lee and a young boy. It had been forty years ago when Jesse Lee had fixed a shoe on Hinges' horse, and the shoe had come loose. The horse fell and threw Peter against a tree. His left leg had been sore ever since, not enough so that he had to limp or that other people noticed, but enough so that Peter remembered and despised Jesse Lee because of it. Jesse Lee was dead now. And so there was Bobby Lee; a young boy to have the right. Peter was old and had been for years. He thought of his youth constantly and with pain. There was nothing colorful or exciting, nothing really to remember, but he did, and when he saw young men and young boys around town, he despised them for the years to pass while he would lie dead on the ground and not know. Yes, he would be a legend, but so would this Bobby Lee—Jesse Lee's son. He squeezed his pipe so hard that he broke the stem, and he slammed his hand on the table, and the pain of the blow added to his hatred of Bobby Lee. Now he must tell this boy the rules—the secrets which for years had been his. He remembered how quickly after Jerry Lyons had told him the secrets that Jerry had died. He thought . . . Now will I die too? He felt terrible. "My God, I'll not die!" he yelled out from the couch.

Almost everybody was turned to the auction stand head high to the crowd. A heavy man, clean, in his thirties, with a red shirt and a tweed sport coat that hung long over his gabardine trousers, carried a briefcase and what looked like radio equipment up to the stand and put the briefcase and the equipment down in front of the faces of the crowd. He looked up from the equipment and at the crowd and told the people that it would take just a couple of minutes to get things ready. He noticed some children playing with some of the equipment he had left near the crowd.

"Hey kids!" he yelled. "Get away . . . Could some of the parents watch that the children don't touch my equipment over there?" He pointed. "It's very sensitive equipment."

Some adults warned the children to get away from the man's things, and the children sat down on the ground and squashed bugs with pebbles to pass the time. The man maneuvered his equipment around, watching the crowd, trying to size them up . . . Damndest bunch of people I've seen yet, he thought. He watched one old woman who hadn't blinked her eyes all the while he had been watching her. Her face carried the same smile as the others. What are they all smiling about? he wondered. Maybe they're just interested? I really didn't expect a turnout like this. The whole town must be here. He bent down and arranged some of his equipment. While the people stared at him—his back to the backs of the broken buildings.

Sun-scarred buildings—paintless, board after board still in place, fashioned into squares then into houses long before anyone still living could remember, except from word of mouth. There was no written history—but there was a history starting with the original thirty who came out of the Ozarks and before that the east coast and before that England, but there weren't thirty then, just a family. But there were thirty who left the mountains and wandered through Louisiana, settling and leaving for thirty years —thirty years and thirty people, by then more than that, who crossed into Texas and the thicket. They cleared land—the thick pine and brush between the swamp, and they set logs into squares to be houses—ax cuts in corners to fit the logs. And the houses were half built and the fields half plowed when the stranger came. It was hot, and there had been a rain, and mosquitoes were thick, and the stranger came from nowhere in the thicket and the men in the fields noticed him and called to other men who brought guns. They watched the stranger as he walked along the ridge of the hill, and then stopped, as if just noticing the men in the valley below him. He turned and ran. He was out of the range of any of the guns so none of the men fired. That night the men waited for the attack and talked in circles around the campfire of sweet pine and crackling sap—the older men passing on to the younger men the truths of their clan. In the morning the thicket burst with men—the attack. Blood and bodies and ten of the originals left. The rest were dead along with all of the enemy. Six—the men left to find the camp of the enemy. Four—the women remained to bury the dead and feed the animals. That night the men returned. They had found the other village and killed the women and children as was their rule. It was a matter of revenge—if any kin of the enemy were left, they would hunt down the sons and grandsons of the originals—their throats cut while drinking at a stream, or their heads crushed by a rock while walking under a tree. It had to be done. The other side would have done the same. It had been so in the mountains these men knew. And the history continues when the ritual began twenty years later—seven times since then till now —during the month of July if a stranger comes near the town.

And the stranger scanned the buildings, and through two alleyways he could see houses with clotheslines, in front, so cluttered that only the upper windows and roofs of houses were visible. He could see cyprus and hanging Spanish moss that led into the swamp. Everything is so dry and dirty looking, he thought. I would come into a place like this—damn radiator overheats, the dirt road and the broken road sign and I say . . . "Is this small enough Boss?" The bastard, putting me on the road . . . "Try the small towns, the small towns," he says, because I couldn't swing the Port Arthur deal. Well here I am. And I better make a deal here. Hell, I can swing it. Damn sure better. Look how interested these people are in me. I'm a special event in a place like this. These people are just the kind who hoard their money, just waiting to spend it. I wonder where the animals are kept? He looked around—far up near a turn of cyprus cutting away from the swamp, up on a hill there were some barns and chicken coops. Cattle are probably grazing along the swamp edge. There's nothing green around here. Damn dry. The chickens are probably out of the heat. I bet they got a bunch of them. Beef is too expensive. They'd be chicken and pork eaters. Well, it's the chickens that I'm interested in. He was setting the dials on the machine. He told the people in just a minute now. If I can swing a couple of deals in towns like these, he thought, then they'd send me to Houston or Dallas. More money then, and Ann would stop bitching about how the kid got no clothes to wear to school. God, is it hot here. Funny there's no dogs around. No cats neither. In this heat though, they probably crawled under one of the buildings. There . . . that's the last dial. Now I better get started.

Bobby Lee was off looking for Peter Hinges. Most of the crowd turned to face the man on the stand. Fred Conley leaned his good ear forward when he heard the man start to talk.

"Well folks, I'm ready now. As some of you must have noticed on my car, I represent the Sound Effects Corporation. We've made radios, TV's, and various kinds of electrical equipment for the past twenty years. Just recently, our scientists have developed a means of tripling the egg output of hens. Triple, I say. And without squeezing the eggs out of the hens . . ."

There was general laughter in the crowd. Bobby Lee crossed the short acre of land till he was to a point where he could see Peter Hinges' house. Bobby Lee was too far away to hear the man on the stand, or care, until later when it came his turn to act. And he knew it would be when he got through talking with Peter Hinges whom he could see on the porch.

Peter Hinges sat on the porch of his house, just minutes before getting off the couch and coming outside. His house was a two-story wood frame building with a flat roof. A large square with a secondary roof jutting out just below the upper windows—this roof to cover the porch. This house was given to him, built for him, started the day after, twenty years ago when he received the right and led the ritual till it was over. Until then he had lived in his old lean-to cabin close to the swamp, and it was by his luck only that he happened to be chasing a stray hog near the road and saw the car, through the trees, way up the road. He could remember that the stranger had lost his way and was looking for directions—a thin man and young, Peter seemed to remember, but it was all too vague now. And it was Jerry Lyons who had taught Peter the rules. Jerry Lyons who was now dead—dead it seemed only weeks after he had told Peter the rules—there was that old saying, Peter remembered, *that when a man had passed on to another what was once his then he might as well die, because it was the owning that made the man in the first place.* And now I must pass on to that boy what I know, he thought. Must I now die? The feeling that he had on the couch came back to him. He looked around at the swamp, at the decay and the gray of it all—it was what he knew. He used to listen to the noises coming from the swamp when there were more of them—that eating that, and being eaten in return. He had heard of some fish in the swamp that when the young are born until they are nearly full grown, the mother fish swims near them to protect them from being eaten by the older fish—cannibal kinds, he thought. What the older fish are really trying to do is protect themselves. The young will do it every time. He watched Bobby Lee coming up the path. That's what he's after, me, really; when he's got what he's come for, I won't be much good to anybody, because they'll be two of us that will know the rules. And people will come to him because he's younger and more spoken out. A boy as young as this one knowing the rules. Damn! Peter could remember each rule as they had come through Jerry Lyons' cracked front teeth—each rule numbered in Peter's mind, one through seven—the commandments—but with no tablet or mountain, just a man on a porch. Peter drew on his pipe and watched Bobby Lee approaching. That the boy was so young seemed to bother Peter most. He had been almost fifty when he gained the right. Fifty years—and only then to be able to walk proud and to really be somebody in the eyes of his people. He never married, or really had a woman. He was a homely man, but he often felt that if he had gained the right when he was younger it might have made a difference. And this boy, he had seen him sneaking into the stores with a girl . . . one time at night, he had awakened and had seen the girl undress by a half-moon's light that shone in the room where she was with Bobby Lee. Bobby Lee had touched her hair, and they both had crouched down below the window. Peter Hinges had stared into the open window for almost an hour, then the girl got up and put on her clothes. There had been the sound of Bobby Lee's bottle as he threw it across the street in the direction of Peter's house. Peter thought that they had seen him and pulled back from the window; then he went to sleep. He thought of that night as he watched Bobby Lee coming closer to the house. He noticed his good looks and it irritated him. He watched from the porch as Bobby Lee crossed in front of the house—the porch shading Peter. His white hair and his heavy belly lobbed over his belt buckle. Peter thought to himself . . . I'll have to tell the boy the rules, but I'll not let him get the best of me, I swear. That he'll not do . . . Even if . . . He squeezed the arm of the rocker.

"Mr. Hinges," Bobby spoke, "I'm Bobby Lee. I guess you know why I'm here? At least I reckon you do." Bobby wiped the dirt and sweat from his forehead with his fingers.

Peter listened, irritated at first by the directness of the boy, then at the boy's unsureness. "People say you got the right, boy? Is that so?"

"Yes sir."

"How old are you, boy? Do you think . . . Come up here on the porch."

"Yes sir, well I'm twenty-one, if you want to know."

"I said come up here. I'll say what I have to tell you just once, and you listen. Hear me?"

Bobby Lee stepped up on the porch. From the porch, part of the crowd was visible through an alleyway. Bobby Lee listened to Peter Hinges.

On the auction stand, the stranger wiped his forehead. He was about halfway through his talk. The sky was still blue, but the air around the field had a thin trace of red dust on it. It made the tanned people appear to have mahogany-stained complexions. The sun was one burst in the sky. It burned deep into the people, always a glare, always the heat for nine months of the year. The animals would move from one side to the other of the house as the sun seemed to pass overhead. And the people, digging at the land of their fathers till the last man or woman dropped and dissolved with the red dust to be blown by the wind and baked by the sun. Cotton still grew and a few crops watered by water carried in pails from the swamp. But babies died before birth and young children coughed so heavy at night that their faces were twisted when they were still in the morning. But the people stayed and died—more dead than born, and there were empty houses fading under the sun.

Out in the crowd the people were feeling the full heat of the sun. They were perspiring heavily and anxious for Bobby Lee to come along so things could begin. They watched the man on the stand and whispered out of the corners of their mouths. Mary Linn Rice fanned herself and Mrs. Ellie Lyons, the daughter of Jerry Lyons.

"Mary Linn," Mrs. Lyons said, "that man does a strong bunch of talking. Like the preacher used to. Rest his soul. Wore his brains out talking. Wasn't that how it happened?"

"Can't say that I remember, ma'am."

"No, you wouldn't Mary Linn, that was a mite before your time." She caught a bug walking across her arm and squeezed it between her fingers. "The years pass by so. Getting old. If Mrs. Lewis hadn't come to tell me someone had come into town, I would have napped right through it and probably be dead by the next time."

"Now that's no such thing to be talking about. Another one might pass by before . . ."

"Before I die. No, girl. This will be the last one for me, and I'm going to get right up close. Coming, Mary Linn?"

Mary Linn held her arm and helped her to the front of the crowd. The man on the auction stand was waving his hands in the air.

"Now the whole setup comes cheap, and its got a service guarantee. I want you to hear some of the music." He leaned over and turned a switch on the machine. The "Moonlight Sonata" blared from the two speakers on each side of the auction stand.

"You think that man up there makes much money talking about things without people buying anything?" It was Mr. Timmons turning his head around to speak to Billy Harris just behind him.

"I don't know, but I reckon he's got more than we do."

"That seems likely, Billy, as we got nothing at all," Timmons chuckled.

"Say, you hear from your papa at all?"

"Nah, but he's still in Colorado looking for work."

"Well, I hope he gets lucky," Timmons said and turned back around facing the stand.

"Thank you, Mr. Timmons," Billy said and lifted his eyes back to the stand.

Bobby Lee was just through talking with Peter Hinges. He walked across the field in front of Hinges' house and stopped when he got to the first cyprus tree. He lit a cigarette and looked up at the sun through a heavy batch of Spanish moss. The sun sort of sparkled as it passed through the moss. Hot as hell, he thought.. He remembered what Hinges had told him—the first three rules. The rest he would be told when Hinges came down to the field. He was to ask the man what tribe he was from, then quickly, were there others waiting with guns, then what hour was the attack to be—this was the meaning. But Bobby Lee would speak in the tongue of the ritual—the old tongue from the beginning—what was spoken by the people before the original thirty—by the family of the myth—not English, not a spoken tongue but the same tongue that comes up in church with the speaking in different tongues. Only this was one not several and none like Bobby Lee had heard in church when there was a church and the family used to go out on some Sundays to go to services.

He thought of the words but then remembered they were not to be spoken or thought about until later. And he would repeat them only after

Peter Hinges had said them first. Bobby took the last drag off his cigarette and put it out on the cypress trunk. He thought he would go find Bess Ann in the crowd. Now, he wouldn't have to hide with her any more. He cut through one of the alleyways to get to the field. He could smell chicken being boiled in one of the houses, and there was a rank smell from another house. Swamp water being boiled for drinking, he thought. Bobby Lee saw Bess Ann with her father—the old man who had dragged Bobby in the street when he caught Bess Ann with him one night near the old livery. But the old man had smiles for him now, he noticed. Having the right, Bobby thought. Having the right can change everything. The old man shook his hand and said, "Come around the house and court Bess Ann proper. I got mad at times, but I always liked you Bobby."

Bess Ann gave Bobby a good look. I'll see her above the drugstore tonight, he thought. He winked at Bess Ann, and told the old man that he had to go, but he'd come around proper like to court Bess Ann. "Do that boy," the old man said. Bobby walked on back to the edge of the field. He chose a place to stand where he could see Peter Hinges when he left the house. The man on the auction stand was still selling. Bobby listened to the man for the first time.

'"Spare parts can be ordered by mail, or you can come down to the factory in Beaumont and pick them up . . ."

Bobby Lee looked up at the sun—it was set just a little off straight up. He figured it was about one or near that. Over to his right, he could see Fred Conley talking to little Sammy Greer. Their voices drifted over toward Bobby when he concentrated on hearing them.

"I'm so nervous and excited," Sammy said, picking a scab off his knee.

"You're like your father, boy. Always moving, fidgeting. You never did know him, did you boy? Fell off that oil rig when you were still crawling, I think."

"Yes sir, but mama got a picture of him at home that I can remember by, when she tells me things about him."

"Well boy, I think it's going to be happening soon. See—that's Bobby Lee over there; he's going to lead this thing. Now stay still boy; it's the heat, I know, but you ought to stay still and listen and watch, so you can remember. It happens quick, boy, like the Lord wills it in church, speaking in different tongues. Now you keep your eye on Bobby Lee so you'll know when things are going to start."

Bobby Lee turned his head back to the man on the auction stand. The man's gabardine trousers were shining from the sun. His voice seemed slow and dry. I guess he needs a pint of water, Bobby thought.

"What I've told you, folks, is what we call our 'first-come-first-serve' bonus catch. What I do is set up all the equipment and make out the payment allowances. We can talk about the liberal terms for your benefit. Sound Effects Corporation serves you. And I represent those who want to . . ."

Bobby Lee watched the man and his mouth moving, but his mind passed over the sound. He watched the man's mouth move, head move, arms move—Just a man, Bobby thought. Never spoke to him, never touched him, or even walked near him—Well it's not a matter of choice. It might have been anybody—except it's him—Still it's not my fault. He looked around at the crowd, paying back respects of people as they passed him by. He was feeling good. It's my day, he thought. He pulled his shoulders back and reached in his pocket for a cigarette. It's my day, he repeated. Feeling a little loose in the stomach but otherwise pretty good. Man, that sun would roast a man. Hinges ought to be coming along soon, though. He looked back up at Hinges' house.

Peter Hinges was sitting on the couch inside his house. He put two cartridges in one gun, then laid it down on the floor. He picked up the other one and loaded it. He ain't going to miss though, he thought. But I'll carry the spare in case. Smart alleck—I bet that boy will be after it's all over with. Bad enough now—like his father used to be. Rotten bastard hurt my leg—ain't been the same since. Damn boy's after me too. Oh, in a different way, but still the same. Have the right, he says. He ain't got the right to nothing—nothing. Peter Hinges fingered a long mole on his face, and then scratched the rough whiskers under his chin. It ain't right for a boy his age to have the right—the same importance as me. Boy'll abuse it. Young do that. Him and that girl will be parading all over the place with "how do you do's." Bastard got no right. It just ain't fair. He crushed the empty cartridge box in his hand—a paper cut split his finger at a joint, but he didn't feel it. He grabbed the two guns and kicked open the front door and went outside heading for the auction stand.

A barn swallow swooped down at the ground, gliding a few feet above the ground, then soaring up again. The bird faced the sun and then swooped down again at the ground. A slight wind began to pick up a little momentum and little dust spirals spun across the ground. Bobby Lee turned in his place in the crowd and saw Peter Hinges walking across the road. Bobby Lee's stomach felt a little dizzy with excitement. Damn, he's coming, he thought. The man on the auction stand was clapping his hands together and asking if anybody had any questions. Bobby looked at the man for a second in a quiet way, then shrugged off any thoughts and waited for Peter Hinges. Peter cut through the same alleyway as Bobby had, and walked straight over to him. He stopped in front of Bobby and stared at the boy. The excitement that he saw in Bobby irritated Peter. "Here," he said, and handed him one of the guns. Then he walked on with Bobby Lee following him.

The same swallow swooped down again but now near the crowd, about ten feet over their heads, gliding, then soaring up again. People heard its shrill cry and looked up, trying to shade their eyes from the sun with their hands. The man on the stand looked up at the bird, following its movements, not noticing the two men who were approaching the stand with guns. Peter Hinges pushed the crowd away, and they left room in front of the stand for the two men. There was a rise of voices and pushing as the people realized it was Bobby Lee and Peter Hinges. The man on the stand looked back at the crowd, seemingly over the heads of the two men. Peter Hinges whispered to Bobby Lee.

"You remember the first three rules now, so repeat after me and then you're on your own. And remember the things you must do—the last four rules that I told you walking over here. I'll be to the right side of the stand and ready in case you miss. Are you ready? Wait, the man's going to say something. Wait until he's finished."

"Now folks, surely someone is interested. Just speak up."

The crowd was tense and excited. A voice broke out above the crowd.

"Hey, watch that. Look at that kid eating those bugs. Where's his mother and father?"

"Shush!" someone yelled.

There was a flair of laughter. The man on the stand smiled. Peter Hinges turned to Bobby Lee. "Now."

Bobby felt a quick chill and waited. Peter Hinges looked around, and then turned back to the stand. He straightened himself and called out the words loudly. The crowd chanted. Peter's voice rose above the slow rising wail of the crowd—there was a rhythm to the words snapping in between the breaths of the crowd, nasal tones—the twang of an old instrument. Then it was all repeated by Bobby Lee, in a younger and richer tone— and it was three times over while the crowd chanted.

"What's that? What?" The man on the stand seemed to strain to hear what was being said. "You men will have to speak up. I'm sorry, but I don't understand you." He looked around at the crowd, staring, bewildered at the chant, at all the faces with a new wild look about them—their silent grins growing broader, and their whispers a thin noise growing louder. The man was frightened, not understanding this change in the crowd. He was slow in moving, slowly edging back.

Peter Hinges walked away from Bobby Lee, cutting through the crowd as people parted to let him through. He felt lost. It would be just a minute from now when it would be over. The people would crowd Bobby Lee, and he, Peter, would stand alone listening.

Bobby Lee stood facing the man on the stand. And he proceeded with the last four rules, a little slow and nervous. While the man on the stand had stopped moving—his eyes fixed on the boy beneath him. The circle must be drawn—the campsite, Bobby Lee thought. He got on his knees and with his finger drew the circle. The trees—he scratched in the trees in the middle of the circle. The people—he marked off three rows of ten people with short lines in the circle. The stranger—he made one mark at the top of the circle. Then he rose from the ground with sure movements and aimed the gun at the stranger. The man on the stand pulled back. A strong wail rose from the crowd. The man yelled "Wait!" just as Bobby Lee fired. The gun thrust Bobby Lee's shoulder back, and the blast hit the man on the stand chest high and spun him off the stand. There was another loud wail from the crowd. Bobby Lee pulled the gun stock back off his shoulder, and stood the gun on the ground. He was still and quiet, then a strong sense of pride burst in him—a smile broke on his face. It's done. I've done it. A great smile broke on his face. People were crowding him.

"Congratulations boy."

"Fine. Fine."

"Well done."

"Thank you. Thank you."

"Boy, we're proud of you. Come over the house anytime."

He recognized the voice of Bess Ann's father. He looked over and could see the prize—a proud Bess Ann smiling at him.

Peter Hinges watched the excitement from the right side of the auction stand. Mr. Timmons had told a few of the men to get rid of the body and car.

"Get that equipment out of here too."

"What was his name? It seems only fitting . . ."

"Come on, come on. How would I know?"

Peter dug the heel of his shoe in the ground. He could hear separate voices at times above the crowd. It was Bobby Lee, and Bobby Lee, and Bobby Lee. What will I do now? What will I do now, he thought. He could see Bobby Lee squeezing through the crowd. Bastard. His old teeth ground together, and he felt the crack as one of his front teeth cracked. The pain caught him off guard. It passed away, but there was a sharp throbbing. Peter held the gun in his hands, reluctant to let loose of it. The sharp pain hit him again. Damn him!

Some of the people had started to return to their houses. They kicked up dust and sand, and children ran around chasing each other. Fred Conley looked around at the crowd as it broke up slowly. He shaded his eyes as he looked up at the sun. He heard the gun blast as it roared from behind him. He immediately turned around and pressed his hand to his mouth, holding back his breath. Slowly he removed his hand from his mouth. "Good God," he whispered. Others that had left were now running back. Some of them were racing to see who would get there first. Bess Ann's father held her from going any closer. She was screaming and struggling. He could feel her tears penetrate his thin shirt. Mrs. Ellie Lyons had turned around quickly when she heard the shot. She held Mary Linn's hand and was struggling through the crowd. "Come on girl—push. There's more to this thing than I thought there would be." She had a broad smile. "Lord yes, there's more to this. And to think if Mrs. Lewis hadn't got me up . . ."

Morris Lurie

Home Is

He lived in New York and in London and on the isle of Rhodes, and in Paris there was always a room for him at Peter Stein's place with a view of gray slate roofs and the Seine, and in Prague Bob Turner who taught English at the University liked to have him but he sometimes chose a hotel (Bob's children were nice, but he didn't like having to tiptoe around when they were asleep), and in Beirut and in Istanbul and in West Berlin and in Rome he always stayed in hotels, though he had friends, good friends, in all these places, and he had friends in Athens too but he preferred the Grand Bretagne, and now, as the plane he was in touched down on Rhodes, he closed the book he was reading (poems; *For the Union Dead*) and sat back and waited for the plane to stop. He closed his eyes. And when he felt no movement he opened them and unlocked his seat belt and reached up for his hat and then made his way along the aisle and down the steps and smiled at the hostess and then he looked up and for a second he was completely lost. It was no place Max Gottlieb had ever been in his life before.

And then it was Rhodes.

It lasted a second, no more, but it was immense, gigantic, and it took all the strength out of his legs and he almost collapsed. One second. For one second he hadn't recognized Rhodes, this airport, hills, trees, where he had been so often, so many years. It was like walking through the door into your bathroom and finding yourself in Africa. Or on the surface of the moon.

Christ, I'm going crazy, he thought.

He shook his head and whistled phew and blinked in the sun. It was gone, but for a few seconds more his legs felt funny as he walked across the tarmac to customs.

Someone was waving. At me? he thought. Who—? *Sylvia*. Of course. And Larry. He'd cabled them from Athens that he was coming. I really *am* going nuts, he thought.

"Hi!" he called, and waved back.

He showed his passport and went through the gate and they came up to him and Sylvia gave him a hug and a kiss on both cheeks and Larry slapped him on the back.

"Max. Welcome home. Max, you're looking marvelous. Good trip?"

Sylvia so exuberant, Larry his smiling self.

"Oh, beautiful, beautiful," Max said. "Sylvia, you're four times as brown as when I left. *Five* times. What have you been *doing,* treading grapes in the sun or something? Larry, how's the painting?"

"Oh, so-so, you know. Just dabbling."

"I *bet*. And winning prizes and getting commissions and making thousands every day. Oh, here come my bags. I'll just get this thing stamped and we can get out of here. *Air*ports, my God."

"The car's right out front," Sylvia said. "Larry, don't just *stand* there. Help Max with his bags, that's what you're here for."

"That's the style," Max laughed. "Earn yourself a handsome tip. Hey, careful with that bag. It's full of Greek cakes and nylon shirts."

"Oh Max, you're gorgeous," Sylvia said.

"The pearl of the Adriatic," Max said.

They squeezed into the front of the Farrells' Citroen—one of those small ones with bug eyes and a canvas roof—with the luggage bouncing in the back. Larry drove and Sylvia sat in the middle and Max lit a cigarette and oh these hills and trees he loved so much, good-by New York forever, who needs it?—they swerved around a peasant girl on a donkey, Larry blasting the horn and the girl sitting sidesaddle and her legs pumping up and down as the donkey trotted along—and again, for a second, the strangest feeling came over him. Where am I? What am I doing here? But he had no time to think because Sylvia, as usual, was talking nonstop.

"How was London? Brilliant? We've been reading all about it in the papers. The *theatre,* my *God*. The things we're missing. Did you see *every*thing? That new thing, what's the name of it?—Larry, what's that absolutely brilliant play the papers have been full of? Oh, he doesn't remember a thing. Old age. Max, you were in *Berlin* too, oh you lucky thing. Did you go into East? How was it? Opera? My *God,* they're foul beasts but they do have the most fantastic opera. Max, hey, you're not listening to a *thing* I'm saying."

"Oh what? Sorry," Max said. "All this flying."

No, he hadn't heard a word. He had been looking at his face reflected in the windscreen. Thirty-five, and still so boyish. Dark, sad eyes and that intense look. But not quite as intense as it had been ten years ago. A little rounder, a little softer. A different intensity. The poet was gone. And in his place?

"Max, I want to hear absolutely everything. Before you tell *any*one else."

"What? Oh." Wake up, wake up, he told himself, what's wrong with you. And he did, all at once, he became his old self, Max the raconteur, charming and casual, full of fun. "Well, before I forget," he began, "Ziggy sends you his love and—"

"*Ziggy*. How nice."

"—*All* the plays in London are awful, completely awful, you have no idea, and—"

The poet had become a gossip. This was Max Gottlieb, aged thirty-five.

And inch by inch, one inch at a time, carefully, he opened the glittering bag of talk and news he had brought with him from the theatres and parties of Europe, trinkets and pearls and tantalizing first inches of multi-colored ribbon—carefully, it had to last for two months. There was love from him, regards from her, stories and jokes and first views of new places and new people, while the bays of the isle of Rhodes opened up before them, the purest sand, the sea that unbelievable blue, and on the slopes of the hills the olive trees so gnarled and centuries old on their pockets of land so small amongst the rocks and the houses so simply white.

"Oh, I must tell you about a party Freddy gave. Someone brought a horse and—Wow, look at that!"

They had taken the final turn and there was the acropolis and the white village of Lindos, which many say is the most beautiful in all Greece.

"Go on about the horse," Sylvia said. "What horse? *Hey.*"

"Sssh," Max whispered. "The view."

It affected him like this every time he saw it, every time he came back. Five years now, going on six. 1961. The year his father died (and the poet too, but he didn't know that then). Max the millionaire on his first world trip.

There were four of them, Roger and Viv and that girl with the red hair—What was her name? Lester? No . . . —and Max, and they were doing the Greek islands, really doing them, Hydra and Mykonos, Patmos and Samos, Santorini, Crete, and from Crete they flew to Rhodes because Roger said there was a famous acropolis there, shouldn't be missed, and as soon as Max saw it, and under it that nestling village like a handful of sugar cubes in the sun—drunk admittedly, the four of them in the back of a cab, Roger and the girl with the red hair on the jump seats and all of them laughing for no reason at all—he decided, I'm buying a house here, and he did. Lindos.

Houses were cheap then, not that it mattered, and he bought a small one overlooking the bay and for three months he had Greeks working nonstop knocking out walls and installing a bathroom and a kitchen and putting up bookshelves and building benches, while Max made a whirlwind trip through Europe and came back with chairs from Denmark, Spanish rugs, knick-knacks from Liberty's in London, German stereo, and a superb print of the defeat of Napoleon at Waterloo for the wall above the mantlepiece.

"This is home," he said, and he had almost decided to get rid of his apartment in New York and his mews flat in Chelsea (which he'd only had for six months) and staying forever in this Greek paradise when he woke up one morning with a great desire for green fields, country lanes, German beer, mountains and snow, and he flew to New York (it was summer there) and stayed for three months. Theatre, parties, old friends, new places.

And after that, to cool down, a month in Paris, which was just as hectic.

Then he came back, stayed two months, and left again. And he had been doing this ever since.

"Here we are," said Sylvia. "Larry, get the bags."

"Ah, isn't it wonderful," said Max.

It was different every time, and always the same. Donkeys, and black-clad women filling their waterjugs at the fountain and old brown men sitting in the sun and everyone talking and making a noise. The same, and so different. Tourist buses and hundreds of Swedes and souvenirs for sale everywhere you looked. There was none of that when he had first come. There were only the Farrells and a Dutch painter (Rembrandt, everyone called him, and my God, weren't his paintings awful!) and an old English lady with a houseful of cats—and now every second house had a painter in it or a writer or a millionaire or a beatnik, and there were two restaurants where before there had been none, and there was a pavilion on the beach and all the Greeks spoke English. Well the dozen words they needed to sell their wares. And Italian and Swedish and German and French. The international gibberish of the merchants of Europe.

"Max! Welcome back!"

Toby, who was from California, a painter with a small talent and the right connections and a taste for whiskey but a nice guy, slapped him on the back.

"How long are you staying this time?"

"Who knows, who knows?" Max said. "Maybe forever."

"It's the same old Max," Toby said. "Listen, come around, say, six? Have a drink."

"Sure," Max said. "Look, I must go up to the house. See if it's still there."

"See you," Toby said.

Max paid a woman to look after his house while he was away. She opened the windows and dusted and when he cabled that he was coming back (to the Farrells; they told Ilena) she washed the floors and made up the bed and picked fresh flowers for the vases and the bowls and bought food and filled up the refrigerator. She lived across the street from Max's house, and she was there in her doorway as they came along the street, Larry with both bags, Sylvia still talking, Max trying to listen and not hearing a word.

"Ilena!" he said, seeing her, and embraced her and kissed her on the cheek.

She was an old woman, and shy, and she had nothing to say but her eyes twinkled with delight. How long has she been standing in her doorway waiting for me, with the key in her hand? Max thought. Oh, she's marvelous. Ilena. Ah.

"Larry," he said, "give me that bag," and there, in the street, he opened his bag and took out a tablecloth of the finest lace and blushing for no reason that he knew, he gave it to Ilena and kissed her again.

"*Efharisto, efharisto*," Ilena said. Her face glowed like the sun, and to hide her embarrassment she made a great business of fitting the key in Max's door and then she stepped aside and they went in first and she quietly followed.

The house was exactly as he had left it, filled with sun and flowers, a bottle of wine and six glasses on a tray on the table on the terrace, the wine cold and the bottle beaded with water, and beside it plates of honey and jams and nuts, sweet things, the traditional greeting.

"Well, you're home," Sylvia said. "Again."

"And let me tell you," Max said, "it's great to be back. Home."

"Home is where your friends are," Sylvia said, smiling broadly. "Oh, before I forget, you're having dinner with us tonight, okay?"

"Well, yes," Max said. "But to tell you the truth . . ."

"Sylvia," Larry said. "Come on, let's go. I'm sure Max wants to relax by himself for a while."

"Oh, no no," Max said. "Please. Have a glass of wine. I'm not tired or anything. Hell, a seasoned traveler like me."

"No, Larry's right," Sylvia said. "You do look a bit drawn and quartered."

"*Sylvia*," Larry said.

"I know, I know," Sylvia said. "I'm going right home to read my Book of Etiquette. But dinner, Max, if you can. About eight?"

"Eight," Max said.

Alone, he sat down on the terrace and lit a cigarette but after two puffs he threw it away. He stood up. The sun was high in the sky and a white yacht was anchored in the very center of the bay and there was a blue flag flying from it. Max took off his jacket. Suddenly he felt very tired, a wave of tiredness he was completely unused to, and he closed his eyes and stood for a minute just like that, not thinking anything, just slightly rocking on the balls of his feet.

Hey, boy, what's wrong with you? he asked himself.

He left his jacket on the terrace and went through the lounge into the bedroom and sat down on the edge of the bed and, hardly able to keep his eyes open, he pulled off his shoes, then remembered his hat and took it off and let it drop onto the floor, and a minute later, in his clothes, he was asleep.

He slept for six hours and when he awoke it was night and quiet and he felt an enormous sense of peace, a peace so total, so complete—and then it was gone. He became aware of the wooden beams on the ceiling, the top corner of a wardrobe, the curtain by the sides of the window billowing in a breeze and for a second he panicked, and then he knew where he was. He switched on the lamp by his bed. He sat up. A rooster was crowing madly in the night. For a minute his head spun with a hundred things, not one of which he could put his finger on, and then he remembered that he was supposed to be eating with Sylvia and Larry tonight—and drinks with Toby at six!—but he knew it was too late even before he had looked at his watch. He lay back on his bed. He didn't feel particularly hungry. He'd see what Ilena had put in the fridge later on.

A moment of peace, a second of panic—it was like that every time he woke up, all that week, and the next, and the week after that. For a few seconds, before he was properly awake, he was somewhere else, in great peace, but where? London, New York, Peter Stein's in Paris, Prague? And of course it was so simple but it took him nearly a month before he pinned it down.

It became an obsession with him.

Each night when he went to bed, after a day of gossip, reading, sitting in the sun, drinking, talking, he thought about those seconds of peace he would feel when he woke up, and when those seconds came, each morning, oh so short, he tried to prolong them, to suspend himself in them, so he could examine them, but each morning they lasted just two seconds, three, never more. As soon as he became aware of that great peace, before he had even opened his eyes, it was gone, and in its place, blind panic. Then nothing.

In the fifth week it came to him, so simple, so obvious. For two seconds, every morning, he was in his father's house, twenty-five years ago, in his room at the end of the house that looked out on the garden and the fruit trees, New England sky, birds in the trees, the first birds of the day, and the house silent with his parents' sleeping. Home. That room he had known so well, photographed on his brain. The ceiling sloping, timber, sixteen planks, and twenty planks on one wall and fourteen on the other wall, and the yellow door. Now, he could still see the lamp, his books, his clothes on a chair, the view from his window, the tops of the trees, bare in winter and in summer green and full. And then his mother getting up and walking in her soft slippers down the hall to put on the coffee for breakfast. While his father still slept.

Home.

Then they went to New York and for a while they lived in Chicago, and then his father went to Rome for a year and they went with him, and they holidayed that year in Venice, in rooms filled with the smell of the sea. Old rooms, yellow plaster, ornate on the ceiling, chandeliers, tiled floors, marble, cold to walk on, cracked.

Then three apartments in New York, each time richer, larger, and then his father's heart attack, and his mother's small apartment, but he didn't move in with her. For various reasons. Beginning and ending with the feeling that she didn't want him to.

The next morning when he awoke, those seconds of being home, that peace, were not there. *Not there.* Nor were they the next morning, nor the morning after that, nor after that, and not for the next ten days, and on the fourteenth day Max awoke with a great and sudden urge to see a friend in Copenhagen, oh that lovely city, so human, so minutely detailed, the ivy growing on the walls and the pigeons waddling unafraid under your feet in the squares.

He left immediately. There was a plane going to Athens at two and he phoned and booked a seat. Then he saw Ilena and told her he was flying off, again (he laughed, and shrugged his shoulders), but would be back soon, as always, he always came back, and then he saw Larry and Sylvia and Toby and a few other friends, and at twelve he was in a cab and on his way to the airport.

He got there in plenty of time, and after the passport formalities he stood with his bags on either side of him and lit a cigarette and watched the mechanics refueling the plane. Then he checked his bags and sat out in the sun with a cup of coffee and waited for two o'clock.

There were less than twenty people flying to Athens, and Max was the first on board. The air inside smelt stale and of plastic and synthetics and the seats looked tired. He moved down the aisle, looking for his seat. It was by a porthole. He put his hat up on the overhead rack and sat back, and all at once he felt relaxed and completely at ease, in this shoddy, soiled, stale, winged metal tube, which was throbbing and the props turning and the light on saying *Fasten your seat belts please,* and he did, and here, on the way to Athens, on the way to Copenhagen, to Paris, to London, on the way to anywhere at all, he felt, at last, completely at home.

Alan Sillitoe

The Road

When Ivan was five his parents took him on a daytrip to Skegness. They wanted to spend a few hours out of the city and see the coast where they had languished for ten days of a misty frustrating honeymoon of long ago, but Stanley said: "Let's take Ivan to the seaside. It'll do him good."

"Yes," his mother said, "he'll love it."

And Ivan, sucking a lollipop as they walked up Arkwright Street, was oblivious to the responsibility they had put onto his shoulders. Yesterday the car had broken down, so they were going by train. To Stanley everything always happened at the crucial moment, otherwise why did it happen at all?

Ivan wore a new navy blazer, and long trousers specially creased for Whitsun. His shoes were polished and tight around his checked socks. Dark thin hair was well parted, and shy blue eyes looked out of a pale face that tapered from a broad forehead down to his narrow chin and royal blue tie. He held his father with one hand, and gripped his lollipop with the other.

"It'll be marvelous to get to the sea," Stanley said. "It's a hard life being a waiter, and good to have a whole day off for a change."

Amy agreed on all counts, though didn't say so aloud. Ivan wondered if there'd be boats, and she answered that she daresay there would be. Stanley picked Ivan up and put him high on his shoulders: "We'd better hurry."

"You'll have a heart attack if you're not careful," she laughed, "like in them adverts!"

"We've got to get going, though."

"There's still half an hour," she said, "and we're nearly there." Such bleak and common rush seemed to expose her more to the rigors of the world than was necessary, so she would never run, not even for a bus that might make her late for work if she missed it. But then, she never was late for work, and it was part of Stanley's job to get a move on.

He fought his way into the carriage to get seats, and even then Amy had to sit a few rows down. Ivan stayed with his father, now and again standing on his gray flannel trousers for a better view. The carriage was full, and he adjusted quickly to his new home, for all the unfamiliar people in the compartment became part of his family. Strange faces that he would be half afraid of on the street or in dreams seemed now so close and large and smiling, loud in their daze of talk, that they could not but be uncles and aunts and cousins. In which case he could look with absolute safety at everything outside.

His blue eyes pierced with telescopic clarity the scene of a cow chewing by green indistinct waterbanks of a flooded field that the sky, having been fatally stabbed, had fallen into. A hedge unfurled behind the cow that stood forlorn as if it would be trapped should the water rise further— which it could not do under such moist sunshine.

Gone.

Railway trucks at station sidings fell back along the line like dominoes.

Gone.

An ochred farmhouse came, and stood for a second to show a gray slate roof, damp as if one big patch had settled all over it, the yard around flooded with mud and a man standing in it looking at the train. He waved. Ivan lifted his hand.

Gone.

A junction line vanished into the curve of a cutting.

Gone. All going or gone. They were still, who were gazing out of the windows, and everything was passing them.

The train found its way along, seemed to be making tracks as it went and leaving them brand-new behind, shining brightly when they turned a wide bend and Ivan stretched his neck to look back. An older boy smiled: "Have you seen my new toy?"

He was sullen at being taken from such never-ending pictures that seemed to belong to him. "No."

"Do you want to?" He put an object on the table, ovoid, rubber, with four short legs as hands and arms. A length of fine tubing ran from its back, to a hollow reservoir of air—which the boy held in his hand. Ivan stared at the rubber, in spite of not wanting to, then at the object on the table that sprang open and up, a horrific miniature skeleton, ready to grow enormously in size and grab everyone in sight, throttle them one and all and send them crushed and raw out of the window—starting with Ivan.

He drew back, and Stanley laughed at his shout of panic, hoping the boy would go on working it so that he too could enjoy the novelty. "Stare at it like a man, then you won't be frightened! It's only a skeleton."

When the boy held it to Ivan's face, it became the arms and legs of a threatening silver spider brushing his cheeks. Fields rattled by but gave no comfort, so closing his eyes he buried his head against his father. "You are a silly lad. It's only a toy."

"Make him stop it. I don't like it." But he looked again at the glaring death-head, phosphorous on black, shaking and smiling, arms and legs going in and out as if i the grip of some cosmic agony. Amy came along the gangway at his cry and knocked the boy away, daring his nearby mother to object. She took Ivan on her knee: "He was frightening him, you damned fool," she said to Stanley. "Couldn't you see?"

The train stopped at a small station. A gravel depot was heaped between two wooden walls, and beyond the lines a rusting plough grew into an elderberry bush. No one got on or off the train, which made the stop boring and inexplicable. People rustled among baskets and haversacks for sandwiches and flasks of drink.

"I want some water," Ivan said, staring at the open door of the waiting room.

"You'll have to wait," Amy said.

"There's an hour yet," Stanley reminded her. "He can't."

The train jolted, as if about to start. "I'm thirsty. I want a drink of water."

"Oh my God," his mother said. "I told you we should have bought some lemonade at the station."

"We had to get straight on. We were late."

"A couple of minutes wouldn't have mattered."

"I wanted to get seats."

"We'd have found some somewhere."

To argue about what was so irrevocably finished infuriated him, but he deliberately calmed himself and rooted in the basket for a blue plastic cup. His whole body was set happily for action: "I'll just nip across to the tap."

"The train's going to start," she said. "Sit down."

"No it won't." But he didn't get up, paralyzed by her objection.

"Are you going?" she said, "or aren't you?" A vein jumped at the side of his forehead as he pushed along the crowded gangway, thinking that if he didn't reach the door and get free of her in a split second he would either go mad or fix his hands at her throat. Their carriage was beyond the platform, and he was out of sight for a moment. Then she saw him running between two trolleys into the men's lavatory as another playful whistle sounded from the engine.

"Where's dad gone, mam?"

"To get some water."

Everyone was looking out of the window, interested in his race: "He won't make it."

"I'll lay a quid each way."

"Don't be bloddy silly, he'll never get back in time. You can hear the wheels squeaking already. Feel that shuddering?"

"You're bloddy hopeful. We'll be here an hour yet." The face disappeared behind a bottle: "I'll live to see us move."

Money was changing hands in fervid betting.

"He will."

"He won't."

At the second whistle he bobbed up, pale and smiling, a cup held high, water splashing over the brim.

"What's dad out there for?" Ivan asked, lifting his face from a mug of lemonade someone had given him. The wheels moved more quickly, and Stanley was half way along the platform. Odds were lengthening as he dropped from view, and pound notes were flying into the bookie's cap. A woman who wanted to place two bob each way was struggling purple-faced to get from the other end of the carriage. Her coins were passed over.

Amy sat tight-lipped, unwilling to join in common words of encouragement even if it meant never seeing him again. Their return tickets were in his wallet, as well as money and everything else that mattered, but she wouldn't speak. He can wander over the earth till he drops, she thought, though the vision of him sitting outside some charming rustic pub with twelve empty pint jars (and the plastic cup still full of water) in front of him, while she explained at the other end about their lost tickets and destitution, didn't make his disappearance too easy to keep calm about.

The carriage slid away, a definite move of steel rolling over steel beneath them all. He was trying not to spill his hard-won water. A roar of voices blasted along the windows as the train gathered speed. "He's missed it!"

The door banged open, and a man who had slept through the betting spree jumped in his seat. He had come off nights at six that morning, and his false teeth jerked so that only a reflex action with both hands held them in the general neighborhood of his mouth. Red in the face, he slotted them properly in with everyone looking on.

"What's the hurry, you noisy bogger?" he asked, at Stanley standing upright and triumphant beside him.

They clamored at the bookie to pay up, and when his baffled face promised to be slow in doing so they stopped laughing and threatened to throw him off the bleeding train. He'd seen and grabbed his chance of making a few quid on the excursion, but having mixed up his odds he now looked like being sorted out by the crowd.

"Leave him alone," the winners shouted. But they clapped and cheered, and avoided a fight as the train swayed with speed between fields

B

and spinnies. Stanley stood with the plastic cup two thirds full, then made his way to Ivan and Amy, unable to understand what all the daft excitement was about.

"What did you have to make a laughing stock of yourself like that for?" she wanted to know.

"He needed some water, didn't he?"

"You mean you had to put on a show for everybody." Their argument went unnoticed in the general share out. "You can see how much he wanted water," she said, pointing to his closed eyes and hung down lower lip fixed in sleep.

The sea was nowhere to be seen. They stood on the front and looked for it. Shining sand stretched left and right, and all the way to the horizon, pools and small salt rivers flickering under the sun now breaking through. The immense sky intimidated them, made Skegness seem small at their spines. It looked as if the ocean went on forever round the world and came right back to their heels.

"This is a rum bloody do," he said, setting Ivan down. "I thought we'd take a boat out on it. What a place to build a seaside resort."

She smiled. "You know how it is. The tide'll be in this afternoon. Then I suppose you'll be complaining that all the sand's under water. It's better this way because he can dig and not fall in."

A few people had been on the beach but now, on either side, hundreds advanced onto the sand, hair and dresses and white shirts moving against the wind, a shimmering film of blue and gray, red and yellow spreading from the funnel of the station avenue. Campstools and crates of beer staked each claim, and children started an immediate feverish digging as if to find buried toys before the tide came back.

"Can I have a big boat?" Ivan asked as they went closer to the pier and coast-guard station. "With a motor in it, and a lot of seats?"

"Where do you want to go?" Stanley asked.

Ivan wondered. "A long way. That's where I want to go. A place like that. Up some road."

"We'll get you a bus, then," his father laughed.

"You want to stay at home with your mam," she said. They walked further down the sand, between people who had already set out their camps. Neither spoke, or thought of stopping. Gulls came swooping low, their shadows sharp as if to slice open pools of water. "How much more are we going to walk?"

"I didn't know you wanted to stop," he said, stopping.

"I didn't know you wanted to come this far, or I wouldn't have come. You just walk on and on."

"Why didn't you speak up, then?"

"I did. Why didn't you stop?"

"I'm not a mind reader."

"You don't have to be. You don't even think. Not about other people, anyway."

"I want to get beyond all this crowd."

"I suppose you want to dump us in the sea."

"I didn't want to sit all day in a café like you did, and that's a fact."

"You're like a kid, always wanting to be on your own."

"You're too bossy, always wanting your own way."

"It usually turns out to be better than yours. But you never know what you do want, anyway."

He was struck dumb by this irrational leapfrogging argument from someone he blindly loved. He stood and looked at the great space of sand and sky, birds, and a slight moving white beard of foam appearing on the far edge of the sand where the sea lay fallow and sleepy.

"Well?" she demanded, "are we traipsing much further, or aren't we? I wish you'd make up your mind."

He threw the basket down. "Here's where we stay, you hasty-tempered bitch."

"You can be on your own, then," she said, "because I'm going."

He opened a newspaper, without even bothering to watch her go—which was what she'd throw at him when she came back. "You didn't even watch me go!" He should have been standing up and keeping her retreating figure in sight—that was fast merging with the crowd—his face frowning and unhappy in wondering whether or not he had lost her forever.

But, after so long, his reactions would not mesh into gear. They'd become a deadeningly smooth surface that struck no sparks anymore. When she needed him to put an arm around her and tell her not to get excited, to calm down because he loved her very much—that was when his mouth became ashen and his eyes glazed into the general paralysis of his whole body. She needed him most at the precise moment when he needed her most, and so they retreated into their own damaged worlds to wait for the time when they again felt no need of each other, and they could then give freely all that was no longer wanted, but which was appreciated nevertheless.

"Where's mam gone?" Ivan asked, half hidden in his well-dug hole.

"To fetch us something."

"What, though?"

"We'll see."

"Will she get me a tractor?"

"You never know."

"I want a red one."

"Let's dig a moat," Stanley said, taking the spade. "We'll rig a castle in the middle."

He looked up from time to time, at other people coming to sit nearby. An old man opened a camp stool and took off his jacket. He wore a striped shirt over his long straight back, braces taut at the shoulders. Adjusting his trilby hat, he looked firmly and unblinking out to sea, so that Stanley paused in his work to see what he was fixing with such determination.

Nothing.

"Shall we make a tunnel, dad?"

"All right, then, but it'll crumble."

The thin white ray was coming toward them, feather-tips lifting from it, a few hundred yards away and suddenly no longer straight, pushed forward a little in the center, scarred by the out-jutting pier. It broke on the sand and went right back.

"She'll be in in a bit, don't worry. We're in the front line, so we'll have to move," the old man said. "Half an hour at the most. You can't stop it, and that's a fact. Comes in shoulder-high, faster than a racehorse sometimes, and then you've got to watch out, even from this distance, my guy you have. Might look a fair way and flat one minute, then it's marching in quick like the Guards. Saw a man dragged in once, big six-footer he was. His wife and kids just watched. Found 'im in the Wash a week later. Pull you underfoot. Even I can find my legs and run at times like that, whether I'm eighty or not."

If it weren't for the trace of white he'd hardly have known where sky ended and sand began, for the wetness of it under the line was light purple, a mellower shade of the midday lower horizon. The mark of white surf stopped them blending, a firm and quite definite dividing of earth and water and air.

"Come here every year, then?" Stanley asked.

"Most days," the man said. "Used to be a lifeboatman. I live here." His hand ran around the inside of a straw basket like a weasel and pulled out a bottle of beer. He untwisted the tight cork, upended it, and swigged it into his bony throat. "You from Notts I suppose?"

Stanley nodded. "I'm a waiter. Wangled some time off for a change. It don't make so much difference at a big hotel. There used to be a shortage, but we've got some of them Spanish chaps now." His jacket and tie lay on the sand, one sleeve hidden by a fallen rampart of Ivan's intricate castle.

Looking up he saw Amy making her way between patchwork blankets of people, a tall and robust figure wearing a flowered dress. A tied ribbon set hair spreading toward her shoulders. She never tried to look fabricated and smart, even on her job as a cashier at the local dance hall. He was almost annoyed at being so happy to see her, yet finally gave into his pleasure and watched her getting closer while hoping she had now recovered from her fits of the morning. Perhaps the job she had was too much for her, but she liked to work because it gave a feeling of independence, helped to keep that vitality and anger that held Stanley so firmly to her. It was no easy life, and because of the money she earned little time could be given to Ivan, though such continual work kept the family more stable than if as a triangle the three of them were too much with each other— which they wanted to be against their own and everyone's good.

She had sandwiches, fried fish cakes, dandelion-and-burdock, beer. "This is what we need to stop us feeling so rattled."

He wondered why she had to say the wrong thing so soon after coming back. "Who's rattled?"

"You were. I was as well, if you like. Let's eat this though. I'm starving."

She opened the packets, and kept them in equal radius around her, passing food to them both. "I didn't know how hungry I was," Stanley said.

"If anything's wrong," she said, "it's usually that—or something else." She reached out, and they pressed each other's hand.

"You look lovely today," he said.

"I'm glad we came."

"So am I. Maybe I'll get a job here."

"It'd be seasonal," she said. "Wouldn't do for us."

"That's true."

While Ivan had his mouth full of food, some in his hand, and a reserve waiting in his lap, she asked if he wanted any more. Even at home, when only half way through a plate, the same thing happened, and Stanley wondered whether she wanted to stuff, choke or stifle him—or just kill his appetite. He'd told her about it, but it made no difference.

After the meal Ivan took his bread and banana and played at the water's edge, where spume spread like silver shekels in the sun and ran around his plimsolls, then fell back or faded into the sand. He stood up, and when it tried to catch him he ran, laughing so loudly that his face turned as red as the salmon paste spread on the open rolls that his mother and father were still eating. The sea missed him by inches. The castle-tumulus of sand was mined and sapped by salt water until its crude formations became lopsided, a boat rotted by time and neglect. A sudden upsurge melted it like wax, and on the follow-up there was no trace. He watched it, wondering why it gave in so totally to such gentle pressure.

They had to move, and Amy picked up their belongings, unable to stop water running over the sleeve of Stanley's jacket. "You see," she chided, "if you hadn't insisted on coming all this way down we wouldn't have needed to shift so early."

He was sleepy and goodnatured, for the food hadn't yet started to eat his liver. "Everybody'll have to move. It goes right up to the road when it's full in."

"Not for another twenty minutes. Look how far down we are. Trust us to be in the front line. That's the way you like it, though. If only we could do something right for a change, have a peaceful excursion without much going wrong."

He thought so, too, and tried to smile as he stood up to help.

"If everything went perfectly right one day," she said, "you'd still have to do something and deliberately muck it up, I know you would."

As he said afterward—or would have said if the same course hadn't by then been followed yet again—one thing led to another, and before I could help myself . . .

The fact was that the whole acreage of the remaining sands, peopled by much of Nottingham on its day's outing, was there for an audience, or would have been if any eyes had been trained on them, which they weren't particularly. But many of them couldn't help but be, after the first smack. In spite of the sea and the uprising wind, it could be heard, and the second was indeed listened for after her raging cry at the impact.

"You tried me," he said, hopelessly baffled and above all immediately sorry. "You try me all the time." And the jerked-out words, and the overwhelming feeling of regret, made him hit her a third time, till he stood, arms hanging thinly at his side like the maimed branches of some blighted and thirsty tree that he wanted to disown but couldn't. They felt helpless, and too weak to be kept under sufficient control. He tried to get them safely into his pockets, but they wouldn't fit.

A red leafmark above her eye was slowly swelling. "Keep away," she cried, lifting her heavy handbag but unable to crash it against him. She sobbed. It was the first time he had hit her in public, and the voices calling that he should have less on it, and others wondering what funny stuff she had been up to to deserve it, already sounded above the steady railing of the nerve-racking sea. An overly forward wave sent a line of spray that saturated one of her feet. She ignored it, and turned to look for Ivan among the speckled colors of the crowd. Pinks and grays, blues and whites shifted across her eyes and showed nothing.

She turned to him: "Where is he, then?"

He felt sullen and empty, as if he were the one who'd been hit. "I don't know. I thought he was over there."

"Where?"

"Just there. He was digging."

"Oh my God, what if he's drowned?"

"Don't be so bloody silly," he said, his face white, and thinner than she'd ever seen it. Bucket and spade lay by the basket between them. They looked into the sea, and then toward land, unable to find him from their mutual loathing and distress. They were closer than anyone else to the sea, and the old lifeboatman had gone. Everyone had moved during their argument, and the water now boiled and threw itself so threateningly that they had to pick up everything and run.

"What effect do you think all this arguing and fighting's going to have on him?" she demanded. He'd never thought about such outside problems, and considered she had only mentioned them now so as to get at him with the final weapon of mother-and-child, certainly not for Ivan's own and especial good. Yet he was not so sure. The horror of doubt came over him, opened raw wounds not only to himself but to the whole world for the first time as they walked toward the road and set out on a silent bitter search through the town.

For a long while Ivan sat on the steps of a church, the seventh step down from the doors, beating time with a broken stick as blocks of traffic sped by. He sang a song, dazed, enclosed, at peace. A seagull sat at his feet, and when he sneezed it flew away. He stayed at peace even after they found him, and went gladly on the train with them as if into the shambles. They seemed happily united in getting him back at last. The effort of the search had taken away all their guilt at having succumbed to such a pointless quarrel in front of him. He watched the fields, and heavy streams like long wavy mirrors that cows chewed at and clouds flowed over and ignored.

He sat on his father's knee, who held him as if he were a rather unusual but valuable tip a customer in the restaurant had left. Ivan felt nothing. The frozen soul, set in ancestry and childhood, fixed his eyes to look and see beyond them and the windows. The train wasn't moving after a while. He was sleeping a great distance away from it, detached, its jolting a permanent feature of life and the earth. He wanted to go on traveling forever, as if should he ever stop the sky would fall in. He dreamed that it had, and was about to black him out, so he woke up and clung to his father, asking when they would be back in Nottingham.

John Banville

Summer Voices

"Shalt thou hope. His truth shall compass thee with a shield. Thou shalt not be afraid of the terror of the night. Of the arrow that flies in the day. Of the business that walks in the dark. Of invasion or of the noonday devil."

The old voice droned on, and the boy wondered at the words. He looked through the window at the countryside, the fields floating in the summer heat. On Halloween people must stay indoors for fear of the devils that fly in the darkness. Once he had heard them crying, those dark spirits, and she said it was only the wind. But to think of the wind in the black trees was almost as bad as imagining devils. And late that night from the window of his bedroom he had seen huge shadows of leaves dancing on the side of the house, and the circle of light from the street lamp shivering where it fell on the road.

"Are you going to ask her?"

"What?"

The little girl frowned at him and leaned close to his ear, her curls falling about her face. She whispered:

"Sh . . . will you? Are you going to ask her can we go? He said seven days and the tide will be up in an hour. Go on and ask her."

He nodded.

"In a minute."

She stuck out her tongue at him. Through his crossed legs he touched his fists on the cool tiles of the floor. The old woman in the chair before him licked her thumb and turned a page of the black missal. The thin paper crackled and the ribbons stirred where they hung from the torn spine.

"I will deliver him and will glorify him. I will fill him with length of days and I will show him my salvation."

She raised her eyes from the page and glared at them over the metal rims of her spectacles. Crossly she said:

"What are you two whispering about there?"

"Tantey, can we go for a swim?" the little girl cried and jumped to her feet. The old woman smiled and shook her head.

"Oh it's a swim is it. You'd rather be off swimming now than listening to the words of God."

"Ah but it's a lovely day, Tantey. Can we go can we?"

"I suppose so. But mind now and be careful. And you're not to stay out late."

She closed the missal and kissed reverently the tattered binding. Groaning she pulled herself up from her chair and hobbled to the door. There she paused and turned, and said to the boy who still sat on the floor with his legs crossed:

"Mind what I say now. Be back here early."

When she was gone the girl ran and sat in the armchair, and with her shoulders bent she intoned, mimicking the old woman:

"Achone achone the lord and all his angels are coming to damn us all to hell."

"Ah stop that," said the boy.

"Nor you needn't be afeared of the divil in the day. Achone achone o."

"I told you to stop it."

"Alright alright. Don't be always bossing me around."

She made a face at him and tramped from the room, saying over her shoulder:

"I'm going to get the bikes and if you're not out before I count ten I'm going on my own."

The boy did not move. Sunlight fell through the tiny window above the stove. Strange silence of the summer afternoon wove shadows about him. Beyond the window a dead tree stood like a crazy old naked man, a blackbird hopping among its twisted branches. The boy stood up and went out into what had once been the farmyard—the barn and the sties had long since crumbled. After the dimness of the kitchen the light here burned his eyes. He moved across to stand under the elm tree and listen to the leaves. Out over the green fields the heat lay heavy, pale blue and shimmering. In the sky a bird circled slowly. He lifted his head and gazed into the thickness of the leaves. Light glinted gold through the branches. He stood motionless, his arms hanging at his sides, listening, and slowly, from the far fields, the strange cry floated to his ears, a needle of sound piercing the stillness. He held his breath. The voice hung poised a moment in the upper airs, a single liquid note, then slowly faded back into the fields, and died away, leaving the silence deeper than before.

"Are you coming or are you just going to stand there all day?"

He turned. The girl stood between the two ancient bicycles, a saddle held in each of her small hands.

"I'm coming," he grunted.

They mounted and rode slowly down the uneven driveway. At the gate he halted, while the girl swung carelessly out into the road. When he was sure of safety he pedalled furiously after her.

"You'll get killed some day," he said when he was beside her again. The girl turned up her nose and shook her hair in the warm wind.

"You're an awful scaredy cat," she said contemptuously.

"I just don't want to get run over that's all."

"Hah."

She trod on the pedals and glided away from him. He watched her as she sailed along, her bony knees rising and falling. She took her hands from the handlebars and waved them in the air.

"You'll fall off," he shouted.

She glanced over her shoulder at him and pulled her hair above her head, and the long gold tresses coiled about her pale arms. Her teeth glinted as she laughed.

Free now, they slowed their pace and leisurely sailed over the road, tires whispering in the soft tar. The fields trembled on either side of them. Sometimes the girl sang in her high pitched, shaky voice, and the notes carried back to him, strangely muted by the wide fields, a distant, piping song. Tall shoots of vicious grass waving from the ditches scratched their legs. The boy watched the land as it moved slowly past him, the sweltering meadows, the motionless trees, and high up on the hill the cool deep shadow under Wild Wood.

"Listen," the girl said, allowing him to overtake her. "Do you think they'll let us see him."

"I don't know."

"Jimmy would. He'd let me see him alright. But there's bound to be others."'

She brooded, gazing down at her feet circling under her.

"How do you know they'll find him?" the boy asked.

"Jimmy said so."

"Jimmy."

"You shut up. You don't know anything about him."

"He's dirty," the boy said sullenly.

"You never saw him."

"I did."

"Well he's not dirty. And anyway I don't care. I'm in love with him so there."

"He's dirty and he's old and he's mad too."

B*

"I don't care. I love him. I'd love him to kiss me."

She closed her eyes and puckered her lips at the sky. Suddenly she turned and pushed the boy violently, so that he almost lost his balance. Watching him try to control the wobbling wheels she screamed with laughter. Then she sailed ahead of him once again, crying:

"You're only jealous."

He stepped down from the machine, and the girl disappeared around a bend in the road. Scowling, he plodded up the first slope of the steep Slane Hill.

When he came round the bend he found the girl standing beside her bicycle, waiting for him, her hand at her mouth.

"Listen," she said and grasped his arm. "There's somebody up there."

At the top of the hill a dark figure was huddled in the ditch at the side of the road.

"It's only a man," the boy said.

"I don't like the look of him."

"You're afraid."

"I am not. I just don't like the look of him."

"Not so brave now," the boy sneered.

"Alright then smartie. Come on."

They began the climb. Sweat gathered at the corners of their eyes and on their lips. Under their hands the rubber grips of the handlebars grew moist and sticky. Flies came and buzzed about them. They lowered their heads and pushed the awkward black machines to the crest of the hill. Below them now the sea, warm and blue and glittering with flakes of silver light. A cool breeze came up over the sandy fields, carrying a faint bitterness of salt against their mouths. A stirring beside them in the ditch. A hoarse voice. Panic stabbed them. They leaped into the saddles and careered off down the hill. Behind them a ragged, strangely uncertain figure stood dark against the sky, querulously calling.

The air whistled by their ears as they raced along the pitted road. The sea was coming to meet them, the dunes rose up green and gold, sea salt cutting their nostrils, the sun whirling like a rimless spoked wheel of gold, sea and dunes rushing, then abruptly the road ended, their tires sank in the sand and they toppled from the saddles.

For a while they lay panting and listened to the sea whispering gently on the shore. Then the girl raised her head and looked back up the hill.

"He's gone," she whispered hoarsely.

The boy sat up and rubbed his knee.

"I hurt myself."

"I said he's gone."

"Who is?"

"The fellow up on the hill. He's gone."

The boy shaded his eyes and gazed along the road. He pursed his lips and murmured vaguely:

"Oh yes."

She caught his wrist in her bony fingers.

"Did you hear what he was shouting? Did you hear what he called you?"

"Me?"

"He was shouting at you. He called you mister."

"Did he?"

"Didn't you hear him?"

He did not answer, but stood up and brushed the sand from his faded cord trousers.

"Come on," he said, grasping her hands and pulling her to her feet. "The tide is up. We'll leave the bikes here."

He walked away from her, limping slightly. She stared after him for a moment and then began to follow. Scowling at his back she cried:

"You're a right fool."

"Come on."

Through a gap in the dunes they passed down to the beach. The sea was quiet, a bowl of calm blue waters held in the arms of the horseshoe of bay. Lines of sea wrack scored the beach, evidence of the changing limits of the tides. They walked slowly toward the pier, a gray finger of stone accusing the ocean.

"I'd love a swim," the little girl said.

"Why didn't you bring your togs?"

"I think I'll go in in my skin."

"You will not."

"If I met some fellow swimming underwater wouldn't he get a great shock."

Giggling, she tucked the hem of her dress into her knickers and waded into the sea. She splashed about, drenching herself. Her cries winged out over the water like small swift birds. The boy watched her for a moment, then he turned away and moved on again.

"Wait for me," she cried, thrashing out of the sea.

At the end of the pier a bent old man was sitting on a bollard, his back turned toward them. The girl ran ahead and began to dance excitedly about him. The boy came up and stopped behind the old man. He put his hands into his pockets and stared out to sea with studied indifference, whistling softly. A distant sail trembled on the horizon.

"And did your auntie let you go?" the old man was asking the girl, mocking her. He had a low, hoarse voice, and he spoke slowly and with care, as though hiding an impediment.

"She did," the girl said, and laughed slyly. "It was such a nice day."

"Aye it's the great day."

He turned his head and considered the boy a moment.

"And who's this young fellow?"

"That's my brother."

"Aye now," he said blankly.

He turned back to the sea, grinding his gums. The boy shifted from one foot to the other. For a moment there was silence but for the faint crackling of the seaweed over on the beach. Then the old man spat noisily and said:

"Well they've took him out anyway."

The girl's eyes flashed. She looked at her brother and winked.

"Did they?" she said casually. "Today eh?"

"Aye. Fished him out today. Didn't I tell them. Aye."

"What did they do with him, Jimmy? I suppose he's been taken away long ago."

"Oh not at all," said the old man. "Sure it's no more than half an hour since he came in. Ah no. He's still down there."

He waved his arm toward the beach at his back.

"Did they just leave him there?" asked the girl in surprise.

"Aye. They're gone off to get something to shift him in."

"Oh I see."

She leaned close to the old man's ear and whispered. He listened a moment, then turned and stared up at her from one yellowed eye.

"What? What? You don't want to see a thing like that. Do you? What?"

"We do. That's why we came. Isn't it?"

She rammed her elbow into the boy's ribs.

"Oh yes," he said quickly. "That's why we came."

The old man stared from one to the other, shook his head, then got to his feet, saying:

"Come on then before your men come back. Begod you're the strange ones then. Hah. Aren't you the strange ones now. Heh heh."

They walked back along the pier, the girl rushing excitedly between the old man and the boy, urging them to hurry. When they reached the sand the old man led them down behind the sea wall. At the edge of the waves a bundle covered with an old piece of canvas lay in the shade of the pier. The girl rushed forward and knelt beside it in the sand. The old man cried:

"Wait there now young one. Don't touch anything there."

The three of them stood in silence and gazed down at the object where it lay in the violet shade. Out on the rocks a seabird screeched. The old man leaned down and pulled away the canvas. The boy turned away his face, but not before he had glimpsed the creature, the twisted body, the ruined face, the soft, pale, swollen flesh like the flesh of a rotted fish. The girl knelt and stared, her mouth open. She whispered:

"There he is then."

"Aye," the old man muttered. "That's what the sea will do to you. The sea and the rocks. And the fish too."

The boy stood with his back to them, looking at his hands.

And then a shout from far up the beach.

"Hi! Get them children away from there! Get out of it you old fool!"

The boy looked up along the sand. Figures were running toward them, waving their fists in the air. The old man muttered a curse and hobbled away with surprising speed over the dunes. The girl leaped to her feet and was away beside the waves, her bare feet slapping the sand and raising splashes that flashed in the sun like sparks. The boy stood motionless, listening to her wild laughter as it floated back to him on the salt air. He knelt in the sand and looked down at the strange creature lying there. He spoke a few words quietly, and with care he gently replaced the canvas shroud. Then he ran away up the beach, after his sister, who was already out of sight.

Some time later he found her, sitting under a thorn tree in the fields behind the beach. She was rubbing the damp sand from her feet with a handful of grass. When she saw him she sniffed derisively and said:

"Oh it's you."

He lay down in the warm grass at her side, panting. Bees hummed about him.

"Did they catch you?" she asked.

"No."

"That's a wonder. I thought you were going to stand there all day."

The boy said nothing, and she went on.

"Jimmy was here a minute ago. He said I was a right little bitch getting him into trouble. He's worried as anything. That fellow's not a bit mad. Anyway he's gone now. I don't care."

She looked down at him. He was chewing a blade of grass and staring into the black thorns above him. She poked him with her toe.

"Are you listening to me?"

"No."

He stood up, saying:

"We'll have to go home. Tantey will be worried."

"Ah sugar on Tantey."

They found their bicycles and started home through the glimmering evening. Clouds of midges rode with them. The tiny flies found a way into their hair and under their clothes. The girl cursed them and waved her hands above her head. The boy rode on without a word, his head bent.

Tantey was angry with them for staying out so late.

"I warned you before you went," she said, glaring at them from her chair by the stove. "I warned you. Well now you can hop it off to bed for yourselves. Go on."

"But what about supper, Tantey?"

"You'll have no supper tonight. Get on now."

"I'm tired anyway," the girl said carelessly when they were climbing the stairs.

By the window on the first landing the boy stopped and looked out over the countryside down to the sea. The sun was setting blood red over the bay. He stood and watched it until it fell into the sea. When it was long gone he heard the girl's voice from above calling to him plaintively.

"Where are you? Where are you?"

He climbed to her room and stood at the end of the bed looking down at her.

"I've a pain," she said, twisting fitfully among the crumpled sheets, her legs thrown wide, her hand clutching her stomach. He leaned his hands on the metal bedpost and watched her. As she twisted and turned she glanced at him now and then through half-closed eyes. After a moment he looked away from her, and with his lips pursed he considered the ceiling.

"Do you want to know something?" he asked.

"What? Oh my stomach."

"You know that fellow today. The one that shouted at us. Do you know who he was?"

She was quiet now. She lay on her back and stared at him, her eyes glittering.

"No. Who was he?"

"He was the other fellow. The one that got drowned. That was him."

He turned to go. She leaped forward and clutched his hand.

"Don't leave me," she said, her eyes wide. "I'm frightened. You can sleep here."

He took his hand from hers and went to the door.

"Alright," the girl cried. "Go on then. I don't want you. You didn't have to be coaxed last night. Did you—mister. Ha ha. Mister."

He left the room and closed the door quietly behind him. Strange shapes before him in the dimness of the stairs. For a while he walked about the house, treading carefully on the ancient boards. All was quiet but for the small sounds of his sister's weeping. On the top landing a black, square object lay precariously balanced on the banister. Tantey's missal. As he passed, he casually pushed it over the edge. The heavy book tumbled down the stairs, its pages fluttering.

He went into the bathroom and locked the door behind him. On the handbasin he knelt and pushed open the small window of frosted glass set high in the wall. Darkness was approaching. Black clouds, their edges touched with red, were gathering out over the sea. Shadows were lowering on the ugly waters. A cold damp breath touched his face. In the distance a long peal of thunder rumbled. He closed the window and climbed down from the basin. He scrubbed his hands and dried them carefully, finger by finger. For a moment he was still, listening. No sounds. Then he went and stood before the mirror and gazed into it at his face for a long time.

Leonard Michaels

Making Changes

The hall was clogged with bodies; none of them hers, but who could really be sure. The light was bad. Too many people had been invited and more kept arriving. There was too much noise, too much movement. I liked it, but it was difficult to get from one room to another and conversation was impossible. People had to lean close and shriek. It killed the effect of wit to find oneself looking into nostrils and saying "What?" But it was a New York scene and I liked it, except that she was missing. I couldn't find her in the bathrooms, closets, bedrooms or on the terrace. I started toward the kitchen. She wasn't in the hall, she wasn't in the maid's room or pantry. I thought of asking people if they'd seen her, but was ashamed to admit I'd lost her; besides I was afraid to discover she was someone's date or inextricably into something. I didn't want to hear either of those things, and I pressed on from room to room.

One couple was in the kitchen, a lady in a brown tweed suit talking to a short, dapper man in spats. She was stoutish, about fifty, had fierce eyes, flat and black as nailheads. Her voice flew around like pots and pans. The man glanced at me, then down as if embarrassed. The lady ignored me. I ignored her and busied around the wet, sloppy counter looking for an unused glass and a bottle of something I hadn't yet tried. She was saying, slam, clang:

"Sexual enlightenment, the keystone of modernity, I dare say, can hardly be considered an atavistic intellectual debauch, Cosmo."

"But the perversions . . ."

"To be sure, the perversions of which we are so richly conscious are the natural inclination, indeed the style, of civilized beings . . ."

I found a paper cup. It was gnawed about the rim, but there were no cigarette butts shredding on the bottom. I sloshed in bourbon and started to leave.

"Wait there you."

I stopped.

"What sort of pervert are you?"

I shrugged and mumbled, hoping she'd forgo dialogue, and let me off with a little animal reciprocity. I'd been stopped before. Lonely types used any pretext for a moment of I-Thou, or just laid on hands. Then there was trouble extricating, feeling guilty about doing it, especially if we'd smeared in a corner and mouths or groins communicated.

And I wanted to find her, with her long, clean stalks and elegant gray eyes. Cecily.

"Speak up fellow."

"I mug yaks."

"Do you hear, Cosmo? A yak mugger."

"Are you married young man?" asked Cosmo, dreamily from left field.

"No."

"Good question," she cried, "for we observe, as necessarily we must, that marriage encourages perversity—assuming the parties agree on specified indulgences, Cosmo, which is paradoxical."

"Indeed, Tulip, the natural perversions themselves, one might well assume," said Cosmo, nearly whispering.

"Let me continue."

"Please, please continue."

Something in her voice, shadowy and mean, threatened to spring out and rip off Cosmo's head. I waited in the door and finished my drink, anxious to leave but curious.

"Paradoxical, I repeat, for the prime value of sex, to an advanced view, lies precisely in its antagonism to society. What, then, dare one ask, must we make of marriage?"

"An anti-social perversion," he said.

"Yes, clearly," I added, "clearly."

The words burst out of themselves with a wonderful feeling. I love logic, and how often did one hear it in simple human discourse. I looked at Tulip, nodding my head at more than the force of her argument.

"Cosmo," she said, ignoring me again, "you're a horse's ass. I say fellow, is there much going on in the living room?" Her black eyes, like periods, stopped mine.

"I just came the other way, from the back of the apartment."

"How fascinating to hear. Do publish a travel book. In the meantime, however, turn your head and look into the living room."

I turned instantly, looked through the dining room over scattered struggling, to the living room piled with dense, sluggish spaghetti.

"It's mainly in there, I think."

"Good. The orgy, Cosmo, our oldest mode of sexual community has moved a bit closer. Let's go watch now that we needn't poke about like vulgar tourists. Oh, Cosmo, what better solvent have we for the diversity of human beings? And needless to add it's such a chic way of breaking the ice."

We started out of the kitchen, her smashing voice flinging in all directions.

They stopped at the edge, standing with the spray in their eyes. Not looking as if they might wade in, but thrilled to contemplate the steamy, heaving sliding, and the whole figures here and there cast up like tidal garbage at their feet, quivering even in sleep.

"Cosmo, the view is breathtaking. Tell me your impressions."

"It's breathtaking."

"Yes, I agree."

I went on again moving down the edge like a beachcomber, squatting, poking, peering at whatever caught some light—blades, nails, brows, paps, hips, tips—looking for her blonde hair and gray eyes.

I went beyond the living room and down the clogged hall, retracing my course to the back of the apartment. I looked into a bedroom where three mirrors showed me looking. I looked into a study with a wall of books, a wall of whips, barbells on the floor, framed diplomas and photos of movie stars and contemporary philosophers, everywhere. I found a bathroom, knocked, shoved in and saw a man, naked, sitting in the tub. "I'll bet you're Zeus," he said. "I'm Danae." I shook my head, backed out muttering, "I'm Phillip." I was in the hall once more, moving toward the living room, dragging rump to rump, hip to hip down the living walls, pardon me and so so sorry until a knee plugged between mine and I pitched sideways. I went down elbow deep in churning, my hand on a hot face, eyes looking up through my fingers. Fingers clapped the back of my thigh and closed. I swung my fist like a hammer and hit a neck. "You want to hit?" asked a man. There was a punch, a slap, and a gibbering girl tumbled over me, nails raking my spine. I scrambled for space and slammed nose flat into shivering thighs, pinwheeled, flapped like a sheet in the wind and went cha cha cha until like a bludgeoned beast I fell out against a wall, wheezing and whistling, and stared back into virtual black. Tulip's voice slashed across like tracers:

"I will say one thing, Cosmo, you meet people in an orgy. Not at all like conventional sex, vicious sneaking in corners, undermining human society, selfish, acquisitive, dirty. I mean everytime one gets laid, as it were, it's conservative politics. On the other hand, orgies are liberal and humane. The ambience of impulse, the deluge of sensation, why orgies are no less than corporate form, the highest expression of catholicity, our modern escape from constricted, compulsive, unilinear simplifications of medieval sex. Don't you think so?"

"They give me a certain cultural feeling."

"Precisely."

I began to see a little, then a little more, and people with no permission went sliding like lizards across my legs. I began inching, bumping buttocks one at a time toward the foyer and the hall door. Then a rat-like squeal of exquisite recognition needled my ear and my hands flew up and slapped a breast, neck, weedy grove. "You!" I shouted.

She collapsed onto my lap and both of us sprawled down the moulding like broken, grateful snakes, clear of the mass and curling into the foyer. Then she quit and lay dead as a ton while I dragged, gasping, snorting, and she babbled, "Gimme, gimme sincere." I reached the door with her, opened it, letting light and air sweep her body, bruised, streaked with perspiration, more limp that any sad deposition I'd ever seen, more tragic than Cordelia in the arms of Lear.

But she wasn't Cecily.

She was all right. Whoever she was, squalid enervation revealed neat, easy lines like vines, lips like avocado pulp. Nose, belly, legs, all in good repair. I helped her to stand and turned her about so she might consider another prospect. Dull raging continued a few feet away and more people were arriving, thickening the stew. Others crawled toward furniture, hung out the windows or crumpled in corners.

I smiled, she smiled, both of us a smidgeon self-conscious, confronting one another this way, a couple in the eyes of the world, standing apart, us, and it wasn't easy to ignore the great pull of the worm bucket and pretend to individuation. She leaned toward the wall, but there was no wall. Her hands flailed like shot ducks, her eyes searched for mine flashing disbelief, horror, dismay as she went down. The tangle squealed, gobbled. She vanished.

Her character was my fate. She was careless, she didn't look, and I'd lost another. But I wanted her back and flung straight into the sticky dismal, thrashing, groping like Beowulf in the mere for a grip on Grendel. I seized a wrist, dragged, and dragged us up to light. She whimpered so at the injustice, the imbecilic ironies.

It wasn't exactly she.

Like her, like her in many ways, and not a speck worse. But another girl. I let go of her wrist, smiled, shrugged, simpered an apology. She gaped:

"You must love me very much."

Such tender imperative. Another time, another place, who knows what might have been. If the circumstances were slightly different, if the light were better, the noise a little less, if, if, if I hadn't shoved her back in, furious with myself, we might have had a moment, a life. To think how much we build on merest chance—marriage, society, great societies. In any event she was well received and I pressed down the shore past Tulip and Cosmo who were still enthralled:

"Cosmo, Cosmo, I think I see a perversion. You'll have to tell me what it's called. If only there were a bit more light. My how it smells. Cosmo, what would you call that smell? The vocabulary of olfaction is so limited in English."

"Communism?"

"I adore your political intelligence, Cosmo. Why is it on every other subject you're a horse's ass?"

I stepped into a bathroom to wash and look for fungicide, slammed the door behind me, flicked the light. *Voila!* A girl was bent over the sink having spasms. Quickly, I pressed up beside her, ran the water, pulled a towel off the rack.

"May I?"

She presented her chin, flecked, runny as it was, and didn't make an occasion of it. Her eyes were full of tears. A speaking picture. In less than a minute there was a bond, soft and strong as silk, holding us. I wiped her chin, we laughed at nothing, chatted, smoked a cigarette and soon we were leaving the party together, but at the door a big man blocked our way.

"I'm glad you came tonight, Harold."

"I'm glad you're glad," I said. "Name is Stanley."

He had large bloodshot eyes, a beard, and an unlit cigar in his mouth.

"I'm sorry you're leaving."

"I'm sorry you're sorry."

"I feel as if you want to say something nasty to me, Harold. You must have had a fight with one of your girl friends. I have to pay for it. Well, what's a fuck'n friend for if you can't mutilate him every ten minutes, eh?"

He laughed, winked at her.

I edged past him, grinning, slapping his shoulder lightly. Not too intimate. I knew the signs and wanted to give no cause for violence. I tugged her behind me into the hall. He frowned, leaned after us saying, "How do you like my beard?"

"Makes you look religious. It's nice."

"You think I'm not religious? Say what you mean, Harold. I hate innuendo. I'm not religious. I'm Satan, right? What should I do, Harold?"

He yelled as we went through the lobby and stepped into the street. She squeezed my hand and pressed flat to my side.

"A moralist like you knows about people. I'd like to be like you and keep my principles intact, but I'm weak, Harold. I lack integrity, Harold. I haven't the courage to commit suicide."

He laughed and nudged my ribs with a big fist. I snickered and looked for a cab. She whispered, "Ignore him. Let's go away." I saw a cab, waved, and it started toward us. She got right in, but he had my arm now and held me.

"Wait a minute, Harold. Which way is better, pointed or rounded?"

He pushed his face at mine and tapped his beard, grinning and winking.

"How about growing it into your mouth?"

He let me go and stepped back a little.

"That would kill our conversation, Harold. And you know when people stop talking they start fighting. For example, if I stopped talking this minute I might kick you in the nuts."

He stopped talking, dropped his hands lightly on his hips, spread his legs. I kicked him quickly in the nuts.

"Ooch!"

I leaped into the cab, slammed the door and locked it. His face smeared against the window as I rolled it up; his eyes were glazed, his upper lip shrivelling and spittle bubbling up oozed between his teeth. His hand clawed across the window as the cab whipped away down the street, and I turned to her. She quivered, dropped her eyes. I inhaled deeply and rubbed my hands together to keep them from shaking. We talked going across town about the people, what they looked like, what they said, who did what to whom, and we talked in my apartment, smoked, listened to our voices, boats on the river, planes in the sky, and it was impossible to say who laid whom and we fell asleep too soon afterward to think about it. Not that I would have thought about it. I'm not a poet. I'm Phillip.

I woke up suddenly as if from a nightmare and it was brilliant morning. She was standing like a stork on one leg, pulling a stocking up the other. She said, "Hello," her voice full of welcome, but I saw she was too much in motion and already someplace else. Her eyes looked through mine as if mine weren't eyes, but tunnels that zoomed out the back of my head.

"Leaving?"

"I'll call you later. What's your number?"

I couldn't speak. I stared. She finished dressing, then sat stiffly on the bed to say good-by. We kissed. I seized her arms.

"Look," I cried, "you can't leave."

"Phillip, please. It's been nice."

She stared at a wall. A toilet flushed, water retched in pipes. I released her arms and went naked to my desk. I picked up a pen, returned and pushed her back onto the bed.

"I'm all dressed."

I shook her hands off mine and wrote on her stomach: "PHILLIP'S." On her thighs: "PHILLIP'S," "PHILLIP'S."

She sat up, considered herself, then me, and as she rehooked her stockings she said, "Why did you do that?"

"I don't know."

"Why?"

"Oh, I'm aware the couple is a lousy idea. I read books, I go to the flicks. I'm hip. I live in New York. But I want you to come back, whoever you are. Will you?"

"I have a date."

"A what?"

"Can't I have a date? I made it before we met."

"You'll come back, though?"

"I'll try."

"Today?"

"I'll try," she said, straightened her skirt, went to the door, out, and down the steps, d'gook, d'gook. The street door opened, eeech. Shut. She was gone. I was empty.

I flopped on the bed, lighted a cigarette, sucked, picked up the phone and called my date for the afternoon. A man answered.

"May I speak to Genevieve?" I said.

He said, "Hey, baby, the telephone."

His voice was heavy, slow, rotten with satisfaction. Heels clacked to the phone. A bracelet clicked. Her cigarette sizzled and she exhaled, "Hello."

"This is Phillip."

"Phillip, hello. I'm so glad you called. What time are you coming for me?"

"Never, bitch."

I dropped the phone, g'choonk.

I flopped on the bed, empty, smoking, listening to the phone ringing and ringing, and fell asleep before it stopped. I remembered no moment of silence, no dreams, nothing but her footsteps going down the steps, then coming up, then a knock at the door. I awoke. It was early afternoon. She leaned over me and I caught her hand. I dragged her down like a subaqueous evil scaly. We kissed. She kissed me. I bit her ear. We kissed and were naked when the phone began ringing. I let it. We had D. H. Lawrence and Norman Mailer, then *triste*.

I lighted cigarettes. She put the ashtray on her stomach. Even tired, groggy and depressed I could see we were a great team. Smoke bloomed, light failed, and before the room became dark I turned on my side to examine her stomach and thighs. A man of property checks his fences. The "PHILLIP'S" were in each of the places. All about them like angry birds were "MAX'S," "FRANK'S," "HUGO'S," "SIMON'S."

"For God's sake," I said.

I looked into her eyes. She looked into mine. She put out her cigarette and turned her back to me. I was about to yell, "Blow ye hurricanoes," when I noticed down her spine: "YOYO'S," "MONKEY'S," "HOMER'S," "THE EIGHTY SEVENTH STREET SOCIAL AND ATHLETIC CLUB'S."

I slumped, my voice trickled slow and feeble:

"All right, we'll do this properly. We'll get to know each other. I see you're difficult. That's good. Difficulty is an excellent instructor, just the one I need. It'll extend the reach of my original impressions. I misjudged you, but I appreciate you. I'll study you like a course. Please turn around. Let me kiss you, all right?"

She turned. I kissed her. She kissed me. We had Henry Miller.

In the shower I scrubbed everyone off front and back and asked what her name was.

"Cecily."

"I'm Phillip," I said, "but you knew that. Cecily? Of course, Cecily."

I couldn't have stopped the tears unless I'd chopped out the ducts with an adz. She giggled, stamped her feet, clapped her hands with glee.

Asa Baber Jr.

My Sister and Me

For fifteen you would say I am advanced. This would get no argument from me because I am proud of my size and I like people to notice me. I am six feet tall but no creep. My sister's girl friends all say they would date me, and more than once I have gone out with them after their show. I am not implying that I am a great lover, but I am advanced in all areas, even though my scores are none of your business.

Suzy got this crazy idea one night when we were at Trader Vic's. I thought it was the rum talking, so I cooled it and didn't argue at first, which was a mistake because when she gets an idea she keeps it. She doesn't have many, but she holds the ones she's got. I was with Dawn that night, and Suzy was with Mr. Loeb, who is a slob but pays the bills. He was giving me pseudo-fatherly advice through his cigar and trying to play footsie with Suzy at the same time. It was funny listening to this moralistic talk while his feet and knees danced around under the table like an organ player's.

"What you need is a good school, Jerry. This life is no good for you. A boy has to be well educated these days or he'll go nowhere."

Suzy picked it up like a cue.

"I keep telling him that. He's got all sorts of big-shot ideas and he won't listen to me. He thinks he can go on like this with me paying for him."

Mr. Loeb just wasn't making it with Suzy, so he decided to do something big.

"You get that boy in school. Already he has missed a year, and he's running around Chicago like an adult with no responsibilities. You take him and find the most expensive school you can get. A check I give you—four thousand bucks I give you for the first year. Like a son he is to me, and I want him to have the best."

And he wrote out the check and handed it to Suzy, who tried to act like it was something that happened every day.

All I could do was gobble egg roll and suck rum through my straw. Dawn and I had ordered one of those big drinks with a gardenia floating in it, and she was drinking, too. I knew she was shook up about the check, not because she wanted the money, but because she didn't want to lose me. Now don't get psychoanalytic about it—she was as old as Suzy, almost twenty-eight, and we had a few things going which are none of your business, but mostly it was just that we could talk to each other. She danced in the same show as my sister, but she had a lead number and she was intelligent in a crazy way. Like before Mr. Loeb had upstaged us all, she had been talking about Machiavelli, which was part of the reading assignment she had given me.

Suzy looked at the check a couple of times. She tried to cry, but it was tough while she read the date and account number to herself and made sure everything was OK. Then she cried real good and excused herself for a minute. Mr. Loeb tried to go out with her, but she stood up to her six feet two and just pushed him back down like the shrimp he was. So he talked big to me about initiative and character and how he'd made it in sausages and refrigerated meats. When Suzy came back we had sweet-sour pork and fried rice and pressed duck and Dawn and I ate with chopsticks. It was too late to have more drinks, so we went right over to the Frolics in a cab, because the girls have to be there a half hour before the show time. Mr. Loeb went to his table and I went backstage with the girls.

Most guys my age would probably play with themselves at the thought of going backstage with the line at the Frolics, but then they have not been going back there for ten years. It was for me a family affair. I knew all the girls and they had known my parents before they were killed, so it was no big deal. That is not to say I didn't keep my eyes open.

Most of the time I was sneaking around the band. I always bothered Sonny during rehearsals, and got him to teach me something about the drums. He said I'd probably be as good a drummer as a white man could be, and I could run through the basic flams and paradiddles pretty well. He let me sit in every once in a while. This particular night I didn't even care, because it'd all be over and I'd be back in school soon. Also, his eyes were glassy. I knew he was on the stuff and wouldn't talk to anyone. So I sat there and listened to the show out front. Mac was on, with his Irish-Jew jokes I'd heard a hundred times, and the poor-johns were laughing it up as if that would bring on the girls. Nothing sounds funny backstage. No, that's not right. If somebody goofs out front, then you laugh your fool head off. Sometimes Mac was a little stewed, and he'd screw up a punch line or something and then I'd laugh.

Dawn came over with a book. Every night she'd give me a new book to read. It's the best kind of education. This one was by Walter Lippmann.

"School will be good for you, Jerry."

"I don't think so."

"This is no life for a kid. I'm bad for you, too."

"Don't start that. I'm not a kid."

"In some ways you are."

"How many guys my age are reading Lippmann?"

"Don't be silly. You aren't in the system, and that's what hurts. You read comics in the system, you win. You read Lippmann outside, you lose. There's my cue."

She stood up and shook her arms like they were noodles. She never talked about it, but I don't think she liked to strip in front of those guys. She had a fast number, you know, lots of business, and she always came offstage out of breath and tired, but cool still, and sweet smelling like jasmine. Some of the chicks, like Candy, smelled like hogs after a set. They were supposed to be sexy because they got sweaty and basic, but they always reminded me of wrestlers.

That night was shot. Suzy tried to make it big and gay, like we had suddenly found the secret to cancer or something. But I knew that she'd given notice, and that the next day we'd head for school, so I sulked, which is the right of any fifteen-year-old. They played like it was a joyous time, like I'd just been circumcised, and we hit the spots after the show. It was useless—we dropped Dawn at her apartment, and Mr. Loeb stayed in our living room while Suzy made a lovely fuss about getting me to bed.

I was wrong. We didn't go to any school the next day. We went to Brooks Brothers. What a joint; quiet, dull, almost holy, with a creepy elevator. Some of the clothes were not bad, a little wild in a queer sort of way. But I couldn't go near them. Suzy had this school catalogue, and she kept talking about a dark suit for Sunday chapel—I thought maybe I could sneak in an Italian silk. Instead, the salesman, who acted like he owned The Drake, brought out a black flannel suit. It felt like an army blanket. That was it. They loved it; the queer little tailor kept measuring me—crotch to instep, crotch to instep—and Suzy paid extra to have it ready in an hour. It fit like a tank. They all kept patting me; you'll keep growing, ha, ha, ha, a pinch on the bicep. Man, I got out of there. The only thing that saved me was one girl with enormous boobs who wrapped the package. She'd try to break the string, and her chest would expand while she stared at me, and then snap! the string would break and she'd shake like jello when she smiled. Suzy didn't like her, but Suzy was jealous.

May I never have another day like that day. From the tailor to the barber, where they shaved my head like it was a white sidewall, nothing left. Shoes I had to buy, no more alligators but heavy red ones, and white ones that made my feet look like balloons. Ties like prison shirts; shirts like button monopolies—buttons on the collar, the back of the collar, everywhere. When they were done Suzy was proud of me. I hated me. It wasn't me.

The next day we flew to New York. I had been in planes before— mostly private ones to Reno and Vegas. Compared to them the big birds are dull. We went first class, of course, because Suzy had Mr. Loeb's credit cards. I was not impressed. The stewardess kept calling me Mr. Lieberman like she'd known me for years and I was about to be President. She was not so hot, but she looked better after a few martinis. Suzy was ordering two of them at a time, and the stewardess—Miss Harris—well, Miss Harris played it coy with a lot of "Are you old enough to drink?" and "Naughty boy" stuff, and about the third round I told her I was old enough to do anything she could think of. She didn't know what to make of it for a second, but Suzy ruined it all because she laughed. Now Suzy's laugh is not exactly dainty—it comes out like a bowling ball and ends in a fit of coughing because she smokes so much. Mr. Loeb always asked her how could a girl with such a beautiful chest have such bad lungs. Did you ever think of that? When you see somebody really good-looking, ask yourself, I wonder what they'd look like if every other day they had to turn themselves inside out; you know, nostrils and lungs and colon all displayed. Anyhow Suzy's lungs are not the best from smoking and years of hoofing it without much on, and she coughed and laughed and coughed, and I lost Miss Harris.

We checked into the Commodore in New York, and Suzy started calling schools. We didn't waste time—we drove down to one that afternoon in a Mercedes convertible she rented.

What a joint it was—like a country club it was, with tennis courts and football fields and ivy walls. Even though it was August, there were people all over the place, and the football team was kicking around like the Chicago Bears training camp.

Suzy pulled up to the red brick building with Administration on it. There were two guys standing on the steps. She showed a lot of leg getting out of the car and they almost dropped their pipes. My sister has no sense of timing. Here we were in a school, and she walks past these jerks like she was on a runway at State and Lake—mince, mince, little steps and lots of jiggles.

No, the Headmaster (that's what they call the cat) was not available. Certainly we could make an appointment, any time next week—the secretary looked like she was scared of everything, especially me; because I kept winking at her. She couldn't believe it, and she couldn't stop looking at me to see if I really was winking.

Suzy tried to stamp on my foot. It was just getting good—up with the eyes, wink, down with the eyes, blush, fluster—when this tall creep comes out of the office and stares at Suzy like he was in the Salvation Army and was there to save her.

Now once a guy looks at Suzy with grace abounding, she's won. And she milked this bit, let me tell you, with the tremulous voice and the teary eyes, all the time pulling her sweater tight across her boobs by pretending to look for a handkerchief in her purse, talking about how we couldn't come back next week, we just had to see him today. He came in on cue.

"Miss Quoon, I've told you before that my door is always open," and Miss Quoon by this time hated all of us. I just kept staring and winking.

The interview—or should I call it Suzy's lament?—lasted for some time. I hardly said a word. I kept watching the guy behind the desk. He sat and swiveled in the afternoon sunlight—the sun came through the windows behind his desk, and as far as I could tell it served two purposes: it made a halo effect for his blond balding head, and it burned the eyeballs out of whoever was sitting and talking to the Headmaster—like the lights in the Hyde Park police station. Suzy began by putting the check on the desk, and the Headmaster looked at it from his chair. I was filling out forms. Suzy explained how brilliant and advanced I was. She made excuses for what she called my "lack of formal education."

All the time they were talking I was trying to write and listen. There was something strange about this guy. Then it hit me: he licked his words! What a gimmick? Every few words and his tongue would flick out after the sounds, then lick his lips.

"Formal education [lick] is, uh, not everything. (Lick.) After all, Aristotle said, 'Let early education be a sort of amusement.' (Lick.) Don't you agree?"

"No . . . sir." (Teachers are like generals, my sister told me. You always call them "sir.") "I mean, I dig the idea, but Plato said it. *The Republic.*"

"Ah yes, that's right, Plato." (I thought he was going to lick, and I waited for it to come, but it didn't) "You've read *The Republic*?"

"Yes, sir. I'm taking an informal course in politics from one of my sister's friends."

"A professor, I presume."

"Yes, sir, of sorts . . . Anyway, I've read it." (I couldn't figure this guy.)

"A distinguished book, the cornerstone of our political thought, don't you agree?"

"Not exactly." (Here Suzy cleared her throat and shot a few daggers but it was too late.) "Plato's got some creepy-crawly ideas about politics— you know, things like democracy giving equality to equals and unequals alike. Plato was a snob that way—five to one, if he were alive today, he'd never listen to modern jazz, for example." (Man, I was in deep—not a muscle moved. I could see the dust on his shoulders in the sunlight—I realized he never listened to jazz either.)

"Your young brother is quite an original boy, Miss, uh, Lieberman. Of course it's late [lick] in the year to apply—tests to take and all that."

So they shoved me in another room and for four hours Miss Quoon gave me I.Q. tests, achievement tests. I asked her for a blood test, too, but that pissed her off. Suzy waited in the car.

Being a Jew, I am aware of the polite brush-off, the extra smile, the false firm grip. Mind you, I'm not neurotic about it, but I am ready for it. After the tests, as we said good-by, I could smell it. Suzy swears I am wrong, that what happened next had no effect on my application. Me, I know better.

First, we got lost on the campus. It was easy. They had roads going in circles, roads into forests, roads around houses. It started to get embarrassing when we passed the same people three or four times. I wanted to ask directions, but Suzy started giggling and driving faster and faster, and pretty soon there was the Mercedes, a cloud of dust, and kids waving after us. We passed football practice five times at least, and the whole team would wave and holler and the coach would blow his whistle.

The fifth time around I made her stop. I got out, trying to cool it, like all I wanted was to watch the practice. Of course she had to follow me and make a big production of taking her heels off and walking in her bare feet, so by the time I got to the field, they were watching her, and I was the only one watching the practice.

Soon a big character comes off the field. He looks like an ape; heavy skin, big hands. He pretends not to notice us, but he stops near us, guzzles water, spits it out, bites into an orange and spits the peel. The big animal number, the watch-me-ain't-I-sweaty bit. Suzy ignores him; I watch him. Among other things, I figure I can make it in this school if he's in it. The coach calls him:

"Landowski, get ready to lead the laps." So he's the captain or something. So what?

He starts to talk to Suzy; she only smiles. He's a wise guy. He's got a mammary-complex, and all the time he talks he looks right at her tits. I try to ignore him, too, until he asks Suzy who the little boy is, and can't she get rid of him.

At that point I ask him if his name is Landowski. He looks surprised and says it is.

"Then," I say real quiet, "where's your frigging harpsichord, Wanda?"

Everything happened at once. Suzy laughed, the brute looked white, then red (he really didn't understand the insult, all he knew was I'd called him a girl's name) and let out a scream, I moved away and he came after me, the team made a circle around us, and I broke Landowski's jaw.

It was over very fast, because you do not live in nightclubs all your life and remain ignorant. I knew enough to take care of myself, what with expert tutoring by the bouncers. I had to go for the jawbone, because he had all that padding and protection on.

I was sorry. The coach came over and almost cried. He chewed me out, telling me how this was the captain, this was the only holder of the Yale Alumni Postgrad Scholarship, this was . . . and he slowed down, looked at me carefully, and asked me why I hadn't tried out for the team.

"Because I'm not in this school."

"What are you doing here?"

"Trying to get into this school."

"Well, you've made a bad start, understand. I don't condone violence or dirty play—but, properly channeled, given the proper rein, aggressiveness can be a virtue." (I'm sure he made this speech once a day, since he was looking around, helping Landowski to his feet, motioning to his team to move away—which they did, like a bunch of cows.)

"You should apologize for your actions. I cannot give you my highest recommendation but, uh, but, uh, run over to the gym there and put on some pads and let's see what you can do, how brave you are in a sporting way."

What the hell, I thought, we're lost and can't get off the campus anyway. Suzy sat down on the bench by the water buckets.

One thing before your heart begins to bleed for a poor youth brought up in a nightclub, who has to go untried onto the football field—I knew more football than any of these jerks. Not that I'd played too much (except at the Bears' training camp in Indiana, where they'd let me go through light workouts, no contact, when Mr. Loeb flew us down. He owned part of the team, I guess). But the pro ballplayers got free booze at the Frolics, just for the publicity, and so I had my own private tutors in that game.

It was not the easiest practice, because I'd hurt their captain, so the line didn't even block on the first play I ran. The second play I called, a roll-out pass, started the same way, but I remembered what Sid Luckman told me and I threw the ball as hard as I could into the linebacker's face. He couldn't even tackle me. They would have blocked for me after that, but the coach took me out, said it was dirty and ungentlemanly, and what was my name?

"Lieberman."

"Well, Lieberman, it is obvious that you have no understanding of this game. That was a dirty thing to do. You have now ruined two of my starting players. Do you know who that was? Do you know who you hurt?"

"No."

"That is the son of the Chairman of the Board of Trustees."

"He was red-dogging."

"Do you see that gymnasium, that huge building? The Chairman gave us that. He gave us that, and he wants to see his son play. That may not be possible now. Lieberman, if you broke his son's nose, anything could happen. The Chairman might . . . he might even change his will. Just because of you."

"What should I have done?" (A little dialectic never hurt a football coach.)

"Run." (He said it real proudly, like a stripper in a police line-up for the first time.)

"Run? It was a pass play. I called a roll-out to the weak side and he blitzed on me."

"You should have run." (Now he had his nose in the air.)

"Look, it isn't logical. You had them in an umbrella with the ends floating. I had no guards pulling out, I had nothing, and with no line-backers left after the red-dog, they were open in the middle and . . ."

"Lieberman, Lieberman, I am not a proud man. You are a big boy. You seem to know some football. Now, Lieberman, do you want to come here to school?"

"No, but I have to try."

"OK. If you come here, do you want to play football?"

"I don't care. Do I have to go to class?"

"Of course you have to go to class."

"No deals?"

"No deals; certain advantages, of course, as any scholar-athlete deserves. But we are a preparatory school and there is no emphasis to speak of."

Now I am a hard-dealer, a player of ice-poker, of cold-chess, and the world to me is Machiavelli-made, good laws and good arms, power and property. But for a few special jerks I would do anything. Suzy being such a jerk, I told the coach I'd play if he'd get me in the school. Suzy was over by the water buckets, but she knew what I was doing, and she looked proud in her dumb way . . .

Now that I've been schnooked, canned, booted, I can look back on the joint as a circus (you know, a clean circus) . . . No more miserable life could I imagine. Why there was no revolution I could not understand —until I met some of the guys there, and realized that this was what they wanted, that this was some sort of guarantee for them, some order and contract with their society, with their parents and friends. But at first I did not know that.

I was put in the Whitney House, run by Mr. and Mrs. Carp. Mr. Carp played the organ in chapel and walked on his toes. He was a little deaf, I think, because he played the organ so loudly that our voices were drowned out. He was a good old jerk, who spent most of his spare time in his garden, talking to his flowers. He was crazy and I liked him.

Mrs. Carp was very much younger, with just a few gray hairs, and with good legs, first-class Dietrich legs. In a place where there are no women, a chick like that can bother you and pull out all your complexes. She did not exactly make it easy, either, as she was not getting enough from him and it made her nervous. After every football game, when I got back to the house, she'd give me a big kiss, and they got bigger from weekend to weekend. Do not begin to read tea and sympathy into this, as I deny everything.

As I look back, I realize that it was tough for them to keep me there through the season. Take the first day:

I'm coming back from class. I get in the house and start to climb the stairs, not paying attention to what I'm doing, thinking about the creeps in the checkered vests and dirty white shoes. Those shoes threw me. I'm wearing white shoes too, but they're really white, not all torn up, scuffed, beaten. I'm thinking how I'll never cut it here, how I try to wear the right things and I still lose.

I walked into the wrong room.

OK. It's a stupid move, but the house is old and confusing. What do I find? Three guys sitting in suits, smoking and drinking martinis. At two in the afternoon. So I stood there, and they looked at me like I was the Grand Inquisitor. Not a word. All the time I'm figuring if I stand there they'll give me a drink. School rules, school schmoos. Finally a skinny big bum gets up. He plays D.A.

"Aren't you a new boy?"

"Yeah."

"You should be in your room."

"Yeah."

"Look here, this may be against the rules, but it's a purely social thing. Now be a good boy and go to your room and don't say anything about this." (He had his arm around my shoulder by then and was pulling me out of the room.)

My sister always told me if it's fair for one it's fair for all. "I want a drink."

"Look here, go to your room. Impudence will not be tolerated." (Here the other two guys looked at me square.)

"I'll go, but on my way I'll leave a little note for Carpy."

(Silence—ugly looks—I smile—he pours me a short one—I drink it.)

"Now get out."

"One more for the road." (They come toward me—I back out—all the time they're calling me new kike, new kike, yid, yid—I slam the door on them and catch a hand—I hear the scream and retreat to my room.)

In those first few days I had broken several of their bones, and this was not good. Soon they stopped leaning on me, crowding me, and the treatment I got was like ice. No one spoke; no one nodded; I was nothing; I was not even there except for a few hours on Saturday, and even then the silence was terrible. I would call signals and hear my voice coming back at me, and pad against pad would echo, the sock and sorrow of the game, knees cracking and shoulders wrenching. For me there was no glory, and once when I scored both sides were silent, one from despair, the other from contempt, and I remember the sun socking my face. I was so pissed I ran through the end zone and threw the ball into the pond. The refs went crazy trying to figure out a penalty for that one.

The last game of the season was the big one. The whole school went crazy the week before the game. There were posters and rallies, and for a time it was kooky. Friday night they had a bonfire in front of the gym. The band was playing, and they were throwing dummies dressed in the uniforms of Pelham School into the fire. The team was standing on the steps of the gym. For me it was uncomfortable watching the dummies fly-flopping into the flames; I kept remembering my sister's stories about Grandpa Lieberman and how he had been burned for soap. But none of the guys screaming and yelling were thinking of that.

Each member of the team was supposed to make a speech. Before that an alumnus from the class of '19 led the school in the cheer he'd composed as a senior. It went:

> "Poke Pelham, Punch Pelham, poke, poke—
> When we're through with Pelham,
> There'll be nothing left but smoke."

They all screamed this, and the poor old alumnus got more and more excited, jumping up and down and spitting the words out through his bad bridge. The Headmaster finally came up and led him back to his seat.

The speeches by the team were ridiculous. There was a great roar from the crowd after each sentence, and I could tell they were not listening, so I played with them, as the bodies were tossed into the fire and the cheers went on and the torches waved.

"And now our quarterback, Jerry Lieberman."

(Moderate roar with some boos.)

"Thank you."

(Bigger roar, with some more boos. A loose figure somersaults into the blaze. They're all frantic now, screaming, blind.)

"Poke Pelham." (That starts the cheer again.) "We're going to win." (Roar) "Unt ve must vin mit der vootball." (Roar) "Ist das ist ein vootball?" (Roar) "Ist you all gut little schnitzels?" (Roar) "Sieg Heil!" (Roar) "Sieg Heil!" (Roar)

I cut it short, because the Headmaster looked pissed. Given a little time to work on them, they might have burned the library.

The day of the game was a special day; no Saturday morning classes, no study halls, no obligations except group hate. Cadillacs and Lincolns filled the parking lots, and it was tweedy as all hell—camel-hair coats, plaid skirts, lunches on the back doors of station wagons, Thermos bottles and flasks. Since no one was visiting me, I sat in my room reading Burke. Dawn was still sending booklists.

Like I said, I'm sitting there reading Burke when I hear these whistles and yells all over the campus. It gets louder. I think maybe the Pelham team has arrived, and I go outside to look. There, way across campus, some kind of movie star has arrived. There's a long limousine, and all the guys are crowding around a big blonde. I laugh and start to go back in my room when I hear it, the voice of the bowling ball, the pickled vocal cords, setting the campus on its ear—"Jerreeeeeeee"—it yells. I look again and this blonde is running across the grass toward me. In her heels and tight dress she looks like a cow on ice, and behind her comes this little fat guy with a big cigar who looks suspiciously like Mr. Loeb. All this is being watched by the whole campus, whistling and jeering, and by Carpy, who has come out on the front porch.

"Jerreeee!" (Smooch, hug, love and sugar kiss.)

"Say there, kid. You're looking great. Have a cigar." (Mr. Loeb is very nervous, and his eyes are glittering like footlights. He keeps looking at Carpy. The Carp just blinks and walks on his toes.)

"No, Mr. Loeb, I can't. I can't smoke here. It's against the rules."

"Slip you one later on the sly, huh, kid?" (Glitter, glitter go the eyes—you'd think it was his first time in a whorehouse.)

"Jerry, we came to see the game. I got the whole weekend off. You like my wig, honey?"

Still the campus was shrieking and wailing and laughing, and I wanted to get those two inside, but that meant steering them by Carpy. It meant I had to introduce them. The Carp was dancing across the porch. He was as uneasy as Mr. Loeb, and he kept blinking like a rabbit. I introduced them. Mr. Loeb decided to make a big show, and it was the first time I ever saw the Carp silent, lost, just blinking.

"Hi there. How's this boy working out, huh? Pretty good, huh? Have a cigar. No, c'mon, have a cigar. Listen, I pay this kid's bills, and I want you to have a cigar. That's better. Pretty good boy, huh? Listen, he's had a few troubles out here. You get him through, I'll see you get a little present. Understand?"

Finally I got them through the door, leaving Carpy with his cigar.

Mr. Loeb was not impressed with my room. He gave me a lecture about the cost, about how it cost eighteen bucks a day, and for that you should have some style, some class. Full-length mirrors, things like that. There was no arguing with him. Suzy thought the room was quaint.

You read a lot about how the course of the world is changed by small responses; you know, what if Luther had healthy bowels or Napoleon comfortable skin. Small responses make up our intelligence—guts and teeth and adenoids all work on us. Me, I am led by my nose, and with Suzy and Mr. Loeb in my small room I was happy for the first time in that room. I could smell the perfume and powder straight from backstage, and Mr. Loeb's Arden hair tonic and cigar smoke and blue-serge sweat, and it all came back, all the crazy confusion and independence. Suddenly none of it made sense—none of the school cheers or white shoes or social contacts. I wanted to be back with drums, breasts, smoke, liquor, light.

So let us make it short, let us cut it here—the chauffeur brought in lunch and drinks, and I got drunk. Training table, training schmable. Give me sausages and fish and spices, all glubbed down with Scotch, smoky Scotch that I had not tasted for weeks. And cigars, and Suzy singing songs from *Pal Joey,* and Mr. Loeb talking bigger, and me, eating and drinking and remembering, waiting for the game.

When they finally broke in on us, I was skunked. Landowski led me away. They threw me into a cold shower, but it didn't help much, and they got me dressed. Somehow they kept me away from the coach, and they pretended to tape my ankles during the warmups. I knew then that they wanted that game, because they protected me, they lied for me, and at the same time they hated me. I kept asking: why should I get my ass busted, why?

Maybe everything would've been OK if Suzy hadn't made her grand entrance just after the kickoff. It was our first huddle, and my head ached, and I was trying to remember the numbers of the plays. Then there was this explosion in the bleachers, and I could see a thousand horny bastards trying to look up and down Suzy's dress. She didn't help, either, taking off her jacket and bending over as she climbed into the seats.

That was it for me. I called a bootleg, and faked it gorgeously, so that when the lines piled up and the whistle blew, I was still holding the ball, standing near the sidelines as if I was already out of the play. Then, as they were untangling the bodies, I walked over very slowly to the ref, and handed him the ball. Man, he was creamed. Immediately they tackled him. Both sides. There was a silence all over, while everyone tried to figure out the situation.

It was time to cut out. The coach was headed toward me, followed by the Headmaster, and behind them the students. I started running around the gym, turned into the golf course, and aimed for the tennis courts. One lap around the campus was all I knew I could make, but it might give Suzy and Mr. Loeb time to get back to the car.

I kept looking over my shoulder. The whole school was chasing me now, screaming, waving their fists, and I could see the Carp running lightly on his toes, surprisingly fast for a man his age, and the Headmaster, almost floating, like a blond angel, and Landowski pumping along, his face tortured by loyalty. I couldn't get back to the parking lot; there were too many people after me, so I had to run out along the highway. With luck the car would be along and pick me up—without luck, they'd use me as the football for the rest of the afternoon.

It was getting very close when I heard the car honking. I could hear Suzy cursing, and the car was beside me. Landowski had just caught me by the shoulder, and I couldn't shake him. I thought it was all over. I could hear Suzy calling, "Landowski, Landowski," and I wondered why she was calling him, but when I felt his hands let go I dove into through the open door of the car, past Suzy, who was sitting there with the top of her dress down and her melons pointed toward an amazed, paralyzed group. The car dug out and Suzy dressed up.

So those were the prep-school adventures of Jerry Lieberman. Now I am back in the free, swinging life, not respectable, never dull. Please do not think that I condemn those schools completely. After all, Burke said that he didn't know the method of drawing up an indictment against a whole people (actually, he said "an whole people," but that's a fruity way of talking these days). And, as I said to Dawn last night, just before we started in on something that is none of your business, if it's good enough for Edmund, it's good enough for me.

Paul Breslow

Before the Operation

Mrs. Schloss wanted to take off the mask. It had been with her for years now, but only in the last few months had it become oppressive, so that she felt herself choking behind the stiff, unresponsive layer of alien skin that hid her true self from the world. The mask had extended itself; no longer could it be avoided by hiding the small mirrors and draping the larger

C

ones; the mask had grown into a costume, sent out veils and roots and tentacles, become a confusion of monsters and plants; it would never let her go. The mask was getting harder; she was afraid that it would soon stop her from speaking. It would not kill her, of course, they assured her of that, but it would keep people from seeing the precise nature of the soul that it enclosed. Its attacks against the rest of her body were still not as bad as its attacks upon her face. Not that she disregarded the palsy of her arms, or the torpid weight of her legs: these things troubled her more, in the course of every day, than did the slight but persistent sense of itself that the mask transmitted to the surface of her face, like hardening clay in a beauty treatment. Yet it was the mask that supported her in her conviction that she, the thinking and speaking and remembering creature, was not ill or infirm, but, rather, in the temporary hold of a rudely visiting disease. Hope for the departure of that disease, which she often called "Mr. Parkinson's" in order further to remove it from herself, was not the only hope that she could summon to her aid on those terrible mornings when she would wake with just the slightest certainty of her own existence apart from the mask. For whenever her body failed for many minutes to do more than twitch in response to the directions that she issued from behind the mask, she would confirm her presence by sending out silent and merciless appeals for recognition of herself to all that knew her and, she thought, loved her. She would call upon her daughter, Beverly; upon her sister, Statira; upon her friend and doctor, Solomon Cotton; upon the maid, the elevator operator, and the man at the mail desk downstairs; and upon the memory of her dead husband, Rudy.

"Beverly," she said to herself one morning from behind the mask, "Beverly, dear child, you are the scandal of Philadelphia. Just the other day, Solomon Cotton, who is a gentle man as well as a gentleman, said to me again that, if he were to meet you on the street, he would slap your face for the way you have treated me. My dear, he said it, not I." Mrs. Schloss imagined that she saw at the foot of the bed the outraged and distorted face of Beverly with her wild hair and expensive clothes—much more expensive than a young girl ought to permit herself—and she silenced, with a gesture all the more authoritative for its source in a body so frail and tiny, the screaming obscenities that were undoubtedly forming behind Beverly's grimaces, and she continued: "In a normal situation all of Philadelphia would be right to expect you to return to your mother and to care for her, for it is true that a stranger is not the same as a daughter. Not the same at all." Mrs. Schloss now observed that the gesture she had imagined herself to have made had in fact occurred, and that her right arm had been withdrawn from beneath the blanket and was moving shakily toward the glass of water on her bedtable. Her success gave her confidence, and she managed to make herself upright. "Your language is so vulgar," she said to Beverly. She swallowed two Dilaudid pills and took a drink of water. She did not *need* the water to swallow the pills.

She was alone, but she began to address her sister. "You know,

Statira, there is strength in money." It would be good for Statira that Beverly was having a wedding. Attending the ceremony would draw Statira out into the world again. The thing that would bring lumpish Ben Kayser into the family would broaden Statira's horizons. *Here it comes,* she always thought when she saw Statira approaching, a large barking woman, always in purple, a green silk scarf around her neck to hide its 'gatorish coarseness, another silk thing wound about her head like a turban, the gold head of a male on a tarnished chain around her neck, the round stomach sticking out like a basketball, the entire creature rooted to thick, laced Red Cross shoes. "Real strength. It takes heavy ledgers . . ." Statira seemed uncomfortable. Poor Statira, she had never seen Rudy's full strength. But what good had it been? It produced miserable, horrible, ungrateful, wretched, beautiful Beverly, the awful growth from friendly soil. She wondered about that business of opening up her tubes, had that had something to do with Beverly's grotesque character? Was it a test? They said it was a test, but she thought that perhaps this pipe, a slender thing connected to a machine, had, by forcing air through the relevant places, removed some foreign clot from her tender vessels. The way had been cleared for Beverly, foul and lovable thing, to whom, no doubt, such penetrations, or even worse, were a familiar matter. The horror of children: they were ruthless beasts disguised as helpless animals, they appreciated nothing while owing you everything; if it had not been for the test, the pressure of air, there would have been no Beverly. Hah! The pleasing thought gave her the strength to answer the doorbell.

Mrs. Schloss, even in her illness, had a large portion of friends and polite visitors; but lately she had not been seeing many people aside from Dr. Solomon Cotton, a bachelor, owner of real estate, surgeon, and amateur composer who had been much connected with the life of her deceased husband, Rudolph Schloss. Cotton was a figure from the past indeed; he had written the music for his own funeral. As a birthday surprise, Mrs. Schloss had obtained the score and had commissioned its performance by a string quartet, but Solomon had not seemed to appreciate the treat. A figure of the present, too, Cotton was a defender of Eros, in theory and practice, whose role of attendant to his splendidly old mother—approaching one hundred now—did not in the least inhibit him from carrying on a variety of affairs with women Mrs. Schloss thought of as "low class." She owed a great deal to Solomon Cotton: he had convinced her to wait when Rudy had implied, if he had not actually said, that he could not marry before the deaths of his adoring father, adoring mother, adoring grandfather, adoring grandmother, and, it seemed, adoring uncle—all of whom, in Solomon's astute opinion, lacked the strength and confidence necessary to compete with his, Solomon's own mother, in active longevity (even then, she was getting ready to last, shrewdly taking out life memberships in country clubs, buying peculiar annuities, cashing in her life-insurance policies).

"Even if I am wrong, and the method gives you no permanent relief," Dr. Cotton said as he settled into Rudy's leather chair and lit a cigar, "it is nevertheless an excellent prophylaxis. The globus pallidus is no more essential to the brain than are the female breasts to reproduction, and, if I were a woman, I would have simple amputations of the breasts carried out as a sensible precaution against carcinoma. The same principle applies to this part of the brain in people with—a tendency to Parkinsonism." He licked his neat little gray moustache.

"I still think it was the flu that did it."

"Conceivably. Nevertheless . . ."

"I will go to New York first, I'd like to see Beverly. She's getting married you know. You didn't know? She is. Isn't it odd? You haven't seen her for so long, I don't suppose you would even have realized she was old enough."

"A very pretty girl." Tight thighs, long hair, erotic revolution, purple contusions and the songs by colored Holy Rollers. They go around with stainless steel rings bobbing about in the uterus, an excellent practice. "I'd love to see her again."

Now why couldn't Beverly have chosen a nice, mature man? Poor Solomon had faced so many disappointments. "I have absolute confidence in you, Solomon," Mrs. Schloss said.

"I am right," he declared. "There is no other way. Freezing the brain: such nonsense is for morticians, not surgeons. Or electricity, you'd think they worked for the power company. At the same time, we could attempt a transorbital lobotomy, but that depends on the state of my feet. You have to stand up for such a long time, Henrietta, you don't know how wearing it is. As I said, the best method is good old hot water. Once you get the holes drilled, there's nothing to worry about . . . .Billions of extra cells in the brain, the brain has its own spare parts, it's quite amazing. So much unnecessary work goes on in the brain, why not cut out the extra stuff? Nobody stays the same anyway, every seven years all of the molecules in the body are replaced by new ones."

Tears of gratitude came to Mrs. Schloss's eyes. Solomon was kind and helpful and good and a friend of Rudy's. Solomon was a great doctor.

"Do you know what the young people are saying, Henrietta? They've turned against circumcision. That Eva Pozner who was always out of line said to me the other day, I met her at a concert in the Academy—were you there?—she said, 'The insertion of the normal phallus is like an unrolling of a beautiful suede glove, but a circumcised phallus enters with agression, like a cork into a bottle.' She said this during the intermission, and it wasn't a bad concert. Too much new stuff, but it wasn't bad. They are in the wilderness."

The phone rang; Solomon picked it up and brought it over to Mrs. Schloss without answering it. He always knew just the right thing to do. How would it sound if a man picked up the receiver and answered her phone? He thought of things like that; he had been the one to suggest that she get a phone with a long cord; he had thought, long in advance, of just such a situation as this.

"Is that you, Henrietta?"

"Charlotte?"

"Can you hear me? I'm fading now, it won't be long."

"You're sounding well."

"Henrietta. I've just had the last rites."

"What?"

"It was very moving."

"But isn't it—symbolic? I mean, you won't really die."

"I am. Now."

"I'm terribly sorry, Charlotte. This is quite dreadful."

"I suppose so. What else has happened?"

"I'm going to have a brain operation, and Beverly is going to be married. To a young man with long hair who doesn't do any work."

"I'm sorry."

"Please don't worry about it. Not now."

"Why not? It takes my mind off the other thing."

While holding the phone in her right hand, Mrs. Schloss made with her left hand a gesture unlike any she had ever made before: she reached up toward the ceiling with her left arm and she acknowledged to herself that she could not touch it. Then she counted her fingers by moving them one at a time. Each calcifying joint was in its turn covered by tiny quivering creases of flesh; then each was exposed, white and knobby, as the finger in which it lived ceased to exert itself and curved again in similitude to a yellow talon. She had not known that she could move her fingers, one independently of the other, and she did not believe it now.

"You will pass on into a better world," she said into the phone. "That's part of the religion, isn't it?"

"It is apparently part of the religion in some form or the other, but I don't believe it."

"Is there something I can do?"

"You will soon be in my condition."

"That's not a nice thing to say. I don't believe you're going to die at all." There was no response. "Does it hurt?"

"Not too much, but I shudder. Like a spring uncoiling. And I can't move my toes. I can't remember what you look like, Henrietta, and I've forgotten almost everything I've ever done. Good-by, Henrietta."

Mrs. Schloss put down the phone. "Charlotte was always very melo-dramatic," she said to Dr. Cotton. She wondered whether it was true, what Charlotte had said. It must have been a joke. People don't call you on the phone when they're about to die. She turned her mask to Solomon Cotton. "I don't want to die, Solomon," she said.

He smiled, touched his moustache with the tip of a manicured nail. "Maimonides gives us some excellent advice," he said. "Maimonides points out that it is extremely important not to delay one's defecations for even an instant. One should not eat unless hungry and unless one has done enough exercise to warm the body. Rise and do your exercises, then rest your soul, defecate—if necessary—and eat while sitting or reclining on the left side. One must not eat large salty fishes. Eat no radishes in hot weather. The stool must be soft; drink honey and water mixed together . . ."

She was grateful for his kindness, for his smooth, deep voice, for his learning and tact. As if Maimonides, through Dr. Cotton, had himself issued the thoughts—they seemed to come from outside herself, from beyond the mask—she found herself transported, conveyed to her wish by the logic of wishes, she saw her property, the *real property,* observed its sagging floors and cracked windows, its cement cornices crumbling, and she knew that the way to its repair ran through her sacrifice, her pain and mutilation; and she saw that the mask, and the rot that had beset her as rot had beset the shoe store, the hardware shop, the stationery shop, the rot and the mask could be sent away, all foul growth brought to an end, revealing the Henrietta of the core within, opening her shell at last. There would be a cavity, or perhaps a knot of dead gray matter deep within her brain. She would be free. It would no longer matter what Beverly thought of her. But now, before the operation, she needed Beverly, needed her love, needed to stop thinking of her as an enemy. She wanted to be seen before she entered a new life. That afternoon she phoned the Gotham and made a reservation, and Solomon Cotton took her to the bus station.

She stayed three days in her hotel room, phoning Beverly every hour, twelve hours a day. Finally, Beverly answered. "You're here? Why?" she cried. Mrs. Schloss said it was for the wedding. "We didn't invite you," her daughter replied. "Ben doesn't like relatives." Mrs. Schloss explained about the brain operation. "Cotton is a quack. He'll kill you." Mrs. Schloss said that she had absolute faith in Solomon Cotton. "That'll really help," Beverly said. "Look," Beverly said, "never in my life did you do anything for me. You wouldn't even let me have a pet. You killed that rabbit. You agreed with your friends whenever they said anything nasty about me. You took my money, it was in his will that it belonged to me. You kept me a prisoner, until I was too old to control. Now that I've got away, you want me back, and that's all this disease of yours amounts to, an excuse to get me back."

"You are very cruel," Mrs. Schloss said.

"Ben says that where there isn't love, cruelty is better than pity. It does less harm, he says."

"Ben? Ben says? Are you marrying a sadist? A Nazi?"

"You don't like the Nazis only because they killed Jews. If they hadn't done that, you would be all for them. That husband of yours was very fond of Germans wasn't he? You always told me so. Did you go to Germany on your honeymoon or not? The Nazis were in power then, weren't they?"

"That husband of mine was your father."

"So you say. But I can't do anything about it, can I? I suppose I'm lucky I never knew him."

The mask grew tighter on Mrs. Schloss's face. She could barely move her lips. "Will you help me to the bus station?" she asked.

"Can't you make it yourself?"

"I don't feel too well."

"I suppose we could help you if it doesn't take too long."

Why do I hate this woman? Ben Kayser thought as Mrs. Schloss spread her arms and came flopping across the lobby toward them. It made him furious, this disease demanding sympathy, and he wanted to knock her head in. Her fur coat, something formed from the hides of a hundred lynxes, spotted with eggs and ketchup, dusty and brown, many sizes too large for her, lacked buttons and moved with her arms. She looked like a bear staggering to its death uncertainly on its rear feet, its skin blown by the wind, a heavy swaying dying monster, stumbling blindly forward toward its young, to die at their feet. "My dears," she shouted, and she nearly fell over in her eagerness to get to them. Not lynxes, not even a bear: a stupid old woman. Beverly cleared her throat; it's her mother, and she hates her, so why am I to blame for acquiring the distaste? The old lady's face; fixed, lined, frozen, the mouth painted on in bright red, the hair artificial. "You came along, my dear Ben . . ."

Kayser cut her off. "Where's the baggage?" he demanded. She frowned at him and gave a thin little laugh. "You want me to carry the bags don't you? That's why I'm here, isn't it? I mean, Beverly couldn't carry them, could she?" Evidently he had suceeded in sounding offensive, for Mrs. Schloss turned around, nearly falling to the floor (Kayser had to struggle with himself to avoid pushing her over), and then she wobbled toward the rear of the lobby. She led them to the entrance to the women's toilet. A smell of moth balls, perhaps they hang the old ladies on racks in there, Kayser thought. Mrs. Schloss had turned herself around, an accomplishment for her, and was thrusting a slip of paper at him. He looked down at it: a check. "For your wedding present," she said. "I can't really shop now," she explained. "So I see. Where is the baggage?" The witch pretended not to hear, she stood there mute watching him inspect the check—five hundred —and put it in his pocket. "Give her a push, will you?" he said to Beverly. "This place stinks of piss, or disinfectant or something." The old lady kept up the pretense of being sick; she was shaking. He got behind her and poked her in the back. She didn't move, either because she preferred to ignore such indecencies or because the combined effect of the heavy coat and the so-called disease muffled its effect. He poked her again, harder.

"Get moving," he said. Beverly looked at him with raised eyebrows. "We don't want to miss the bus," he said.

"What?" said Mrs. Schloss.

"It stinks of piss here," Kayser said.

"I always ignore such things," Mrs. Schloss told him.

"Move your ass," Kayser said.

"I do very well," Mrs. Schloss said, looking up at him with her expressionless eyes; apparently the eyes did not tremble, although her head shook a lot.

"You can hardly walk," Kayser pointed out, feeling that he ought to instruct her on the truth of her condition. "You seem to be getting worse," he added. With a few more shoves he got her to the door. "Where are your bags?" he demanded. "I can't carry them if they're not here." She pointed to a heap of canvas rucksacks and a plastic wigbox. "What's in there, a bomb?" Kayser said. "Pretty stupid of you to leave the stuff on the sidewalk in this city, you can't trust anyone here. But I suppose it's all worthless anyway."

Mrs. Schloss addressed herself to Beverly. "This was your father's luggage," she said, "which was handmade for him in Paris." Kayser grabbed a rucksack.

"I suppose he also wore a wig," he said.

"The wigbox," said Mrs. Schloss, "is mine, and so is that." She pointed to another canvas container, apparently holding golf clubs. Kayser suspected her of trying to steal someone else's stuff; old people became kleptomaniacs, he remembered reading somewhere.

"How can you play golf when you can hardly move your arms?"

Beverly laughed; "My mother keeps food in there," she said.

In the cab, Kayser decided that he had been too polite; he didn't want the old girl to get the idea he liked doing favors for her. "This is a fascinating way to spend the day," he said. She said, "What?" to indicate that she had heard but that she hadn't liked what she had heard. "Acting as your porter," he explained. He wished Beverly would say more and stop inspecting her lips in the mirror. "Some people would be better off dead," he said, "at least as far as society is concerned." He regretted this remark; he didn't want the old bag to die, just to stay away from him.

"My dear Rudolph had a cutting wit," said Mrs. Schloss. Beverly's head jumped up, as if she had been startled.

The bus terminal was infested by the poor; deformed, resentful figures, carrying their own bags and forcing themselves onward to the Middle West or California. "This is awful," Beverly said, "but I suppose it's cheaper to go by bus." Kayser thought it was interesting to see all these victims of a rotten society gathered in one place, but he didn't think he should say so. "Watch the luggage," he said, "you can't tell what might happen here. These people have no respect for bourgeois values. Of course, they're right." He turned to Mrs. Schloss. "Get your ticket," he shouted. She'll have to be satisfied with my carrying her bags, he thought, I'm not buying her ticket for her. "Why can't she stay in Philadelphia?" he said to Beverly as Mrs. Schloss shuffled off for the ticket. "She'll be gone soon," Beverly said. Kayser waited for some more positive expression of dislike. "She's disgusting," he said. "Oh," said Beverly. "Well, I suppose so." She seemed to be dreaming; about killing her mother, perhaps. "Odd that she didn't get a round-trip ticket," he said, "almost as if she's been planning to stay here." Beverly looked frightened. "You're right," she said, "she's disgusting."

Groaning to call attention to the weight of the bags, Kayser led Beverly and her mother to an escalator. A bevy of incipient corpses stood at the departure gate in postures of fatigue and decrepitude. One of them, a Negro, dressed in a black suit and stiff collar, was carrying a single pair of old shoes; this shortage of luggage apparently caused him shame, and he explained aloud, to the crowd at large, that he had been in New York only two days and therefore he did not need more. "No cause for big cases," he said. Mrs. Schloss pretended to be moved. "He takes it with such dignity," she said. "That's what he gets for a lifetime of ass-kissing," Kayser said. "Old Uncle Tom and the boss's cast-off shoes." Beverly smiled at the Negro. A voice called the Philadelphia bus. "I can't understand why you haven't asked me to your wedding," Mrs. Schloss said. "You'll miss the bus," Kayser said, gathering up the bags.

Beverly told her the truth: "There isn't going to be a wedding. Ben doesn't believe in weddings." Kayser observed that Mrs. Schloss was pleased by this information; perhaps she wasn't so bad after all. "You're better off in Philadelphia," he said, "where your friends can look after you." He pushed her toward the bus with the edge of a suitcase. "Stay well," he called to her.

Mrs. Schloss was put into a white room with blue drapes, a color television set, a foot massager, and an electrically operated bed. "You won't mind being baldy for a while, will you dearie?" said a nurse as she applied electric shears to Mrs. Schloss's thick brown hair. "It grows back dearie." She was left with prickly coldness and a pink bonnet and the thought that it was all Beverly's fault. Beverly Schloss, before this court hear that you have abandoned your mother in hate, be cast in dung and smitten with sore boils from crown to foot, be scummed with ashes and chastened with arrows flung into your hard heart. As she fell asleep, she thought of the freedom to come: bowls of silver nuggets, a new image of Rudy in her mind, soft French cheese, a pear, and a glistening gold knife with tiny cutting teeth. When she woke, she thought of her living room, its chairs with small glass discs under their feet, chairs prohibited from ever touching the carpet. It was wrong to do that to the chairs; when she was better, she would throw away the glass discs, or use them, perhaps, as ashtrays; they had little depressions in them, surely good enough to hold cigarettes. Hands grabbed her, lifted her to a cot on wheels, strapped her down, wheeled her to a swimming pool of a room smelling of old cuts and dental repairs, lifted her again, clamped her into a chair, clamped her head and her feet and her arms, and told her she would feel nothing. She had thought they would put her to sleep.

"Science, shmience, it's just a way of cracking skulls," said dear Solomon Cotton's voice.

They gave her an injection. Not to knock her out, just to keep her dazed.

They swabbed her skull with icicle brushes.

"I'm cold," Mrs. Schloss said. Chickens, why did she think of chickens, then of turkeys? Oh I'm thinking of them because of the bones, the wish-

c*

bones, the snaps you hear, and it must be the noise of cutting my skull open, my bones. A feather duster revolved behind her nose. A bubble burst in her forehead. Her hands opened and closed around the padded tips of the armrests. Her teeth hurt, as if she had bitten her fork while eating. Sweet, sugared soup in her veins. She felt herself a falling phantom in an elevator dropping rapidly through dense dark silted channels. She remembered the story Beverly had made up and told as a child, the funny, precocious child, the strange story about raccoons, it was a lovely story.

Once upon a time an old woman looked outside to get her milk in, and she found a raccoon there, so she put out a pan of milk and she went away.

The next morning she looked out and there were two raccoons. So she put out a pan of milk and went away.

The next morning there were three raccoons. She put out a pan of milk again and went away.

The next morning she looked out and there were a hundred raccoons. She put a pan of milk out for them and she tried to go away, but the raccoons climbed on her and bit her and ate up all the food in the house and drank up all the milk and the old woman ran away and then the raccoons had the house all to themselves. And they lived happily ever after. The raccoons.

Austin C. Clarke

The Collector

By chance Nick saw the landlady get off the Sherbourne Street bus at the stop three doors from the rooming house. He snatched up his hat, his coat, and his old shopping bag, lined with three others; and he slipped through the side door. The landlady was coming for rent. His rent was thirteen weeks in arrears. She had given him four o'clock this Saturday afternoon as the deadline. But she had come early as usual, to sit the whole day in the hallway, like a guard, waiting for the other roomers.

Shuffling along the laneway of blackened winter-weary palings to reach Wellesley Street, a block of safety away, he could feel the force of wind and dampness climbing his urine-and-vomit-starched trousers, as it lodged itself round his thighs. Nick had forgotten to put on his underwear. But it was more than mere forgetfulness: last night he had tottered home drunk from the beverage room in the Selby Hotel where he had drunk twenty-three draughts of fifteen-cents-apiece beer (having begged strangers for twenty of them; and having taken a long time to get them, because the beverage room clientele was always changing, transient as the roomers and prostitutes in the houses along the street. Some of these Friday pay-night drinkers despised him; and some pitied him. Some threw a quarter on the oval, ringed and salt-sprinkled table top in front of him); and he had vomited on his clothes, on the street; and was fortunate to escape the cruising eyes of a police car which got abreast of him just as another car stalled. The car hid him from the police. And it was this same man who helped Nick up the shaking front steps of his crumbling entrance. That was at two o'clock in the morning. It was now seven.

Shuffling through the laneway now, Nick tried to remember all the events of last night. But to think, so early, on an empty stomach, in the cold, and with his head going round and round like a ferris wheel coming to a stop . . . well, Nick had to think about rent money: seven dollars which (after forty-five minutes of pleading and abusing and being arrogant, crying and pleading again, on the telephone at seven o'clock Friday morning when the landlady woke up the whole house, as the pay-phone in the hall bellowed for ten piercing minutes) he had promised to put into her hand first thing Saturday morning at nine o'clock (or "if not, at four, the latest, 'cause I not have time sitting here all day, Mr. Evans!") as a token of his intentions—though not ability, as was obvious this morning—to bring his arrears up to date. Last night, wondering how to get the money without having to work for it, and wandering near the Selby where he thought he would get it; and then going there to see if he could get it there, he had seen Indian Johnson who loaned him two dollars (from his daily car-washing wage of eight dollars) to help him with his rent. But he had helped Indian drink out *his* six, on beer, and then had spent the loan on Indian and himself. "You just loaned me two. I loan you back two. Now we squared-off. Right?" Indian Johnson grabbed him by his neck and hissed, "Who say so?" Rubbing the circulation back into his neck, Nick said, "All right, all right. I was only joking, Indian boy. Only a joke." And the transaction was forgotten.

On this cold morning at seven o'clock before the garbage trucks came out like cockles, he was now retracing his steps along his favorite, fruitful route, searching for empty soft-drink bottles. He had to go out before the crawling white trucks got all his empties of Pepsi, Coca Cola, Teem and Ginger Ale, which were among the most merchandisable merchandise of bottles.

It was following his attack of pneumonia in January 1965, and the beginning of an arthritic tenseness in his limbs, that Nick first experienced the taste of chronic hardships. He lost the job he had washing cars, in a semi-automatic, jet-fast car wash, because his limbs were suddenly like the Tin Man's and he was no longer the whizzing wizard of shine and tone among cars; because too, he came to work too late too often, too drunk.

He never could impress the manager that he had to drink a lot to help the pain, a little to soothe the unbearable stings that rambled through his legs and right arm. (He never could understand why the needles of torment never entered his left arm: "If only I was a south-paw! Why, I couldda licked this job.") He hadn't worked from February until late in May, when hunger and the exhaustion of friends and strangers (from whom he could trick a few pennies with "mister-spare-a-dime-for-a-cuppa-karfee?" while standing too near the entrance to the Selby) drove him onto the streets, to experiment with his body; and also, to tread like a postman over garden paths, over lawns and broken bottles, dog filth and human filth of old mattresses and forgotten shoes and handbags, for three sweating, sore days in the dilapidated Parliament Street area, to stuff samples of Dial Soap which "kills bacteria and prevents odors" into letter boxes, thrown onto rotting porches, or left in the front yards, like the children and the snow. He was distributing them for a large downtown advertising agency. And scarcely had he received his wages in the small collection-size brown envelop before he was sitting in the beverage room of the Chez Moi tavern, comfortable as if he was in his room, drinking draught beer and eating potato chips and cursing "them goddamn kooks," the Frenchmen and the Canadiens "who beat the balls off Toronto Maple Leafs" in the hockey championships just concluded. But the money was shorter than his hatred for French Canada. And after a few gracious "loans" and gifts of a dollar here and seventy-five cents there, and after several "buy me one, mister?" he was plunged into the gutters of early morning Toronto Saturdays and Sundays, searching for empty wine bottles. He found them in laneways and parking lots and garbage pails. In those collecting days he used to drink wine: cheap, throat-corroding wine; and sherry too. The retail value of an empty wine bottle was high as the wages of sin. But one night he and his friend Indian Johnson parked in a parked cold car in winter, beside the car wash where Indian still miraculously held his job, and where Nick used to work, and they drank and talked; and drank; and talked about boxing, that "Cassius Clay gonna burst Floyd's kisser"; and they drank some more, and talked some more about Clay's left jab, ("Goddamn, Indian! I can see myself with Clay's left. Bam! bam! bam! Right in a copper's goddamn face! Bam-bam-bam!") and they drank until they couldn't talk anymore, until the yellow cruiser with two policemen in it found them, early that Sunday morning the 16th of May, in the little Model T 1928 Ford on display, their bodies locked together by the paste and the thickness of their vomit, and joined by some sort of homosexual glee. Nick said afterward, he could smell alcohol on the breath of the ruddy-faced policeman who drove the cruiser. Nick was charged with being drunk in a public place. And Indian Johnson was given a stiff, sobering beating by the other, older, graying policeman in the cruiser, before they reached the station; and afterward laid to rest on the doorstep of the house in which the identification on his Blue Cross slip said he lodged. From that night, Nick's mind turned against wine, and collecting empty wine bottles. Instead he set his affection on soft drink bottles, with the occasional beer bottle, when stumbled upon.

Early this morning, before the dogs, before the hearse-like city collec-- tion of garbage, before Indian or any of his friends could crawl from their drunken haphazard rest under the stairs of basements (for three uninter- rupted weeks, last winter, Nick slept in the furnace room of a downtown hotel bar, before the waiter who had sneaked him into this resting place, in exchange for the use of his body, grew tired with it, and then gave him a heavy beating. And only God knew how Nick didn't burn himself to death in that furnace room!); before the yawning, stretching first passengers of nurses going to hospitals, you can see Nick, large and billowy in a too-large brown winter coat, dark glasses ("Never show the true look in thine eye, Indian Johnson! Never!"), shoes as large as a clown's, shuffling along Church Street, going north to carry out his minute examination of the symp- toms of last night's illegal drinking and illegal happiness and love, in parked alleyways. Nick knows the city better than anyone, including Mayor Givens; because he knows the city's garbage. Ah! a bottle! Nick sees it glimmering like sun and snow against a stunted post, in the parking area of a supermarket. Nick shuffles up, on feet that have no arches, their hav- ing fallen many years ago (from marching in the War; from walking through the grounds and halls of the university, where he was a porter-messenger before they found him and a philosophy student, in a telephone booth, in the basement, a breath away from the liniment and sweat of the men's gymnasium, one night during the Michaelmas term), here he is now, archless, a man with a fallen past and spirit, broken finally when he worked for one week and two days as an orderly at the Doctors Hospital, shuffling to take up the bottle. "Five cents! A wine bottle, goddamn! Need a wash- ing, though!" . . . There is a note inside. Nick pounds the mouth against his palm, and he does not see the small black cockroach crawl out: but when it touches his skin, he catches fright, and drops the bottle, all five cents worth. "Goddamn!" He stomps his foot like a ton of slab on the small cockroach, three times (although it was already killed from the slap he gave it to knock it off his sleeve), and said, each time with increased venom, "Bugger! Bugger! Bugger!" He wiped away the corpse of the cockroach, leaving only a ghost of a stain, to register that once there was a cockroach in a bottle. He kicked away the crystals of the green bottle; and then he re- membered the note. It was written on a half page, torn from a child's writing exercise book, with double lines. It said: *Norman, I am not making no more fun with you. I have taken the baby to my mother. You can find me there, if you want me. Elaine.* Nick pondered for a long time on the plight and flight of Elaine and Norman and the baby; wondering whether Norman would "chicken-out" and go to Elaine's mother's place; whether Norman should go ("Mother-in-laws're bitches, all o' them! Why in hell does a man got to have a mother-in-law?"); and whether Elaine's flight came through the plight of Norman spending all his wages on wine and strong drink, and didn't remember milk for the baby; whether the room and the baby were cold . . . ("That's goddamn kindness from Norman! No milk of human kindness for little Norman the second.") But he soon shrugged their plight out of his mind, for he had more bottles to look for; and there was no point worrying about Norman's problems, when he had to find seven dollars worth of empty bottles before his landlady left the rooming house, at four this afternoon. Plus, finding a storekeeper to buy them off him. "Some o' the bastards think they own the city." He was now out for twenty minutes; and not a bottle yet. So he scoured the parking lot a little more, efficient as a vaccum cleaner on a rug, and he found three more beer bottles near a pile of cigarette butts and some balls of Kleenex, stained with lipstick. He put the bottles into his shopping bag, and the butts into his winter coat pocket. "Gonna be a good day!" He saw himself, within a few hours, before the morning got colder, with his rent paid, sitting in his warm room, emptying all his butts into the old battered Macdonald cigarette tin, its label now peeling off (a gift from Indian, three Christmases ago, when the tin was filled), spending his time of afternoon rolling cigarettes, and waiting for Indian to call (as he said he would) to share the bottle of Bright's wine, which Indian said he "had found."

But he couldn't put Norman and Elaine and the baby out of his mind. "You finds some funny things in empties, damn funny things," he reminded himself, trying not to think about Norman and family. "You could almost tell what kind o' person a person is, that throws away a certain kind o' bottle, whether in anger or when hiding from a police cruiser, and even the way the person feels when he throws it away. Like that empty VO bottle I picked up last Sunday, beside the Christadelphians church place, on Asquith. Why, that bottle even had a French letter in it, and the stuff was still in it, too! Christ! they mustta had a hell of a time, Saturday night! Wonder if they belong to the Christadelphians?" And once, in the dripping clothes of a sudden morning rain, Nick found a small ginger ale bottle, on top of a pail of garbage, in front of an apartment building on Jarvis Street. And when he looked into it, putting his eyes to the bottle as if he were a captain spying out to sea, he almost dropped the bottle, when he saw the bills rolled round inside. It took him two shaking, nervous minutes to get the money out. And it was twenty-one one-dollar bills he got. Somehow, he felt it belonged to an old person, probably an old woman, on pension: only old women kept their money in empty bottles. He thought of returning it to the old woman: he was sure it belonged to an old woman! ("Press every goddamn buzzer in this big apartment building? I ain't no goddamn postman.") But he was glad there were so many names under the buzzers, and no address in the bottle. He kept the money. That morning, he collected no more bottles; and he didn't even remember his landlady, nor his rent. He and Indian Johnson found Cabbie the bootlegger, and they spent the twenty-one dollars on a bottle of Canadian Club whiskey, and three bottles of Bright's cheapest wine. "Indian, when I saw them dollars in that ginger ale bottle, what you think I did first?" "You whistle?" Indian said. "No! I say, Thank God!" They had just finished the whiskey, and Nick was opening the first bottle of Bright's. "Christ! first

time, in I don't know how many years, I haven't even remembered God,
or prayers. But! One man's losses is another man's profits." Indian wasn't
impressed. "Wine taste good, Nick Evans. If old woman lost money, and
Nick Evans find it, then finders is keepers. I see wine in this glass, not a
old woman. Not even money! But wine. Luck it is, Nick Evans. Look, we
two here, sitting down, watching football on television, drinking like two
kings. King Nick and Chief King Indian Johnson. Man wants no better
life, Nick Evans." (When Indian called Nick *Nick Evans* he did it derisively.
Deluded by success in business, and by discrimination and prejudice in the
business world—he was once an insurance salesman for Manufacturers
Life, when he came back from the war — he had anglicized his name to
Evans. But the social and financial benefits that were to follow this change
never came. At least Indian Johnson never saw them. "Nick, I tell you
something," Indian said, once, in the beverage room of the Selby, "I's a
Indian, and my name is Johnson. You'se Ukerranian, and you have a name
like Evans! We's brothers." "You want to know something?" Nick said,
after the wisdom of Indian's words had soaked in, like the drinks going to
his head. "You want to know something, Indian? I am a man, fifty-five
years of age. And you, you must be about the same age, fifty-five, give-or-
take a year. Me and you, sitting down here, goddamn, drinking out twenty-
one dollars in liquor, and perhaps, right at this very fucking moment of
our drinking, perhaps an old woman might be weeping somewheres out
there, in Toronto, right at this moment as I raise my glass to my . . .
burp! . . . head. And something else. Listen! This twenty-one bucks could
have paid my rent for three weeks. But I did not even conceive of rent, or
paying the rent, the same way you have not considered the old woman who
rightly is the owner o' this money. And you want to know something else,
too? If I pay, if I had paid the rent, why, if not next week, the next week
after that, I would still have to look out for more rent, *and* wine! And after
we drink this wine, as we intend to do, I still have to look for more wine,
and rent!" Indian took a large mouthful of wine, and said, "Six o' one, and
half dozen of the next, Nick Evans. I am glad you's a man of wisdom,
Nick Evans. You didn't have to invite me to share in your good fortune,
but you have invite me, nevertheless. Out of kindness. So, stop talking
concerning rent, the old woman, the landlady, and drink the damn wine."
"You want to know something, Indian? You's a goddamn genius! I am glad
you's my friend." They watched the football game from two until it went
into the final period, drinking and not saying a word. Suddenly Nick said,
"Indian, you want to know something? When my eyes rested on this twenty-
one bucks, that twenty-one bucks, I had a damn funny feeling as if I was
seeing my whole future in front o' my eyes. Why, it is not once or twice,
but many times, countless, that I lay down on this bed that me and you
sitting down on now, watching that bastard Jimmy Brown chew up that
New York line, right here! many times I dream that I am searching under
hedges for empties, and I don't see a' empty, not one lousy empty, but I
spot a quarter, twenty-five cents; and the more I search, the more I seeing
quarters coming at me from out the ground. Like water springing from a

goddamn spring! And the more quarters I throw in my shopping bag, the more quarters coming at me. Why, only last week, I had this same dream. And I had to say to myself, Nick Evans. . ." "You's a lucky bitch!" Indian put in. "One day, you will get rich as a millionaire. I see that in your zodiac. So keep looking for empties! If not this sunset, then tomorrow's sunrise." They had watched television right through till seven o'clock, when the news came, when they both fell off to sleep, sitting up, and snoring, with the television bemoaning the above-average highway traffic fatality in Canada, that holiday weekend.

Nick emerges out of his reminiscences and spots three Coca Cola bottles beside a bus stop, at the corner of Wellesley Street. He hurries, shuffling like a Chaplinman in a rush. And just as he crosses the street (against a red light: but "what the hell?" what's a red light in an empty street when three empty nickle-apiece bottles are so close?) and as he is almost there, already bending down in his imagination, and picking up the empties, a boisterous boy on a bicycle bears round the corner, riding on the sidewalk, and shouting, "Hey! Hey! Rocket Richard! He shoots, he *scores*!" And looking at Nick, he asks, "You see that, mister?" Transfixed by hate, and still in the middle of the road, Nick sees the three bottles crash against the corner stone of the bank, on the opposite side of the street. The boy had not even lost his balance for a second, as he kicked them flying into a hundred sparkling stars. Nick watches him maneuvering and contorting like a snake, as he raised himself off the saddle, and punched the pedals, zigzagging to overtake the wind. "You bastard!" Nick shouts into the wind, and walks on. On and on, up one street, on one side; and down the same street, on the other side; on and on, walking and looking. "Coke bottle! Five cents. Need a washing, through . . . hey! Half dozen beer empties. Six more to make a quarter!"; and kicking a useless whiskey bottle back into the gutter of all evil; searching with his left foot (he always searched the cluttered hedges with that foot) and occasionally having that left-foot shoe polished with the brown Vaseline of a dog's defecation. "Shit!" But mere defecation cannot deter Nick this morning; and so, as always, he would shine his shoe in the snow, until his foot would almost be numb, before he walked on, shuffling on his right foot, and pounding the numbness out of his left.

All of a sudden he is not alone on the street. All round him are women and men, holding their coats and hats and scarfs with their early-to-bed-early-to-rise unskilled calloused hands. Nick sees them bulbing out on to the sidewalks and corners, waiting for streetcars and buses in the blowing, flowering snow. 'Twas a time when he himself was respectable and fat; not stunted by the necessary abuses to which he submitted his body; nor shamed by this present collecting occupation of degrading empty bottles. Nick glares at them, and hates them. He wishes them short lives, long as the halos of vapor that linger around their heads. Nick does not like people; does not like people to see him collecting garbage: 'twas a time, when he would be standing like a thawing snowman at one of these corners, waiting for a taxicab to take him to Manufacturers building, on this very street;

'twas a time when the skin on his face was not peeling off like a lizard's; before the wine flushed blood to his face in a perpetual sunset of red, and made it look raw; before the arthritis; before the pneumonia; before the Greek waiter and the army sergeant and others used his body as if it were a banana, and afterwards threw away the peeling. But now, Nick, there is a blind man, tapping with his long white eye on the sidewalk, just in front of you. Nick sees the blind man about to cross the street, walking just outside the double-lined crosswalk: he sees him picking with his stick, his tapping way off the curb, heading into the rushing, late, Italian construction traffic. And he did not even touch the blind man's arms to say, Look out! The rushing panel truck cannot see the white stick through the white windshield of winter. But the brakes scream. *"Madre! Conon! Madre!"* The blind man jerks. He stumbles. Men and women, walking and working, do not look. The blind man picks his way back to the tapping corner; and in the seconds of hushed guilt and carelessness and hate and abuses and pity, he comes and stands beside Nick. And when he smells, for the second time, Nick's presence, he looks toward him and asks, "You can't see?"

Shuffling away from the blind man, he approaches the insurance section of the city: tall buildings of granite and glass and with the best Christmas trees and lights and front lawns in the whole city, with their double indemnities of ugliness and vaults: Crown Life, Continental Life, Mutual Life and Manufacturers Life, where, had this morning been January 3rd 1946, Nick would have been heading. " 'Twas a time, Indian, 'twas a time when I would be taking the elevator to the ninth floor . . ." A graying streetcar conductor, looking like a mouse in his uniform of gray, stealthily drinks the last two gulps of a small bottle of Pepsi Cola, in haste; and looks around to see who sees, to see where he could put the bottle. But Nick is there, holding out his shopping bag. The inspector hops into the moving streetcar; and just before the doors swallow him, like two gigantic jaws, he has time to look back. "Nick?" he shouts. Before the doors close, he recognizes him *as* Nick. *"Nick!"* Nick has recognized him too; and he suffers now the humiliation of having taken an empty bottle from the hands of the same man who beat up his friend, Indian Johnson, that night when they got drunk in the parked car, beside the car wash. It was about six months after this brutality to Indian Johnson, that this same man, then a constable in the metropolitan police force, next beat up a West Indian night club singer, and was dismissed from the force because "of a heart condition" and not, as one newspaper asked, "was it because of the recent alarming occurrences of police brutality against Toronto Negroes?" And remembering it now, and recognizing this man, Police Constable Broda Van Pistle, ex, Nick felt a thick spittle forming in his throat; and the more he relived that violent night (he remembered that the constable who drove the cruiser had a red face and was kinder to him), the more he shuddered, and the thicker the spittle formed in his throat. And he could not even spit it out. But he did the only thing, the only remaining dignified thing he could do: he searched in his shopping bag among the dozen assorted empties for that Pepsi Cola bottle; and when at last his shaking hands and faltering sight allowed him to grab the bottle (with a draining of spit and drink still in it), he pulled it out and aimed for the middle of the street, to crash it . . . but a police cruiser was cruising by; and he was conscious of eyes and the street looking at him. Instead, he went inside the restaurant at the corner. He felt eyes and people were following him, although the restaurant was almost empty. The manager looked at Nick and said, "What's your order?" Nick wanted the warmth of the restaurant. He also wanted a coffee; but he didn't have a penny in his pocket. He thought of his bottles. "I have some empties," he began, timidly. The manager, a tough-looking Greek, with thick eyelashes and thick moustache, listened. Nick hated Greeks more than he hated policemen. Greeks in restaurants he knew always made him "drink-up, drink-up!" even though they knew his soup was still too hot. "I have some empties, here . . ." Something like blood and anger replaced the eyelashes and moustache, and coursed through the manager's face. "Git, git!" he screamed. Before Nick shuffled out, all the time hearing the manager saying something about "decent business people eat here, their lunch . . ." he got a glimpse at the clock above the cash register, which said something to twelve, noon. (" 'Twas a time, during the war, when I had a helluvva time. Even after the war. I could spend forty, fifty bucks on a broad, in a bar, and another twenty on a meal, in the King Eddy, on a Friday night, on a broad. 'Twas a time, when I could lose sixty, seventy bucks on a Saturday night crap game, without even thinking about supper for Sunday; a time when this goddamn country didn't have no goddamn DP's, no goddamn sweaty Greeks, was a time when this country was *clean* . . .") But now, all he could hear were the screaming air-raid sirens in the Greek's curses, "Git! Git!" He shuffled back across Bloor Street, on his way to the back streets to hide from the front street, to be among the broken like himself, to be where he knew he wasn't conspicuous. The curses screamed louder and faster, like a pneumatic drill in the hands of a new immigrant from Italy: *git-git-git-git-git-git! git-git-git! gitgitgitgit-git!*

Nick was now obsessed by time. Time was against him. It was past twelve-thirty. And he not only had to collect enough bottles, but also find a storekeeper willing to exchange them all for money. The landlady had bellowed over the telephone, two or three days ago, "Four o'clock! Not a minute later, Mr. Evans! *Cash!* If it ain't in my hands by four . . ." and she had left the remainder of the threat and its consequences to the imagination of his experiences. He knew the cruelty she was capable of: she had thrown his clothes and his transistor radio in the snow in front of the house once before when he was two weeks behind in his rent. That night when he came home tottering, arm in drunken arm with Indian, and he saw his Japanese transistor, half-buried in snow, its batteries probably freezing, but still playing rock 'n' roll music ("I Want To Hold Your Hand"), everything scattered like an unmade bird's nest in public view. He was so broken and so ashamed that Indian was there to see it all . . . "You see, Indian, one thing about this goddamn country is that it is free and that it belongs to we, we Canadians!" he had told Indian during an argument at the Selby, earlier that evening . . . Nick sat down on the snow on the front steps and cried, and called his landlady "this goddamn German immigrant!" Indian tried to sympathize. "Goddamn, we was fighting them Germans in the last war. And now the government letting them come to this country, *my* goddamn country, and they treating me this way? But you want to know something, Indian? Far's I is concern, the war still on! And I still killing Germans. In my sleep I dreamed I was killing Germans, and the landlady is one o' them. Why, only last night, thinking 'bout rent, I dreamed I had to strangle that bitch. This goddamn country, this goddamn government we have, it isn't no blasted good, Indian. Why, we was enemies only twenty years ago. How come a German woman could throw my clothes and my transistor that I pay thirty-nine ninety-five for, on the fucking sidewalk? Ain't we still in Canada? Ain't we Canadians, Indian?" "I am a Indian, Nick Evans," he said; and he picked up the transistor radio, and changed the station. Nick kicked his clothes into the road; and after a car passed over them, he gathered them up and was invited to spend the night in Indian's six-dollars-a-week room on Parliament Street. He spent the next five sweating days collecting bottles to raise the ten dollars, before the landlady allowed him in his room again. Since that time, Nick made a point of not acquiring too many possessions: he had learned a very humiliating lesson. But he was still deeply troubled this afternoon about whether he could indeed find sufficient bottles to make up his rent money; whether he would have any money left for beer—he seldom thought of groceries—whether he would have to suffer the deeper humiliation of having to beg his landlady for time; and whether—and this was more important to his sense of pride and independence—he could collect the empties in time to have them cashed in for money.

He stopped beside a garbage pail which disclosed one large Canada Dry bottle. He felt it was time to check his collection; but when he did so he found he had only fifty cents worth in empty bottles. And the time was two o'clock. "Goddamn! I been sweating my ass off this whole morning, and for what? Fifty cents? Fifty lousy cents?" He thought of spending the fifty cents in the Chez Moi beverage room; but he changed his mind. "Rent first, Nick! And Indian, that bastard, might be sitting down in there." He decided instead that the Selby might be a better place to hide, to spend this chilly afternoon in a dark corner drinking a cool draught. "Indian might be there, too. And I not spending *one* penny on that bastard. Not today, Mister Indian!" He didn't know what to do. Bottles were scarce today. Here he was, a grown man, a war veteran, a Canadian, outside in the chilly wind shuffling up and down like a dog, sniffing in gutters for bottles. A feeling of isolation, a kind of open-air imprisonment, came heavily upon him. All of a sudden he started to hear again the curses of the restaurant manager: *git-git-git-git!* The abuses came after him, like pebbles thrown at a dog poised to pee on a freshly raked-and-watered lawn. And when each insult hit him, it was like a stone hitting and bouncing on his frame, git-git-git-git! "I feel like a goddamn dog." Although he was not conscious of it, he was now crawling instead of shuffling; and he carried his shopping bag as if it were tied onto a dog collar, instead of being held in his hand. His shoulders drooped and the arthritis in his legs became heavy and painless, like legs of logs. He was struggling very hard not to shuffle more than normal; not to walk with his neck between his shoulders; not to hang his arms too loose to look like a long-eared spaniel, which was the way he looked. Suddenly he was dog-tired. And the next front steps he came to, which had no snow on them, he sat on, and relaxed his weight on them; and just as he was about to sigh and exhale all this heavy feeling and take in a little fresh winter air, a head above him, at a window screamed, "*Scoot!*" He looked up. And he got up. And when he looked down to walk on the tricky steps, a police cruiser, eternal in this slum as poverty, had slid to a stop on the ice-covered road. It was beside him. The face that looked out on him was the face of a man who knew the world and the world's drinking bars. It was a ruddy face. "Get in, Nick!" It was a command. "Git! Come *on*, git!" And Nick got in.

Time, and the meaning of time, were now slipping from him. He did not recognize the streets through which the cruiser was taking him. He did not think of the charge that would be laid against him. He scarcely regretted being picked up. He was too tired. And after many turns (which, even in his normal condition of hazed sobriety, he would have known like the bottom of his beer glass), the police cruiser stopped and the officer said, "Okay! get out." And Nick got out, obedient as a marionette. When the cruiser sped away, Nick was standing beside a mountain of empty bottles: Canada Dry, ginger ale, Teem, Coca Cola, Pepsi Cola, one bottle marked Wink, and many others with names he didn't even know existed. His dream had come true. His dream of searching under hedges and seeing quarters springing up out of the ground had come true. This time, instead of quarters, it was bottles; and although each bottle wasn't worth as much as a quarter, there were enough to make up his three weeks rent. He thought of Indian, and of what he always said about his recurring dream of riches. Keep looking for empties. *If not this sunset, then tomorrow's sunrise.* "Indian and me gonna have a ball tonight, at the Selby! Goddamn! There's more bottles here than whores on Jarvis Street! Goddamn! I could feel it in my luck this whole bloody morning . . ." Nick was overjoyed. The time was only three-fifteen. Time was with him again. He took up a Pepsi Cola bottle and holding it close to his eyes looked at it, and saw clearly before him the television commercial that that young generation of swinging teen-agers sang, as they "got with it" and stayed alive, for this, goddamit, Nick, this's the goddamn Pepsi generation. "Get with it, Indian!" And he laughed out, aloud. And he started to put the bottles into his shopping bag. He noticed he was standing beside the ugly green-painted paling of a construction site; and that just a few yards from him a crane with TEPERMAN marked in scandalously bright orange letters was swinging debris from the ground and depositing it on the building. Nick wasn't sure whether TEPER-MAN was building the wreckage or wrecking the building.

His shopping bag could hold only about thirty bottles. Thirty bottles was quite a load for him; and he didn't know how far he was from the nearest store. So he decided to count the bottles, figure out exactly how much money he could get for them, find a drugstore, or a taxi to take the bottles . . . no, he would count the empties first, then take a taxi to a drugstore, yes! Starkman's, that big never-closing drug store on Bloor Street; third, tell them how many bottles he had (not counting in the beer empties which he could always drop off at the nearest Brewers Retail); take the taxi back to collect the bottles and "goddamn Nick, you's gonna be a happy bastard tonight! Yah-hooo! Indian! Wah! wah-wah!" . . . There were two hundred and eighty-two bottles, including five whiskey bottles, which he broke immediately; and thirteen wine bottles which he pushed aside, "Goddamn winos!"

"Starkman's!"

"Which one?" the taxi driver asked; and immediately laughed as if he had told a marvelous joke. "Okay, bud! *I* know."

"Instead, make it the first Dominion Store you come to."

"Okay, buddy!" the taxi driver said, and immediately settled back for an intimate chat. "You married?" Nick shook his head, and the driver caught the remark in the mirror. "You're goddamn lucky! Me? Five years I married this broad, and last Friday night she takes up my kid and runs to her mother. She leaving me, she says. Goddamn her mother, my mother-in-law! Ha! Well, that's something else . . ." Nick was thinking of Norman and Elaine and the baby and their life in the small bottle of wine; he was thinking about their plight and their flight. When he got into the cab he was as cheerful as happy hands rubbed together in winter. Now he wasn't happy anymore.

"Stop here," he said. Shuffling back out from the store he told the driver, "Back where we came from."

On the way back the taxi driver started to whisper through his teeth, singing a popular song. "Hey! Whaddya think 'bout that nut who tried blow up the House o' Commas? Crazy, eh? God! Jees! There's more nuts outside of 999 Queen Street than those inside. Hell! Just the same, it wouldda been fireworks like hell on Parlment Hill, eh? But you know something, bud? There's a lotta nuts in Parlment, too. Yeah! He shoudda sent the whole bloody place sky-high! That's what I wouldda liked to see. Things so blasted hard, and those nuts in the . . ."

"I wouldda hang that bastard. This is a great country. He is a goddamn traitor. I fought in the last war, and I know that . . ."

"Hey! you's a bigger nut than that nut who killed himself trying to blow up the Commas! Great country? With so many Americans running it? . . . hey! here we are!"

At first Nick couldn't believe this was the same laneway where the taxi had picked him up. He looked round, like a man emerging from the bad dream of a morning movie, to face the afternoon glare of reality: yes! goddamn green construction paling's still here! TEPERMAN still banging mortar and dust! Yes, yes . . . The taxi driver was shouting, "Keep the meter running? Or you stopping here, Mack?" . . . Nick had walked further along the paling, muttering, "Two hundred and eighty-two empties! Two hundred and eighty-two empties! Two hundred and eighty-two, I just left them here . . ." (The taxi driver was following, and nodding and smiling, because he was sure now that Nick was a nut; but a nut with lots of money for taxis) . . . "Just before I take the cab I counted them myself, two hundred and . . ."

They were standing now over the pile of broken glass, in a heap, where the wrecking crane had come to rest on the dot of the coffee-break hour. There was no dust flying. No hammering. No thudding of concrete on concrete. At the long end of the green paling, an Italian was passing water. Nick bent down and picked up the bottom of a broken Canada Dry bottle. He looked at it and dropped it on the glittering pile.

"Come on, Mack. Three-fifty. Come, this is a bad night! And it's almost four o'clock and I ain't made a penny yet, and I have to get some money 'cause the Family Court judge . . . Come, you owe me three-fifty . . ."

"My empties. I just left them here, two hundred and eighty-two . . ."

The taxi driver did not let him finish. He grabbed Nick by the throat and shook him like the wrecking crane had been shaking the old insulated walls. "Goddammit! If you wasn't such an old worthless bastard I would beat the living shit outta you, you *nut!*" And he gave Nick one last push, and when he dragged his feet through the angry half-frozen mud of the building site, back to the taxi (the meter was still running), and even after he slammed the door and roared off, Nick was still sitting on the remnants of his collection, just where the taxi driver had thrown him. Gazing round him at his shattered collection of bottles, some of them matching the color of the construction paling, he heard shortly afterwards the chiming of the clock on the roof of Manufacturers Life, which whispered four times.

Jerome Charyn

Sing, Shaindele, Sing

At the Shamrock Gardens I was either Little Annie Rooney, the pride of Killarney, or Mary O'Reilly, the queen of County Cork, but at the Loew's Pitkin or the Henry Street Theatre I was always Shaindele Berkowitz, the Molly Picon of East Broadway. In 1943 vaudeville was already on the way out, but my father could still count on a two-week stay at the Henry Street for the summer and winter revues. After all, it was with "Shaindele" that I always scored my biggest successes. When I sang *"Yussele"* or *"Oif'n Pripetchik,"* even the penny pinching furriers in the first row wept and threw dimes and quarters without a stop, and my father kept hopping across the stage and retrieved every cent. God help any of the stage boys who tried to chisel my father out of a dime. He caught them after the show and taught them a lesson for life. My father paid Greenspan the tailor two dollars a week to teach me all the latest Jewish songs, and I spent night after night in the back of Greenspan's shop, singing and sipping tea with strawberry jam. His son Itzie was around most of the time, and he was always ready to pinch my behind or peek under my dress. But when his father caught him in the act, he would throw up his hands and complain, "Pop, pop, why should I want to start up with her? She's only a kid. Pop, the girl doesn't have a tit to her name." So I learned how to sing *"Oif'n Pripetchik"* like an expert, and had to put up with Itzie's antics. Greenspan showed me off to all his friends. "A goy," he would say, raising his right hand solemnly, "so help me God. A goy, but she's another Molly Picon. I should know. I taught her myself." I would have gladly performed for all of Greenspan's friends, but my father didn't allow me to give concerts for free.

Twice my Aunt Giuseppina sent the truant officers after me, but my father hopped from hotel to hotel so fast that no one could keep up with us. And once, after a session with Greenspan, I decided to visit my old neighborhood in the East Bronx. But as soon as I came near Webster Avenue, Father Farinella hailed me down. First he hugged me and asked me about my father, and then his face darkened, and he told that every soul in purgatory was wailing for me because of all the Masses I had missed. "Fannie Finocchiaro," he said, "you're a lost soul." What could I tell him? What could I say? Call me Shaindele, Father. I'm the Molly Picon of East Broadway. So while he kept up his harangue, I ran off and promised myself that I would stay away from Webster Avenue for good.

I was fifteen in January, but my father still wouldn't let me wear a brassiere. "Fannie," he complained, "if they ever find out you're over twelve, they'll banish us both." But even my father couldn't hold back nature, and when I started to grow in the right places, he made me wear a towel around my chest all the time. So I remained flat-chested Fannie. And, God forbid, if I ever went downstairs without the towel, he pulled my hair and made me drink cod-liver oil for a week. "You'll ruin me yet," he said, but we both knew with or without the towel, my vaudeville days were near the end of the line. The Shamrock Gardens burned down in late '42, and the Loew's Pitkin cancelled its weekly vaudeville show. So, in '43, we had to settle for the Henry Street. I also sang at weddings and Bar Mitzvahs, and we made enough to get by. And when Breitbart, the stage manager at the Henry Street Theatre, told my father that he wanted "Shaindele" for the winter revue, I was shipped back to Greenspan for more songs. And now Itzie followed me around like a spider. But after four or five sessions, Greenspan told me that I was ready for the revue. "Fannie," he said, "Molly Picon better watch out. You'll drive all the stars out of Second Avenue with your singing. I mean it." So my father unpacked his accordion and we went over to Henry Street.

Even in 1943 the Henry Street Theatre was already ancient. Everyone waited for the theatre to close down or fall apart. Half the seats were broken, cockroaches and rats used the floor for a playing field, and the curtains caught fire at least once or twice a month. Fire inspectors kept coming around and condemning the theatre, but Breitbart's brother knew the captain of the Clinton Street precinct, and the theatre stayed open. Breitbart's biggest problem was the balcony. It collapsed the summer before, but Breitbart claimed that the Ludlow Street Theatre hired some hooligans from Brownsville, and while Yankel the talking monkey was performing on stage, the hooligans brought hammers and hacksaws into the theatre, and destroyed the balcony. Nobody knows if the story is true or not, but Breitbart sued the Ludlow Street Theatre for thousands, and even the police department was on his side. Breitbart himself installed two metal supports, but the balcony still kept rocking, and all the old-time actors started betting that the balcony would collapse again, with or without the help of any hooligans. So when we went over for rehearsals, my father warned me: "Fannie, if you want to stay alive, don't stand under the balcony." And, believe me, I took his advice. When Breitbart saw me, he called me over and started pinching my cheeks and hugging my behind. "Shaindele," he said, "Shaindele." My father stood in the corner and tuned up his accordion. Breitbart winked at me. "Shaindele," he said, "a cup of coffee after the show? Don't worry, I'll send your father on an errand." He winked again. Breitbart had a whole harem full of wives, daughters, and nieces, and he also had a double hernia and a punctured lung, and he spat blood regularly, but he still ran after all the girls in the show, and it didn't make any difference to him if they were twelve years old or sixty. Breitbart was always ready for action. "So, Shaindele?" he said, but he heard my father tuning up the accordion, and he stopped squeezing my behind. "Shaindele." The beams that supported the balcony began to shake. "Doomsday," my father said, and he dropped his accordion and hid behind one of the broken seats. I ran over to him. I heard him mumble a "Hail Mary" under his breath and promise Jesus, Joseph, and Mary that he would send me back to St. Agnes' Secretarial School. "Notte," Breitbart said, "come down from the balcony. Notte, move, before I skin you alive." A strange head peered over the balcony rail. Breitbart slapped his sides, complained to me, and spoke to the wall, all at the same time. "My nephew Notte. He's half an idiot, but what can I do? He's part of the tribe. Give him a job, my wife tells me, give him a job. But can he sweep the floor or draw a curtain? No! Not Notte. All he can do is scribble poems that no one can understand. Notte, Notte!" My father stood up and went back to his accordion. Breitbart's nephew Notte jumped over the railing and climbed down one of the beams. The whole balcony shook, but this time my father stood his ground. Notte's back was slightly humped, his nose was crooked, each ear was huge and red and shaped like half a bell, several of his teeth were missing, and he hardly had a chin. A pair of stretched and worn suspenders supported his unbelievably baggy pants. And he was a little bowlegged. All in all, he looked like a missing member of the Marx Brothers. Breitbart rushed over to Notte, and gripped his bell-shaped ears. "This is what I pay you money for, hah? To hide in balconies. My philosopher! Every bone in your body I'll break. Nephew or not!" My father laughed and worked the keys of his accordion with nimble fingers. Notte started to cough; his suspenders heaved and he had to told up his baggy pants. "Breitbart," I said, "leave him alone." Breitbart looked at me and released Notte's ears. "Notte, look—you found yourself a protector." Then he flung Notte halfway across the theatre. "Pick up a broom. Sweep. Make a little trouble for the cockroaches, or I'll send you packing without a dime. Nobody gets paid here for nothing." Notte picked up a broom. Breitbart turned his back for a moment and shouted at one of the stage boys. Notte's ears perked and one of his suspenders popped, and I thought he was going to throw the broom at Breitbart or leap across the theatre and pounce on him, but he wiped his brow instead and smiled. All his missing teeth showed. He dropped the broom and started to perform for me. He scowled and mimicked Breitbart's motions. I laughed. Breitbart turned around. He cursed Notte seven times and chased after him. "A clown yet, a clown." Notte dodged between the seats. His baggy pants flopped and his unhooked suspender kept swinging back and forth. "Uncle, Uncle," he shouted, and then he ran behind the stage. I retrieved Notte's broom. My father came over to me and pinched my neck. "Fannie, you want to get us in trouble, huh? Don't interfere."

"What did I do, papa, what did I do?" My father pushed me toward the stage. "Shut up and sing," he said. I almost fell into the orchestra pit. My shoulder banged against an abandoned drum. I stood in front of the stage, and holding Notte's broom, I sang, *"Shain Vi Di Levone."* All the stage boys stopped working and listened to me. Breitbart came over and congratulated me. "Shaindele," he said, "with you in the show, how can we lose?" Then he walked over to my father. I saw Notte standing behind the curtain. He smiled to me. I climbed up the steps of the stage. He took my hand and led me to one of the dressing rooms.

"Notte," I said, "why do you take such abuse?"

"Uncle's all right," Notte said. "He needs someone to knock around once in a while. It keeps him calm. And now I can afford my own room." He tugged his one workable suspender. "I'm a poet," he said, "and every poet needs a part-time job." He removed a crumpled cigarette from a pocket of his baggy pants and broke the cigarette in half. Lumps of tobacco began to fall on his left shoe. He stooped over, scooped together the shredded lumps and stuffed them inside both cigarette halves. He straightened one of them and offered it to me. "Smoke, smoke," he said, "it's good for the brain." He lit both cigarettes. I coughed, and Notte patted my back. The tobacco was stale, and the cigarette tasted bitter, but I didn't want to disappoint Notte. So I smoked. He started pacing back and forth in the tiny room. "You'll see. One day Uncle will stage a play of mine, and then I'll be the one who gives out the orders. Uncle, raise the curtains. Uncle, add ten more seats. Uncle, put Mrs. Dushkin behind the pole. Her son crucified me yesterday in the *Forvartz*."

I started to laugh, and I almost swallowed the cigarette.

Notte kissed me. I kissed him back. We sat on the floor and Notte taught me how to play *show* and *tell*.

"Shaindele, Shaindele," he said. He opened my blouse and saw the towel. "What's this? A new kind of underwear? *Vey iz mir!*"

"My father's orders," I said, and I took off the towel. Notte taught me another game.

I heard Breitbart and my father call me. "Shaindele."

"I'm telling you," Breitbart said, "she's with that monkey, Notte."

I buttoned my blouse. Notte hid the towel in his pocket. We tiptoed out of the dressing room and went through a dark passageway. Notte held my hand. We came out near the other end of the stage. Notte draped the curtain around us and we kissed for the last time. I heard Breitbart and my father tramp across the passageway. "Notte!" Breitbart shouted. Notte disappeared. My father saw me standing behind the curtain. He was ready to tear my hair out. Breitbart stopped him. "She's a valuable piece of property. You want to ruin the revue?" My father glared at me. He could see that I wasn't wearing the towel. "Where's Notte?" Breitbart said. "That's the question. Notte, Notte, Notte!" Notte's head appeared suddenly behind the balcony rail. "Uncle, Uncle," he said, "I'm tracking down a cockroach."

Breitbart shook his fist at Notte and the balcony. "Wait, wait. I'll beat you black and blue." Notte stood on the ledge of the balcony and laughed. "Wait."

My father had rented a room at the Hotel Delancey, and when we came home, he locked the door and went to work on me. He pulled my hair, twisted my nose, and pinched me in seven places. He wanted to know what happened to the towel. I didn't tell him a thing. "Papa," I said, "no more towels. Either you let me wear a brassiere, or I don't sing. That's final." He pulled my hair again, but he could see that I already made up my mind. He took out a soiled handkerchief from the laundry bag and started to cry. "I'm a ruined man."

"Papa," I said, "no tricks. A brassiere, papa, or you can kiss Shaindele good-by."

He wanted at least a little satisfaction, so he pulled my hair again, and then he gave in. "But I'm warning you, Fannie, it has to be the smallest size."

So the next day I appeared at the theatre wearing my Maidenform. All the stage boys whistled. Breitbart looked at me and marvelled. He clapped my father's back. "Congratulations, Berkowitz, the girl grew up overnight. Never mind the Molly Picon of East Broadway. Now we have the Lana Turner of Hester Street. Berkowitz, she will be the star of the show. This I guarantee."

My father was a little overwhelmed. "Fannie," he whispered, "go out and buy a bigger size. We can't lose."

Only Notte seemed disappointed. "Show-off," he said.

"Notte," I told him, "if you want, I'll wear the towel again."

"The damage is done," he said, and picked up a broom.

Breitbart called me over. While my father's back was turned, he pinched both cups of the Maidenform. "*Oy*," he said, "I'll die. It's the real thing! Shaindele, Shaindele, meet me after the show." He took out his wallet. "Shaindele, a dress, a coat, a hat, whatever you want. It doesn't have to be Klein's. Let it be Saks or Gimbels even. Buy. Buy. What is money to me? Shaindele, is it a deal?"

"That's not in the contract."

His eyes closed and his nostrils dilated lasciviously. "*Oy*, and she's particular yet. That's what I like. A girl with spirit. Shaindele, refuse me all you want. It's good for the blood. Tonight I will feast on Gluckstern's a steak. Punctured lung or not. The girl gives me a hearty appetite. Shaindele, Shaindele . . ."

I walked away. I heard Notte mumbling to himself. "Nalewski Street, Niska Street, Muranow Square . . ."

"Notte," I said, "what are you doing?—going on a tour of Brooklyn?"

His thick brows began to knot. "Sure, there is no Niska Street in the Bronx. Notte where is—"

"In *Warsaw*," Notte said, "where else! Jews are dying all over the world, and I'm stuck here. Uncle is right. A fool, a dope, a clown, this is what I am."

"Notte," I said, "I thought you wanted to be a poet."

His lips twisted fiercely. "A machine gun in the right hands is also poetry."

"Notte, if you want to fight, join up with the army or the marines. My Uncle Dom is a captain already."

"Who would take me?—I'm only sixteen." He raised his crooked shoulder. "And a cripple to the bargain! And suppose they took me, where would they send me?—to fight the Japs. Better I'll stay here and collect *zlotys* for the resistance. Later I'll join the Jewish Commandoes in Tel Aviv, and then we'll all parachute over Niska Street, and send Germans to Gehenna."

Breitbart saw us standing together. "Notte, Notte," he shouted across the theatre, "make an appointment with the broom before I hang you from the ceiling. Shaindele, it's time to sing."

"Notte," I said, "Notte . . ."

That evening I asked my father for two dollars.

"Papa," I said, "a girl that wears a brassiere has to have an allowance."

He pulled my hair for five minutes and finally gave me fifty cents. The next day I saw Notte standing under the balcony and gave him the fifty cents. "For the resistance," I said. "That's all I could raise." His ears shone. "Shaindele," he said, "Shaindele." Breitbart was standing behind us. "Later, in back of the stage."

So I sang three songs for Breitbart and the stage boys and met Notte in the dressing room. We didn't waste any time. Notte gave me a marathon kiss, but he boycotted my brassiere. He refused to even let me unhook it. Notte taught me a few more games, and I kept my brassiere on. Then he pinned a cardboard medal on me, and congratulated me. I was now a Jewish Commando. We kissed some more, and he handed me a crumpled sheet of paper. I was a little baffled. "A poem," he said, "a poem."

"Notte, I'm not a dope. I know, I know." The poem was in Jewish. "Notte," I said, "read it to me. I can't see so good without my glasses."

Notte read the poem. "*Du hast mein hartz* . . ." I didn't understand a word, but I cried anyway. I'm sure it was a beautiful poem. I heard Breitbart call me. "Tomorrow," Notte said, "same time, same place." He disappeared before I could kiss him, or thank him, or anything.

Greenspan came over to the theatre the day before the opening of the show. He wanted to see his prodigy. He brought Itzie with him. When Itzie saw me with my Maidenform on, he ran over right away with his hands outstretched. "Fannie," he said, "Fannie." Notte held him off. He had a broom in one hand and a hammer in the other. "Fannie," Itzie said, "call off the hatchetman. I'll break him in twenty pieces. I mean it." Notte raised the hammer.

"You I'll fix," Itzie said, but he walked away.

"Shaindele," Notte said, "who, who is Fannie?"

"Fannie," I said. "Notte, that's my nickname in the Bronx."

Itzie left the theatre. Greenspan came over. He stared at my Maidenform. "*Mazel tov!*" He clapped his hands twice. "Shaindele, sing. Sing for me, Shaindele, sing." So I sang the whole afternoon. Greenspan kept kissing me. Breitbart called me over a dozen times and made more proposals. "Shaindele, a Persian lamb coat, a room at the Waldorf, anything you want. Name it and it's yours."

Itzie came back. Two of his friends were with him. They were carrying something under their coats. I saw Notte walk behind the stage. Itzie and his friends followed him. "Shaindele," Breitbart said, "if you don't trust me, I'll bring over my lawyer. We'll sign an agreement. Shaindele, you want the theatre? Take it, it's yours!"

"Later, Breitbart, later." I ran behind the stage. Itzie and his friends were in the dressing room. Notte was sitting on the floor. His nose was bleeding, and his forehead was bruised. Itzie's friends were holding baseball bats. "Notte," I said, "what did they do to you, Notte?" Itzie locked the door. "Okay, Fannie," he said, "now we'll find out what you're worth. And if you make one sound, your friend gets a dented head for himself." Itzie's friends brandished the bats over Notte's head. They found some rope and tied Notte to a chair. Then they held my arms, and Itzie tore off my Maidenform and everything else. They wound the brassiere around Notte's head. And they made Notte watch while they had their fill of me. Notte's eyes looked haunted, and I cried all the time. Itzie's friends picked up the baseball bats and then they left. I untied Notte. His body was shaking. I kissed his nose, his forehead and his eyes. "Notte," I said, "Notte." We left the dressing room.

I told my father that I didn't want to sing. "Fannie," he said, "you'll ruin me for life. Breitbart can throw me in jail. And believe me, he will. What happened to your brassiere?"

"I threw it away."

My father slapped his sides. "The girl is an idiot, Notte number two!" He went down on his knees. "Fannie, it's the poorhouse for me."

I finally agreed to sing. "Remember, papa, after this, no more shows." He kissed my hands. "Papa," I said, "get off the floor."

The theatre was packed. Every seat in the orchestra and balcony was taken, and Breitbart gave out cushions to all the latecomers and told them to sit on the floor. "I never saw such a house," Breitbart said. "It's even better than before the war. Even Michel Michelesko never drew such a crowd." But when Breitbart saw me without my Maidenform, he became furious. "What's the gimmick, Berkowitz, what's the gimmick?"

"The girl's depressed," my father said. "She'll be all right by tomorrow. You'll see."

"I'm not worried about tomorrow. It's today what's on my mind. You see them out there. You want them to tear up the place!" Breitbart sent home one of the stage boys to borrow a brassiere from his wife. The boy came back with a brassiere that was three sizes too big. But I had to put it on. "That's better," Breitbart said. "No more gimmicks."

Yankel the talking monkey went on stage first. With the help of Rosenblum the ventriloquist, Yankel told dirty stories in Jewish, Polish, Russian, and Roumanian, but the crowd was bored. I could hear the men and women in the first row stamp their feet and shout, "Shaindele, Shaindele." Breitbart called Yankel off the stage. "Enough, Rosenblum, before they tear off the seats and throw them at you. Enough." Next Minna Mendelsohn sang, *"Der Rebbe Eli Melech,"* and her husband Boris leaned one knee over a chair and strummed his balalaika. I opened the curtain an inch and looked out, I cupped my hands over my eyes and saw Itzie sitting in the first row of the balcony. This time he had nine or ten friends with him. They were stamping their feet and shouting, "Sing, Shaindele, sing!" My Notte was standing near the orchestra pit. He still looked a little dazed. Breitbart pushed me away from the curtain. "You want to spoil the show? Nobody is allowed to see you before you go out on stage." Everybody kept hooting and stamping their feet. "Sing, Shaindele, sing!" Minna Mendelsohn never even finished her song. Someone climbed up on the stage, stole her husband's chair, and flung it into the orchestra pit. "Cancel all the other acts," Breitbart said. "Bring out Shaindele." My father's knees were knocking. "Berkowitz, you want to get us all killed? Pick up your accordion and let's go." Everybody stood up and cheered when they saw me. My father brought out his accordion, and someone booed. He ran behind the curtain. "Breitbart, please," I heard my father scream. "They don't want me. They want only Shaindele." Breitbart cursed him and let him stay behind the curtain. The stage lights blinded me for a moment, but after a while I became used to them. A man in the second row started to dance across the aisle. He must have been about seventy years old. "*Mommenu*," he said, "look at the tits on her! Better than a seven-course meal." Everybody sitting next to him started to laugh. I heard Itzie shout, "Sing, Shaindele, sing!" Notte was still standing near the orchestra pit. He saw that my hands were shaking, and he smiled for the first time. "Notte," I said, "Notte," and I started to sing. I didn't sing for Breitbart, or Itzie, or my father, or anybody in the second row. I sang only for Notte. "*Yussele*," "*Shein Vi Di Levone*," "*Oif'n Pripetchik*," "*Gai Ich Mir Shpatzieren*," "*Ot Azoy Nait A Shneider*," all for Notte. The man in the second row clapped his hands. "Never mind the *titzgehs*. The girl has a *golden shtimme*. Such a voice. "Sing, Shaindele, sing." They wouldn't let me off the stage. Itzie and his friends kept stamping their feet. I sang "*Yussele*" for the fifth time. Notte's face started to brighten. I saw the beams that held up the balcony start to shake. First there was a rumbling sound. Breitbart peered through the curtain. "*Oy*," he said, "stop the show." I heard a woman scream. Then the balcony came tumbling down.

We stayed in the hotel for two days. My father wouldn't let me see Notte or anybody. He kept making phone calls. "Fannie," he said, "pack your underwear. We're going to Chicago. Who needs trouble? If anybody finds out that we were associated with the Henry Street Theatre we're finished. Breitbart is in jail. Even his father-in-law is suing him. He was sitting in the balcony. Fannie, pack, pack."

I refused.

He started rocking his head back and forth. "Fannie, they're opening up a theatre on Maxwell Street in Chicago. They want an accordion player. You won't even have to sing. We'll be back in two, three weeks."

"I don't go before I say good-by to Notte."

"Go, go, but put on some kind of a disguise. If they catch you in the street they'll burn you alive."

I wore a kerchief and one of my father's old coats, and I went looking for Notte. The Henry Street Theatre was boarded up, and I couldn't even get inside. I called up Breitbart's home, but no one answered. I even went to the Clinton Street precinct. Then I tried all the rooming houses. "Notte," I said, "Notte." I didn't even know his last name. I came back to the hotel without finding Notte. We left for Chicago the next day.

There were no theatres on Maxwell Street, only meat markets. My father apologized. "Fannie, I was desperate. We had to get out." He became a butcher and worked in a kosher meat market. In April I heard about the uprising in the Warsaw ghetto. "Niska Street," I said to myself. I still had my Jewish Commando badge. I wrote over a hundred letters to Notte. They all said the same thing. "Notte, please come and get me. I live on Maxwell Street over the Morgenstern Meat Market." I mailed ten of the letters to Breitbart, a few to the Henry Street Theatre, one to the Clinton Street precinct, one to the Hotel Delancey, one to Greenspan, and the rest to people I knew who lived near Delancey Street. Most of the letters came back. I put on different envelopes, and sent them out again. Notte never showed up.

Daniel Spicehandler

Black Barbecue

I met them at the neon city just outside Savannah. They drove up in an old Checker cab whose original yellow streaked beneath the black coat that was obviously painted by hand. I accepted the logic of their invitation which claimed that three can live more cheaply than two. I hopped into the back of the car, and soon the road whined me to sleep.

They did not ask me where I was going until we approached the Florida border. By then it didn't much matter, so I told them, "South."

"How south?" asked the driver. He was a dark man of about thirty and was sucking on a bottle beer.

"Till you turn west," I answered. We were traveling along the shore and there was no possibility of turning east.

"That's no answer," said the one sitting on an airplane bucket seat next to the driver, and he grabbed the wheel and spun it to the right. The car swerved off the road and stopped dead in a sand embankment which glittered with tin cans and amber bottle necks. "Now we're going west. You want out?"

I was sunk in some gray padding, the remains of an arm rest, my legs slung over the back of a folding seat. The man watched me through the mirror above the driver's head as he took out a pack of cigarettes from his shirt pocket. He held a match between his two fingers and cupped it with his thumb. I took out a cigarette, and untangling my legs, leaned forward and drew his hand toward me in order to catch his light. High on his forehead, he wore a felt hat.

"You through?" he asked.

"I'm through."

He took back his match and extinguished it on the tip of his tongue, all the while watching me through the mirror.

"Where you heading?" I asked.

The driver reached down between his legs and brought up another bottle of beer. He pried it open with his teeth. "Miami Beach," he said. "Maybe."

"Suits me."

"Maybe further," said his companion.

"Swell. I've got no real plans."

The driver backed the car out of the sand and soon we were driving south again. He had to slow down as we came up behind a trailer truck whose great rear doors were marked with the name HEMINGWAY. Each time he weaved out in order to pass the truck, the oncoming traffic drove him back behind those tall letters.

"They must've abolished Social Security," he said. "Everyone's heading back north."

"I had a sergeant once," said the man with the felt hat. "His name was Hemingway."

We finally passed the truck and followed the road along the ocean. The highway was built on a sea wall made of piled ashes that sloped down into the water so that the crashing surf rose in a rainbow spray onto our windshield. The whining of the wipers, which the driver now turned on, and the drone of the sea in the tires made me doze off once again.

"You from the South?" asked the driver.

I sat up in a start. "New York," I said.

He shook his head back and forth and kept repeating, "Great! Great!"

His companion lowered the window and flicked out his cigarette. "I'm going swimming," he announced, and without any objection or hesitation, the driver pulled over to the shoulder of the road. He had to use his hand brake to bring the car to a full stop. By the time he got out of the car, the man was half undressed.

"Pretty cold in January," I said, trying to act cool.

"It's the South, ain't it?" said the swimmer. "They show all them pictures of swimming in the snow time, don't they? I'm going to see if they lie."

The driver got out and then lifted the door open for me. He held a bottle of beer in his left hand. "Cracked it up on our last night in New York. Great! Great!" and he turned to the other man and said, "Ain't it great, Benjy?"

The man called Benjy looked at him. "You going swimming?" he asked.

"Shit no. I'm from Duluth," said the driver, and he took a swig from his beer. "Ain't it the hell, though."

Stark naked but for his shoes and socks, his friend now walked down the charcoal beach. The driver began to laugh, "Ain't he a gas though," and he raised the bottle to his pursed lips.

"What's your name?" I asked.

The bottle came crashing down on the embankment, splattering what remained of the beer on our shoes. Then he leaned over and spat out a mouth full of foam. His lips shone from the beer. "Carl," he said. "Just ole Carl with a C." He walked back to the car and sat in his seat letting his feet dangle out onto the ashes. The road smelled of tar and salt.

Down on the beach, Benjy had squatted and was trying to wet his fingertips in the ocean, when a huge wave rolled in and fanned out, encircling him. His shoes squeaked as he came walking by me and back to the car. "They lied," he said, and began to dress.

Carl was for eating breakfast. Benjy, who did not even look at his friend, ordered, "Drive!"

I was back in my sleeping position when I felt a hand nudge my knee. I opened my eyes and saw Benjy's palm stretched beneath my nose. "The toll," he said. "You pay it."

I didn't see any toll gate. "What for?" I asked as I dug into my pants for some change.

"Back there. A dollar."

I handed him a crumpled bill, figuring that if this was all he would want, I would still be ahead of the game when they let me off.

"This a poker dollar?" Benjy asked.

"What?"

"Poker, poker," and he rolled the dollar between his palms, then tossed it up and caught it.

"No. Just habit. I keep money all over me just in case of an accident. It really shakes up the cops. Mystery, you know."

"Cops," he said indifferently, and blew into his khaki handkerchief, the kind that had been issued during the last year of the war. "We're gonna need gas soon," he said, and he pushed the handkerchief back into his jacket pocket. "We share that." He took out another cigarette.

"Have one of mine," I said, and I reached over to offer him my cigarettes. He turned from his hips as if he had a stiff neck and looked at my pack of king-sized, filter-tipped, hard pack with contempt. "I like my own smokes," he said. "They burn different." He did not offer me a cigarette, nor did he accept the light I held out to him. He looked at the flame of the lighter and then lit his own cigarette with a match cupped around his nail-bitten thumb.

"You do something?" he asked.

"Depends. If I like it. You?"

He drew in his breath in a low moan and then swallowed. "Yar. It all depends." He stretched out his hand and began to tap a drum call on the dash board. Carl pressed down the accelerator. "That's Florida out there," he said. "The bend in the road out there is St. Augustine."

"Oldest settlement on the continent," I said.

Benjy looked up through the mirror. "Yar," he said, and then lowered his window and spat.

We were now on the main highway into Jacksonville and there was

D

very little traffic. By late afternoon it became warm and Benjy removed his shirt. The wind from the open window burned in my eyes. I had had nothing to eat all day and I was very hungry.

"How about a beer, Carl?" I asked the driver.

He leaned down and from under his seat he drew up a bottle. He opened it with his teeth and raised it over his head. "How!" he said, and then swung it back to his mouth and drank.

I decided to abandon this cheerful couple at the first stop we would make.

It was eight o'clock when we rattled into a place called Kaloochee—a gas pump, a porch without a building and an unlit sign which said, CITY CAFE. Carl and I got out.

"Aren't you for eats?" he asked his partner.

"Goddamn liars," was all Benjy said.

The café was one of those chrome and formica joints that cater to the local dog lovers and the stale hunger of transients. On the counter stood two large jars stained with salt and oil, and filled with little bags of peanuts. There were trays piled with packaged cookies whose sugar filling pressed sloppily against the cellophane wrappers. The cook was busy draining coffee grounds from the steaming urn through a spotted cheesecloth. A cigarette burned slowly in a glass ashtray next to two opened packs of bread.

Carl was nicer when he saw that they had steak on the menu. While we waited for our orders to be filled, he took out a pack of cards from his breast pocket and began to shuffle them expertly. "I got a trick," he said to the cook, who set two mugs of white coffee before us.

"I'll bet," said the cook. Some of the coffee spilled on the counter.

Carl proceeded to perform a simple trick I remembered from my childhood, and the cook and two grim-faced men, tanned and wearing hats but no jackets or ties, watched as well. The men were seated at the one table in the café and between them there squatted a coon dog whose chin rested on one of the men's toes. The dog too stared at Carl.

Five minutes later the cook set before us two plates filled with food. Carl reached over and pulled out a napkin from the overstuffed holder and meticulously wiped each piece of silverware. Then, hunching over his plate, he cut the meat into little, neat squares. The cook watched him as he gripped his knife and fork in his fists, tapped them once against the counter, and then proceeded to eat quickly, alternating between bites of meat and gulps of coffee which he drank from the mug without raising it. Carl was a serious eater.

"Wonder if they skinned this animal?" I asked, as I myself picked at the peas that pressed like eyes into a mound of cold mashed potatoes. Everyone turned to me, including Carl. He was about to spear his fork into a slice of bleached bread that he had dipped into his gravy. The steak was very tough.

"Know each other long?" I asked Carl. He was busy adding sugar to his coffee and was slowly stirring it. The coffee, I knew, was already sickeningly sweet.

Carl leaned over and examined a pineapple pie, half-used, which lay under a plastic dome. He raised the lid and smelled the pie. Without uttering a word, he signalled the cook and nodded to the pie. He continued to stir his coffee.

"Who?" he asked.

"Benjy. Your buddy."

"Who's he?"

"Johnny Weissmuller, outside."

"That's not his name." He ate the pie in three bites.

"But you told me—"

"I lied."

"Then what's his name?"

"Never said."

"What's he do?"

"Pimps."

"What?"

"How in hell should I know. I met him two hours before you did."

"OK. What do you do?" I lit a cigarette.

Carl snapped his finger at me impatiently. I handed him my pack, but instead he took the cigarette from my mouth. His hands were tanned and chipped and his nails were blue and encrusted with tar.

"Let's pick it up and move it out," he said, getting up and adjusting his stomach. He was not a thin man.

We drove on till midnight. I offered to relieve Carl at the wheel, but he merely chuckled. Just as I was dozing off, Carl pulled up before a square white building of two stories. "Sack time!" he declared, and began to laugh.

We parked on a dark street where only the light of the hotel sign shone. As we climbed the stairs leading to a gallery, Benjy reached up and unscrewed the bulb. He wiped the moth powder on his pants.

Inside, Carl said, "Rooms are on Benjy," and then he signed his name to the registry. An old man, who looked as if he slept only in the sun, read our names with his fingertips and then reached over and handed Carl a red rubber ball attached to a key. "Three thirteen," he said. "It's got two winders."

"This place got a name?" asked Benjy.

"Colonel Hendrix House," said the old man. "Three cities chain."

"No shit?" said Carl, who was already ascending the staircase.

"You gents need anything, just ring the maid. Any luggage?"

"Him," said Benjy, pointing to me.

We had to find the room ourselves. An old scraped runner, weighted down by brass poles, clinked as we walked down the hall. Once inside the room, Carl took off his shoes. "I'm for a beer," he said, and he rang the bell that hung by the bed. They had left the door open.

Benjy stalked the room, investigating the sparse furnishings. He picked up an ash tray and slipped it into his pocket. He tried one lamp, which did not work, and then another. The lamp shades were stained from old light and a faded swan on one was rubbed headless. He raised and then lowered the green window shade which was perforated like a used stamp, and finally, he walked over to the sink that stood on two lion's paws over in the corner of the room. "Ain't worth it," he said, and gathered up the small packets of soap on the shelf above the sink. From a paper bag that he carried, he pulled out a towel that smelled of old beach and exchanged it for the clean, well-ironed one that hung on the rack near the window. The night tables—three of them—were all scarred with cigarette burns.

Carl was sitting on the bed and running his fingers through his toes. He wore no socks. When he finished, he lit a cigarette and fell back upon the bed. "Man! I sure am for something." And now he scratched his crotch.

A chambermaid stood in the doorway, her arms laden with fresh towels and soap. She was about seventeen, flat and very black. When he saw her, Carl perched on his elbows and with a wet leer in his voice, he said, "Yeah, something."

I went over and took the soap and towels from the girl. She didn't move. "Can we get something to drink?" I asked.

She stared through me, only raising her thin, brown hand to her lips. The movement was enough to show life beneath the colorless dress. I nodded to her encouragingly and then almost in a whisper, I said, "Beer."

She turned toward me, her black eyes meeting mine for the first time. "Beer," she repeated, neither in question nor in response, and then she backed out of the room.

When I turned back to the room, both men were staring at me. As usual, Carl was first to speak. "Nothing," he said. "Nothing at all. Just her ole little snookie. Just nothing at all."

He saw that I was puzzled. "I mean, Boy, it was black and bare and nothing but that little ole rag of cotton between it and you." He began to laugh and then it turned into a hacking cough.

Benjy's lower lip drooped and trembled. He too laughed, the way you'd imagine a snake laughed.

"Ever get any black meat?" Carl asked me.

"What?"

"Nigger snout. Pussy. It's different. It's way in a hell hole different. They smell sex. Like minx. Once you whiff in on the ole black oyster, man, just lie down and let it slide."

"You wouldn't kid me, would you?"

Benjy giggled. "He ain't the first and he ain't the last. That's on a fact."

"OK, Mister Freedom Rider. OK." I walked into the bathroom and tossed more soap at Benjy. "Only you don't drive, do you?"

Benjy's hanging jaw tightened. "Depends, friend. Depends on the horsepower." Carl was resting his head on his folded arms. His toes curled around the brass bar at the foot of the bed. Benjy came up to him and reached down and shook him. "But you know for sure," he said. "Don't you, old sport? For sure." And he jabbed a finger into Carl's paunch.

Carl's body tickled with laughter. "Well, I can't rightly say," and he kept right on laughing as he swung himself to a sitting position. "Because I wasn't that close yet."

Benjy turned toward me. "You was close enough, weren't you?"

I pulled off my shirt and walked over to the sink. The water came out rusty and left a red rim on the bowl. I waited till it cleared and was about to take a drink off the palm of my hand, when there was a knock on the door. Carl stopped laughing and looked over toward me and then at Benjy.

"Only this time I'm going to get close enough to find out forever," and he leaned over and opened the door.

The young Negress, chewing gum, stood silently in the doorway, her spindle legs together. She held a small tray with three iced bottles of beer, but no glasses. One bottle had lost its label.

"Com'on in, Honey. No one's going to take nothing away from you all." Carl rose from the bed and led the girl by her elbow to the table where I stood. "You been hanging here long, Doll?" he asked.

The girl shook her head.

"How long?"

She looked at me.

"Leave off, Carl. Let the kid alone," I said.

Her eyes darted back to Carl.

"Do you smell something funny, Benjy?" Carl asked.

"Yar," said Benjy. His lower lip began to tremble again.

"What you smell, ole buddy boy? Tell the doll what you smell?"

Benjy's hands rubbed hard against his trousers. Carl's fingers danced up and down the girl's arm.

"Tell you what *I* smell," said Carl. "I smell girl. Nice, young, wet girl."

The girl's eyes blinked once. Her legs did not move.

"Hear me now, Honey," Carl went on. "We are three young fellers and you are one. Let's have a little ole basket party."

She looked at him with vacant eyes. "Six," she said.

Carl backed off. "Six what?"

"Been six months," she said, blinking once. "You asked me."

"Well then, you're just an ole hand at packing lunch for the guests."

Her large black eyes again turned toward me. "Lay off," I said. "She's a scared kid."

Benjy's fingers touched her lips.

"Easy, Benjy man," said Carl. "We got to finesse this," and then he pulled out his deck of cards and began to shuffle them. "How you want them, Honey. One at a time," and he began to toss single cards at the girl's feet. "Or all at once." He let the rest of the deck fall in front of me. "You don't want none, as I understand it," he said to me. "That's a mighty fine shame. So, little girl, there'll be but two. You all think you can take care of me and my ole billy goat over there, Ma'am?"

"Ah got to go now," said the girl.

"Now, Honey. Where you got to go at one ole o'clock in the morning?

Com'on and set down over here and have us a little drink." Carl took the tray out of her hand, placed it on the table and then led her over to his bed. He eased her down without her resisting. She sat stiffly on the edge of the bed, her feet at attention.

Benjy brought her a beer, and without looking up at him, she said, "Ah don't drink that."

Quick as an eel, Benjy whisked out a flask and began to pour a drink into its silver cap. Carl frowned and took the cap from Benjy.

"Ah got to go," said the girl.

Carl drank the whiskey and screwed the cap back on to the flask.

"Hell with this noise," Benjy swore. "Let's see if it smells." And he grabbed the girl and forced her down on the bed.

Carl pushed him away and sat down next to her, shaking his head and patting the girl's thigh. "She's got to read out her hand," he said. "First she's got to do her reading." Carl held his belly which now quickly filled with laughter. "It ain't no good, Benjy man. Ain't no good at all. Now you went and scared the little ole pussy cat." Carl reached over and took the girl by her waist.

The girl chewed her gum once. Carl's hands moved more quickly. He played with the row of buttons that ran down the front of her dress, and as he cooed and cajoled, one at a time the buttons came off in his hand. Before I could move, the girl lay sprawled on the bed, her dress open and her black, flat belly breathing evenly and calmly, accentuating the color of her underclothes.

"Lock the door, Benjy! I'm going into the pool first."

Carl was about to press his knee down upon her groin when he must have realized that she was not resisting. He pushed her down across the bed and ran his hands along her body, gently parting her thighs with the back of his hand. There was no mistake about it. She did not resist at all. Carl sat up in a shudder.

"What in hell's the matter?" hissed Benjy. He had been leaning close to Carl in order to get a closer glimpse of the girl's body.

"Skin and bones," said Carl, breathing heavily. "So damn skinny her bones are like drumsticks."

"Com'on," said Benjy, who now kicked the bedpost. "Just up and let me if you can't. Come off or get off."

The hulking matron who came through the door would have torn Carl to shreds had not her husband, who stood in the doorway, held on to her monstrous arm. She sent Benjy sailing against me and then, dragging her husband with her, went for Carl. "Get out!" she ordered.

Carl rolled off the girl, almost with relief, and scatted into the bathroom. The girl still lay with her dress open, her head hanging over the side of the bed.

"You go home now, Cora," said the matron. "Go home and fix up some sleep."

Carl's drool had left a wet spot on the pillow.

We had been driving for about an hour, skirting the Everglades, when Carl finally spoke. "Where'd you get that whiskey?"

Benjy, gazing ahead, following the beams of the headlights, did not answer at first. Then he turned to me and said: "Never did get a chance to see the color. You pushed it before I had a chance."

"Pushed what?"

"The mother-grabbing bell. You rung it and all I seen was the black."

"Me? Why—why I saw him push it when he couldn't—"

"Lies," grumbled Carl. "All of you are little ole lies."

Benjy lit a cigarette and held a match close to Carl's ear. "Just you drive, Stud Boy. Just you roll." The eager and dependent note in Benjy's voice of the hotel room was gone. He raised his flask and took a long pull.

"You and your goddamn whiskey," mumbled Carl.

We drove through the effluvial night, listening to the moil of insects and the bark of raccoons. Carl turned off the highway and followed a muddy country road until the grass whistled against the sides of the car. Without warning, he stopped, threw open his door and with his legs hanging out and his head thrown back on the seat, he collapsed into immediate sleep. Benjy remained seated in the same position he had been in since we had left the hotel. The mist on the windows dripped with dead bugs.

I climbed out of the car and walked into the glade. Noises darted and rustled as I moved between the flexed vines the size of pythons. The grass sucked at my shoes and I felt the dip and swell of the earth.

There was a small pool packed with moon and slime. Occasionally a ripple broke across the viscous green and was quickly dissipated in a blot of silt that lay upon the surface of the water. I sat down on a rock at the edge of the pool and listened to the thrumming frogs. The stone I threw into the water hardly made a splash, and as I raised my arm to toss another, something held my wrist. In terror, I whirled about and saw Benjy glaring at me.

"War is hell," I said in relief.

He stood behind me, holding my hand, not uttering a word. I tried to yank it free, but his grip tightened.

"You!" he said. "You spoilt it."

"Spoiled what?"

"The girl. You spoilt it."

"She was a scared kid."

"You spoilt it. I didn't even get to see."

"See what?"

"The color. I told you. To see the different color."

"What the hell you talking about?"

"If it's different. Down there. Like their palms."

"Jeezus! You're sick."

"Just wanted to see and you spoilt it." He released my hand reluctantly. I watched him undress and plunge into the pool. The smell of honeysuckle hung in the blackness, and I heard the thickness of the water. It was a long time before he surfaced and in the moonlight his body was the color of bile. "Thought you were dead," I said.

"Like piss," he said. "It's like clapped piss. And my name ain't Benjy. It's R.C."

"R.C. what?" I asked, turning away in disgust at the sight of scum and slime that clung to his body.

"Just plain R.C." He climbed back into his clothes without bothering to wipe the green off his body.

"You must have been named for someone."

"Yar. My sonofabitch old man."

"OK. What's his name?"

"He's dead."

"Was?"

"R.C. I told you."

"Benjy's a nicer name," I said. "More legal."

"It ain't my name," he said, threateningly.

"All right. Well, what does your mother call you?"

He looked at me and spat. "Horse," he said, and then he walked back to the car.

Benjy made us stop at the edge of the swamp, in front of a ramshackle boathouse moored to the first palm tree I had ever seen. A slab of wood, nailed to the stern, announced in green paint, ICE BEER. Carl bought out their stock and said to me, "You pay!" while he stacked the car trunk with the bottles. He set a cake of ice, wrapped in a gunny sack, upon the beer and then brought down the trunk lid with a crash. Benjy meanwhile went behind the boathouse, followed by a slip of a girl.

When he reappeared, Carl, who had regained his insolence, asked: "Did she whistle?"

Benjy ignored him. He came back carrying two amber bottles plugged with newspaper. Uncorking one, he raised it to his mouth and took a quick pull and shuddered. "Beer takes too long," he said. "Drive!"

Carl spat between his legs.

By noon we were out of the glades. We drove by a wide pasture where the tips of grass were dappled with brown and hung over the shoulder of the road. Benjy had stripped to his waist and was slowly nursing his flask which he had earlier replenished from one of the bottles. As he gulped the whiskey, his ribs convulsed up and down over his sunken diaphragm. He had an old chest and his skin was hairless, like leather. Occasionally he poured a few drops on his palm and then rubbed the liquid on his chest and shoulders.

"Whatcha call for lunch, Benjy?" Carl asked.

"Ain't had BK yet."

"We'll skip breakfast, like them movie actors."

"Steak," said Benjy.

"Check! You look while I drive."

A breeze came up and Benjy leaned way out the window, causing the rim of his hat to turn up rakishly. "Knew a guy once," he said, "a duster pilot. Said you can tell the wind the way their asses faced," and he nodded to the steers that stood in a half burnt out field. He raised the flask to his lips and drank. This time when he finished he passed it on to Carl.

Suddenly two steers began to gallop across the pasture. A cloud of dust rose before us and the next thing I knew, I was tossed against the front seat. The car had swerved off the road and had jerked to a halt between two trees. Through the shattered windshield I saw a big brown eye staring at me. For a moment I stared back, until Benjy's rasping cough made me reel back against the door which swung open, and out I tumbled into a puddle of blood that was already encrusted by the settling dust. A black calf, half squatting, lay blinking over the left fender of the car.

"Check the payload," Carl called to me. And I saw how he slumped lower in his seat and puffed out short, noisy breaths. Benjy cleared his throat and then spat across Carl's chest and out the window. He picked up the two bottles of whiskey and pushed himself out of the car.

He stood in front of the calf, shaking the bottles in its face. "This will cost you, cow. This will damn cost you!"

"Let's get it on its feet," I said. "It's just stunned a little. That's all." Benjy didn't move.

"Must have charged with the others," I said. "Only it was slower and didn't quite make it. Give us a hand."

Benjy didn't move.

I looked down a moment at the passive animal. It was all black except for its face, which was patched with white and one splash of brown.

Benjy moved. He drank from one of the bottles and then poured some whiskey on the gash at the side of the calf. It was from there that the puddle of blood had formed. "Like I said. We ain't had no breakfast yet."

Carl came out now and he, too, eyed the poor beast. He took one bottle from Benjy's hand and began to laugh. Before I could protest, Carl ordered me to look for kindling. "Me and him will do the rest. Move!"

Meanwhile Benjy held the other bottle of whiskey like a candle as he examined the calf. He poked a finger into its belly and the animal shuddered in an attempt to rise.

"You're really serious," I said, beginning to back away.

"Breakfast," Carl giggled. "Nice little ole veal chops for good ole BK. Get the wood!"

Benjy moved. He walked over to the car and came back with a large monkey wrench. He stood over the calf and stared into its blinking eyes. Then without warning, he raised the wrench and brought it down hard against the triangular skull of the animal. The calf's legs convulsed, and then, raising its face slowly, it lowed once and fell back against the car. Blood spurted out of the beast's nostrils.

It took them over an hour to beat the calf to death. When Benjy tired, Carl removed his shirt and took up the wrench in both his hands. Each time

D*

he raised his arms, the fat of his flesh quivered as he pounded death into the animal. They worked in shifts.

I do not know what made me stand and watch as the indomitable beast slowly leaked its life away. Even after the head lay smashed and battered, the big eyes remained open and never quite dead.

"It's let go its pee," Carl finally said. "It's dead for sure now."

Both men sat down on the grass and rested. Blood splattered their clothes and the grass in which the animal now lay was wilted and brown. A fly flashed its green belly to the sun and then plunged down into the tear on the skull of the beast.

"Hear me, you!" said Carl. "You want to eat? Get kindling!"

I reached over for one of the whiskey bottles which was propped in the grass near the calf's dead tail. It took three long swigs for me to say, "Better hurry before the flies get at her," and then I walked off into the brush.

By the time I returned, the sun had begun its work on the carcass and the air was choked with the sweet smells of dung and blood. Benjy was busy getting up a spit, while Carl peeled dead flies off his wet body. A small fire was already smoldering.

"Get the jack," Benjy growled at me. He had jammed two Y-shaped branches at either side of the fire and was now trying to pry open the mouth of the calf.

I was too drunk to move. Carl sneered and as he went by, on his way to bring the jack, he flicked a squashed fly off his chest and at me. On a rock near the car, Benjy's flask lay half empty. I picked it up and took a few gulps. I began to giggle when I turned and saw Benjy struggle to ram the jack handle down the gullet of the dead calf. The whiskey was very hot.

"Sonofabitch got too many teeth," he said. He picked up the bloody wrench, and like a batter at the plate, took a stance, and pivoting gracefully on heel and toe, began to clobber the mouth of the calf.

"You want to eat?" Carl said to me. "Then push." And together we rammed the long bar down the mouth of the animal.

The problem was how to get the carcass up and over the two sticks. Holding the jack handle, which by now was slippery with blood and bile, I raised the head of the calf. Benjy had his hands dug into what was by now mud under the haunches of the calf, as he struggled to raise the rear of the animal.

"You," I panted at Carl. "Get in the middle."

Carl was laughing and drinking. He came over and holding a beer bottle in one hand, he slipped the other under the calf. "That's me," he said. "Always on the serious part." Together we managed to lift the carcass.

"It's hotter'n hell," said Benjy. "Won't need too much cooking." Some hairs of the calf had become pasted to his chest.

Then the animal slipped. Carl passed around the bottle of whiskey.

"Let's get it one side at a time," he suggested, and they both came over to my side.

We managed to get the jack handle over and into the groove of one stick and then we raised the hind quarter of the animal onto the other one. The weight of the carcass made the branches sink into the ground and tilt away from the fire. Benjy pushed the burning twigs over with his foot so that the fire was centered under the carcass, and then he tossed some more kindling on the flames which made the hairs on the hide snap and hiss. The flies had all disappeared.

The three of us sat down, exhausted and wet. Benjy passed the flask around for the last time.

"Smells Nigger," he said.

"Look at the ole tail burn," said Carl.

"It's a little bit of a calf," I said.

Benjy got up and tried moving the animal by the jack handle, but all that turned was the bar. One eye flashed in the sun.

We must have sat there for an hour without saying a word, just watching the fire roast the hide without having any effect on the flesh. The flames began to smolder.

"Any of you ever do this before?" I finally asked.

"Do what?" asked Carl.

"This. Roast a live cow."

"Barbecue," said Benjy. "It's called barbecue."

"All right. Barbecue. It appears to me we forgot something."

"Yeah, City Boy. What? What did we all forget?"

"The skin."

"Hide," said Benjy.

"Hide. We didn't strip the hide."

Both men looked at me with hurt expressions.

"Tell us, City Boy," said Carl. "Tell us how to cook the ole cow."

"It's wrinkling up like wet shoes. The fire'll never get through to the meat."

"Shut up!" said Benjy.

"Yeah. Shut up," said Carl, who now rose to toss some more kindling on the dying fire.

Some time later, one of the sticks collapsed, and the carcass came crashing down on the flames. No one moved to raise it up again. The head of the calf was now hanging down into the smoking fire.

Soon the flames were out. Carl went back to the car and carried over some beer.

"This'll have to do breakfast," he said, as he handed a beer to me and then one to Benjy.

"Got an opener?" I asked.

"Use your teeth," said Carl, biting his beer bottle.

Benjy leaned over and shook his flask over the fire. There must have been a few drops left in it because suddenly a claw of flame shot up and then simmered back into the smoke. Carl spat the bottle top into the fire.

"You spoilt it again," Benjy said to me.

"Spoiled what?"

"The barbecue. The goddamn barbecue," and he set his beer down in the grass and began to swat flies.

Malcolm Bradbury
The Adult Education Class

Once a week, on a Tuesday, Stuart Treece taught an evening class at the Adult Education Centre, a large grimy building in the center of the town. Heavily invested with Victoriana, its rooms were the haunt of evangelizing vegetarians, seasoned protestors with the stains of Trafalgar Square on the seats of their jeans, and young teachers and secretaries taking courses in speedy reading. Tonight he passed the book display— "ALL ARE available for YOUR WINTER reading"—and went into the men's toilet, where he took off his oilskin cycling suit. Then he washed off the dust that had flapped up from the books he had been working on all day, and sat on the edge of the sink reading through a page of notes, his preparation. Then he was ready for the fray.

In the common room there was a fire, the new *New Statesman,* and an elderly lady who wore a large *vol-au-vent* hat and was one of the students in his group, which studied modern poetry. "What's a nice book to give for a Christmas present?" she said, looking up from her knitting, "you know all about books." "Oh, I never read *nice* books," said Treece, "only nasty ones. Isn't the best thing to give a book token?" "I think they're so tasteless, so impersonal," said the lady, putting away her knitting and following him into the classroom.

They were the first there. On the board was a diagram, left over from the night before, of what Treece realized, a little belatedly, to be the female sexual organs. He rubbed it out while the class jostled in—fat motherly ladies who counted how many pullovers he was wearing, and worried about him; little men with small bushy Grimsby moustaches who were furniture salesmen, bus inspectors and newsagents; two nuns; a few bearded local Bohemians smoking cigarettes with black cylinders; and Louis Bates. "What do you think of this, for a sofa," said one pleasant lady, sitting down and producing a piece of furnishing fabric from a shopping bag. "I like it," said Treece. "Did you see Connolly's bloody review on Sunday?" asked one of the Bohemians. "I've written to them about it. Again." A man who now owned a bookshop but persisted atavistically in calling himself a bricklayer—he was the class's worker—began selling copies of a little literary magazine called *Hooligan,* published at Leeds University. They all drew in their chairs around the oblong table and waited for things to happen.

"Are we all here?" said Treece. The class secretary put ticks down the register. "Mr. Smart's not here," she said. "I expect it's too cold for him," said one of the old ladies. "Yes, that'll be it," said the class secretary, "but he is a tryer and he'll put in his attendances. He suffers with the cold a lot." "Well," said Treece, "we ought to start, because I want to finish on time this evening." "Going out, Professor Treece, then?" asked one of the ladies. "Yes, I'm going to a party." "Lovely," said the lady. "We used to have marvelous parties when the children were young," said a housewife, "balloons, gingerbread men, everything." "Dr. MacElwee used to have a class party," said one of the insurance men. "Meeting before Christmas he'd come in loaded up with buns. Everyone would bring a bit of something, cakes and such like." "Of course," said a housewife, "we have to remember that Professor Treece isn't married like Dr. MacElwee was. His wife was lovely. She often used to come and make comments."

Dr. MacElwee hovered over the class, a persistent ghost. He was the previous tutor. He had come up through the old tough days of the WEA and had a steadfast commitment to working-class culture and the critical analysis of newspaper advertisements. The middle-class housewives found him marvelous. Now he had been translated to higher things, running a liberal studies program in a college of advanced technology, but Treece knew all about him, though he had never actually met him. He knew about the kind of ties he wore, and how he always lost the key of the book-box, and how he hated James and Proust, and how he and Mr. Smart used to quarrel about the First World War. Some of the class remembered tutors even before MacElwee; they seemed to Treece like possessors of an illness who were not satisfied with one, but wanted a second and a third opinion. And so they came along, year after year to compare Mac-Elwee's D. H. Lawrence and Potter's D. H. Lawrence with Treece's D. H. Lawrence, noting similarities with pleasure and differences with doubt, and building up great accretions around the one book, which they read time and time again. There were moments when Treece asked himself why they did come. As week succeeded week, he grew to suspect that they weren't really understanding what he had to say, as he discoursed on and on about *The Four Quartets,* juggling subtleties of interpretation and differentiating between various states of visionary perception. The odd thing was that none of them *stopped* attending, save for one conspicuous defector who had objected to the inclusion of Eliot on political grounds and had been disliked by the rest of the class. On the other hand, the things they said seemed to bear almost no relation to the things *he* said. They appeared often to sit, on three sides of the oblong table, following out little private trains of thought in the interstices of his own observations.

Treece believed in education, and he was sure that it was all very profitable, all the same. But it was true that the only person who seemed to be following at his heels was Louis Bates. Bates was one of his undergraduate students at the university, an odd persistent man in his first year, older than the others. There were, indeed, times when it seemed to Treece (and he suspected, to Bates too) that he was the *only* undergraduate at the university. Mrs. Mary Baker Eddy once instructed her followers in Christian Science that they were forbidden to haunt her house or her drive; Treece felt the need of the same instruction for Bates. He was a dogged pursuer who popped up in the most unexpected places; at foreign students' weekends, at staff cocktail parties in the bookshop, on the doorsteps of various faculty members. Treece had suggested to him, when he appeared at the first meeting of his class, that he had enough work on his hands with the university course without attending an adult education class as well. "Well," Bates had said, licking his lips thoughtfully, "I do feel that in the honors course we do less than justice to the moderns— who are, after all, converting contemporary experience, for us primary experience, into literature. That's just a little belief of mine." Treece had had to grant some justice in this, and Bates had sat there week after week, nodding his domed head at the better *aperçus,* getting angry with the weaker brethren. The rest of the class didn't quite share his view about primary experience. They were interested, but writers seemed to annoy them rather, critics annoyed them a little bit more, and though they respected everything Treece said, he sometimes thought they respected him mainly for two things—the fact that he got his cup of tea, served at midway point in the two-hour meeting, free, while everyone else paid fourpence; and the fact that he could actually earn his living doing this kind of thing.

In consequence of this analysis of his class, Treece in more recent meetings had changed his technique somewhat. Instead of working on line-by-line analyses of major works, referring back learnedly to Donne and Jessie Weston, he had curbed his scholarship and tried to apply what he called, rather pretentiously, the Socratic method. This meant that he read poems and passages of prose to the class and then asked them questions. Tonight he began with Auden's song, "As I Walked Out One Evening." He produced from his briefcase a wad of cyclostyled copies of the poem and pushed them to the people sitting nearest him. "Would you pass these round the table?" he said. There was a good deal of fuss as everyone took the sheets and stared at them with blank fascination; they always enjoyed, to the full, any teaching aids, and there were hisses of awe and delight when he wrote words like "free verse" on the blackboard. "Would you like me to read it aloud?" he asked. "Yes," said the housewife nearest to him, "and I'm going to mark bits with my pencil." "I did give you copies of this last week didn't I?" asked Treece. "Did he?" said a lady. "Yes, I think you did," said an insurance man. "You asked us to *read* it," said a

Bohemian, "for this class." "*Did* you?" asked Treece. "Yes," said the Bohemian. "No," said everyone else. "I didn't really," said the Bohemian. "Well, I think you're going to find this fairly easy and straightforward, after the Eliot. So just listen and tell me afterward what sort of purpose the poem has; what it says and why it says it in that way. Watch the tone, the diction, the verse form."

Treece then read the poem. It was followed by a silence. "Well, what do you think?" asked Treece. "I would say this," said one of the class, a schoolmaster, after a moment, "he's a real poet." "Why?" asked Treece. "He's a technician, a consummate technician," said the schoolmaster, "he knows exactly what he's doing, where he's putting words and so on." "Yes, good. Well, what do you all think it means? How clearly is that meaning expressed?" "Can you say what a poem means?" asked a Bohemian. "Who was it said a poem should not mean but be?" "MacLeish," said Treece, "but that doesn't indicate that it has no paraphrasable meaning at all." "I didn't like it," said a lady. "Why not?" "It's cruel," said the lady, "and it isn't fair." "Why should it not be cruel? And to whom is it cruel?" "I don't quite know," said the lady, "it just sounds cruel." "It must be cruel to someone." "Well, then, to everyone, I suppose. I think he's accusing me of wasting my life, and you can't say that sort of thing to people." "But surely there's a sense in which nearly all literature is saying that? Arnold once said that poetry is at bottom a criticism of life and surely we do expect literature to do more than entertain us. We expect that it should reflect upon the nature and responsibilities of man, don't we? And that it touch us at a very deep level of our experience? It's a form of high civilization, to produce and read literature; and all really great literature is a record of the worth of man, and a criticism of the deviations from the highest kind of living."

"But writers are only other people, after all," said the woman. "But very dedicated and refined people who are really concerned with this question of quality," said Treece, beginning to glow with excitement. "What do you live for? What do you want life to provide you with?" "Are you asking *me?*" asked the lady. "No," said Treece, hastily, "I mean, that's what literature asks us." "Of course," said Bates, "some people just *live* life away." Treece laughed, and Bates looked very pleased with himself. "But, but," cried an insurance salesman, "poetry needn't be about life at all, need it?" "How can it avoid it?" asked Treece. "Well," said the man, "some of the best poetry in the world is about birds, and flowers, and the wind. Look at Keats. Now there's a poet. I'd say that was pure poetry. Keats knew what poetry was about." "But isn't the question one of Keats's relationship to those things?" "No, not really," said the salesman firmly. "Well, what you're saying sounds very depressing to me. I teach literature because I believe it does do those things, does have that sort of quality and concern. But doesn't that mean anything to you?" Treece looked around the room, suddenly puzzled and unacquainted; what he was saying was so much at home with him that he felt it odd that here might be people who did not think, deep down, in the way that he did. It was a matter on which he was persistently innocent, and he realized now, as he had been forced to realize on other occasions before, that here were assumptions that were not commonly shared. "Well, of course, literature is about life in a sense," said one of the housewives, "but it's got to be pleasant and entertaining, hasn't it? Otherwise it doesn't interest you. What's the good of reading a sad, depressing book, like so many of these modern books, when you spend all your life trying to avoid those things? I don't know about you, but I have enough trouble of my own without reading about other peoples'."

From the far end of the table a voice suddenly spoke. "You people surprise me," said the voice, which was Louis Bates's, in very loud tones. "Here's a man telling you what literature is really about, trying to raise you up, and you don't recognize what he's saying." At first Treece wasn't clear about whom Bates was talking, whether he meant Auden or himself; he *hoped* that he meant Auden. But then, as Bates went on to condemn the ingratitude of the class, he recognized with unease that this was a paean of praise directed toward himself. His first response, when he knew this, was one of fury. He was prepared to believe that Bates's comments were sheer flattery, spoken with the intention of bettering his own position as a student. But then he realized that this really wasn't true; it was evident from the flash of his eyes and the spittle flying from his lips that somehow what was said had violently engaged Bates, that he had, and in an extravagant form, values that he shared very exactly with Treece. Then Treece's reaction was shame—shame in his apologist, who, by behaving in this ridiculous way, by committing this solecism, was virtually guying all that Treece was trying to state and stand for. It wasn't enough to have someone say the right things; they have to be said by the right persons for the right reasons. And when he saw that, Treece became embarrassed by another kind of shame, shame for being ashamed of his apologist; the two shames existed together and were the same emotion. Bates went on, elevating and murdering Treece's case; he extended it and parodied it and made it absurd. He spoke for about five minutes and the view became not the view of Treece's commitment but of Bates's maladjustment. "Here is a man who can teach you how to put depth into your lives," said Bates. "You're privileged to read these things with him." Treece knew he had to stop Bates or destroy his class; Bates had to be sacrificed to preserve the cause he was arguing. Treece said: "That's enough, Bates. This is my class, not yours. And I'm afraid neither you nor I will convince anyone with that kind of rhetoric." Bates's round eyes grew large, and sad, and he stopped in the middle of a sentence. Treece expected he'd then go on to excuse himself; he had heard many such Bates excuses. But he dropped his head and said nothing. The class, already looking uncomfortable, looked more uncomfortable still. It would look to them like a private quarrel. To restore atmosphere, Treece said he would read the poem again. He did this. When he had finished, the housewifely lady who had spoken before spoke again. "Well,

I still don't understand it," she said. "I didn't before and I don't now. I
wish someone would explain it. But it doesn't seem very poetic to me."

"Well, let's talk about that," said Treece. "What is a poetic poem? Or
to put it another way—aren't all poems poetic?" "Oh, no," said the housewife. "Well, then," said Treece, "what is it that Auden is doing with
language that gives you a sense that this isn't poetic?" "Well, it's sort of the
way everyone speaks," said the lady. "Yes, it is, to a point. What's different
about it?" "Oh, some of the words." "Pick them out," said Treece. "But
shouldn't all the words be poetic?" asked the lady. "Well, how do words
become poetic? Doesn't a poet have to use the language of his time?
And heighten it and sharpen it and concentrate it?" "To communicate
better," said the lady. "Yes, in part," said Treece. "Well, what I'm saying
is that this poem doesn't communicate to me at all." "Does it to anyone?"
asked Treece. "Well," said a bank clerk, "this is by D. H. Auden, isn't
it?" "W. H. Auden, yes." "Well, what I was going to say was, wasn't
Auden trying to use the language of the common man?" "Yes, that's right,
Mr. Hope, he was," said Treece, "up to a point." The class all looked
pleased at this victory by one of their members; they now felt they were
getting somewhere. The man smiled. "Yes, well if this is the language of
the common man, why doesn't it communicate to Mrs. Wilkins? That's
the key question, isn't it?" Treece admitted it was. "Well," said the man,
"if I might suggest a few things, I think it's because the common man
doesn't want poetry in his language."

"Balls," said a bluff man at the other end of the table. "Mr. Tinker,
please," said Treece. At once the class was in uproar; an old lady hit Mr.
Tinker with her scrap-pad. Mr. Hope, in uncovering Treece's pattern of
thinking, had endeared himself to all; whereas Mr. Tinker, who was a Com-
munist and smelled at the armpits, was not at all popular. Perceiving his
isolation, Tinker, proud of it, rose to his feet. "Ladies and gentlemen,
I want to apologize to all you comrades for a momentary indiscretion.
Passion drove me to words I wouldn't normally have used before you, but
what I meant to say was this: I think our friend is overlooking the signi-
ficance of the whole working-class movement since the French Revolution.
Fascist poets and critics have too long obscured the value of the language
of the common man. Even in poetry." Mr. Tinker sat down.

"Go on, Mr. Hope, with your argument," said Treece. "Well, Professor Treece, what *I* was going to say, when Mr. Tinker burst in like that,
was that poetry has to delight us as well. Now, what D. H. Auden is saying
here isn't difficult to see. I think he's saying that time defeats us all and
prevents us from realizing our youthful hopes. But he doesn't say it to
please." "Very good," said Mrs. Wilkins. Then above the heads Treece
saw an arm waving; it was Bates's. "May I speak?" said Bates. All the
members of the class turned to see what fresh shock was in store. "Go
ahead, Bates," said Treece. "Well, I'd like to read an almost identical
poem—that is, a poem on an almost identical subject. I won't tell you
yet who it's by. If you do recognize the author, don't shout out. Then after

I've read it, I'd like, if you don't mind, Professor Treece, just to ask the class and Mr. Hope one or two questions." Treece looked at this indestructible character with renewed amazement; Bates said, "It's all very relevant." "All right," said Treece.

Bates beamed and then read from a large tome, the title of which he obscured behind an immense hand, the song from *Cymbeline,* "Fear No More the Heat O' the Sun." The reading over, Bates turned to Mr. Hope and asked him whether he thought the piece was any more delightful than the Auden song. "Yes," said Mr. Hope firmly. "Why?" demanded Bates. Treece watched his class slip away from him and with a tired hand plucked at the straps of his briefcase. "Because it's more poetic," said Mr. Hope. "Well, then, I suggest the reason is not that Auden hasn't succeeded in his poem but because he hits home too hard." "That's right," said Mr. Tinker. "It has relevance to your own life; he describes your own situation," said Bates. "That's it, comrade," said Mr. Tinker. "The glacier's in *your* cupboard. *You're* in the land of the dead. He's pinned *you* down, hasn't he?"

Uproar was renewed. "I think it's awful," said Mrs. Wilkins. Mr. Tinker got to his feet again and shouted: "Good lad, good lad." "I think Mr. Tinker is drunk," said the old lady. "Please sit down, Mr. Tinker," said Treece, "and please pay attention to me." The class quieted down. Then Treece, cutting off any further comments from Bates, who was now well prepared to make some, went on to another poem. "Perhaps this one seems more poetic," he said. It was by Dylàn Thomas. Treece read the poem, "Lament," slowly, to give time for passions to subside. "Well," he said after he had finished, "did you prefer that?"

"Yes," said Mr. Tinker. "Why?" asked Treece. Mr. Tinker preferred it because it was about sex, and said it would improve everyone present if their bedsprings squeaked a bit more often. "Let's leave sex until after tea," said Treece, wearily. Mr. Tinker misunderstood this and said that in his view it was better in the afternoons and in the open if possible.

"I think Mr. Tinker should be expelled from the class," said the elderly lady.

Tea came in, and this restored some order. The two nuns, who had not been looking happy, revived. After tea followed a more controlled discussion of the Dylan Thomas poem, in which Treece managed to extract a sense of its meaning and design from various members of the class. At the end when Treece stopped the evening just on nine, Mr. Hope stood up and said, "Well, I don't know how the others feel, but I think this evening's been most instructive. I think it's shown one thing, though, and that is whether you ask of poetry what these ladies want, or whether you want it to be about life, Keats stands out above all the rest," Everyone began to stand up and put on their coats. "*Don't* forget to avail yourselves of the book-box," screamed Mrs. Tubbington, the class secretary, "and *don't* forget your tea-money please, to me or in the saucer by the door." The two nuns took out separate black purses: "We each pay for our own," said one of them to Treece, with a giggle. Everyone was filing out, except for the few people who always stayed on a little afterward to ask him personal questions, encourage him to get married, take up little points of discussion. "I don't like to say this," said the elderly lady, "but I don't think Mr. Tinker should be allowed to stay in this class. Several people are signing a little petition. He's spoiling it for everybody." "Wah!" shouted Mr. Tinker, who was standing in the middle of the room putting his coat on and scratching his crotch. "It's a free country, you can't throw a man out. Ye all can't help envyin' a man wi' a spot of blud in his veins." "Mr. Tinker's right," said Treece, "but I do hope you will control your language, Mr. Tinker. We do have nuns here." "I've seen them," said Mr. Tinker.

There were a few more questions, and then only Louis Bates was left, looming large by the doorway. "I wondered whether we were going in the same direction," he said. "I've been wondering the same thing myself," said Treece, putting papers into his briefcase. "You realize you spoiled this class." "A number of people commented that it was the best class they've ever had," said Bates, "we certainly made them think, didn't we?" "We?" asked Treece. "Well, you and me and Mr. Tinker," said Bates. "I thought you behaved rather badly, Bates," said Treece. "You certainly have a way with the dramatic gesture, don't you?" "I suppose I did behave rather ill," said Bates, speculatively. "You did," said Treece, firmly. Bates looked enormously flattered at this; all attention was a compliment to him. "Perhaps we could discuss it," he said, "perhaps I could come round to your house one evening." "There's nothing more to say," said Treece, "except that I expect you either to act in a responsible way or not come to this class in the future." Bates grew pathetic. "But this class is the most rewarding thing in my week," he said, "it's the only time I get to hear you in detail. Someone ought to tell you that you're a most stimulating teacher." But as he stood in the washroom, putting on his cycling suit, Treece felt only the deepest sense of failure. It seemed to him that the only man he could convince, the only man who shared what he most believed in, was a preposterous madman. To this man he was fettered; this was his own half-self; and he suspected that there was nothing in the world he could do to set himself free. He watched Bates walking ahead of him down the street, pacing out his strange long step, and his shoes seemed to fit in the same footprints. "I wondered whether we were going in the same direction," Bates had said. "Perhaps we are," thought Treece, getting on his motorized cycle, "perhaps after all we are."

John Updike
During the Jurassic

Waiting for the first guests, the iguanodon gazed along the path and beyond, toward the monotonous cycad forests and the low volcanic hills. The landscape was everywhere interpenetrated by the sea, a kind of metallic blue rottenness that daily breathed in and out. Behind him, his wife was assembling the hors d'oeuvres. As he watched her, something unintended, something grossly solemn, in his expression made her laugh, displaying the leaf-shaped teeth lining her cheeks. Like him, she was an ornithischian, but much smaller—a compsognathus. He wondered, watching her race bipedally back and forth among the scraps of food (dragonflies wrapped in ferns, cephalopods on toast), how he had ever found her beautiful. His eyes hungered for size; he experienced a rage for sheer blind size.

The stegosauri, of course, were the first to appear. Among their many stupid friends these were the most stupid, and the most punctual. Their front legs bent outward and their filmy-eyed faces almost grazed the ground; the upward sweep of their backs was gigantic, and the double rows of giant bone plates along the spine clicked together in the sway of their cumbersome gait. With hardly a greeting, they dragged their tails, quadruply spiked, across the threshold and maneuvered themselves toward the bar, which was tended by a minute and shapeless mammal hired for the evening.

Next came the allosaurus, a carnivorous bachelor whose dangerous aura and needled grin excited the female herbivores; then Rhamphorhynchus, a pterosaur whose much admired "flight" was in reality a clumsy brittle glide ending in an embarrassed bump and trot. The iguanodon despised these pterosaur's pretensions, thought grotesque the precarious elongation of the single finger from which their levitating membranes were stretched, and privately believed that the eccentric archaeopteryx, though sneered at as unstable, had more of a future. The hypsilophoden, with her graceful hands and branch-gripping feet, arrived with the timeless crocodile —an incongruous pair, but both were recently divorced. Still the iguanodon gazed down the path.

Behind him, the conversation gnashed on a thousand things—houses, mortgages, lawns, fertilizers, erosion, boats, winds, annuities, capital gains, recipes, education, the day's tennis, last night's party. Each party was consumed by discussion of the previous one. Their lives were subject to constant cross-check. When did you leave? When did *you* leave? We'd been out every night this week. We had an amphibious baby-sitter who had to be back in the water by one. Gregor had to meet a client in town, and now they've reduced the Saturday schedule, it means the 7:43 or nothing. Trains? I thought they were totally extinct. Not at all. They're coming back, it's just a matter of time until the government . . . In the long range of evolution, they are still the most efficient . . . Taking into account the heat-loss/weight ratio and assuming there's no more glaciation . . . Did you know—I think this is fascinating—did you know that in the financing of those great ornate stations of the eighties and nineties, those real monsters, there was no provision for amortization? They weren't amortized at all, they were financed on the basis of eternity! The railroad was conceived of as the end of Progress! *I* think—though not an expert—that the key word is this over-all industrio-socio-what-have-you-oh nexus or syndrome or whatever is *overextended.* Any competitorless object *bloats.* Personally, I miss the trolley cars. Now don't tell me I'm the only creature in the room old enough to remember the trolley cars!

The iguanodon's high pulpy heart jerked and seemed to split; the brontosaurus was coming up the path.

Her husband, the diplodocus, was with her. They moved together, rhythmic twins, buoyed by the hollow assurance of the huge. She paused to tear with her lips a clump of leaf from an overhanging paleocycas. From her deliberate grace the iguanodon received the impression that she knew he was watching her. Indeed, she had long guessed his love, as had her husband. The two saurischians entered his party with the languid confidence of the specially cherished. In the teeth of the iguanodon's ironic stance, her bulk, her gorgeous size, enraptured him, swelled to fill the massive ache he carried when she was not there. She rolled outward across his senses—the dawn-pale underparts, the reticulate skin, the vast bluish muscles whose management required a second brain at the base of her spine.

Her husband, though even longer, was more slenderly built, and perhaps weighed less than twenty-five tons. His very manner was attenuated and tabescent. He had recently abandoned an orthodox business career to enter the Episcopalian seminary. This regression—as the iguanodon felt it—seemed to make his wife more prominent, less supported, more accessible.

How splendid she was! For all the lavish solidity of her hips and legs, the modelling of her little flat diapsid skull was delicate. Her facial essence seemed to narrow, along the diagrammatic points of her auricles and eyes and nostrils, toward a single point, located in the air, of impermutable refinement and calm. This irreducible point was, he realized, in some sense her mind: the focus of the minimal interest she brought to play upon the inchoate and edible green world flowing all about her, buoying her, bathing her. The iguanodon felt himself as an upright speckled stain in this world. He felt himself, under her distant dim smile, impossibly ugly: his mouth a sardonic chasm, his throat a pulsing curtain of scaly folds, his body a blotched bulb. His feet were heavy and horny and three-toed and his thumbs—strange adaptation!—were erect rigidities of pointed bone. Wounded by her presence, he savagely turned on her husband.

"*Comment va le bon Dieu?*"

"Ah?" The diplodocus was maddeningly good-humored. Minutes elapsed as stimuli and reactions traveled back and forth across his length.

The iguanodon insisted. "How are things in the supernatural?"

"The supernatural? I don't think that category exists in the new theology."

"*N'est-ce pas?* What *does* exist in the new theology?"

"Love. Immanence as opposed to transcendence. Works as opposed to faith."

"Work? I had thought you had quit work."

"That's an unkind way of putting it. I prefer to think that I've changed employers."

The iguanodon felt in the other's politeness a detestable aristocracy, the unappealable oppression of superior size. He said gnashing, "The Void pays wages?"

"Ah?"

"You mean there's a living in nonsense? I said nonsense. Dead, fetid nonsense."

"Call it that if it makes it easier for you. Myself, I'm not a fast learner. Intellectual humility came rather natural to me. In the seminary, for the first time in my life, I feel on the verge of finding myself."

"Yourself? That little thing? *Cette petite chose?* That's all you're looking for? Have you tried pain? Myself, I have found pain to be a great illuminator. *Permettez-moi.*" The iguanodon essayed to bite the veined base of the serpentine throat lazily upheld before him; but his teeth were too specialized and could not tear flesh. He abraded his lips and tasted his own salt blood. Disoriented, crazed, he thrust one thumb deep into a yielding gray flank that hove through the smoke and chatter of the party like a dull wave. But the nerves of his victim lagged in reporting the pain, and by the time the distant head of the diplodocus was notified, the wound would have healed.

The drinks were flowing freely. The mammal crept up to him and murmured that the dry vermouth was running out. The iguanodon told him to use the sweet. Behind the sofa the stegosauri were Indian-wrestling; each time one went over, his spinal plates raked the recently papered wall. The hypsilophoden, tipsy, perched on a bannister; the allosaurus darted forward suddenly and ceremoniously nibbled her tail. On the far side of the room, by the great slack-stringed harp, the compsognathus and the brontosaurus were talking. He was drawn to them: amazed that his wife would presume to delay the much larger creature; to insert herself, with her scrabbling nervous motions and chattering leaf-shaped teeth, into the crevices of that queenly presence. As he drew closer to them, music began. His wife said to him, "The salad is running out." He murmured to the brontosaurus, *"Chère madame, voulez-vous danser avec moi?"*

Her dancing was awkward, but even in this awkwardness, this ponderous stiffness, he felt the charm of her abundance. "I've been talking to your husband about religion," he told her, as they settled into the steps they could do.

"I've given up," she said. "It's such a deprivation for me and the children."

"He says he's looking for himself."

"It's so selfish," she said. "The children are teased at school."

"Come live with me."

"Can you support me?"

"No, but I would gladly sink under you."

"You're sweet."

"Je t'aime."

"Don't. Not here."

"Somewhere, then?"

"No. Nowhere. Never." With what delightful precision did her miniature mouth encompass these infinitesimal concepts.

"But I," he said, "but I lo—"

"Stop it. You embarrass me. Deliberately."

"You know what I wish? I wish all these beasts would disappear. What do we see in each other? Why do we keep getting together?"

She shrugged. "If they disappear, we will too."

"I'm not so sure. There's something about us that would survive. It's not in you and not in me but between us, where we almost meet. Some vibration, some enduring cosmic factor. Don't you feel it?"

"Let's stop. It's too painful."

"Stop dancing?"

"Stop being."

"That's a beautiful idea. *Une belle idée.* I will if you will."

"In time," she said, and her fine little face precisely fitted this laconic promise; and as the summer night yielded warmth to the multiplying stars, he felt his blood sympathetically cool, and grow thunderously, fruitfully slow.

Hugh Allyn Hunt

Acme Rooms and Sweet Marjorie Russell

A puce romance, this is. Small towners hover round, for this romantic message comes to you straight from the hinterland heart of fields, farm houses and gentle, leafy communities of less than 20,000. These words figure to be nostalgia-ladened, memory-aimed. Youth and love, those ever-warm states of being and mind, are about to be reheated. Sit down and prepare an indulgent smile for rural, boyish things recalled.

My town has exactly 16,548 easy-going, rather unanxious folk in it at the time all this takes place. It's bigger now, but this was faraway in the days of my youth, four thousand years ago in 1949. We're not, of course, going to deal with *all* those people. Just about a dozen or so.

For a helpful point of identification, I'm the long, skinny, flax-headed kid hitching his shoulders nervously over thère at the drugstore counter. Notice this is not the usual adolescent cliché: I am *not* plagued by acne; beneath my straw sloshes a green river, *not* a coke; my levis, *not* corduroys or khakis, are hooked lethally low, the belt loops sliced off and the bottoms carefully cut the right length with a razor blade. I do have to admit to a letter sweater, but there's a switchblade knife in my pocket to offset this. The sweater and the blade, incidentally, more or less typify a division of opinion within myself at this time. With normal high school aplomb I am supporting two opposing and totally unintegrated points of view of the world. It is the co-presence of these two incompatible attitudes that, I think, I sincerely hope, will provide the dramatic tension of this purple-hued reminiscence.

Around me, in similar stagged pants, sweaters and lazily drooping cigarettes, stand my fellow-adolescents. There are six of us, all of different sizes, everyone an eleventh grader and to a man sixteen.

If our sallow and fatigued features seem to indicate that we are plotting unspeakable degradations, good. For after all, the most significant and exciting hours of the day are just commencing: After School. Moments given completely over to teen-age evil. We are here at this particular hour —four o'clock in the afternoon—too, because it is between the end of basketball season and the beginning of track season. All of us at this counter attend Catholic high school and in this Protestant town we fish-eaters are known as deadly, fanatical competitors—not especially good, but competitive. At the moment, our six pallid faces are open testimony to the dissolute relief we're taking from months of tendon-stretching athletic combat. In a very brief time we've worked hard to relax, getting little sleep, losing our spending money at the poolhall, breathing numberless cigarettes and doing other things.

In plotting our boyish iniquities we have, naturally, come across such unimaginative things as getting into fights and stealing automobiles. But such things are not it; not what we are after. What we are seeking with undeviating single-mindedness, has to do with girls. We call it many things, most of them fanciful and extravagant. It is, of course, *sex*. Mysterious, furtive, condemned and immeasurably fascinating.

At sixteen, all of us have had our initial and incomplete little grapplings in cramped back seats. It is, in fact, this minor kind of experimentation that emboldens several of us (me, for instance) to keep an old American myth alive—that we are rampant swordsmen, that we've "gone all the way" with this or that girl, long ago last month—carefully selecting for these lies older females, usually recently graduated from public high school, who possess well-known reputations and who are totally removed from the possibility of knowing any of us. Against this unsatisfactory behavior and this unsurprising dishonesty, we relentlessly prepare and verbally rehearse keen teen orgies. What we impatiently seek now is the raw, unclothed act, fact, confrontation, the great entwined spasm. We are at the counter, behind our emerald drinks, waiting—nervously.

One other community or municipal (if you will) fact should be pointed out here. My home town is at the time of this story a division point for a Midwestern railroad and as such possesses the remarkable total of thirteen whore houses. There's really little more to add about this at the moment, except that ours is no sin city. The houses, regulated by the mayor and the city council, are quite sedate and rather spectacularly unobvious.

"Look," I tell Jerry Donovan, working hard to keep my cigarette balanced at the side of my lip and grab the position of chief evil-artist of the group at the same time, "what we'll do is pool all our loot, get two cases of beer, go up, ask for a big room and for as many girls for as long as we can afford." It is a long sentence for me and I am confused. I end by nodding rapidly, persuasively.

Jerry, who tries to be swift and clever, but is really good-natured and kind of slow, quickly wags his broad head and grins. "Yeah, yeah. Two blondes, a brunette and three redheads." He rubs his hands together hungrily. When and how he has worked out this ratio, I don't know, but every time girls are mentioned lately he offers this ambitious numerical proportion. Since he's agreeing with me, I agree with him.

"Sure," I tell him, trying to sound authoritative. "If we've got enough money. Now, how much loot do we all have?" The five prematurely worn faces around me turn childishly reticent and doubtful at this. Like small grade-schoolers they tug hesitantly, almost shyly, at their pockets.

Tom Murray finally flips out fifty cents and suggests cockily: "How about making up a pot and I'll go down to the poolhall and double it, huh?"

"Not my money, by God," Jerry squeezes his fist shut. Tom Murray is our school's hot-shot football player, really pretty good, and this leads him to believe he's the world's greatest everything. Actually, he's an erratic pool player who usually loses all his money if he plays very long. Usually, he loses to Don Brandon or me. Now, belligerently, Brandon reaches over and punches Tom on the arm with wicked force.

"You couldn't win a game of slop from a blind, back-busted whore." Don has a thin, prisoner's face with a slit mouth. The first time I met him, I was immediately frightened. At eight years old, he was the only child I'd ever seen who looked as if he might at any moment, coldly, premeditatively murder a close relative—his mother, say. He wasn't that tough at all, though he worked awfully hard to live up to that grim face of his.

Between the six of us, we place on the counter an unpromisingly small pile of gritty coins and a single faded bill. Acting as temporary treasurer I count it. "Four dollars and seventy-three cents. Not even a buck apiece. God. What a bunch of duds." I shake my head. "What the hell do you think this is going to be, anyway—a sodality meeting, for Christ's sake? We need . . . Well . . ." I don't really know how much we need. "At least five bucks apiece for the whore house," I say recklessly, immediately appalled by the vast fortune that must be mounted to bring this orgy off.

"Damn," murmurs Curly Franklin. "That's . . . that's thirty dollars." Curly is the mathematician in our group. There is a long silence as the monumentality of this sum sinks in.

"OK, how many want to chicken out? Say so now, before we get started," I challenge them, abruptly able to do so for the first time in the many years of our boyhood lives together. Compulsively, I am pushed to this exceptional brashness, this ferocity, by the dazzling, lustful visions writhing in my imagination, refusing to be dimmed or stilled by something so minor as thirty dollars. I sneer at my companions so unpleasantly that no one says a word. We all order another green river and ponder how we're going to get more money.

"A dice game," announces Tom Murray who has never been in one.

"You're nuts," says Jerry fretfully.

"We could steal it," Don Brandon grins, trying to be evil.

"Crap," Curly Franklin tells him. "Crap. We'll have to work for it." This announcement depresses us even more and silence wades through our ranks.

"Work," someone murmurs incredulously. "Wow."

"We could borrow it," says Franky Shea suddenly.

"Sure." Curly nods. "Just walk up to the bank teller and say "We want thirty dollars to go to the whorehouse, how much is the interest on that?"

"Yeah," says Franky disheartedly. "I don't know anybody that'd lend it to us."

"Look, it's about five bucks apiece. Now each of us ought to be able to scrounge up that much some way." I'm still flexing my newly discovered and unfamiliar organizational abilities. "What things can we do to make money?" I ask. "That's the way to approach it." But unfortunately that's a hard question to answer. It's mid-school year and most of the after-class and weekend kind of jobs are already in the anemic grip of creeps that don't go out for sports. Then too, there is the fact that we are in a terrible hurry, both because we're impatient and sweaty to get to those simmering, purchasable female bodies, and because track season will start next week.

"Let's cop something to sell," says Don Brandon, still trying to live up to his face. His unlipped mouth smiles criminally, but we know he'll do nothing unless we all tag along to help.

"Look," says Curly, pretending to be smart and logical and, I think, maybe trying to ace me out of my just-gained foothold on temporary leadership. "Look," he says solemnly, and I've already got three good reasons why whatever it is he says is wrong. "There are little things like, let's see . . ." He's playing it big, pretending to think. "Like collecting bottles and selling them—"

"Oh, man, man," both Jerry and Don moan in unison. "You're kidding."

That's good, that's practical, I think. Maybe Curly and I can make a team. "Fine, fine," I declare with as much superiority as I can muster in a hurry. "What else?" Generously giving him the lead, but thinking fast now that there's a challenger. "Maybe hook a job as a grocery boy after school this week," I say, before anybody else can get it out. "Or mow lawns, do yard work." Here I lose momentum because the grass isn't growing that fast yet; it's just spring, not summer. But my brain joggles and spins out a better one: "Con your parents into paying you to do something around home. Clean the garage, the basement, something."

Curly nods his head in admiration. The challenge dies and I suck noisily at my straw, and then calmly light a butt. "This is Monday," I snap in a company commander's voice, imitating the infantry captain in the movie I've seen over the weekend. "Friday is five days away. By then we should have it. That means we've got to come up with a buck a day. All right?"

"No sweat," declares Tom Murray, easing his fifty-cent piece out of the sandy pile on the counter.

"Anybody showing up without a full five dollars is out. Right?" I glare at them like a two-star general. They all agree: "Sure, sure." After that, I don't really know of anything else to say and neither does anybody else. Silently, we wonder about the money, chew the melting ice in our glasses and then, finally, split up, each going his acquisitive way, elaborate financial schemes sprouting in his head.

Skating with infinitely lewd dreams jerking my limbs toward the rear door of the drugstore, I spy blonde and pink Marjorie Russell snuggled in a back booth with other public high school girls. I slow my pace, lecherous hopes losing their evil focus, changing to something I can't quite grasp.

My pulse and breath maintain the same rambling race, but some hidden mechanism has shifted ever so slightly. My speed diminishes, my path wavers and I casually lope over to Marjorie Russell's booth, draping myself with careful ease across the back of it. "Hi," I grin with the sensible face of an idiot since the presence of a lot of girls confuses me. "Hi, Marjorie." I want to let the others know they don't exist, not for squishy emotional reasons, I think, but for convenience.

Marjorie is sipping a cherry phosphate demurely and can only nod. To fill the silence, I snarl at her companions and sardonically light a cigarette.

"Hi," she says at last. "How are you?"

I mumble rudely and blow smoke at her. For a moment I grit my teeth. Marjorie's nice, I like her and am anxious to do things with her, but she often says these very formal, stupid type things that drive me nutty. Like "How are you?" For Christ's sake, I just saw her last night. I'm fine and whatever trouble I've got she knows it.

Sawing my head up and down, I try to signal her out of the crowded booth, but she just giggles a little and blinks. The other girls laugh and I flinch at their pitched syllables. Behind a fog of smoke, I poke Margie's shoulder and growl: "Hey, I want to talk to you." At this she glares and turns away. Irritably, I flick ashes on the splotch-faced girl next to her. "Come on Marjorie," I plead, weary already. "Please. Just a minute."

At this, signaling her friends she has won, she simpers, smirks into her phosphate and considers my request. In my private presence, she is not like this at all, and while she makes me wait for my answer, I puzzle this curious adolescent warfare of the sexes. Finally, slowly, she comes out of the booth, sighing wearily as if it were costing her dearly, plopping books down, asking friends to stand up, at last stepping into the aisle with a very public expression of condescension on her girlish features. At the moment, I could easily strangle her and wish wildly for Don Brandon's cruel face with which to frighten them all. Instead, I grab her hand and stalk to the telephone booth for our intimate exchange. At once, dumped unceremoniously onto the booth seat, she is demure, quiet, no longer simpering. Such changes jostle me, and I stand in the doorway squinting, my brow undoubtedly doubled, for she asks: "What's wrong, honey?"

"Jesus, Jesus," I say to that pretty face and blonde hair, abruptly unable to explain why I'm angry. Marjorie is wearing the soft, pale pink sweater I like so much and within it her small, round breasts press gently outward. That is Marjorie: small and round and smooth. My alternate opinion of the world: soft, poignant, immeasurably emotional, infinitely hushed and gentle—Marjorie. My other astigmatic affliction. "Marjorie," I say, neither beginning nor ending a sentence. Then: "Look, let's walk home, huh?"

I wait at the telephone booth as she goes back and picks up her books, laughs at someone's joke and says good-by to her friends. Outside in the street, I take her school things and put my hand around her plump, childish fingers. This is my girl, and as I ramble on about school and tease her easily, now that we are alone, I am troubled by the contrast between my whorehouse plotting and the dreams I have for Marjorie. Though I know intimately how Marjorie's small breasts feel, I do not know what they look like and I have never made successful explorations elsewhere. Though we are not going "steady," we date no one else and I believe we have ambitious plans for each other, romantically. Marjorie's present physical reticence does not offend me outrageously, really. I'm infatuated with her, I cherish her and am trusting the future—tonight, tomorrow, the next night—to provide the opportunity, the right responses so that our romance may be consummated. I am young and incorrigibly American. I have little real evidence how she feels about our sexual destiny, nor am I clearly positive how I feel about it at this exact second; but nervously, jerkily, I believe we both think it's a certainty. I want to believe that, need to. As we stroll along, I saunter and strut, grimace and boast, entertaining her. I nip her ear and tell her how much I love her. On her porch, I've become so nervous that I kiss and hug her quickly even though her mother stands watching in the doorway. Then, embarrassed, I run off shouting back that I'll call her later. Instead of seeing her after dinner tonight, I will be busy launching my fund for carnal purposes.

All week long opposing instincts within me cut across one another. I dream of Marjorie in soft colors: pinks, faint blues, lavender—and she is cuddly, vulnerable, innocent yet passionate. In my other, darker dreams, I ruthlessly, coldly drive with abandon into the faceless, twitching bodies of dark-haired women, my passion there as close to rage as my unwieldly love for my dreamt Marjorie is to a kind of physical prayer. During the long hours of emptying the family garage of five years' accumulated junk, of running endless errands for my mother, for neighbors, of doing fifty odd little jobs, these two warring fantasies clash behind my sweaty brow. And diminish only slightly each night as I count the dimes and quarters. By Wednesday I am determined to get enough for a case of beer. My own. And Thursday afternoon I rush away from school and begin cleaning the backyard of a neighbor, bruising my sore hands with rakes, shovels, hoes, brooms. Then from that yard I go on to the next, pocketing with secret greedy glee the money these women pay me. From female to female these coins will pass, I think with exultant cynicism.

That night, after a hurried and rattled call to Margie, I count my money. I know, almost to the penny, how much is there, but I must count it, nonetheless. All the dimes I arrange in careful columns, side by side, the nickels, quarters, fifty-cent pieces, the few pennies. I smooth out the bills, turning them all green side up. There are ten amazing, potent dollars marching in little totem rows across my desk. I gloat. I giggle and clutch my sides and glee hiccups loose. At the locked door my mother knocks and asks what's wrong, am I sick? Painfully suppressing my bouncing spirits, I gasp as calmly as I can: "No. No. Everything's fine." Indeed, it's glorious, uproarious. Troubled by my sniggering and gurgling, she stands outside my door as if waiting for prolonged cries of illness. But finally, with a sigh, she leaves and I topple onto the bed, burying my hysterical head in the pillow.

The endless moments of sunny Friday morning crawl by with incredible slowness. By ten o'clock, I've fretted and fidgeted myself into a state of near exhaustion. At the break, we feverishly confer, interrupting each other, demanding to know if everyone's brought their money. But the really big question is, where's Don Brandon? He isn't in school. Is he chickening out? He can't. We'll go to his home and get him, pull him out of bed if he's pretending to be sick. Nobody cops out. Standing in the crowded school hallway, squirting down cokes and peanuts, we curse Brandon for his cowardice. Then, we count the money. I put down my five. Everyone has theirs, except Franky Shea. He has only three dollars and twenty cents. I curse him and then Tom Murray slugs him, starts slapping him, venting his rage at Don on Franky.

"Hey, hey," I yell. "Maybe the girls are cheaper than we think. Anyway, if he needs some more money, I'll loan it to him." This surprises all of us, especially Franky and me. We both know I don't really like Franky that well. But at times like this, I dislike Tom more than enough. So . . .

Gravely then, with uneasy glances flickering between us, we recount the money and speculate on exactly how much we'll really need. That's the unknown quantity—how much does a girl cost? A whore? Standing in the close hallway of this Catholic high school, we can think of no one who knows such facts.

Then, evil leader of them all, I announce: "Hell, I'll call them. They've got a phone, haven't they?" I grin smugly, proud to have thought of it first. But the bell rings and we have to wait until lunchtime to call.

At noon, across the street from the school, I sit in a service station telephone booth, carefully looking up the number of Acme Rooms—all such places of business hide behind this ingenious disguise. I find the number, write it neatly in my palm, open the door slightly and murmur to my friends: "Bless you my sons. When was your last confession?" They all grin and I close the door and theatrically dial.

An indifferent feminine voice answers and replies to my question. "All rooms here are five dollars, mister." There is a click as the connection is cut.

"Five," I announce solemnly as I climb out of my confessional. The remainder of the afternoon, we plot vengeance against Brandon and wish time, time, time would hurry. We are not going to the Acme until after dark, seven o'clock. As I listen to talk about parallelograms and side-angle-side, I wonder doubtfully how we'll ever last until seven. My muscles are fluttering and jumping.

At three-thirty, as we race with relieved shouts and ragged laughter out of school, Don Brandon is waiting for us across the street, a patronizing smirk fixed on his thin lips. Before we can grab him, accuse him, he waves a five-dollar bill at us. He's got more, he declares. Since six this morning he's been driving a truck for a dollar an hour. As soon as he'd earned eight dollars, he'd quit. He has a total of ten, he brags, and is not going to lend *any* of it to *any*body. "Beer," he grins thirstily. "Beer and broads, bring them on." And all of us, wrestling and punching one another, chant, "Yes, yes." Passersby stare at us. We leap down the street, pent excitement jerking our limbs, voices, thoughts. We are anxious for the Big Game.

At the drugstore we swarm into a booth, crowding each other, smoking, arguing, ordering, sipping, hoping time will disappear. Behind our bright, agitated eyes we are all planning just how we're going to act with the girl we'll buy at seven o'clock. Cool and steady, I direct myself. And unrushed. Get your money's worth, is my basic consideration.

As other students come and take booths about us, we eye them with open superiority. They instantly become objects of our scorn, pitifully unsophisticated and innocent. Dull, unimaginably cleanminded, they sit around us mindlessly munching their Cokes and sundaes. We laugh outrageously and they look up, puzzled by our outbursts, and this drives us to further hilarity. Those pathetically sinless, bewildered expressions. The manager comes back and asks us to please be a little quieter and we grin false obedience at him.

Then I see Marjorie. As I stand up my companions hoot and yell, kidding me, warning me in merciless, loud voices to be careful, not to become too exhausted before we meet at six-thirty. Luckily, Marjorie doesn't understand any of this as I hurry off to the counter in front. There, I buy her a phosphate and smile exaggerated innocence: "Margie, uhn, the track team has a meeting tonight at about seven at the gym, so I guess I can't make it over." Intently, I concentrate on my drink.

"What about after?" she asks. For a week I have devised elaborate excuses for not seeing her. By now she is becoming hurt and distrustful. I can't blame her. I just hope she holds on until after tonight.

"Sure, if it's not too late." I try to be positive, yet vague.

Solemnly, she finishes her drink. Then, with exceptional quiet, she watches me. Doesn't say anything, merely looks at me steadily. Immediately I begin hitching my shoulders and scratching and wiggling.

Pretty soon, Marjorie breaks the silence: "Are you going to come over tonight or not?" That's all, just that simple question.

"Yes. Yes, I am," I promise—both her and myself. "But it might be kind of late."

"Are you *really* going to a track team meeting?"

"Yes, I am," I lie and grit my teeth. In spite of my recent desire to be sinister, I dislike lying to Marjorie. Once more, she gazes silently at me with her smooth, little-girl's face. Scratching my ear, I grin back, senselessly. After a moment, she picks up her books.

"I'll walk you home," I tell her.

"No. I'm meeting Mom over at the dime store. I'll see you tonight. OK?"

"Sure." I grab her hand and squeeze those small, doll-like fingers.

Six-thirty, six-thirty, six-thirty, I tell myself giddily. By the clock at the back of the drugstore, it now *is* six-thirty—rendezvous hour for the Sinister Six. Cleverly, I have fortified myself for the ravages of this evening with a healthy supper and eight multi-vitamin pills . . . which make me belch. Presently, I am watching the clock and holding my breath, hoping to cure the belches.

Spang. In bursts my fellow evildoers, shouting. They are practically rubbing their hands in anticipation. Spilling nervous excitement about us, we huddle and count the money again. Don has relented and contributes part of his ten dollars for the beer, as do I.

When we arrive at the Acme Rooms, we scurry almost soundlessly up the steps to the door and, as chief evil-one, I press the buzzer. A little nervously, I set myself for this first, peripheral encounter. For tonight's occasion, I have carefully dressed in my adventurous best: a blue and white polka dotted long-sleeved shirt, pressed levis, white sweat socks and newly shined shoes. With a clever flair for the needs of the evening, I have worn no underwear. The polished door before me opens slightly and a woman stares at me. "Just a minute," she says, and I can hear her trundle away.

"What the hell," mutters Curly Franklin impatiently. "What's going on?"

Then the door swings wide and a plump, henna-haired woman of about forty-five or so examines us. "Well, boys, what can I do for you?"

"Girls," cries Brandon. "Girls, girls."

The woman chuckles. "How old are you boys, anyway?"

"Old enough," I tell her with ingenious brashness and move into the doorway. My companions hoot and laugh approvingly at this.

"Looks like you've come prepared," she flicks a red fingernail at the case of beer under my arm.

"Did you bring any money?" she asks with a smile.

We all wave dollar bills at her and she stands back, inviting us in with a generous gesture. Like eager children, I'm afraid, we crowd in, gawking around with immense, unrestrained curiosity.

"Hey, hey," chants Jerry Donovan, pushing past me, snapping his fingers in time to some personally heard music. "Hey, hey."

With an amused expression, the woman takes us into a parlor-like room furnished with a couch, several chairs and a juke box. "Hey, hey!" Jerry cries and pushes a quarter into the machine.

There is no one in the amber-lit room and we all look at one another a little nervously, disappointedly. To indicate we mean business, I slap the case of beer down on the couch and tear it open.

"Girls," Tom Murray says. "We'd like to see some girls, huh?"

Nodding, the woman counts us and hurries out.

Then, as Jerry's quarter begins to work and music comes bouncing out of the jukebox, we hear spiked heels in the hallway and swing around in a single, intent group. The girls—they are women, to my surprise—are all dressed in short, fluffy costumes. Like chorus girls, I think dimly. But the material is awfully thin and you can easily see their breasts through it. We stare. We stare with great intensity. Here it is. This is *sex*. The women we'll possess in a few moments. The confrontation threatens for an instant to become almost grim. Then, thumb and forefinger clicking nervously, Jerry whispers: "Hey, heaayh." And we all grin at the lightly clad women across the room.

For a moment, I wish the lights were just a little dimmer, that we were each alone with a girl, that it was more . . . more romantic, I guess. But the long-checked lust coiling hungrily in my stomach, rapping impatiently at the base of my skull, overcomes all hesitations and I leer eagerly at the women. For an instant, I vaguely remembered our plans for a mass orgy, my particular aim to select the best-looking, most gorgeous, most appealing whore in the world. But these are misty, evanescent thoughts, vanishing as one of the young ladies steps toward me and, with rather candid charm, smiles and administers a pleasant, professional caress. That is it—all my planning, my careful considerations disappear. There is really nothing at all in my mind, just the clotted web of blank desire. That's all. Sensation but no thought. Laughing gently, she leads me from the parlor and, two doors down a carpeted hall, into a small room.

The room, I vaguely notice, has a table, a lamp and a single straight chair. Plus the bed, of course. The girl is quite merry and whispers something appealingly obscene in my ear. I don't really understand her, but I grin anyway and comment that the light is awfully bright.

"All the better to see you with, honey," she smiles and touches me again. As she unbuttons me, I ask what her name is.

"Shirley," she says, and with warm water swabs me off. Squinting with embarrassment, I watch her pink-nailed fingers move efficiently over my skin.

"OK. Now, if you'll give me the money, I'll be right back, sweetie."

"Uh," I shrug uneasily. "How much is it?"

"What? Oh, haven't you been here before? My, my." She grins and squeezes my arm. "It's five dollars a round, sweetie. More, if you stay longer."

Rather blankly, I blink at her, wondering if she's overcharging me. Then automatically I nod and hand her the money.

"Just take off your pants baby. I'll be right back."

All these cold, directional remarks are reviving me from my trance and I stomp resolutely back down the hall into the empty parlor and get a couple of beers. Back in the room, I take off all my clothes, draping my polka dotted shirt over the lamp, dimming it provocatively, I think. Then, naked, I open a beer and lay back on the bed, momentarily in command of myself.

"Hey," Shirley exclaims when she comes in. "You've got all your clothes off." Unzipping her dress, kicking off her shoes, she grins at me. "You're not bad looking, for a kid."

"I'm not a kid," I correct her. "You want a beer?"

E

"Well say, you know if you're in here too long, it's going to cost you more."

"Fine."

"OK, I'll take one." She gets a glass off the table and sits down beside me. She has rather long, pale brown hair and a wide, friendly mouth. Opening the beer for her, I stare at her breasts. They seem nice—I really have few comparisons, books, primarily. And below her navel her hair is black. This seems disturbingly incongruous to me and I realize that her long, light hair is dyed.

She takes the beer and, with a slim hand on my thigh, drinks.

"Humm, that's nice." Quickly, she finishes her glass and leans over me.

"Come on, honey, let's go," she purrs roughly.

And then, then, with a deft, practiced movement, she runs her tongue from my ear downward, downward . . . I'm sure I groan, at least, for I'm close to crying out in surprise. Sensations totally unexpected break in on me and after a moment she skillfully pulls me over on top of her. Desperately trying to clear my head, to refocus my vision, I blink against the red, clogged web of turbulence and amazement—totally without result. And then, easily, still smiling, she eases me off and steps away from the bed. Quite numbly, quite bereft of any feeling at all now, I blankly study the ceiling above me. What has happened? I ask myself. What has really taken place? What did I really do—I mean, feel? I don't know. I haven't the slightest idea. A stirring numbness is the only impression reaching my mind.

"OK, honey. Better get up and into your clothes," Shirley announces with that ever-present grin in her voice. Did she experience anything? I wonder. No. Whores aren't supposed to. Then, in spite of her indifferent, abrupt instructions, I have a difficult time believing Shirley is really a whore. I have the impression that she'll now get dressed in street clothes and we'll walk out of this place together, preferably hand in hand. She's become my girl—even if I haven't felt anything, nothing that I can remember, at least. This fact and the money I gave her doesn't matter. The act does. That makes her my girl. Watching as she stoops, picking up her little dress, I see her breasts sag and as she bends beside the lamp, wiggling a foot into a shoe, the light cuts unbecoming lines beneath her eyes and all at once I understand that she is older than I, much older. She is, well, maybe almost my mother's age.

"How old are you, Shirley?"

Frowning, she glances at me, then shrugs carelessly. "Oh, about twenty-seven."

Eleven years older than I am, maybe even more. Slowly, I get up and dress. In the hallway I pull myself along despondently, wearily. From the parlor comes the clatter of my friends' noisy banter and as we enter, I put my hand on Shirley's loose flank, wondering silently if I'll ever see her again.

Laughing at the girls, patting them familiarly, we tumbled with our beer down the stairs. On the street, we exultantly brag to one another, replacing old lies with new ones. Elaborately, we gesture and giggle how it was with the whore we had. Confidently, we tell one another we're coming back as soon as we have another five dollars. Great, it's absolutely great, we all declare, agree.

Then, as we approach the corner, I unaccountably, fiercely, feel I must see Marjorie—immediately. Handing the remaining beer to my companions, I leave them, offering no explanation, and their jeers echo down the sidewalk as I hurry away.

In the front room, she is waiting for me. As I say hello to her parents I am certain they can see the stains of my lechery, my wantonness, the new strangeness on my face, hands. Insistently, I pull Marjorie out onto the porch, away from her parents' eyes.

"Margie," I say with a big breath. "It's good to see you." And I try to kiss her.

"Is your meeting over already?" she asks coolly.

"Yes." I hunch my shoulders and look out at the lawn. "Margie, uh, you know . . . that I like you. You know that, don't you?"

Her blonde hair swings softly and I want to touch it.

"After last week," she says crossly, "I don't know anything. I mean," her voice arches unhappily, "I mean, what's going on, anyway?"

"Nothing." I want to reassure her. "Nothing at all. Really. Just this track thing. It's all over now." At this moment, I am ready to tell her any fantastic lie I can think of. Now, close beside me, the warm scent of her floating around us, she's infinitely more real, more *possible* than ever before; both abruptly close and very far from tonight's experience. "Margie, I love you. I really do." This is not a lie, I realize at once. Yet, I am not sure it is the truth. It is something I feel, a lush unstoppable longing reaching my limbs, startling my fingertips. It is something, something absolutely new. For an instant I possess a totally unfamiliar confidence that I know much more about her than she can possibly know about me. In that moment, as our bodies lightly touch, I understand what it is I desire; that portion of her, of me, is no longer frightening and thoroughly dangerous. I want to share my total physical discovery, the immense freedom of it with Margie. And tell her much, much more: How this emotion I feel for her now is a gift of the *instructive*, nerveless lust that broke over me in that room at the Acme. That there is no longer any reason to be afraid of each other.

Immediately, I sense that these things will only frighten her. Besides, I have no truly accurate words for it. Instead of saying any of this, I touch her velvet hair, the deep curve of her cheek and whisper the word love, love, love, helplessly, happily—my alternating dual dreams of the world narrowed, abruptly, to one.

Jay Neugeboren

The Zodiacs

When I was in the seventh grade at P. S. 92 in Brooklyn, Louie Hirshfield was the only one of my friends who wasn't a good ballplayer. Which is putting it mildly. Louie was probably the worst athlete in the history of our school. He was also the smartest kid in our class and you'd think this combination would have made him the most unpopular guy in the world. It didn't. He wasn't especially well liked, but nobody resented him. Maybe it was because he let you copy from his homework—or maybe it was just because he didn't put on any airs about being so smart. In fact, Louie didn't put on airs about anything. He was one of the quietest kids I've ever met.

The only time I ever saw him excited—outside of what happened with him and our baseball team—was when our fathers would take the two of us to baseball games at Ebbets Field. Louie lived one floor under me, in my apartment building on Lenox Road, and we had grown up together, so I knew lots about Louie that nobody in school knew. He was an interesting guy, with lots of hobbies—tropical fish, rocks, stamps, Chinese puzzles, magic tricks, autographs.

That was the one thing the guys in school did know about. I don't know how many days he'd waited outside of Ebbets Field to get them, all I know is he had the best collection of baseball players' signatures of any guy in school. Lots of them were addressed personally, to—like, "To Louie, with best wishes from Jackie Robinson." What amazed me most about Louie, though, was that he could figure out a player's batting average in his head! If a guy got a hit his first time up in a game, Louie would say, "That raises his average to .326—" or whatever it was, and sure enough, the next time the guy came up, when the announcer would give the average, Louie would be right.

Louie had no illusions about his athletic ability either; he was never one of those guys who hang around when you're choosing up sides for a punchball or stickball game so that you *have* to pick him. And whenever he did play—like in gym class at school—he did what you told him and tried to stay out of the way.

That was why I was so surprised when he came up to my house one night after supper and asked if he could be on my baseball team.

"Gee, Louie," I said, "we got more than nine guys already—anyway we're not even an official team or anything. We'll be lucky if we get to play more than five or six games all year."

"I don't really want to play," said Louie. "I—I just want to be on your team—"

"Well, I suppose you can come to practices and games," I said, "but I can't promise you'll ever get in a game."

"Honest, Howie—I know all the guys on your team are better than me. I wasn't even thinking of playing. What I'd like to do is be your general manager—"

His eyes really lit up when he said that. I looked at him, puzzled.

"Look," he said. "What do you think makes the Dodgers draw almost as many fans as the Yankees—? What was it that made people stick with the Dodgers when they were hardly in the league?"

"I don't know," I said. "They were just Dodger fans, I guess."

"Sure—that's it. Don't you see? Being a Dodger fan means something because being a Dodger means something colorful to the fans. And you know why? Because the Dodgers have what my dad calls 'a good press'—they know how to get headlines in the papers whether they're winning or losing."

"I guess so," I said. "But what's that got to do with us?"

"What's your team like now—? I'll tell you. It's the same as ten thousand other teams of guys our age all over Brooklyn. Nobody cares if you win or lose—except maybe you guys. If I'm general manager, Howie, I'll promise you this—your team will be noticed. Guys won't say 'we got a game with Howie's team'—they won't come to the Parade Grounds to see all the older guys play. They'll come to see the *Zodiacs*—!"

"The who—?"

Louie stopped for a second, and I realized that I'd never heard him speak so fast before. "That's—that's the first thing you have to do, it seems to me." He spoke more hesitantly now, the way he usually did, not looking right at you. "You have to have a name that's different."

"What's wrong with calling ourselves the Sharks?"

"Nothing's wrong with it—but don't you see, nothing's right with it, either. I'll bet there are a hundred teams in Brooklyn alone called the Sharks. Sharks, Tigers, Lions, Phantoms—every team has a name like that. But calling ourselves—I mean, your team—the Zodiacs, will make them different—"

"Sure—but giving us a crazy name isn't going to win us any games."

"Right. What will win you games? I'll tell you—a good pitcher. I've been going down to the Parade Grounds to watch games, making a study of the teams there, and I've found that pitching is about *ninety* per cent of winning. Especially at our age, when we're not built up yet. Did you know, for example, that on high school teams pitchers average about eleven strike-outs a game? It's like with baseball teams in spring training—the pitchers are way ahead of the hitters because the hitters' reflexes aren't developed yet."

"Izzie's a pretty good pitcher," I said. Izzie was my best friend, and the pitcher for our team.

"Sure, but let's face it, he's not a top-drawer pitcher. He's just not big enough to be. He's got good control, I'll admit that—but his fast ball is almost a change-up. If you let me be general manager, Howie, I'll get the best pitcher in our school to play for us—"

"Who's that—?"

"George Santini."

I gulped. *"Him?"*

"That's right."

George Santini was a year ahead of us at P. S. 92 and he was always getting in trouble with the teachers and the cops. He was about six feet tall, had black greasy hair which was long and cut square in back, and the biggest pair of shoulders I've ever seen on a guy. He was also the best athlete in our school. The coaches and teachers were always talking to him about going straight and being a star in high school and college. But George never seemed to care much. He was the leader of this gang, which as far as everybody in our section of Brooklyn was concerned, was the most dangerous gang the world had ever known.

What made George's reputation even worse was his older brother, Vinnie. Vinnie was about nineteen years old and had already spent two years in jail. He was a skinny guy—not at all like George—and the word on him was that he was really chicken. To listen to George, though, you would have thought that Vinnie was the toughest guy ever to hit Brooklyn. Whenever he wanted an audience, George would sit down on the steps of the school—on Rogers Avenue—and start telling tales of all the jobs he and Vinnie had pulled off. Sometimes, if we'd pester him enough, he'd tell us about the gang wars he had fought in with Vinnie—in Prospect Park, in Red Hook, in Bay Ridge. If he was sure no teachers or cops were around, he'd show us his zip-gun, the gun that Johnny Angelo—one of George's lackeys—claimed George had once used to kill a guy with.

"I don't know," I said. "If my mother ever caught me hanging around with him, I'd really get it—and anyway, how would you ever get him to play for us?"

Louie smiled. "You leave that to me."

A few days later I got all the guys together at my house, and I let Louie speak to them. He told them what he'd told me about how he would make our team special, maybe famous—and he also told them that George Santini had agreed to pitch for us. A few of the guys reacted the way I did to this news: they were scared. But when Louie insisted he'd be able to handle George, Izzie and I were ready to back him up.

"I say it's worth a try," said Izzie. "Even though I'm pitcher and he'll take my place. I'll bet we could beat lots of high school teams with him pitching for us—"

"Sure," I said. "You ever see the way he can blaze a ball in?"

A few more guys followed our lead, and after a while we all agreed that we'd probably be invincible with George Santini pitching for us.

"One thing, though," asked Kenny Murphy, our second baseman. "How'd you get him to play for us?"

"Simple," said Louie. "I offered him the one thing he couldn't refuse —fame. I told him I'd get his name in the newspapers—"

"Really?"

"Sure," said Louie. "It's not hard. All you have to do is telephone in the box score to the *Brooklyn Eagle* and they'll print it. My father knows the managing editor there. We go to the beach with him sometimes."

For the next few weeks Louie was the busiest guy in the world—calling up guys at other schools, arranging games, getting permits from the Park Department, talking to George and keeping him happy, coming to our practices . . . When he started giving us suggestions on things, nobody objected either. He may have been a lousy ballplayer, but I'll say this for him—he knew more about the game than any of us. Izzie and I gave up playing basketball in the schoolyard afternoons and weekends and spent all our time practicing with the Zodiacs.

Our first game was scheduled for a Saturday morning, the second week in April. Louie had gotten us a permit to use one of the diamonds at the Parade Grounds, next to Prospect Park, from nine to twelve in the morning, and we were supposed to play this team of eighth-graders from P. S. 246. I was at the field with Izzie by 8:30, but the other team didn't get there until after nine. We ran through infield practice and then let them have the field for a while. Kenny Murphy's father, who had played for the Bushwicks when they were a semi-pro team, had agreed to umpire the game. By a quarter to ten neither Louie nor George had shown up and the other team was hollering that we were afraid to play them.

Since George had never come to any practices, some of us were a little worried, but at about five to ten, he showed up. He was wearing a baseball hat like the rest of us, with a Z sewn on the front, and he looked a little embarrassed. He was smoking and he didn't say much to anybody. Just asked who the catcher was, and started warming up. He wore a T-shirt, with the sleeves cut off. Looking at him, you would have thought he was too musclebound to be a pitcher, but when he reared back and kicked his left foot high in the air, then whipped his arm around, he was the most graceful, coordinated guy I'd ever seen. As smooth as Warren Spahn, only righty, with this natural straight overhand motion that every coach spends his nights dreaming about. Stan Reiss, our catcher, had to put an extra sponge in his mitt, but he was so proud, catching George with all the guys looking at the two of them, that I think he would have let the ball burn a hole in his hand before he would have given up his position.

"C'mon," said George, after a dozen or so warm-ups, "let's get the game going."

"We were waiting for Louie," I said. "He should be here any minute."

"Okay," said George. "But he better hurry. I got better things to do than spend all day strikin' out a bunch of fags—"

He said the last thing loudly, for the benefit of the other team. Then he turned and spit in their direction, daring one of them to contradict him. None of them did.

A minute later I saw Louie. He was getting out of his mother's car, on Caton Avenue, and he was carrying this tremendous thing. From my position at shortstop I couldn't make it out, but as he came nearer, running awkwardly, holding it in front of him like a package of groceries, I realized what it was: his old Victrola.

"Hey, George!" Louie called. "You ready to break Feller's strike-out record?"

George laughed. "Anytime they get in the batter's box—"

"Wait a second," said Louie. He put the Victrola down next to the backstop. He started fiddling with it, cranking it up the way you had to to get it to work, and then he started playing a record. At first it wasn't cranked up enough and you couldn't tell what kind of music it was. But then Louie cranked some more—and I whipped off my hat and stood at attention as the strains of "The Star-Spangled Banner" came blasting across the infield. I looked at George and he was smiling as broadly as he could, holding his cap across his heart, standing rigid, at attention. The team from P. S. 246 must have been as shocked as we were, but by the time the music got to "and the rockets' red glare—" both teams were standing at attention, saluting, listening, while Louie kept cranking away so that the music wouldn't slow down. People sitting on benches, guys playing on other diamonds, men and women walking along Caton Avenue, a few park cops —they all stopped and started drifting toward our diamond. When the record was over, Louie—in the loudest voice I'd ever heard—shouted "Play Ball!" and we started the game. We must have had a crowd of over fifty people watching us play our first game, and I'll bet if George had been pitching for a major league team that day he would've pitched at least a shutout.

He struck out all but two of their men—one guy hit a grounder to me at shortstop, and another fouled out to Corky Williams at first base. He also hit four home runs. I got a double and two singles, I remember. We won, 19-0, and the next day, as Louie had promised, our box score was in the *Brooklyn Eagle*.

Louie got us six more games during the next two weeks, and we won all of them. George gave up a total of three hits in the six games, and he was a pretty happy guy during that time. He had clippings of the box scores of all the games in his wallet, the way we all did. Clippings of the box scores—and then, the first week in May, the best clipping of all: an item in Jimmy O'Brien's column in the *Brooklyn Eagle* about our team, mentioning George, and Louie's Victrola. I think I carried that clipping around with me until my third year in high school.

After that, we began getting even more attention and teams from all over Brooklyn were challenging us to games. We played as many of them as we could—and George kept shutting out every team we played.

In the meantime, Louie had devised another plan. He called a meeting of the team the second week in May to discuss it. He told us that a team of our ability and prestige had to live up to its name. We said we were. We were winning games, weren't we?

"Sure," said Louie. "But what do you look like out on the field? People are starting to come in pretty large numbers to see us play—they hear about us, we got a reputation—and then when they see us, we look like a bunch of pickups."

"What do you think we should do?"

"We have to develop some class," said Louie. "And I have a plan worked out. It's not a new one, I'll admit—lots of the high school guys use it, but it's a good one. I say we run a raffle and use the money to buy ourselves jackets and uniforms."

We all liked the idea of jackets and uniforms, naturally, but they cost a lot of money—especially the kinds of uniforms and jackets we wanted to have.

"I got it all figured out," said Louie, answering our objections by pulling out some pieces of paper. Then he started talking about numbers, and once he did that, I knew we'd get those uniforms and jackets. It turned out that Louie could get a clock-radio at a discount from an uncle of his. Then he said he could get Levy's Sporting Goods Store, on Flatbush Avenue, to donate a glove and ball for the raffle. He also said they'd sell us the uniforms and jackets at cost if Jimmy O'Brien would mention them in his column sometime. Louie said his father could take care of that. We'd make the radio first prize and the glove and ball second prize, but we'd tell the kids at school that if they won first prize we'd give them the glove and ball anyway. There were fifteen of us and if we each sold five books of ten raffles at a quarter apiece, that'd be almost two hundred dollars. Louie said that he himself would sell at least fifteen books, and he expected most of us to sell more than five. If we took in three hundred dollars in the raffle we could have the uniforms and jackets.

George was at the meeting this time—right in Louie's house—and he volunteered to get his gang to sell chances, and I think all of us were pretty glad then that we'd be on the selling end of the raffle during the next few weeks. Louie said he had already had the raffle books printed and that the drawing would take place on Friday afternoon, June 1st. On June 2nd, we all knew, we had a big game with the Flatbush Raiders, a team from P. S. 139 that had lost only one game. Louie said that if we could give Levy's a down payment of one hundred dollars they'd go ahead and get the uniforms and jackets made in time for the game against the Raiders.

We had only two games during the next week, and the rest of the time all of us were running around getting everybody we knew—friends, relatives, neighbors, teachers, store-owners—to buy chances. By the following Friday, Louie reported that we had more than a hundred dollars and that Levy's had already started making the uniforms and jackets. The uniforms would be gray with orange lettering and the jackets were going

E*

to be made of this orange and black material that felt like satin, with *Zodiacs* written across the back in bright yellow.

By the middle of the following week, Louie reported to us that if we went over three hundred dollars, as it looked like we would, the extra money would be used to get Louisville Sluggers and official National League baseballs for the team. Louie also told us that his father could probably get Jimmy O'Brien to come down to see our game against the Raiders.

On Wednesday afternoon, two days before the raffle-drawing, Louie rode out to Marine Park on his bicycle where the Raiders were playing a game, and when he showed up at our big meeting on Friday, June 1st, he had a stack of scouting notes.

"Before we get to our skull session on the Raiders," he said, "we have to get this raffle business over with. First, some of you haven't given me all the money—or the leftover raffles."

While Louie took care of the final accounts of the raffle, George stayed by himself in a corner, looking through Louie's sports magazines. Although he spoke to a few of us a little more, you couldn't really say that any of us had become pals with him. At school he still stayed pretty much with his gang, and after school—on the days when we didn't have games—we knew that he still hung around with his brother.

"Okay," said Louie. "I got it all figured out. Just a few things don't check. You, Marty, you took out seven books and only gave me fifteen dollars."

"I forgot," said Marty. He handed Louie a book of tickets. "I didn't sell these."

Louie crossed his name off. He seemed to be stalling, because he kept adding and subtracting figures and I knew that he never had that much trouble figuring things out.

"George?"

"Yeah?"

"According to my records you gave me raffle stubs from sixteen books, which means you owe forty dollars."

"So?"

"You only gave me twenty-eight so far."

We were all quiet. George wasn't looking straight at Louie. He had a magazine out, with a picture of Sal Maglie on the cover, and he made believe he was thumbing through it.

"Maybe you didn't give me sixteen books," said George.

"I did. It's right here in writing."

"Hell, anybody can phony up figures."

"I didn't phony them up." Louie's voice was loud. "You still owe twelve dollars."

"Prove it."

"Prove it?—It's down here in black and white—"

"Oh yeah?—My word's as good as yours."

"It's not—!"

"Are you callin' me a liar?"

George stood up now and walked toward Louie.

"I'm just saying you owe twelve dollars.—You better pay up, or—"

"Or what, smarty?"

"Or—" Louie stopped. "—or you can't play tomorrow."

George laughed. But his laugh was forced. You could tell. "Who needs to play with you guys, anyway? You can't win without me and you know it."

"You pay up or you don't play. I mean it, George. You won't get your uniform and you won't get to play in front of Jimmy O'Brien either . . ."

"I don't give a damn," George said. He walked up to Louie and pushed his fist into Louie's face. Louie didn't move. This surprised George. "I never should of given you the twenty-eight dollars either. And you know what you can do with your raffle—"

George didn't finish his sentence. Instead, he picked up the clock-radio, raised it over his head, and then flung it to the floor, splattering its parts all over the room. Louie leapt at George, screaming cursewords, but with an easy push, George shoved him to the floor. Then he kicked him a few times and Louie started crying. He got up and went after George again, but this time I was ready. I grabbed George's right arm.

"C'mon, you guys, help me hold him. Nobody's gonna ruin our raffle and get away with it—!"

Izzie jumped on George's back and got him in a strangle hold. George tried to throw him off, but by this time, Kenny and Corky and Stan and the other guys were all holding George. He fought and it took all our strength to hold him, but it was fifteen to one, and these odds were too much even for him.

"C'mon, Louie," I said. "Give it to him now."

"Yeah, c'mon," the guys yelled. "Let him have it . . . right in the gut . . . he deserves it . . . give it to him good . . ."

Louie was still crying, but he came at George. "You're—you're nothing but a *bum!*" he screamed.

George spit at him.

"C'mon," said Kenny. "We can't hold him all day. Just give it to him—"

"Yeah, c'mon, ya little sawed-off runt—I hear they're gettin' up a girls' team at school for you to play on—"

"You're just a big bum," said Louie, whimpering. He was breathing heavily. "I wouldn't waste my knuckles on you. Just get out of my house. Get out. We—we don't need crooks on the Zodiacs. Get out. Get out . . ."

Then Louie started crying again. We all pushed and pulled George to the door and somehow we managed to slam it with him on the other side.

We ran off the raffle anyway—Louie said that the money that was going to go for bats and balls would be enough to get another radio—and a few hours later, we all left Louie's house. I was glad I lived in his building.

The next morning there were over two hundred people gathered around the backstop and baselines at the Parade Grounds. Izzie warmed up and he looked pretty good. I think the new uniforms made us all play a little over our heads that day. The pitcher on the Raiders was really fast and our only chance, we knew, was if his control was off.

When Louie cranked up his Victrola before the game, most of the onlookers started laughing. We ignored them. In fact, I think hearing the National Anthem, the way we had in all our other games, made us play even harder, because in the first inning, Izzie held the other team, and in our half, Kenny Murphy doubled and then I hit a single which drove him in. That was the last time we had the lead, though. The Raiders tied it up in the third inning, and went ahead in the fourth, by 4-1. The final score was 7-2.

When the game was over and we were picking up our gloves and stuff, and changing out of our spikes, nobody said anything to each other, and nobody looked at Louie.

We waited for one another and were walking away from the diamond, when Stan spotted George.

"Uh-oh," he said, pointing. "He's got his gang with him."

We all looked and sure enough there they were, about ten of them —in their motorcycle jackets and pegged pants.

"Hey!" George shouted, coming nearer. "Ain't those guys got pretty uniforms."

"Yeah," said one of his guys. "And look at those jackets. They look like my mommy's underwear—"

This seemed to strike George's gang as a pretty good joke.

"Hey, you bunch of fags," George said. "Who won the game?"

Nobody answered. George and his gang had almost reached us now.

"Aw, c'mon—you don't mean you let those other fruit-boots beat you, do you? How could anybody beat a team that's got a manager like Louie? He's real smart, ain't he?"

George was in front of us now, about fifteen feet from Louie, his hands on his hips. Louie stopped.

"C'mon, smart boy. Cross my path. I dare you."

"Don't do it, Louie—" I shouted. I looked around, hoping a policeman was nearby. I wasn't in any mood for a fight. Louie put down his Victrola.

"I don't want any trouble," he said.

"Hey, listen to this, guys. He says he don't want no trouble. Ain't that nice—I don't want none either, see. Only I say you called me a liar and a crook and I don't take that from nobody—"

"I—I didn't mean to call you that," said Louie. "Why don't we just forget the whole thing?"

"I don't forget easy."

I was holding one of the bats and I gripped the handle firmly. The other guys had already let their gloves and equipment drop onto the grass.

I spotted a cop about a half block away. He was moving toward us. I tried to stall.

"What's the gripe, George?" I asked. "You mad 'cause you didn't get to pitch today?"

"What's the matter? Can't Louie fight his own battles?"

"We just don't want no trouble, that's all."

The guys in George's gang began to move toward us and then George shoved Louie. I ran at him, the bat raised over my head. "We got bats, George—one of you is gonna get a bloody head."

"You don't scare us with your toothpicks—!"

Somebody grabbed my arm and then the fight was on. It didn't last long—probably less than a minute, but by the time the cop got there and started bopping guys on the head with his night stick, most of us, myself included, were glad it was over. I had managed to get a leg-scissors on George and even though he was really blasting me in the gut, I held on long enough so that he couldn't get at Louie. A few more cops were on the scene pretty quickly and when we were finally separated they asked the usual questions about who had started the fight. When they saw that nobody was going to give them any answers, they told us to beat it.

"Okay, all of you—get on home. You, kid," the cop said, pointing to Kenny. "You better get some ice on that eye in a hurry—"

George's gang started to move away, then George turned and called to us. "We'll get you guys at school—"

One of the cops ran after George and grabbed him by the front of his jacket. "Okay, tough boy," he said. "If I find out that one hair on the head of any of these kids was touched I'll throw you and every one of your cronies in jail. You hear that?"

George nodded.

"Hey," said the cop. "I know you. You're George Santini, ain't you? Vinnie Santini's brother?"

"So what?" George tried to squirm out of the cop's grip.

"It figures," the cop laughed. "You know who Vinnie Santini is," he said to one of the other cops. "He's that punk we had down at the station last week. I never saw a guy turn yellow so quick."

"It's a lie!" George shouted. He almost broke away. "You shut your damned mouth—"

George kicked at the cop, and the cop whacked him across the arm with his club. Another cop held George while the first cop put his nose right up to George's face and continued: "I never seen a guy yellow so quick," he said. "We didn't have the light on him more than ten minutes when he started ratting on every petty thief this side of Bensonhurst. And you're probably the same."

George didn't say anything. He just sort of hung there, held up by the cop. "Get goin', punk," said the cop, shoving George. "And I better not hear that you touched these kids."

George and his gang walked away. We all picked up our stuff, Kenny and Marty carrying Louie's Victrola, and then, suddenly, Louie started running after George.

"Hey, wait a minute! Wait—"

George turned and waited till Louie caught up to him.

"Yeah?" George said.

Louie stopped, as if he had forgotten why he had told George to wait. Then he spoke, in that slow, hesitant way of his. "I was going over the records last night," he said. "And I discovered that I made a mistake yesterday. You really only owed eight dollars. I was thinking that if you gave me the eight dollars, then—then you could pitch for us against the Raiders. We play them a return game next week."

"Who'd wanna play on your sissy team?" said one of the guys in George's gang.

George looked at Louie, then at the guys in his gang, then back at Louie.

"I'll let you know," he said, and walked off.

The next day he gave Louie the eight bucks. On the following Saturday, with George pitching, and wearing his new uniform, we beat the Raiders, 4-0, and were we happy! George too. We won about a dozen more games that month. At the end of June, though, lots of the guys, myself included, went away to camp or to the country, and the team had to break up. The next year when George was a freshman at Erasmus Hall High School he didn't play for us.

When he was a sophomore at Erasmus—I was a freshman that year —he played fullback on the football team and was starting pitcher on the baseball team. In the middle of his junior year, though, he quit school. The next time I heard about him, somebody said he had taken off for Florida with his brother.

Joyce Carol Oates

Dying

"Come closer, sit here on the edge of the bed. Or are you afraid of me?"

"Why should I be afraid of you?"

"You might catch my disease."

"You don't have any disease."

She saw that he was irritated, in spite of his smile. It was too warm in this room again, everything crowded and musty; as usual he had not opened the window. Each time she came to visit him she felt herself more tediously familiar with the furniture of his life, now narrowed strangely to this room in a half-empty old apartment building with a TV-radio repair shop on the first floor. Things lay where she had seen them last: a pile of old newspapers, books from the city library, dirty trousers collapsed on the floor. The man himself, sitting propped up in bed, watched her distaste with a kind of malicious triumph, as if he were proud of presiding over this particular kingdom.

"Well," she said, setting down the bag she carried, "how much do you weigh today?"

"I didn't bother weighing myself."

She sat at the little kitchen table, only a few yards from his bed. As she crossed her legs he could not help but glance down at them, and this annoyed her; she said coldly, "What's wrong with you now? As soon as I came in you were irritated."

"That isn't true—"

"It's true."

He scratched at his bare chest. She could hear his fingernails against his skin and smiled at the familiarity of the sound. "So I suppose you won't be coming anymore," he said.

"Please, not that again."

They were silent. She could hear the sound of machines from somewhere, not far away. These sounds and even the sight of his room pleased her, as if she were coming home to something, and now their routine disagreement seemed to fit in precisely with what she had expected. He made a sound of impatience. His hair was tousled, yet she could see clearly that he would be bald soon; that sandy boyish hair was a disguise that had never fooled her. They had met years ago at college, both of them dissociated from the larger social world of the university by their having the wrong clothes, the wrong mannerisms, the wrong nervous intensity. To her he seemed to have changed little. To him, she guessed, she was more attractive than she had been; surely her blond hair wound in thick braids about her head and her expensive clothes must draw all the light of this shabby room to her. "Here, look what I brought you today," she said suddenly. "Why should we always fight?"

"Is that all for me?"

"Of course, everything." She sat with her back arched as if she were a princess, elegantly conscious of sitting this way as he watched her, and began to take things out of the bag. "Some wonderful fresh fruit, look at these colors. Look at this apple, isn't it beautiful? No, seriously. Do you want an apple now?"

"I don't like the skins on apples. The noise they make—"

"How preposterous," she said, laughing.

"I can't help it."

"But how can you be so weak?"

"Are you going to start that again?"

"No, no, look at these bananas—but they're not ripe. I bought you some eggs, here. And some oranges, do you want an orange?"

"I don't care."

"Well, do you want it or not?"

"Oranges make a mess."

"Do you want me to peel it for you?"

He shrugged his shoulders. She watched him through her lowered lashes, as if trying to reconcile this man with the man she had once known, whose shoulders and arms had been broad, not muscular exactly but solid, while in this man hints of bone had begun to assert themselves fragilely beneath his flesh. "I'll put these things away and peel one for you," she said. She looked around; he said, "You can use that newspaper there." She nodded and put the paper on the table. Peeling the orange with her short chipped nails she smiled at him as if she were performing an intimate gesture, parodying some intimate gesture. "Of course I'm coming to see you again," she said. "Why do you always ask that? Of course I'm coming. I like to take that bus, I even like to walk past that damn construction area. Those men in the white helmets—"

"What are they doing for so long?"

"I told you, widening the street. Putting an overpass in too."

"What about the men in the helmets?"

"The sun glares off the helmets, the men work with their shirts off, they're very tanned—"

"Not like me."

"When it's sunny like today everything is hot and gleaming. On overcast days it's something else again, another scene. All the light drains out and everything is sluggish, even the machines seem slower."

"How have you been this week?"

"Oh, fine. Wonderful. And you?"

"The same."

"You didn't get out, I suppose."

"No."

"I'm glad you're so pleased with yourself."

"What do you mean by that?"

"You promised you'd get out somewhere, go downtown or to the park, any goddam thing. Now you tell me you stayed here."

"I wasn't up to it."

"You'll never be up to it, then."

"Look, for a bag of fruit I don't have to put up with this. I'm not your husband."

She frowned; then she laughed. Her laughter surprised her, for she knew it was not the right response to his eager, sullen tone. "No," she said. If she were to look at him, she knew, he would be staring at her with his big angry eyes, grown larger now that his face was thin, trying to involve her in some mysterious hurt. But this was familiar. Always he led her to talk about her husband, angrily and wistfully, as if trying to trap her in a lie.

"What do you mean by that *no*? Is the idea so absurd?"

"Certainly not."

"You do mean it."

"Here's the orange, it smells wonderful. Do you want a plate or something? I'd better get you one." Dishes were piled in the sink, some still dabbed with food. She took a saucer and rinsed it and brought it to him. "I suppose I could wash those dishes for you, but I don't want to. I can't stand to do dishes."

"Okay, thanks," he said. He put the saucer on his thigh and picked up the orange carefully. "Why don't you sit here? On the edge, there's room."

She sat on the edge of the bed. "My feet áche. I wore these shoes without stockings. It's so hot, even for July. Can I ask you why this window is never open?"

"Noise from outside."

"But you open it at night?"

"Yeah." He was eating a section of the orange, self-consciously. She saw him glance at her crossed legs. "Your shoes got dirty."

"All that dust out there, yes."

"Do you wear high heels like that to attract attention?"

"Whose attention?"

"I don't know, anyone's. Is that why women wear them?"

"I don't know."

"How stupid!"

"Yes, stupid. Why don't you get out of bed?"

He ate the orange angrily. Now a spurt of juice appeared on his chin. "Why don't you come in here with me?" he said.

She smiled and looked vaguely away—at a calendar on the wall, with half its numbers X'd out. "You don't really want that," she said.

"Look, I'm sick as hell of your telling me you know what I want. You know me better than I know myself, crap like that. Maybe you talk to your husband like that, but—"

"I never talk to him like that."

"Then to your friends."

"No, only to you." She paused. "You're my only friend."

He laughed. Then an unpleasant mottled flush appeared on his face. She was fascinated at his embarrassment, which came and went for reasons she could never understand. It was true, she thought, watching him eat, that he was her only friend, only to him could she talk, he existed for her as a face and a voice, a presence, a spirit, as no one else existed. Yet it was her husband she loved. Her love for her husband was so secure that it could be neglected and returned to, forgotten, and nothing would ever happen to it. Now this strange man, lying in his rumpled bed and supposing himself sick, was so moved by her having said that he was her friend that he could not for a moment even look at her. He ate the orange slowly and deliberately, sullenly, as if it were a duty he did to please her. "Yes, my only friend," she said, touching his shoulder. At his look of irritation she withdrew her hand. "You were my only friend at college, too. Later on, when I didn't see you much anymore, I still thought about you. That was what upset me—I always thought about you, you were always there. I didn't always want you so close to me, do you understand? You created something in me that stayed alive . . . And just last year I thought that you couldn't be dead, nothing could have happened to you or I would have known it. And then our meeting like that, by magic . . ."

"Magic, hell. Accident."

"By accident . . ."

"Did you ever tell your husband about me?"

"I told him about every man I had been involved with."

"What do you mean, involved with?"

"Made love with."

He stared down at the saucer. She felt his muscles tense as if he were stiffening himself against a blow. "We didn't make love," he said.

"Yes."

"We didn't, no, for Christ's sake. You say that now—you've imagined that now—to keep us apart. We never did."

"We did, yes. I remember."

"Look, this is ridiculous, every time we argue about it! We never made love, you never let me touch you, you were never any closer than this and you know it. What the hell are you trying to pull?"

"You've forgotten it, that's all."

"I've forgotten nothing."

"Why are you so angry?"

"Because you're lying—it's a trick to keep us apart now, when you know how I feel about you—"

She lowered her gaze. When he talked like this she felt a peculiar comfortable lassitude overtake her, as if he were safely set upon a speech already written and memorized, something she might have helped write herself. "No, honey," she said, taking the saucer from him, "that's not true. I don't involve myself with other men now. I'm not interested. You don't seem to understand about my marriage, you have the idea that marriage is—"

"You've never admitted the truth about your marriage."

She set the saucer on the bureau. There were a number of bottles there, a stained spoon, an ash tray. "What's this?" she said. She picked up a small blue bottle filled with capsules. "Is this new?"

"No. Herzog's tranquilizers. He said nothing was wrong with me, just to keep calm. No anxiety."

"Well?"

"The fat old bastard! Seven dollars for those things."

She set the bottle down and forgot about it. "Well, let's not argue,

I don't want to waste time that way. Why do you always want to talk about my marriage when it only upsets you? It has nothing to do with you, nothing at all. I shouldn't have told you about him, that time, but I thought you'd be pleased to know what my life is like now. After all, when we knew each other I wasn't very happy. Would you like me to be that way now?"

"Yes."

"But that's a—" She stared. Before her gaze little bluish lines seemed to appear beneath his eyes and at the sides of his nose, near his nostrils. "That's selfish," she said.

"So what? Who isn't selfish?"

"How am I selfish?"

"You talk to me about him, to make me miserable. You lie. You lie to me and you won't—you won't—"

"But I said it wasn't going to be that way, the first time I came. I love you as a friend. Don't you know how important that is, what it means to me? What does a lover mean, beside a friend? Doesn't that mean anything to you?"

"Christ, you really believe that." He drew his hand across his eyes; she could hear the slight elastic sound of his eyeballs being rubbed. "I hate that, stop it," she said, pulling at his wrist. "That noise—"

"Huh?"

"Oh, nothing."

"What noise?"

"Oh, nothing, it's silly. Nothing."

He stared at her, saw she was embarrassed about something. After a moment he said, "Doing any painting?"

"No."

"Anything wrong?"

"Of course not."

"Well, I just asked."

"I'm not angry, I'm sorry. I haven't been working but I think I have an idea. For two weeks or so . . . ."

"You never did a portrait of your husband, did you?"

"No, I'm past that stage. Anyway I wouldn't call it that, I never did portraits. That thing of you wasn't a portrait."

"Did you really see me that way?"

"Oh, I don't know."

"You never talk about your painting, why is that?"

"I don't know anything about it, I suppose."

"How old are you now?"

She laughed. "Why do you ask? You know I'm thirty-four."

"You're still young, then."

"Why do you say that, that way? You're the same age."

"Well, the success you've had with it, without trying, and you're so healthy—" Nervously she caressed his wrist, avoiding his sticky fingers.

She could feel waves of hatred in the stuffy air between them. "If that magazine had carried that story of you last year, how do you know what might have happened?"

"I never expected them to run the story."

"So you were crowded out, but look how close it was, that stupid news magazine with the artsy-craftsy color section! Just like that. Some half-wit takes a liking to a painting and there you go, easy as that."

"It hasn't been easy, I wouldn't say that."

"For Christ's sake don't tell me that. You've never worried about it, not once. You don't give a damn about it."

"But it isn't my life, I'm not like you—"

"Not your life!" He drew away from her. Now he did look ill: perhaps he was not imagining everything after all. His lips were dry and loose and contemptuous. "Of course it isn't your life. You're married. You're in love. You've got money. You've even got a friend you can show off to, that you visit surreptitiously."

"What a foolish word—"

"Surreptitiously? What else should I say?"

"Nothing."

"You've got everything, why should you worry about your work? Your career? You worry about nothing. You sleep at night. You have no headaches, no fears, no moments of darkness when you know absolutely that everyone is going to die and that you—you can't escape it."

"But you're not going to die. Don't torture yourself with it."

"I wasn't talking about myself, what makes you think that!"

"You never talk about anything but yourself."

"And look at my work, all scattered around here, those goddam papers on the floor there . . ."

"Oh, have you been working?"

He grinned contemptuously. "What do you think?"

"But you said last week you had an idea."

"No good."

"But if you started to write, something might happen. It used to be that way, didn't it? I still remember one of your stories, the one that was dedicated to me—about that German woman who worked for the family—"

"Forget it."

"But I liked that story."

"I didn't. So forget it."

"What was wrong with it?"

He had begun to breathe heavily. His eyes narrowed as if resisting pain. "I should think you'd play some music, at least," she said softly. "Should I put something on?" He seemed not to hear her at first; was he truly in pain, did he imagine it, or did he pretend? "No, thanks, no," he said rigidly. "Don't you like the records I bought? Is something wrong with them? That fifth symphony is supposed to be a perfect cutting—" "No, forget it," he said. "Are you all right?" she said. He nodded impatiently.

"But you don't want any music on?" she said. "Not while you're here."
"But in the background—to blot out that noise—" "I don't put music
on to blot out noise!" he said shrilly. He closed his eyes. She touched his
chest and was surprised at how cool and damp his skin was. "That goddam
orange," he muttered.

"Do you want a pill? Anything?"

"No."

She bowed her head and caressed his chest, vaguely. While she waited
for his pain to pass she looked down at the floor—unfinished boards
painted an ugly brown. Something had been spilled near the bed. "I'm
going to exhibit some things in Chicago, by the way," she said. "In September. *He's* going to go down with me and help."

He pushed her hand away. "I'm all right."

"Are you going to see the doctor this week, then?"

"I suppose so."

"But how have you been, worse?"

"I weigh a hundred fifty-six."

"Oh."

"So that crap you made me eat, that goddam nutritious cereal, didn't
work. Matter of fact it made me throw up."

"Maybe if you went out sometime—went for a walk—"

"Out here?"

"You could move closer in to the city. Near a park, why not? How did
you ever find this apartment, it isn't in the city or in the country, there
isn't anything here but vacant lots and buildings half torn down and that
factory or whatever it is, down that way—what a stupid place! It's inconvenient for me, too, since I don't drive—"

"Inconvenient for you!"

"Well, I mean—"

"I thought you liked to take that bus. Liked to walk by the men
working out there, so they can watch you. In your high heels."

"What's wrong with you?"

"Nothing."

"If I took a taxi out here next time, would you come back with me?
We could go to that doctor near my house, I told you about him. I think
your doctor at the clinic is too busy."

"Near your house? I couldn't afford it."

"Don't be silly."

"What? On that check they send me? How could I afford it?"

"I mean, don't be silly, I'd pay for it myself. Of course I'd pay for it.
I always said that examination they gave you wasn't complete—"

"Your husband would pay for it."

"I have my own money."

"And his money too, you have his money! I saw his ads in the paper,
real estate in a commercial area, will build to suit tenant—I was proud to
see it."

"Don't talk about him, please. Be sensible, be nice. We've got to do something about your health. You keep losing weight, we've got to do something about it. Why don't you look at me?"

"What do you want from me, anyway? Why do you keep coming here?"

His face was brittle with anguish. She knew in that instant that she had never been apart from him, during all those years, but that they had been regarding each other with this same inexplicable anguish, always, confusing other faces with the one face they desired, confusing other voices with that single unique voice neither of them could quite reject. She was humiliated by her bondage to this whining, helpless man.

"Why do you keep coming here?" he said.

She stood. She turned away. "I don't know."

"You never know anything!"

"Leave me alone. I'm going now."

"What time is it?"

"I'm going."

"Is it time for the bus?"

"You exhaust me, for God's sake—"

"But don't go yet, I mean it isn't time for the bus, is it? What time is it?"

His desperation shamed her. She stared over at the sink. "I know, I'll do your dishes for you," she said.

"No, the hell with them—"

"It's dirty this way, you'll make yourself sick," she said. "Don't you ever want to get well?" She inhaled slowly, feeling tears about to come into her eyes. She waited. Nothing happened, no tears. "Don't you ever want to get well?" she repeated, as if this remark were a cue that would inspire her to sorrow.

He had heard her coming on the stairs and opened the door for her. "Well, hello," she said. "How good you look! What's happened?"

"Oh, the weather change, after the heat wave, I guess," he said. He was leaning back against the sink, smiling. Behind him the grimy window faced nothing—she could not tell if it looked out upon another anonymous building or upon the gray sky. "Come on in, sit down. Sorry about last time."

"Last time?"

He glanced at her. She was still smiling, pleased at his being out of bed and dressed, but now she saw that she had said something wrong. "Oh, yes, last time," she said. She recalled their argument vaguely—he had refused to come with her to a doctor. "Then I know what," she said, not sitting in the chair he had offered her, "let's go out for a walk. Not that way, where they're working, but up this other way . . ."

He hesitated. She saw that his hair had been dampened and combed recently, that it looked thin. For a moment he was about to agree; then as if terrified by something, he turned slightly away. "Maybe later on."

"Please, a nice walk. You said yourself the weather is nice. Come on."

"No." He went past her and sat on the edge of the bed. His movements were cautious, even rigid, as if he were in some kind of danger. She sat in the chair and felt the atmosphere of the room go heavy with failure. "So," he said, "how's your work been going?"

"I've started a painting." She saw that he was barefoot. His long, bony, white toes cringed as she spoke. "I've been working on it for three days."

"Yeah, how is it? Anything like the last one?"

"I guess not." Watching his toes she heard her voice go thick with embarrassment. "Men working on a road, a lot of white, in fact everything's white or black or gray. No colors. The weeds alongside the road have been whitened by dust . . . they look like bones of something, skeletons . . ."

He smiled sourly. "Not putting this place in, are you?"

"Well, no. I don't want any buildings."

"Why not? This is a picturesque dump and you like picturesque things. Television antennas on the roof. Quaint things."

"What do you mean, quaint?"

"You like quaint things, don't you? Men working, with white helmets. What happened to their sun tans? Transfixed weeds, transfigured weeds—"

"Just what do you mean, quaint? What do you mean?"

He was still smiling but she knew he was nervous, ready to back down. "Forget it," he said. "I'm doing some work too."

Her heart was beating rapidly. For a moment she did not hear what he had said. Then she said, "Oh, that's nice. Really. Are you going to let me read it?"

"Maybe, when it's done."

"What is it?"

"A story."

"Oh, a story," she said. The flatness of her voice startled her. "But how are you? How do you feel?"

"The same."

"I'm so glad to hear you're working . . ." She glanced over at the kitchen table, which was cluttered with dishes and newspapers, as if seeking out evidence of his work. "A story, did you say? About what?"

"A man and a woman."

"A love story?"

"Yes."

"You'll let me read it when it's finished."

"Sure."

"I always liked what you wrote. In college . . . I thought you were the most intelligent man I ever met."

"Now you know better, huh?"

"I didn't mean that."

"You think I've changed some?"

"No. But we've all changed . . ."

"Some of us for the better."

"We've grown older. Grown into adults. Surely there's nothing wrong with that."

"What are you suggesting?"

"I don't understand you."

"Are you suggesting I haven't grown up?"

"I didn't say that, my God. How touchy you are! As far as I'm concerned you were always grown up. You had no childhood." And now she could see that he was not well, really, that she had imagined when she first came in that his being up, his smiling so confidently, had meant much more than it did. "How much did you say you weigh?"

"A little less."

"But how much?"

"A hundred forty something. I don't know."

She winced. Her hand came up before her in a gesture of pity, or defense, as if she supposed he expected some movement from her. "Please tell me what you're doing for yourself."

"I'm resting. Thinking."

"Be serious, will you? This is important."

"How can anything about me be important?"

"It's important to me!"

"But why to you? Who are you?" He stood up, excited. Then he sat down again and lay back on the bed, laughing. "My God, if you could explain that to me. Why you bother with me."

"Because you're my friend," she said contemptuously.

"I'm your friend," he said. "But why? Why? If this is the last time you come everything should be settled between us. Right now you're thinking—"

"You don't know what I'm thinking."

"You're wishing you hadn't come. A sick man isn't a man at all."

"But what has that got to do with it?"

He swung his legs around off the bed. "What has what got to do with it?"

"What you said—"

"What? What?"

"Oh, I don't know. You're giving me a headache. And I wish you'd open that window, noise or no noise, it smells in here—"

"A sick man isn't a man, huh? That's what you think."

"I never said that!"

"You don't let me be a man!"

"Look, please, if you're—" She made a gesture of rising that was insincere; he did not respond. They were silent for a while. "So you lost more weight," she said. She looked over at his little calendar, something from a service station, on which the new month was being X'd out. For some reason this pleased her, as if it were a landmark.

"Yes. And you, you're looking very good."

"With these lines under my eyes?"

"What? Let's see. I don't see anything."

"You never notice anything. I was up until four last night, drawing weeds. Don't laugh. Then I couldn't sleep, when I did go to bed." As she spoke a wave of exictement rose in her that she had to hide from him. His narrow glittering eyes were hostile.

"You're looking very good, just the same. Very healthy."

Her excitement was transformed suddenly into a sensation of dismay. She put her hands to her eyes in a melodramatic gesture. "Why do you hate me so?" she said.

"What?"

"You hate me, I can feel it. You hate me. There's something inside me that was born when I met you—when a woman meets any man, it happens—and this thing, this creature that becomes me when I'm with you, you're killing it, you hate it and want to destroy it—"

"That's not true," he said quietly.

"You want me to come to bed with you so you can kill it. We're fighting each other, I bring you love and we're antagonists, what's wrong with us? The other time it wasn't like that. We were close to each other and it was beautiful—" He said nothing. She went on, in spite, "But of course you don't believe that ever happened. You've forgotten it, like all men."

He made a gesture that indicated nothing. He looked confused and ill. A hand might have been pressing against his chest, pushing him back down on the soiled pillow that was propped up against the headboard. He took a package of cigarettes out of his pocket, as if for something to do.

"Anyway," she said, "you should open that window."

"I open it at night."

"You're so remote here, my God this is the end of the world. That window is all you have and you keep it closed. How can you live like this?"

He lit a cigarette. "You're very generous, then, to come here in spite of everything. To come here and let me admire you. See what I can't have."

"Do you think that's why I come here?" she said sharply.

"How do I know? Why you began, or why you're stopping—"

"Why I began? When I saw you downtown that day I couldn't have walked away. Are you serious? Don't you know what you mean to me? You looked so sick—I guess I thought you were drunk—there was never any question about my coming to see you."

"Is that true?"

"Yes."

"And about stopping?"

"Why do you always bring that up?"

"Because I'm afraid."

She got up slowly. In spite of his watching her, she stretched her arms and stifled a yawn. "I'm still sleepy. I got up at seven this morning . . . Now you say you're afraid, afraid of what? How strange you are—" She came to sit by him on the edge of the bed. He was pleased at this; she saw the cunning rigidity of his face relax. "Afraid of what?"

"The usual."

"But what nonsense—something you can't even explain—" She watched him closely, as if jealous of something. He took hold of her hand and caressed it without affection. She smiled sharply. "Tell me what you're afraid of."

"I'm not sure."

"Not that thing that bothered you once before, I hope. That awful accident—"

"Oh, that. The woman by the bus? No, not that, but I still dream about it sometimes. No. Something else. Earlier than that, years ago . . . But hell, I don't want to talk about it."

"I want to talk about it. I want to know."

"Do you? I was working at the hospital, then, I told you about that. I was twenty-seven—where were you at twenty-seven?"

"Married."

"To him?"

"I've only been married once."

"At the hospital, then . . ." But he said, with a harsh burst of laughter, "Hell, I'm crazy, what's the difference? Do you think I don't know absolutely every truth about myself, even how I look to you?"

"That's not possible."

"Do you suppose your mind is so impregnable? I can see everything— everything. And if I'm crazy, do you think I don't prefer this to something else? Huh?"

His fingers had become hard against her arm. She seized his hand and brought it to her lips. "Don't hurt me," she said.

"Don't hurt you! You come to watch me suffer and you're afraid of getting hurt yourself!"

"Do you think I come to watch you suffer?"

"Why else? Why? You could let me lie in bed and rot, what the hell does it matter? It occurs to me now that you won't let me alone until I'm dead, dead and stinking. Then you'll go back home and wash your hands."

"Please don't talk like that—"

He jerked his hand away. "And I didn't do any writing either. A lot of crap, I was lying. I did nothing."

"I know."

"I wish I could tell you what I thought, when I heard you coming up the stairs. I feel I'm learning a new language, that this is a prison and I have to talk in code . . . You have a key that lets you in and out and you're a spy they've sent in here, and I have to talk to you, I can't help it. I lie here and wait for you and think, What if she doesn't come! What if she's left me! And then when you leave I feel worse, I wish you had never come. And you're a spy, you want to get that secret from me and show it to them, paint it up, transfigure it so that it becomes symmetrical and quaint— ending up in five colors, reproduced in that news magazine! Do you think I don't know you? Everything about you? You might be a character in something I've written, that's how well I know you! A woman, a devouring woman—"

"If that's so, then you wanted me that way. If you created me you created me that way."

He smiled bitterly at this. "To hell with that psychological crap! And you want me to go for a walk—as if I can go for a walk! As if I can walk down those stairs! And so sympathetic with suffering—other people's. So appreciative of suffering. So sweet, solicitous. And all you ask in return is that I love you. And if I did tell you what I dreamt about, could you understand it? No. Could you feel it? Only as a picture. You'd get a vision, a sight, the picture of what happened but you wouldn't know what I know. You weren't there. People like you never happen to be there."

"Tell me about it."

"And then what?"

"What do you mean?"

"What will you do for me?"

She half-closed her eyes as if seriously thinking. Then she said, "What I've always done for you."

He turned away with a grunt. His hatred for her made him shudder; she watched with fascination the convulsive jerking of his hand. "So I'm your jailer, now," she whispered.

"I didn't say that."

"I'm a spy, then. That your jailers have sent."

"Hell, I know I'm crazy, that was just talk. No one cares about me except you. Forget it." He shivered. She was frightened, physically frightened, by the shift in his expression: his anger had been overwhelmed by a look of passive terror. "But what's wrong with you?" she wanted to cry. "What is it? What do you know that I don't know? Why are you dying?" But she said nothing. She held his hand and pressed it against her throat and would not let him pull it away.

She believed she heard something, it must have been him telling her to come in. So she opened the door. He lay in bed, evidently just waking, his eyes narrowed and vague as if out of focus. A stale, sharp odor was in the room. Immediately she began to breathe shallowly as if in the presence of danger. "Did I wake you?" she said. She had brought him a bag of groceries and some magazines; she put the things down slowly on the cluttered table. A coffee cup was nearly overturned—half-filled yet with coffee, with a cigarette butt floating in it. "Are you all right?" He raised himself on his elbow. The sheet fell away to show his pale, bluish chest. He stared at her and began to smile. She faced his smile with fear, for it seemed to her ghastly, its very eagerness terrifying. "You didn't forget I was coming, did you?" she said coquettishly. But the lilt of the remark was ludicrous in this musty room and she felt her cheeks burn with shame. He did not notice. "Come in, sit down," he said. "I guess I was asleep." She came to him and stood nervously by the bed as he sat up and tried to smooth his hair down. She wanted to pull the sheet up about him, to protect him. "God, what a taste in my mouth," he said, making a face. "Could you get me some water or something?"

She brought him a glass of water. He drank it eagerly. The side of his face was crisscrossed with reddened wrinkles from the pillow. She took the glass from him when he finished. "I was lying here thinking about you, I wasn't asleep," he said, touching her arm. "I was thinking how I loved you. And if you didn't come this time . . . If I thought it was the wrong day or something . . . " Then in mid-sentence his tone changed; she could see him swallow, and then struggle not to show something—anxiety, malice. He tugged at her wrist. "Come down here with me. Just this one time, will you? It isn't too hot in here. I can brush this off the bed—crumbs or something, what is it?" He began brushing something off angrily. "I've been thinking about you ever since you left last time. And a whole week in between—that goddam exhibit you had to go to—of course you had to go to it. Come on here."

She laughed nervously and tried to pull away. "I brought you some magazines—"

"Look, God damn you, you—" But he stopped. He grated his teeth. "You don't know how I've been waiting for you," he said softly.

"Please, let go. What's wrong with you?"

"With me?"

"I come in here and see how you've let yourself go—see what you've done to yourself—there's nothing wrong with you, don't you know that? Nothing! You're weak, whining, and now you want—"

"What?"

She turned away from him. She was overcome with disgust and shame and could not look at him. "How can you think I'm like that, that I would want to make love with a dying man!" she said.

And, as soon as this was said, the tension between them dissolved; even the foul air of the room seemed to weaken. She looked over her shoulder at him. He was sitting up, the wrinkled sheet fallen down to his stomach, his body hunched and skeletal and contemplative. So that is what he looks like, she thought sharply, and could not remember if he had really changed or if she had never seen him before. After a moment he glanced up and smiled shakily. "Magazines, huh?" he said. "What kind?"

She brought them to him. She sat on the edge of the bed. He looked at the glossy covers, smiling, and leafed through the pages perfunctorily. "And how have you been this week?" she said. She saw that his vague familiar smile did not change, that he had not heard, and she had to repeat her question.

Penelope Gilliatt

The Redhead

When the skulls in the crypt of St. Bride's Church were disinterred the wisps of hair remaining on them were found to have turned bright orange. The earth lying under the paving stones of Fleet Street had apparently had some extravagant chemical effect. This was what Harriet's hair looked like: when she was born she had two sprouts of what seemed to be orange hay on her head, shocking in its coarseness, and to her gentle Victorian mother alarmingly primitive, nearly pre-moral. It was like having some furious Ancient Briton lying in the crib.

Neither the color nor the texture ever changed. The hair stayed orange, and to the end of her life it was as tough as a rocking horse's. When she was a child it was left uncut and grew down well below her waist. The tangles were tugged out three times a day by a Norland nurse who attacked the mane in a moral spirit as though it were some disagreeable piece of showing-off. By the time she was thirteen the routine of agony and rebellion on one side and vengeful discipline on the other had worn everyone out, and she was taken to a barber. The barber took a knife to the thicket, weighed it when it was off, and gave her 2½ lbs. of hair wrapped up in tissue paper which the nurse briskly took from her as soon as they were outside because she didn't believe in being morbid.

The operation had several effects. One of them was that the nurse, robbed of her pleasure in subduing the hair, turned her savagery more directly onto Harriet and once in a temper broke both of her charge's thumbs when she was forcing her into a new pair of white kid gloves for Sunday School. Another was that the child, who had always been sickly and scared, as though all her fortitude were going into the stiff orange fence hanging down her back, seemed to begin another kind of life as soon as it was cut off. She grew four inches in a year. Her father, a dark, sarcastic, pharisaically proud man whom she worshiped, started to introduce her to people as "my fat daughter."

She wasn't really fat at all. With her hair cut she didn't even look like any normal Victorian parent's idea of a daughter. She looked more like Swinburne streaming up Putney Hill. Her lavender-scented mother began to watch her distastefully, as though she were a cigar being smoked in the presence of a lady without permission. Mrs. Buckingham's dislike gave

Harriet a sort of bristling resilience. She had from the beginning an immunity to other people's opinion of her, which isn't a characteristic that is much liked in women; later in her life it made her impossible. Her critics thought it crude of her not to care what they thought of her. It meant that she started off at an advantage, for just as they imagined they had caused her misery they found that they were only confirming her grim and ribald idea of the way things would always be. She lay in wait for pain, expecting no rewards from people, and this made her a hopelessly disconcerting friend. Her peculiar mixture of vehemence and question caused people discomfort. If she had had any talent, if she had been born in another period and perhaps if her spirit had been lodged in the body of a man, she might just have been heroic. As it was, her flamboyance struck people as unbecoming and her apparent phlegm as not very lovable. The only person who might have respected her independence was her father, and he was the one man in whose presence she lost it. His mockery, which he meant as love, frightened her and cut her to the bone. At thirteen she felt trapped by the system of growing into a woman, which seemed to be separating them, and longed more than ever to be his son.

A year later her back began to hurt. At the girls' establishment where she had been sent at huge expense to learn music and French and to carry out the ornate disciplines conceived by the headmistress—which included communal teeth-washing in the gardens, winter and summer, and then communal gargling into the rosebeds, which the headmistress regarded as a form of manure-spreading—the pain was put down to growing too fast. It was only after she had fainted at tennis that her father took her to a specialist who found that she had an extra vertebra. For the next two years she was supposed to spend five hours a day lying flat on her back on an old Flemish seat in the hall of her parents' London house. Formal education was shelved, which was a relief, because the unctuous kind of diligence expected of her at school had convinced her that she was both stupid and sinful. The physical privation of lying for hours on cold wood anyway suited her mood. She began to feel that she would like to become a Roman Catholic, partly to frighten her mother, who was one of the pioneer Christian Scientists in England, and partly because the rigorousness of the experience attracted her. Her father was a Presbyterian and when she confronted him with her decision, as pugnaciously as usual in spite of her nerves, they had a furious and ridiculous quarrel: a man of fifty for some reason threatened by the vast religious longings of a fifteen-year-old. She found herself capable of a courage that startled her. Maybe it was temper. She went upstairs, emptied her jewelbox into her pockets and left the house.

In 1912 this was an extraordinary thing to do. For two nights she slept on the Thames Embankment. It was really the misleading start to her whole punishingly misled life, because it gave her an idea of herself that she was absolutely unequipped to realize. She started to think that she had a vocation for taking heroic decisions, but it was really nothing more sustaining than a rabid kind of recklessness that erupted suddenly and then left her feeling bleak and inept. As a small child, sick with temper when she was forced to do something against her will or even when she was strapped too tightly into a bed, she had risen to heights of defiance that genuinely alarmed her family. She had a ferocious and alienating attachment to independence, but very little idea of what to do with it. The row about Catholicism got her out of the house and carried her through two euphoric days, during which she thought about the Trinity, existed on lollipops and stared at the celebration of the Mass from the back of Westminster Cathedral. After that, the fuel was spent.

The priest whom she eventually accosted took one look at her, an ill-proportioned, arrogant child with slides in her gaudy hair, and started grilling her for an address. She was furious that he refused to talk about religion except in terms of duty to her parents; what she wanted was a discussion of Peter Abelard and an immediate place in a convent. She had an exhaustive knowledge of Sunday Schools and it was depressing to find him full of the same bogus affability that she met every Sunday of the year. She wanted harshness, remote ritual, a difficult kind of virtue. What she got was an upholstered smile and an approach like a cozy London police-man's to a well-bred drunk on Boat Race night.

Declining to lie, she let him take her home, planning to swear the maid to secrecy and slip out of the back door again as soon as the priest had gone. When she got there she found that her father was dying. The truancy was forgotten. Her mother, supported by two Christian Science practi-tioners, was in another room "knowing the truth," trying to reconcile her hysteria with Mary Baker Eddy's teaching that passing on is a belief of mortal mind. The child was allowed into the bedroom and for two hours she watched her father die. He was in coma, and as he breathed he made a terrible bubbling sound. The nurse and the doctor left the room together for a moment, and she grabbed him by the shoulders and shook him des-perately, with an air lock in her throat as though she were in a temper. When his bubbling stopped and he was dead, it seemed to her that he suddenly grew much larger. He looked enormous, like a shark on the sand.

After that no one in the family really bothered about her. Though it was Edwardian England and though Harriet was the sort of upper-class child who would normally have been corseted with convention, Mrs. Buck-ingham's resolve collapsed after her husband's death. Her natural passivity, encouraged by her religion and perhaps by the fact that she was pregnant, committed her to a mood of acceptance that was sweetly and hermetically selfish. The nurse was sacked to keep down the bills and the incoming maternity nurse was not interested in an unattractive fifteen-year-old. It was agreed by Mrs. Buckingham, who had always resisted the false belief about the pain in her daughter's back, that Harriet should stop lying on the hallseat and go to a school founded in the 1840's for the further education of gentlewomen. Having lost some of the true Christian Scien-tists' sanguinity about money and the faith that good Scientists should be able to demonstrate prosperity, she suggested faintly that Harriet had better take a secretarial course and equip herself to learn what she called a hat allowance, by which she meant a living.

The classes that Harriet in fact chose to go to were logic, history, English literature and Greek. Logic, when she came to it, seemed to her as near to hell as she had ever been. She felt as though her brain were clambering around her skull like a wasp trying to get out of a jam jar. History was taught by a whiskery professor who thundered about the Origin and Destiny of Imperial Britain. His ferocious idealism made her think over and over again in terror of what her father would have said to her, and what she would have replied, if he had woken up when she shook him.

The English master baffled her. She hated Lamb, who was his favorite writer, and once terrified the class by saying so by mistake. Her own tastes were all wrong for the times; she liked the flaying moral tracts of the Christian Socialists and a kind of violent wit that had hardly existed since Pope. She felt a thousand miles away from the gentle professor who used to cross out the expletives in Sheridan and even bowdlerized *Macbeth*. "Ladies," he said sweetly to the class one day, "before proceeding further we will turn to the next page. We will count one, two, three lines from the top. We will erase or cross out the second word and substitute the word "thou." The line will then read: "Out, out thou spot. Out I say!"

To begin with she made friends. There was one girl called Clara whom she used to meet in the lower corridor an hour before classes began: they had long discussions about Tolstoy, Maeterlinck and Ibsen, and were suspected of immorality. But soon she began to detach herself from the girls sitting hand in hand in the Bun Shop and from their faintly rebuking way of going at their books. Life, she felt vaguely but powerfully, was more than fervent chats about great literature. Life as she wanted it to be was momentarily embodied by the don who taught her Greek, a brave and learned man who had fought the Turks in modern Greece. As usual her excitement burnt out fast, like her courage. She had no gift for academic work; she simply longed to be able to dedicate her life to it.

Six months later she went to prison as a suffragette, having lied about her age and enrolled as a militant. It was the only time in her life when she was free of Doubts. She had found a cause, and the cause wasn't yet debased by her own incapacity to believe. She was thrilled with the suffragettes' tenacity and the expression it gave to her feelings about being in some kind of sexual trap.

But feminism, far from letting her out of the trap, turned out to be a hoax. She suddenly saw herself and her comrades not as prophets but as a howling, marauding mob. She prayed for faith, addressing a God whom she had never altogether managed to believe in, but clinging to the structure of the Roman Catholic Church as though it might do instead. During a hunger strike she asked to go to Confession. The prison doctor refused unless she agreed to drink a cup of tea and eat a piece of bread and butter.

Confused, she agreed, and wrote a letter confessing the weakness to a friend outside, asking her not to tell the stonyhearts at Suffragette Headquarters. When she came back from Confession, uncomforted, she found her cell mate kicking the doctor who was trying to feed her, and at the same time yelling that he should take his hat off in the presence of a lady.

For Harriet this was the end of Votes for Women. She had no idea what she wanted, but it wasn't a license to have it both ways. She felt cold and fraudulent. After making several trips to Headquarters in Lincoln's Inn and each time letting the bus take her on to Aldgate East, she managed to resign from the movement. Characteristically, she did it in the most abrasive and insulting way possible. Everyone was disagreeable.

Six months later the Great War had broken out and she had found a new cause. She became a ward maid in a hospital. For a girl brought up in a Christian Science home there was a certain frightening kind of excitement about medicine, like drink for a teetotaler; but otherwise she found the work harrowing and repellent. Everyone else seemed to be roused by the War, but she saw it as a giant emotional hoax. The romanticism of the period upset her more than the blood. All the house surgeons started to avoid her, preferring the pretty V.A.D's. Her unnecessary decision to do the dirtiest work in the place struck them as alarming. By now she was six feet tall and to the patients she looked like Boadicea with a bedpan; none of them found her calming, and the sisters regarded her hair with secret fear. The people she liked best were the consultants. Longing as usual with her spirit to enact the role that her flesh shrank from, she pined to be a doctor. She knew that the one thing that her mother would never provide money for was a training in medicine, so she wrote eventually to the "Boys' Own Paper" to ask them how to go about it, inventing a letter that was supposed to come from a badly off boy whom she thought would enlist their sympathy. The bullying answer appeared in the correspondence columns:

"Medical training is long and arduous. It is unsuitable for the working boy. Our advice is that you learn a trade."

So the huge, blundering, privileged girl, now 17, went back to her mother's comfortable house. She prayed, and she took up vegetarianism, more as an extra religion than as part of the war effort; after a while she made herself go back to the hospital, and eventually she found Higher Mathematics. She bought textbooks, studied in bed at dawn, and went every night to evening classes given by a frock-coated seer who spoke about calculus as though it were a way of life. "The language of Newton!" he cried, scribbling figures on the blackboard and immediately wiping them off with a damp rag as though he were doing vanishing tricks. "O Newton!" He was the only living person whom she had ever heard using the vocative case. He talked as though he had learned Latin constructions before English. "To read the language by which Galileo explored the harmony of the celestial system; To look backward to the time when first the morning

F

stars sang together!" He treated the mad redhead as though she were a fellow spirit, and she responded, until the moment when she finally admitted she was incapable of understanding a word he was saying. After two months she loosened her grasp on the subject like a drowning man giving himself up to the sea.

Slogging away at the military hospital, sickened by the pain she saw and more muddled than ever, she decided that when the war was over she would become a tramp. She thought of it first when she spent her two nights on the Embankment, which was littered as soon as dark fell with sad, wild men and women stuffing bread into their mouths out of brown paper bags or staring at the barges on the river. She was attracted by the rigor of the life, which she always linked with virtue, and she liked its sexual freedom. One woman derelict told her that after living with three husbands for twenty-five years she had decided to give them up and devote herself to the task of viewing the cathedrals and abbeys of the British Isles. This woman also had a passion to visit Russia, and she seemed to look on herself as a sort of tramp reformer. Besides being keen on Bolshevism she was deeply religious and a great admirer of the Court of St. James. She told Harriet that she often met King Edward VII in her dreams, and looked on him as a sort of uncle.

At the end of the war the Buckinghams decided that something had to be done; not Mrs. Buckingham, who was still repining, but Harriet's vast web of paternal relations. At Christmas her Uncle Bertie assembled the clan at his manor house in Wiltshire and announced that as a start she had better be presented at Court.

"But I don't want to be," she said.

Girls didn't speak like that then.

"Nonsense," he said breezily. "Fun for you. Get you out of yourself for a bit. Put some roses in your cheeks." And he bore down on her and pinched them, smelling of horse sweat and sherry. "Agnes will see to it, won't you?"

His wife stopped eating marrons glacés and nodded grimly.

"It's a waste of money," said Harriet, looking out of the window at the parkland, which seemed lush enough to feed the whole of the East End of London until the next war. She remembered going to harangue working women in the East End when she was in the Suffragettes: their pale, pinched dulled faces, dulled with years of lost endeavor. She had told them that once women got the vote everything would be all right: "Poverty will be swept away! Washing will be done by municipal machinery!" Not that she knew anything about washing; at home she had never been aware of it; but it seemed to her that the women in the East End never got away from it. Everlasting wet linen in the kitchen, smells of flatirons and scorching, burns on their knuckles and puffy skin up to their elbows.

Bertie was furious. His performance of the lecherous uncle collapsed. His glass eye—he had lost the original when he was cleaning a gun—seemed to swivel further out of true than usual and stared pleasantly at the fire; the real one looked like a razor.

"Waste of money! Question of yield, my girl. £1,000 for a season and we might get you married off. No £1,000 and your mother might find herself supporting you all her life. How much do you think you cost in a year? Eh? Add it up. Add it up." The married women in the room looked righteous as though they had made the unselfish decision. Harriet's Aunt Gertrude, a nervy spinster who lived with Uncle Bertie's household, sat as still as possible.

When they got back to London Harriet packed and left forever. The fact that she had no money of her own didn't strike her as an obstacle; the Suffragettes had reinforced her natural contempt for people who worried about money. One of her few friends in the movement, whom she used to meet at Lockharts in the Strand for a poached egg once a week, had come down from a mill town in Lancashire in 1916 with nothing but two brown paper parcels. (The smaller was her private luggage; the larger, which she called her public luggage, was full of pamphlets.) Harriet got a job as a dentist's receptionist and lived on lentils and poached eggs in a hostel until the dentist asked her to marry him. To her surprise, she said yes.

She was surprised, because she had thought that she had a vocation not to marry. Her heroines were Queen Elizabeth and Mary Wollstonecraft and Edith Cavell and, when she was miserable, Mary and Martha, the maiden ladies of Bethany. Queen Victoria, whom she made perpetual coarse jokes about in a way that struck people as uncalled for, had put her off marriage, in the same way that she had put her off Scotland. But the dentist supplied her with a religion for a while, the religion of giving up everything for someone else. As she saw it, this meant becoming as drab and acquiescent as possible, and until her temper and gaiety erupted again it worked.

They lived in a depressing house in Finchley. She cooked abominably, boiled meat and blancmanges. After the birth of her second child, during the Depression, she began to dream violently of hell and her father and the Book of Revelation. The Queen Victoria jokes got more ferocious and they upset the dentist a good deal. There was one terrible day when she came into his surgery and found him sitting beside the gramophone playing "Soldiers of the Queen" with tears pouring down his face. She launched into a long mocking invention about patriotism and monarchists and the Army, inspiring herself with hatred and feeling pleasurably like a pianist going into cadenza. Afterward she repented it bitterly, but she was hopeless at apologizing; instead of retracting her feelings, what she always did was to say that she was sorry for expressing them, a kind of amends that costs nothing and carries the built-in rebuke that the other person is unable to bear the truth.

The fanatic voice of Revelation built up in her head like the air in a pressure chamber. "Nevertheless I have somewhat against thee, *because thou hast left thy first love.*" She went over the final quarrel with her father again and again, and left her present loves to fend for themselves. She brought up her children in her sleep; her husband, who was a silent, kindly man, did a lot of the work. In the front room she started to hold prayer meetings that were almost like seances. Presently she found that she had the gift of tongues: notions of sacrifice and immolation and a saviour with hair of sackcloth poured out of her mouth like a river of lava.

When the war began her husband was too old to be called up. He became an Air Raid Warden and they kept allotments. She made rather touching things for the children called mock devil's-food-cakes, concocted out of cocoa, golden syrup, carrots and soya flour. Her back by now was giving her constant pain. She looked more odd than ever, and her movements were beginning to stiffen. She smoked cheap cigars, and the ash lay on her cardigans like catkins. On her fortieth birthday, in 1943, she was taken to hospital for a cancer operation and no one expected her to live. When she found she had survived she felt like Lazarus. She noticed that everyone was slightly embarrassed by her; she reminded them too much of the death around them, and they put on brutish cheerful voices with her. She felt, as so often, fraudulent, a corpse stuck together with glue.

In 1944, when she was out shopping, a flying bomb killed her elder child. It fell on a crowded school, and when she ran to the site from the High Street she could see some bodies still moving. The youngest children had been out in the playground; some of them survived. She found one little girl of about four under a pile of masonry. The child was on her back, unconscious. Just before she died she began to bicycle furiously with her legs, like a bee not quite crushed under a knife. Harriet carried the memory around with her as an image of horror, like the sickness in her own body.

After the war it became clear to her that the one heroic thing she was even faintly equipped to do with her life was to teach herself to die honorably, by which she meant without fear. This meant grappling with a panic that was like asphyxiation. Her wisps of belief in an after-life had gone irrevocably with the flying bomb. "It is not death that is frightening, but the knowledge of death"; she started from this. After cooking her watery stew one night and seeing her younger daughter into bed she went to the public library and looked up "Death" in a concordance. She brought home piles of books every week: Seneca and the Stoics and *Measure for Measure* and the Jacobeans. Her husband watched her reading and finally lost touch with her. The daughter fidgeted through her long wild monologues and wished she wore prettier clothes. People said that she had become nicer, quieter, but harder to get at than ever, if you knew what they meant.

"I've got to go up to Harriet's tonight."

"Oh God, she's so unrewarding."

"You feel you have to, she might be gone next week."

"I thought they got it out."

"You never know, do you."

"But she's as tough as old boots."

"I can't bear her really, but I feel sorry for her husband."

"How can people make such a *mess* of themselves."

She is still alive. When she dies I think she is going to be much more frightened than she expects. It is an absurd ideal really: a huge carcass inhabited by a blundering speck of dust and hoping to die as well as Nelson.

I put this down only because I have heard her daughter's friends call her "mannish," and her own generation "monstrous," which is true perhaps, but not quite the point.

Edward Franklin

Girl in a White Dress

With the car safely parked beneath a broken street lamp, he walks west on Taraval Street, downhill against the wind. Ahead stands the liquor store. The owner is in his usual place guarding the scotch. He reads a newspaper spread flat on the counter.

"Pong!" goes the alarm as the light beam is broken. Quick now, before he looks up, full ahead toward the ninety-eight cent Liebfraumilch, fake left, then right oblique. Like a dirt farmer, he squats before the magazine rack to consider, first, the newcomers, then the standbys. He wears a uniform for this, dark slacks, checkered shirt, black tie, tweed coat. And sunglasses. The coat belongs to his brother-in-law Malcolm, way too big for him, affording room in which to hide.

Time's up, choose something, no, not that, this. No. Never see anyone buying one of these magazines yet they sell and sell and some sex fiend has taken the last copy of *Femme Spice*. He stands up with empty hands and frowns at the collection, frowns to reflect indecision should anyone be watching. As if he might suddenly dart right and seize a copy of *Real Love*. Fat chance.

"Pong!" A pregnant woman comes into the store. Caught in his awkward stance, one foot pointing the escape route, he chooses what he knows is an unlikely book, replaces it, and takes a second magazine without even looking. The woman has him trapped, scuffing closer in her beaded moccasins, the bottom flaps of her coat spanning the full width of the aisle. He faces her, the magazine proffered in his loose grasp. Here, slap it out of my wormy fingers. This is worse than sin.

Above the collar of her coat her hair is a sea of tight pin curls that he knows will be loosened and combed out for someone else. But on this fluorescent-lit night before the man who sells these magazines and the disgusting boy who buys them, she parades uncaring. Coming to a halt she stoops down, selects a bottle of Liebfraumilch and straightens with a dutiful groan. She glances at his magazine, takes a moment to study her own reflection in his glasses, then, with a gentle smile, turns away.

What was that, forgiving or accusing? He must know. He takes a step toward her but stops when she gives a checking glance. Mustn't scare her, remain in place until she leaves then go bounding after her, pounce, and drag her to the playground across the street. Sacred Parkside motherhood sent down the slide backward and wrong side up into the tanbark chips at the bottom to be followed by her dark-glassed lover. But what's this?

In his hands is *Mister He-Man*, a magazine he's never seen before. Flipping it open he finds some familiar friends, one in the water with parts floating, one with levis unbuttoned four inches below the navel, one crawling over the back of the sofa with thirty feet of curtain draped over and around. Not really friends, not with those faces, some cruel, some vacant, some accusing. Accusing me! a nice, clean-cut person. Everybody says so.

The pages fall open to another photo and he bends close in disbelief. A girl with long dark hair sits on a couch in someone's apartment wearing a white dress. The dress is undone and pushed down at the top, pulled up from the bottom. "Gaye Karr," he reads aloud, "rhymes with star."

"Pong!" the pregnant woman leaving, but he doesn't look up.

"Really, Jeffy, couldn't you find something besides Malcolm's coat to wear?"

"Hero worship. Though he's gone his smell stays on and on," but Mother has already turned away, back to concentrating on the gin game with Daddy. Raising only an eyebrow from the game, Daddy says, "Now now."

"All right," he says while sitting on the edge of the sofa, paying his guilty respects before rushing upstairs with the prize. The prize is flat against his stomach, inside the waistband of his slacks, held fast by the alligator belt cinched in an extra notch. "I suppose it's just that Malcolm took Janey away from us. To a honeymoon at Hoberg's no less. Completely ruined our foursome for bridge."

"We could still play if you'd be a good sport about it," says mother, looking at her cards.

"Don't wanna."

She looks up. "What are you doing, sitting there? Why don't you go pour yourself a drink?"

"No, thank you."

"Pour your Mother one at the same time." She finishes the last of her bourbon, spits an ice cube back and hands him the glass.

"Dad?"

"I'm fine."

Yes you are, Sir, newly promotionalized, tranquilized, with one son donated to the war, and another talented in trampoline and subterfuge. But tell me, Dad, what about Gaye Karr. Why does her cleavage travel on and on?

"Jeffy, are you listening? Not too much water in that."

"Yes, I know," weak kidneys and all, but how can it, huh? How can it do that, just run on and on so? In the kitchen he finds out, belt apart, zipper down. Gaye, Gaye, forty-three.

"Thank you, Sweetheart."

"You're welcome. Going to bed now."

"So soon?" glancing up from her cards. "Early class tomorrow, Dear?"

"Yes."

"Oh too bad. Come and give your Mother a smooch first."

"Yes, Ma'am."

"And tie your laundry and leave it near the door. Annie doesn't look very hard for it, you know."

"Yes'm." You I love for your weak kidneys and because you spit all the time. I do. But Gaye, Gaye I love for her face, just her face, staring right into the camera with a hint of a wise smile, a slighter hint of intelligence. Yes, intelligence lurking behind those dark eyes but no accusation, not Gaye. Yes, says her expression, I know you are all out there, my vast audience, but feel free, I do not condemn you. And I? I only do this for philanthropic reasons.

"Jeffy, did you hear?"

"No, I . . . "

"I said, sleep well . . ."

"Oh I will. I will."

Miss Gaye Karr
C/o Z. Speed
Box NZ 189783
North Hollywood

Dear Miss Karr:

Well! I just finished reading my April copy of Mister He-Man *and I must say, Miss Karr, that you are the loveliest and most talented girl in the entire periodical. And what a generous thing for the people at* Mister He-Man *to do, running an article entitled, "Bounty of bountiful beasts breathless for correspondence from cute, cuddlesome, He-Cats," and then going right ahead and listing the personal addresses of all you ravishing girls. Well!*

I know the busy life you models and show-business girls lead but should you have just one free minute, just one, Miss Karr, I would appreciate hearing from you. You absolutely must tell me all about yourself, like whether you might have any

*additional snapshots of yourself lying around that you would
care to send me. I would be heartily grateful, I assure you.*

*If you do write, Miss Karr, I wonder if you would please
do me a great big favor—here we are, barely acquainted and
I'm already asking favors, isn't that something?—anyhow, it's
rather a silly problem but I think you'll understand. The wife
of my landlord is terribly infatuated with me. Now mind you,
I give her no cause for this emotion and besides, she's quite old
and keeps me awake all night running to the bathroom. This
woman is extremely jealous and has been known to tear up any
mail I may receive from unrelated ladies, so if you could just
refrain from placing your name on the outside of the envelope
it would be nicely appreciated.*

*Well! Here I am talking about how you should do your
envelope and you might not even write to me. But I hope you
do. Again, I certainly enjoyed to the fullest your place in* Mister
He-Man *and hope you will allow me to list you among my very
close friends. Do take care.*

Sincerely yours,
Jeffrey Sutton

Malcolm takes his cigarette out of his mouth, stares pointedly at his
wife, and says, "Janey, remind me to pick up that old sportcoat of mine
when we leave. Keep forgetting the darn thing."

Janey merely turns to Jeff and smiles but Mother speaks up with
irritation.

"Yes, Malcolm, please take that thing out of my house, won't you?"

"Sweetie, consider it done."

Jeff is pleased to see Malcolm rate an eyebrow from Daddy who is
pouring cocktails. No speech. Come, you must have something to say even
though Malcolm looks as if he's going to end up being more successful and
more tranquilized than you are.

"Jeffy," says Mother, "you're fidgety, can't you stop it?"

"Worried about having that coat torn off his back," says Malcolm.

"Not very."

"Har."

Stepping up with the tray, Daddy says, "Well, do you think you're all
old enough for Manhattans?"

Jeff hunches his shoulders, pulls the coat tighter about his neck, slides
his right hand toward the inside pocket and touches a corner of the envelope
then quickly retracts it in time to take a glass from the tray.

Dear Mr. Sutton:

*Gosh, Jeff (hope you don't mind me calling you Jeff cause
I want us to become real good friends). I was thrilled with your
letter. Honestly. You sure were right about us showbiz girls*

being busy, but never too busy to write a friend and send along some pics. I hope you'll excuse these, Jeff, kind of unpro, if you know what I mean. My roommate, Ruby, snapped them of me doing ordinary things around the house. Sure don't want to shock you but my roommate (she's a rascal) really caught me in some indiscreet poses.

Would love to send you scads more but you can't imagine the cost, Honey, specially the studio poses (which show just about everything I have) which are going for about $1.99 per 3 x 5 glossy. I sure hope you'll want some 'cause I can't think of anyone sweeter I'd rather pose for, and Jeff, please write again real soon and tell me about yourself and how you want me to pose 'cause I'll do anything for you. Honestly.

Love 'n' stuff,
Gaye

P.S. Forgot something, Sweets, send a money order for the pics. No checks. Remember, $1.99 per.

In one picture Gaye bends over the stove wearing only high heels and a gossamer cocktail apron. Hey everybody, I got to see Gaye's heinie.

"That's absurd," says Daddy.

And a nipple in the other one, I think.

"No!" says Malcolm, "no, I don't think so. Not really."

Or else a flyspeck on the camera lens.

"Nonsense."

"No, we'll be forced into recognizing China eventually, why not do it now? Positive move and all that."

"But Malcolm," says Mother, "think of those poor Tibetans."

Can't tell, medium-distance shot. Ruby must have been hanging from the moulding or else they have a camera crane in their living room. Anyhow, ten feet below Gaye stares wistfully through the curtains. On her white panties is stitched, "Sunday."

"Shall we play one rubber before dinner or wait 'til after?" says Mother.

"Wait 'til after."

"Now Jeffy, you don't count."

"We'd best eat first," says Malcolm, "or else he'll just stand there and breathe in my ear."

"I'll run and get things started. And remember, you two, you're coming down for Memorial Day weekend."

"Oh Mother, that's a whole month away," says Janey, "a lot can happen in a month, you know."

Yes, like two more incoming letters if I'm prompt with the money orders.

F*

"How was it today, Sweetheart?"

"Same. Any mail for me?"

"Another one of those strange little letters for you. Strange, thick little letter for my strange little son. That's right, run off, go to the bathroom and read your strange little letter . . . son."

> *P.S. Well, Honey, this is it. What I mean is, guess which person you know is about to make their San Francisco debut at the Del Mar Theatre in Oakland? I can hardly believe it. Imagine, appearing in Mr. Sutton's home town!!! I'll be there Sat. before Labor Day. Let me hear from you. Please.*
>
> *P.P.S. Ask for Adrienne Steinberg.*

And then, at the very bottom of the furry skinned page, a curious line printed in hastily built letters.

> *You're real first string. Luck.*

"This is Adrienne Steinberg."

"Hi. I really wanted to speak with Miss Gaye Karr. You can tell her it's Mr. Sutton . . . Jeffy."

"Oh yes, Zack warned me about you."

"Zack? Warned?"

"Zack Speed, my agent. Gaye Karr is my stage name."

Z. Speed. Good-by. "You have a very nice voice, Miss Karr." Silence. "I suppose you've been told that before."

"Yeah."

"Well . . . I hope you enjoy your stay in Oakland." Hey, I can hear a bass drum. That's something, at least.

"Zack said to be nice to you. Why?"

"He did? I mean, that's great. He's a nice man." A real first-stringer. Silence. "Well gee, he's right because I am nice. Honestly. Know what I do every morning on my way to . . . downtown? I take this piece of bacon, see, that I've saved from . . . you don't have to go on any minute, do you?"

"I have ten minutes."

"I don't want to wreck your coffee break."

"You aren't."

"I mean, I know how little time you get between . . . are you there? Hello, Gaye, are you there? Gaye?"

"I'm here."

"I thought we'd been disconnected. No, what I really thought was you'd gotten sick of all this talk and hung up. Was that close to right? Well I'll hurry up and get off the phone so you can get a little rest before . . . you aren't chilly standing there, are you?" The drum goes on and on and maybe that other sound is her steady breathing. Her breathing. Gaye, I looked at your heinie and I'm sorry. I'm so sorry I could die. "I guess you're wondering if I'm ever going to finish my shaggy dog story. Well, you know, actually there is a dog in this story. He's in this bare yard and nobody ever plays with him . . ." and finally, his voice cracked and dying at the end of a breath, "Gaye. Gaye, can I see you?"

Incognito, he stands on San Pablo Avenue staring through a blue tinted window. In the center of the window is a diamond of clear glass. Gold letters in biblical scroll spell the word, "Beer." On the other side of the glass sit two dark-haired girls in trenchcoats. One of them is Gaye Karr. He isn't sure which.

"This is Candy Matther. A co-worker."

Oh. A curt nod for her because people are watching closely from the bar. Scowl for them, let them see their miserable faces in the glasses. There. Now sit down. "Well." Wary little animals. Can't blame them. But all she sees in my glasses is her own pale face, tired in the eyes, almost innocent. Too much makeup. All that goo . . . kiss me. "The service here is sensational, isn't it?" That's right, don't answer, you desirable creature, just drink your coffee and stare over the rim at San Pablo Avenue. See, Candy has a wristwatch under the sleeve of her trenchcoat. She brings it into sight and shows it to Gaye. They both nod. Two minutes to zero. "How's the show going?" Candy shrugs, but wait, she's opening her mouth for speech.

"The crowd hasn't been too good today. It's the same situation all up and down the coast, wouldn't you say, Adrienne?"

"This is an improvement over Spokane."

"We've just come from Spokane."

"Hence the raincoats."

Cut, cut. "Tell me, Gaye . . . Adrienne, are you going to be here long?"

"What did Mr. Henry say, two weeks?"

"One, I think. It's that bad, you know."

"I know, I just thought he said two."

"No, one."

Cut, for Christ sake. Should have brought Malcolm along and we could all discuss Red China. Tapes running out and the two girls sitting at my table just exchanged another glance. They resisted a nod. "Let me get you both some more coffee."

"No thanks, I've got to run back," says Candy.

And Gaye? Gaye is definitely staying. Wait a minute, do I look that safe?

"I'm glad to have met you, Jeff."

"So long." Good-by, you look awfully promising, voluble too, but good-by. Sit down. "Tell me, is Mr. Zack Speed really a nice man?"

"Yes, I suppose he is."

"That's good to know," since I've written him several intimate letters since April. Her hands go to hold her face. "Are you tired?"

"A little."

"One more show to do?"

"Yes."

"May I drive you home afterward?"

"I'm staying only one block away."

"I still want to drive you home. May I?"

"No. I don't think so."

"Oh." Zero. "I'll walk you back to the theatre." At least I can see what you look like standing up. Can't see your heinie though. "It's this way, isn't it." She has a nice walk. "Hey, is the reason you won't see me because you think I'm too young? Look. Look at me without my glasses. I'm old, I really am. I'm an old guy."

She laughs. "No you're not. I'm glad you took those things off though."

"I'm ancient. Maybe it all doesn't exactly show but I'm not nice, Gaye. I'm not nice at all."

"Who said you were?"

"Everybody. Everybody is always saying I'm such a nice, clean-cut boy. I'm not. I swear I'm not. Now will you see me?"

"No. I only go out with nice boys."

"You're kidding me, I know, but how about tomorrow? Can you come to my house for Sunday dinner? Malcolm will be there, and Janey, and of course Mother and Daddy and it'll be . . . Gaye, what's wrong?"

"Now you're kidding me."

"What, about tomorrow? No, it'll be absolutely stupendous. It'll be a wonderful family afternoon and we'll talk about Red China and we'll watch Malcolm play bridge. Say you'll come."

"You're not kidding?" She stops walking. "Of course I'll have to do the matinee first. I can skip the evening show though, if you really . . ."

"And I'll take you home tonight." Got Daddy's Buick. "We'll drive around awhile." Got his credit card too. "Show you the Oakland Estuary, or something."

"Jeffy, you really shouldn't."

If only there was somebody to see me. Turn on the light. And look, no glasses, not even Malcolm's coat.

"Don't."

"Gaye Gaye Gaye."

"What is it?"

"Don't you like the view?"

"All I can see is a warehouse and a bunch of boxcars."

"Yeah, I know, didn't I deceive you? Here, give me your hand. No, this one, and tell me I'm not a nice boy."

"Well you're not. What are you giggling about?"

"I'm so happy."

"Jeffy, just what is the matter with you?"

"Tired."

"Hungover, if anyone was to ask your Mother."

"And I wish you wouldn't lie on the floor, Buddy. My coat, you know."

"Jeffy, sit up."

Yes, Daddy. He sits up on the floor, his back against the sofa. Through half-closed eyes he watches the bridge players.

Mother says, "Malcolm and I are up one. Let's play another and Jeffy'll fix a round of drinks."

"Isn't dinner rather late?" asks Daddy.

"Darling, I told you."

"Yes, but is he sure the young lady is definitely coming?"

"Jeffy, Dear. Jeffy, wake up please and listen to your Mother. What time do you expect your lady friend?"

"Any second now. Play more bridge."

"You're absolutely sure she's coming?"

"Certainly." Oh please, Miss Gaye, you promised. Just like I promised. Promised a lot of things, promised to show you the Oakland Estuary. Lied.

"Hey, Tiger," says Malcolm, tipping back in his chair, "better check outside."

"Why?"

"Malcolm's right," says Janey, "there's a taxi stopped out there."

"Here," says Daddy, "don't let the girl pay her own fare."

Magic, ten dollars out of Daddy's tweed coat.

"Here, take this."

"I don't need it. See? Magic money waiting in Malcolm's pocket."

"Better hurry."

"Yes, Dear, don't keep the nice girl waiting."

Gaye is still counting out money for the driver. "Hello, Jeffy, I'm sorry I'm so late."

He stops at the door of the cab, staring at her. The driver, in turn, is staring at the forgotten sheaf of bills in Jeff's hand. Gaye finishes counting. "Gaye, how could you. How could you possibly do this to me?"

"Jeffy, what's wrong."

"Everything. Your . . . your hair."

"That's what took so long." She steps out of the taxi and he slams the door. The forgotten money flutters to the ground, a few bills lodging in the pyracantha bush. Gaye kneels down to help him. The taxi leaves.

"That dress. It's white, isn't it."

"Yes, it took me half an hour to decide. Is it really all right?"

No, it's awful. Big bow, frills down the front, full skirt. Hair in a pony tail. And no makeup. "You look so . . . so nice."

"Oh, I'm glad. I worried so about this dress."

"Ouch."

"Careful, Jeffy, this stuff has thorns."

"Yes, I know it does."

"Why are you sitting down on the lawn? Are you badly hurt?"

"Yes," he says, squeezing his finger.

"Jeffy, I'm sorry. Is there anything I can do?"

"No." He sits there holding his finger, staring into the gutter.

"Shouldn't we be going in? I feel bad keeping your parents waiting so long."

"They're occupied with their carding."

"I love cards. We play a lot, you know, when we travel."

"You play bridge, I suppose. Yes, I see you do. Never mind. I'm awfully tired, would you be so kind as to give me a hand up? Thank you, now we can go in and meet Mother and Daddy and Malcolm and Janey."

"But Gaye . . . Adrienne, burlesque! Burlesque is so fascinating. How do you stand the excitement? Oh God, I've always wanted to be a burlesque dancer. I would have been good, I'm positive."

"Dear, I'm sure Gaye is a good one."

"Oh I'm sure she is, I was just saying . . ."

"It's a dying art, I understand," says Malcolm, blowing cigar smoke over Gaye's bowed head. She is the last one eating, finishing her cake. She smiles for him. "Not that it should be. Dying, I mean. Of course I haven't seen one since . . . since my bachelor party. Hey Janey, you didn't know that's where we went, did you?"

"Thought you all went to Cinerama."

"Har."

Hey everybody, funny thing happened to me last night, saw Gave's heinie. But that won't move them. She could have worn her makeup, her upsweep, her lowcut, it all would have been completely absorbed here.

"Are you through, Gaye dear?"

"Yes, it was a lovely dinner, Mrs. Sutton."

"Can't go wrong with roast chicken. Now why don't we all move to more comfortable chairs. We'll have coffee in the living room. Do you play cards, Gaye?"

"Jeffy, I think they're holding up the game for me."

"Just want to show you my room. Actually belongs to my brother and me but he's away on a business trip. That's his desk. Got it for his fifteenth birthday. Here, let me close the door."

"I don't know that you should."

"There's my bed, as you can see."

"Yes."

"See that hat with the feather? On the dresser? Got that at Y Camp years ago. Feather Merchants' Club. Neat, huh?"

"Yes, very."

"If you'd be more comfortable with your dress off, or anything, just go ahead." Not very horrified, just surprised, now watchful. "Oh you're too much, Gaye, can't hide all that stuff in a little girl's dress. Come here."

"No, Jeffy, we shouldn't. Not now."

"I just want to ask you something. Come closer. There. Now tell me what happened last night in the car. I can't remember a thing today."

"Please don't feel bad about anything . . . stop that! Jeffy, you're ruining everything. Please take your hands away and we'll go join your folks. Jeff, did you hear me?" And then she smiles up at him, presses his hand harder against her breast, and says, "Later, Darling."

"Later."

"Later. Now let's go join the others. And you might be a little nicer to your Mother. I couldn't help but notice during dinner . . ."

"Well, here you are, you two. We're all set up for you, Gaye. Sit over there, Malcolm insists on having you as his partner. Janey, why don't you run and bring the coffee."

"I'll get it, Mother."

"Why Jeffy, how nice. Don't forget the cream. It's in the refrigerator in the door. The sugar's on the sideboard."

Norma Meacock

Changed

The minute I woke on the far side of the bed on the day I left, I snapped: "Are you going?" and I looked and thought how beautiful, how pink and blowsy and warm from bed in a green cotton calyx. Perhaps the walls were yellow as lemons. And the curtains. I think they were yellow.

I'd bought her a salmon-pink dress for the mayor's ball and paid by check. I've still got the counterfoil and other mementos: twelve red roses, scrolls of paper—little love-messages—and letters, letters. Not all from Girly, of course.

She said: "Yes, I'm going," in a prim, chill mode, without turning. I knew if I kept on at her, if I taunted and jeered, if I gnaw-gnawed in stealthy, monotonous, rat-like persistence, she'd have hysterics, scream, tug her hair and be quite beyond my control. I wouldn't be able to do anything with her. So I was silent (but not for long enough). I didn't say: Why don't you try taking an interest in somebody besides yourself?

Just because you feel guilty about your mother you needn't make *my* life a misery.

You wouldn't have treated me like this in the beginning; you loved me then.

You don't seem to realize how much your behavior has changed.

You've been deceiving me for the past three years.

Why did I believe your promises?

You're sham inside.

Outside as well.

I wish we'd never met; I curse that day.

You told me you loved me, and all the time you were thinking of men.

What a conventional sort of person you are at bottom.

You're not as intelligent as you once appeared.

Haven't you any human sympathy?

I really think you ought to see a psychiatrist.

I kept very still, but words burst. "You know what this means," I said. "Poldy," she besought. "What time will you get back?" I screeched. "Two at the earliest. And then? He's bound to see you home. How am I expected to feel, upstairs, in the bedroom, listening? Or perhaps you want the bed. Perhaps I'm to sit in the garden watching the light. The situation's impossible. I'm going." I sat up. "Poldy," she wailed. "You might have chosen someone intelligent," I said, "instead of turning me out for a shop assistant. One day you'll know what it feels like when he gives you the push. By the time he's thirty you'll be nearly forty, and past it, don't forget." I slumped down and tugged the blankets. "I'll be gone," I vowed, "forever. You can keep my books." I withdrew, a crescent hump.

I was heartbroken. I wanted to stay. And in the afternoon I went. I piled coal on the fire. She sponged herself over a tin basin. Heat reticulated her thighs, as she knelt, till they looked like the skin of a foetal giraffe. "Help me," she said. "Can't you see I'm burning?" So I moved the soaked newspaper, the sponge, the washbowl; she shuffled after them. "I'll never be ready," she said. "I'm meeting him at five. We'll have dinner in town, then go on to the dance." "I'm not interested," I said. "Remember what you promised three years ago." "Don't start again, please," she said.

She didn't flinch; she told me: "You've just got to face up to it, Poldy. I love you, and I'll always love you best in the world. But I need experience. My body's asleep and you can't rouse it. Your touch is not enough, some-how, or it's bizarre, somehow: it's the burn of ice."

She stood upright, dropped the towel. Her belly billowed like pink silk. She stooped and gripped the bowl by the rim. I carried it away without a word; my eyes smarted. The gray suds spun, then rose, then sank, then rose in a pustule, festered, burst, whirled and were gone.

"I'm just a phase in your development, you mean," I shouted. "I lose all patience with you when you sum things up," she said. "That silly remark has nothing to do with me and my love. You've got to admit new elements into our relation. It would happen to any couple, however viable they were in the beginning. It's not enough for me, this isn't, what we've had. I don't want to lose it, but I must have more. I've only got one life to live. Our partnership was free and loving. You don't want me to turn into a stunted nagger."

"What about the animals," I said, "and symbiosis? They batten on each other. I want to be a master. I want a slave. Life must satisfy my deepest want. It's got to. What else can?" "There you are," she said, "our aim's the same but our wants are incompatible. And I'm off to the mayor's ball, tra la la." She pulled on a stocking and left it rolled in a bangle under her knee. "Get my corset," she said, "there's a love; I think it's in the second drawer down." I muttered: "You ought to ask your fancy-man," and fetched it. It girdled her thighs snugly, this cummerbund embossed with silver flowers. "Yank it up behind," she commanded. "But it makes you look like an armadillo," I said. " 'The splendor falls, or should fall.' " I raised her buttocks and let them drop; they wobbled. She moved a pace. "What do you think I am," she said, "an animal?" "We're all animals," I intoned placidly. "You're always doing this," she said. "I'm just an object to you, a thing: not a person at all. It's the alienation Marx talks about. You're an adept at it." "Don't be bloody daft," I said. She raised her voice: "You want me as an ornament to fondle and drool over. It fits in with your need to dominate." "It would," I said. She stooped, caught her breasts in her bra cups and hooked herself up high. "They say woman ought to walk on all fours," I told her. "Because she's got a straight birth-canal. I mean, you'd expect it to be curved in a biped, biologically speaking." She didn't believe me. "That's what they say," I told her. She powdered her fat, white back.

"What about Doris?" she said. "You swore you loved her passionately one Thursday evening after work as you walked along High Street. You helped her do a bit of shopping. 'O, let me carry the potatoes, please.' Under the street lamps leaves trembled like chandeliers. I can picture it all. You approached her doorstep. Doris petite, head bowed, dainty ankles, to vanish in an instant for another week—a week! You stumbled. 'Doris,' you besought. 'I must tell you; I love you. Forgive me.' And you sheered off, elated, hot with embarrassment, back home to give Muggins all the details."

"Big Mouth," I protested. "It was different. You know I don't love anyone else. And I'm a fool. I'm not like you. Perhaps it's vanity; I don't intend any harm. I just seem to end up in a position where only one thing is required. I'm seduced all the time." "We are what we do, you know," she said. "And more besides," I pleaded, "or it's a very hard doctrine." I begged her not to go out. "Let's try again. How can we part? You're my memory, my past." Irritation cross-hatched her brow. "It's clear you don't understand me and the pressures on me," she said. I shut up and sat wiping my eye quietly in an armchair to the right of the fire. She moved from place to place, troubled, picking up clothes and baubles, hiding dirty underwear behind cushions. Humdrum and familiar. Impossible to go. This was life, wasn't it, my own, my only? And we'd reached the point of parting. Out of the question. Step back a bit; I smelt the cold. We weren't here yesterday. The rift in our lute had widened into an abyss. But you can't have an abyss in a lute. Go back. Go back. Perhaps shock saved me. Always. For a fool is a fool. And my cupboards howl with lute-strings. The anomaly saves me. As in "I die." Unbelievable. Oxymoron. Yesterday I ran down the stairs onto the platform, swung through an entrance and shouted "Wheeee!" for gaiety, for warmth, and the people there and running. Then it dropped like snapped elastic. Knickers tumbling down. Change of world. Same event under different conditions. We are what is done to us.

As she fastened her stockings she reflected: "It's been coming a long time now, but I don't want to part. Let's take it in our stride. Let's meet everything together and see it through together." I sniffed. "Silly optimism." She snapped her compact shut, the first present I'd ever given her, pearly swans riding a wave. She stepped into the salmon dress. "You don't dress up for me, any more," I carped. She smacked her lips together, spreading the lipstick. "It's a month since you touched me," she said, "and then you only poked around outside." "How crude you are," I said. "You hope to hurt me by debasing our love-language. There's a tough streak of sadism in you, Girly. You push me away so much it's like a wound. You know I'm delicately poised. I walk an androgynous knife-edge." My voice quivered. I hesitated. "It's not easy," I said. "I'm wide open to rebuff." "I've always loved your vulnerability," she confessed. "I don't mean to put you off. Only, you're not enough any more." "So you keep telling me," I snapped. With a knife I could have split her lobster shell. She turned away. Tears pricked her eyes, perhaps. She gathered her coat, her bag, put on her shoes, pulled on gloves, glanced in the mirror and again, patted her hair, pouted her lips, wiped away a fallen eyelash, arrayed her fringe. Was she reluctant to go? I think her heart was sad, though she performed every customary act. She approached, kissed me. "Keep a good fire," she said, "and try to stay." Then she crossed the room, opened the door, crossed the hall, opened the house door, closed it with a little bang. I ran to the window. Her heels tip-tapped away. They receded slowly, but they receded. I moved aside the net curtain and peered through the slice. Three fences down the road her dark head swayed an instant and was gone. I dropped the net. Lips tight, eyes slit, I ran upstairs, pulled six Books of Thoughts (my own) from under the bed, ran downstairs, unhooked a carrier bag off the pantry door, picked up a little knife, a cup, a spoon, emptied half a pound of sugar and half a packet of tea into paper bags, and dropped them all in the carrier. I put on my coat and went.

The room was narrow, with a narrow bed and a squat window. Yellow bars trickled like lymph down the wallpaper. The air smelt of fog and gas. A rusty gas bracket projected out of one wall. I sat on the bed and stared at a gray washstand. I thought of gas. I sat there. My eyes wept and dried. I sat thinking of gas. I'd always had bouts of depression. This didn't resemble them at all. "Do it," I said, "at last, get rid, be shut. Everything's broken. This pain has no anodyne," I said aloud. "I wanted private joy, domestic bliss, and I haven't any fragments to shore against the ruins. But I wouldn't bother. She's not for me. I can't hold her, and I don't want what isn't freely given"—I repeated this declaration—"and couldn't have it if I did." The room darkened. I got up and turned the light on. Shadows slid out of corners and pressed flat against the walls beyond the gold globe of light. I touched them with my hand, then explored the wall as far as I could reach, rubbing cheek and breasts against it. Round and round I went. I snuffed damp plaster and sagging ovals of paper. The cold wall of this untenanted room licked my nipples, and I pulled my jumper up and squeezed them onto the lymph. It was solace of a kind. I sniffed at the gas bracket, made sure the tap was off, opened the window, and got into bed fully dressed for warmth.

And there, for a month, I stayed, eating little, sleeping scarcely at all. I accumulated nothing; my nest-building impulses withered away. At work I confided in Doris and felt no better. "I'm not surprised," she said. "I saw it coming: everybody saw it coming. You must be awfully miz. If you take my advice you'll go straight out and find yourself a nice, understanding man. These Lesbian affairs never work. One side always cracks in the end." Well-wishers beset me: "Why don't you see a psychiatrist?" "A woman's missing something if she doesn't have babies." "You'll never keep a partner for life." "But what exactly do you do, if you don't mind my asking?" "It's just a phase." "You're well out of it." "How old are you?" "Haven't you fancied a man, not for a minute, ever?" "It'll get you in the end; it's biological; women need more security than men—family life and so on." "Why kick against the pricks?" "You really ought to consult Doctor Blank; no strings attached; mention my name; he's a personal friend (and a pet)."

Etiology? Psychological beyond a doubt. I'll ask you a few questions. Was your childhood unhappy? Did your parents want a boy? Were you strongly attached to your mother? It isn't somatic at all. Prognosis? Good, where the patient co-operates. You've no intention of co-operating? You want to change your sex? Now listen, my dear, supposing I told you I want to be a woman? Haw-haw-haw. It's ridiculous. What's that? Clitoris rather big? Common enough. I've seen a perfectly normal female with a clitoris three inches long. You'll have to adjust, Dear, dear, me. He wiped his watering eyes. Would you like an examination? No, I'm sure you wouldn't. Run along now, and try not to worry. If you have any difficulties come and see me again. Just drop in. And we'll straighten them out. With a chat. Smiles.

Clematis, an invert from the provinces, on hearing the news, came tootling south in a clapped out Ford Prefect colored like a barge and inscribed Sappho of Lesbos. She sported a suit, a cravat, an Eton crop, a black eye. We toured the pubs. She slapped me on the back over pints of brown. "Cheer up, old man," she jollied. "You can't depend on women. They're not always loyal to a chap. Mind you, I think I've fallen on my feet at last. Nothing ersatz about Gloria. Tell you what, come up to Batley for a few days. I expect you could do with a break. If we leave in an hour . . . Look, old man, I insist. You'd be no trouble. The little woman'd love it. She's as hot as hell on the domestic side, cooking, cleaning, all that guff. Of course, she's sorry we can't have any kids just yet—she loves kids—but we're saving our pennies to get across to Sweden, and then we'll see. Any idea how long the operations take? She says she'll wait, "til the sands of time are run" (she thinks the world of me). We reckon about three years: then I'm hooked, and that's the way I like it. No, this one's on me. I don't give a damn who bought the last round. I'm drawing a good salary. Gloria gets fifteen quid a week—two steady incomes, and by God we've feathered our nests: you'll see for yourself. And then there's Sappho; she costs a packet. It's all expense, but we're able to meet it." "You'll have to excuse me, Clem, this time," I said. "I don't feel up to travelling." "Why ever not?" she said. "We'll go on a real orgy."

I left work, turned the corner, and there was Girly, waiting. "I'm so relieved," she said. "I was worried about you. Where are you living? You do look thin. Let's go and find a caff." "I'm not hungry," I whined. "I can't eat; I don't eat anything at all, just tea, without sugar. I feel very weak." The street lamps flickered on, then glowed huge bowls. "Here we are," she said, and pushed a door hung with fog-yellow net. Silence in the café as the door opened. One unified inquisitive soul. Then murmur again, and the café fell apart into private lots. An ungainly poster depicted Clacton. I sat on the nearest chair while she walked between rickety tables to the counter. I watched nothing. She returned with tea, cake, Woodbines, and gave me half (and slipped a fiver in the Woodbine packet). She wore a blue poplin mac with saddle-stitching faded almost to white and the cuffs frayed. The wide collar covered her shoulders very gently. I wondered whose hands had smoothed it at the back, and tears stung my eyes. So I wondered again, and tears coursed down my checks. "I can't help it," I blubbered. "Please don't let it affect you." I tried to swallow a lump of fruit-cake; it stuck in my throat like a cardboard box and I sprayed it across the table in a choking sob. She pressed her hand over mine. More tears, dripping onto my plate. "I can't live without you," I said. "You can see that. You'll have to come back. Or else I'll die. I've lost a stone already in one month." "Impossible," she said. "I mean, that I'll come back. He's more or less living with me now . . . as man and wife." "How smug you are," I sneered. "You sound like a silly woman who's got one up on somebody, as if there's a value in experience for its own sake." "Quantity turns into quality," she said. "Not yours," I said, "you fat, complacent cow." "Don't start," she said. "I haven't started anything," I said. "You started this," she said. "Who met me in the first place?" I said. "I didn't ask to come." "I'm going," she said, stood up and walked out. I ran after. "Girly," I pleaded, "stop a minute. I didn't mean it. This is my life. I've only got one. You're smashing it to bits." I had to run to keep up. "Wait just a minute," I panted. "Forgive me. I'm overwrought. Make allowances. I don't eat or sleep. You can see my condition. I'm bound to behave like an idiot. It's psychosomatic. Don't be tight-lipped," I begged. "This isn't a game. It's very real. It's me this is happening to, and you of course. You'll only regret it. When you get home," I warned, "you'll wish you'd turned and spoken. You'll wish you'd turned when you're wondering whether I'm alive—or dead. Or perhaps you'll be too busy with your *husband*." A bus pulled up. She jumped on it. I ran like hell. They were off. The conductor barred the platform with his arm. "Never," he pronounced, "attempt to board a moving vehicle. 'Nother behind." And there was. I didn't hail it. I shoved my hands in my pockets. I gripped the dust at the bottom. Ribbons of light streamed past my eyes, which were blinkered by interior dialogue. "I think you're about the most self-centred person I've ever come across," I told her. "Oh, I know I'm egoistic. I've plenty of self-confidence and self-esteem. Like Nietzsche I could stand up and say 'I'm right; the rest of the world is wrong.' But I'm not egocentric. Not like you. There's many a time I ask what you're thinking—and it's always about yourself, whenever I ask. You're totally absorbed with self. Now don't get huffy. There's no need to be ashamed of it. I'm describing, not prescribing, merely recording a state of affairs, what is."

William Trevor

A Meeting in Middle Age

"I am Mrs. da Tanka," said Mrs. da Tanka. "Are you Mr. Mileson?"

The man nodded, and they walked together the length of the platform, seeking a compartment that might offer them a welcome, or failing that, and they knew the more likely, simple privacy. They carried each a small suitcase, Mrs. da Tanka's of white leather or some material manufactured to resemble it, Mr. Mileson's battered and black. They did not speak as they marched purposefully: they were strangers one to another, and in the noise and the bustle, examining the lighted windows of the carriages, there was little that might constructively be said.

"A ninety-nine year's lease," Mr. Mileson's father had said, "taken out in 1862 by my grandfather, whom of course you never knew. Expiring in your lifetime, I fear. Yet you will by then be in a sound position to accept the misfortune. To renew what has come to an end; to keep the property in the family." The property was an expression that glorified. The house was small and useful, one of a row, one of a kind easily found; but the lease when the time came was not renewable—which released Mr. Mileson of a problem. Bachelor, childless, the end of the line, what use was a house to him for a further ninety-nine years?

Mrs. da Tanka sat opposite him, drew a magazine from an assortment she carried. Then, checking herself, said: "We could talk. Or do you prefer to conduct the business in silence?" She was a woman who filled, but did not overflow from a fair-sized, elegant, quite expensive tweed suit. Her hair, which was gray, did not appear so; it was tightly held to her head, a reddish gold color. Born into another class she would have been a chirpy woman; she guarded against her chirpiness, she disliked the quality in her. There was often laughter in her eyes, and as often as she felt it there she killed it by the severity of her manner.

"You must not feel embarrassment," Mrs. da Tanka said. "We are beyond the age of giving in to awkwardness in a situation. You surely agree?"

Mr. Mileson did not know. He did not know how or what he should feel. Analyzing his feelings he could come to no conclusion. He supposed he was excited but it was more difficult than it seemed to track down the emotions. He was unable, therefore, to answer Mrs. da Tanka. So he just smiled.

Mrs. da Tanka, who had once been Mrs. Horace Spire and was not likely to forget it, considered those days. It was a logical thing for her to do, for they were days that had come to an end as these present days were coming to an end. Termination was on her mind: to escape from Mrs. da Tanka into Mrs. Spire was a way of softening the worry that was with her now, and a way of seeing it in proportion to a lifetime.

"If that is what you want," Horace had said, "then by all means have it. Who shall do the dirty work—you or I?" This was his reply to her request for a divorce. In fact, at the time of speaking, the dirty work as he called it was already done: by both of them.

"It is a shock for me," Horace had continued. "I thought we could jangle along for many a day. Are you seriously involved elsewhere?"

In fact she was not, but finding herself involved at all reflected the inadequacy of her married life and revealed a vacuum that once had been love.

"We are better apart," she had said. "It is bad to get used to the habit of being together. We must take our chances while we may, while there is still time."

In the railway carriage she recalled the conversation with vividness, especially that last sentence, most especially the last five words of it. The chance she had taken was da Tanka, eight years ago. "My God," she said aloud, "what a pompous bastard he turned out to be."

Mr. Mileson had a couple of those weekly publications for which there is no accurate descriptive term in the language: a touch of a single color on the front-floppy, half-intellectual things, somewhere between a journal and a magazine. While she had her honest mags. *Harper's. Vogue.* Shiny and smart and rather silly. Or so thought Mr. Mileson. He had opened them at dentists' and doctors', leafed his way though the ridiculous advertisements and aptly titled model girls, unreal girls in unreal poses, devoid it seemed of sex, and half the time of life. So that was the kind of woman she was.

"Who?" said Mr. Mileson.

"Oh who else, good heavens! Da Tanka I mean."

Eight years of da Tanka's broad back, so fat it might have been padded beneath the skin. He had often presented it to her; he was that kind of man. Busy, he claimed; preoccupied.

"I shall be telling you about da Tanka," she said. "There are interesting facets to the man; though God knows, he is scarcely interesting in himself."

It was a worry, in any case, owning a house. Seeing to the roof; noticing the paint cracking on the outside, and thinking about damp in mysterious places. Better off he was, in the room in Swiss Cottage; cosier in winter. They'd pulled down the old house by now, with all the others in the road. Flats were there instead: bulking up into the sky, with a million or so windows. All the gardens were gone, all the gnomes and the Snow White dwarfs, all the winter bulbs and the little paths of crazy paving; the bird baths and bird-boxes and bird-tables; the miniature sandpits, and the metal edging, ornate, for flower-beds.

"We must move with the times," said Mrs. da Tanka, and he realized that he had been speaking to her; or speaking aloud and projecting the remarks in her direction since she was there.

His mother had made the rockery. Aubretia and sarsaparilla and pinks and Christmas roses. Her brother, his uncle Edward, bearded and queer, brought seaside stones in his motorcar. His father had shrugged his distaste for the project, as indeed for all projects of this nature, seeing the removal of stones from the seashore as being in some way disgraceful, even dishonest. Behind the rockery there were loganberries: thick, coarse, inedible fruit, never fully ripe. But nobody, certainly not Mr. Mileson, had had the heart to pull away the bushes.

"Weeks would pass," said Mrs. da Tanka, "without the exchange of a single significant sentence. We lived in the same house, ate the same meals, drove out in the same car, and all he would ever say was: 'It is time the central heating was on.' Or: 'These windscreen wipers aren't working.'"

Mr. Mileson didn't know whether she was talking about Mr. da Tanka or Mr. Spire. They seemed like the same man to him: shadowy, silent fellows who over the years had shared this woman with the well-tended hands.

"He will be wearing city clothes," her friend had said, "gray or nondescript. He is like anyone else except for his hat, which is big and black and eccentric." An odd thing about him, the hat: like a wild oat almost.

There he had been, by the tobacco kiosk, punctual and expectant;

gaunt of face, thin, fiftyish; with the old-fashioned hat and the weekly papers that somehow matched it, but did not match him.

"Now would you blame me, Mr. Mileson? Would you blame me for seeking freedom from such a man?"

The hat lay now on the luggage-rack with his carefully folded overcoat. A lot of his head was bald, whitish and tender like good dripping. His eyes were sad, like those of a retriever puppy she had known in her childhood. Men are often like dogs, she thought; women more akin to cats. The train moved smoothly, with rhythm through the night. She thought of da Tanka and Horace Spire, wondering where Spire was now. Opposite her, he thought about the ninety-nine year lease and the two plates, one from last night's supper, the other from breakfast, that he had left unwashed in the room at Swiss Cottage.

"This seems your kind of place," Mr. Mileson said, surveying the hotel from its ornate hall.

"Gin and lemon, gin and lemon," said Mrs. da Tanka, matching the words with action: striding to the bar.

Mr. Mileson had rum, feeling it a more suitable drink though he could not think why. "My father drank rum with milk in it. An odd concoction."

"Frightful, it sounds. Da Tanka is a whiskey man. My previous liked stout. Well, well, so here we are."

Mr. Mileson looked at her. "Dinner is next on the agenda."

But Mrs. da Tanka was not to be moved. They sat while she drank many measures of the drink; and when they rose to demand dinner they discovered that the restaurant was closed and were ushered to a grillroom.

"You organized that badly, Mr. Mileson."

"I organized nothing. I know the rules of these places. I repeated them to you. You gave me no chance to organize."

"A chop and an egg or something. Da Tanka at least could have got us soup."

In 1931 Mr. Mileson had committed fornication with the maid in his parents' house. It was the only occasion, and he was glad that adultery was not expected of him with Mrs. da Tanka. In it she would be more experienced than he, and he did not relish the implication. The grillroom was lush and vulgar. "This seems your kind of place," Mr. Mileson repeated rudely.

"At least it is warm. And the lights do not glare. Why not order some wine?"

Her husband must remain innocent. He was a person of importance, in the public eye. Mr. Mileson's friend had repeated it, the friend who knew Mrs. da Tanka's solicitor. All expenses paid, the friend had said, and a little fee as well. Nowadays Mr. Mileson could do with little fees. And though at the time he had rejected the suggestion downright, he had later seen that friend—acquaintance really—in the pub he went to at half past twelve on Sundays, and had agreed to take part in the drama. It wasn't just the little fee; there was something rather like prestige in the thing; his name as co-respondent—now *there* was something you'd never have guessed! The hotel bill to find its way to Mrs. da Tanka's husband who would pass it to his solicitor. Breakfast in bed, and remember the face of the maid who brought it. Pass the time of day with her, and make sure she remembered yours. Oh very nice, the man in the pub said, very nice Mrs. da Tanka was—or so he was led to believe. He batted his eyes at Mr. Mileson; but Mr. Mileson said it didn't matter, surely, about Mrs. da Tanka's niceness. He knew his duties: there was nothing personal about them. He'd do it himself, the man in the pub explained, only he'd never be able to keep his hands off an attractive middle-aged woman. That was the trouble about finding someone for the job.

"I've had a hard life." Mrs. da Tanka confided. "Tonight I need your sympathy, Mr. Mileson. Tell me I have your sympathy." Her face and neck had reddened: chirpiness was breaking through.

In the house, in a cupboard beneath the stairs, he had kept his gardening boots. Big, heavy army boots, once his father's. He had worn them at weekends, poking about in the garden.

"The lease came to an end two years ago," he told Mrs. da Tanka. "There I was with all that stuff, all my gardening tools, and the furniture and bric-a-brac of three generations to dispose of. I can tell you it wasn't easy to know what to throw away."

"Mr. Mileson, I don't like that waiter."

Mr. Mileson cut his steak with care: a three-cornered piece, neat and succulent. He loaded mushroom and mustard on it, added a sliver of potato and carried the lot to his mouth. He masticated and drank some wine.

"Do you know the waiter?"

Mrs. da Tanka laughed unpleasantly; like ice cracking. "Why should I know the waiter? I do not generally know waiters. Do you know the waiter?"

"I ask because you claim to dislike him."

"May I not dislike him without an intimate knowledge of the man?"

"You may do as you please. It struck me as a premature decision, that is all."

"What decision? What is premature? What are you talking about? Are you drunk?"

"The decision to dislike the waiter I thought to be premature. I do not know about being drunk. Probably I am a little. One has to keep one's spirits up . . ."

"Have you ever thought of wearing an eye-patch, Mr. Mileson? I think it would suit you. You need distinction. Have you led an empty life? You give the impression of an empty life."

"My life has been as many other lives. Empty of some things, full of others. I am in possession of all my sight, though. My eyes are real. Neither is a pretense. I see no call for an eye-patch."

"It strikes me you see no call for anything. You have never lived, Mr. Mileson."

"I do not understand that."

"Order us more wine."

Mr. Mileson indicated with his hand and the waiter approached. "Some other waiter, please," Mrs. da Tanka cried. "May we be served by another waiter?"

"Madam?" said the waiter.

"We do not take to you. Will you send another man to our table?"

"I am the only waiter on duty, madam."

"It is quite all right," said Mr. Mileson.

"It is not quite all right. I will not have this man at our table, opening and dispensing wine."

"Then we must go without."

"I am the only waiter on duty, madam."

"There are other employees of the hotel. Send us a porter or the girl at the reception."

"It is not their duty, madam—"

"Oh nonsense, nonsense. Bring us the wine, man, and have no more to-do."

Unruffled, the waiter moved away. Mrs. da Tanka hummed a popular tune.

"Are you married, Mr. Mileson? Have you in the past been married?"

"No, never married."

"I have been married twice. I am married now. I am throwing the dice for the last time. God knows how I shall find myself. You are helping to shape my destiny. What a fuss that waiter made about the wine."

"That is a little unfair. It was you, you know—"

"Behave like a gentleman, can't you? Be on my side since you are with me. Why must you turn on me? Have I harmed you?"

"No, no. I was merely establishing the truth."

"Here is the man again with the wine. He is like a bird. Do you think he has wings strapped down beneath his waiter's clothes? You are like a bird," she repeated, examining the waiter's face. "Has some fowl played a part in your ancestry?"

"I think not, madam."

"Though you cannot be sure. How can you be sure? How can you say you think not when you know nothing about it?"

The waiter poured the wine in silence. He was not embarrassed, Mr. Mileson noted; not even angry.

"Bring coffee," Mrs. da Tanka said.

"Madam."

"How servile waiters are! How I hate servility, Mr. Mileson. I could not marry a servile man. I could not marry that waiter, not for all the tea in China."

"I did not imagine you could. The waiter does not seem your sort."

"He is your sort. You like him, I think. Shall I leave you to converse with him?"

"Really! What would I say to him? I know nothing about the waiter except what he is in a professional sense. I do not wish to know. It is not my habit to go about consorting with waiters after they have waited on me."

"I am not to know that. I am not to know what your sort is, or what your personal and private habits' are. How could I know? We have only just met."

"You are clouding the issue."

"You are as pompous as da Tanka. Da Tanka would say issue and clouding."

"What your husband would say is no concern of mine."

"You are meant to be my lover, Mr. Mileson. Can't you act it a bit? My husband must concern you dearly. You must wish to tear him limb from limb. Do you not wish it?"

"I have never met the man. I know nothing of him."

"Well then, pretend. Pretend for the waiter's sake. Say something violent in the waiter's hearing. Break an oath. Blaspheme. Bang your fist on the table."

"I was not told I should have to behave like that. It is against my nature."

"What is your nature?"

"I am shy and self-effacing."

"You are an enemy to me. I do not understand your sort. You have not got on in the world. You take on commissions like this. Where is your self-respect?"

"Elsewhere in my character."

"You have no personality."

"That is a cliché. It means nothing."

"Sweet nothings for lovers, Mr. Mileson! Remember that."

They left the grillroom and mounted the stairs in silence. In their bedroom Mrs. da Tanka unpacked a dressing gown. "I shall undress in the bathroom. I shall be absent a matter of ten minutes."

Mr. Mileson slipped from his clothes into pajamas. He brushed his teeth at the washbasin, cleaned his nails and splashed a little water on his face. When Mrs. da Tanka returned he was in bed.

To Mr. Mileson she seemed a trifle bigger without her daytime clothes. He remembered corsets and other containing garments. He did not remark upon it.

Mrs. da Tanka turned out the light and they lay without touching between the cold sheets of the double bed.

He would leave little behind, he thought. He would die and there would be the things in the room, rather a number of useless things with sentimental value only. Ornaments and ferns. Reproductions of paintings. A set of eggs, birds' eggs he had collected as a boy. They would pile all the junk together and probably try to burn it. Then perhaps they would light a couple of those fumigating candles in the room, because people are insulting when other people die.

"Why did you not get married?" Mrs. da Tanka said.

"Because I do not greatly care for women." He said it, throwing caution to the winds, waiting for her attack.

"Are you a homosexual?"

The word shocked him. "Of course I am not."

"I only asked. They go in for this kind of thing."

"That does not make me one."

"I often thought Horace Spire was more that way than any other. For all the attention he paid to me."

As a child she had lived in Shropshire. In those days she loved the country, though without knowing, or wishing to know, the names of flowers or plants or trees. People said she looked like Alice in Wonderland.

"Have you ever been to Shropshire, Mr. Mileson?"

"No. I am very much a Londoner. I lived in the same house all my life. Now the house is no longer there. Flats replace it. I live in Swiss Cottage."

"I thought you might. I thought you might live in Swiss Cottage . . ."

"Now and again I miss the garden. As a child I collected birds' eggs on the common. I have kept them all these years."

She had kept nothing. She cut the past off every so often, remembering it when she cared to, without the aid of physical evidence.

"The hard facts of life have taken their toll of me," said Mrs. da Tanka. "I met them first at twenty. They have been my companion since."

"It was a hard fact the lease coming to an end. It was hard to take at the time. I did not accept it until it was well upon me. Only the spring before I had planted new delphiniums."

"My father told me to marry a good man. To be happy and have children. Then he died. I did none of those things. I do not know why except that I did not care to. Then old Horry Spire put his arm around me and there we were. Life is as you make it, I suppose. I was thinking of homosexual in relation to that waiter you were interested in downstairs."

"I was not interested in the waiter. He was hard done by, by you I thought. There was no more to it than that."

Mrs. da Tanka smoked and Mr. Mileson was nervous; about the situation in general, about the glow of the cigarette in the darkness. What it the woman dropped off to sleep? He had heard of fires started by careless smoking. What if in her confusion she crushed the cigarette against some part of his body? Sleep was impossible: one cannot sleep with the thought of waking up in a furnace, with the bells of fire brigades clanging a death knell.

"I will not sleep tonight," said Mrs. da Tanka, a statement which frightened Mr. Mileson further. For all the dark hours the awful woman would be there, twitching and puffing beside him. *I am mad. I am out of my mind to have brought this upon myself.* He heard the words. He saw them on paper, written in his handwriting. He saw them typed, and repeated again as on a telegram. The letters jolted and lost their order. The words were confused, skulking behind a fog. "I am mad," Mr. Mileson said, to establish the thought completely, to bring it into the open. It was a habit of his; for a moment he had forgotten the reason for the thought, thinking himself alone.

"Are you telling me now you are mad?" asked Mrs. da Tanka, alarmed. "Gracious, are you worse than a homo? Are you some sexual pervert? Is that what you are doing here? Certainly that was not my plan, I do assure you. You have nothing to gain from me, Mr. Mileson. If there is trouble I shall ring the bell."

"I am mad to be here. I am mad to have agreed to all this. What came over me I do not know. I have only just realized the folly of the thing."

"Arise then, dear Mileson, and break your agreement, your promise and your undertaking. You are an adult man, you may dress and walk from the room."

They were all the same, she concluded: except that while others had some passing superficial recommendation, this one it seemed had none. There was something that made her sick about the thought of the stringy limbs that were stretched out beside her. What lengths a woman will go to rid herself of a horror like da Tanka!

He had imagined it would be a simple thing. It had sounded like a simple thing: a good thing rather than a bad one. A good turn for a lady in need. That was as he had seen it. With the little fee already in his possession.

Mrs. da Tanka lit another cigarette and threw the match on the floor.

"What kind of a life have you had? You had not the nerve for marriage. Nor the brains for success. The truth is you might not have lived." She laughed in the darkness, determined to hurt him as he had hurt her in his implication that being with her was an act of madness.

Mr. Mileson had not before done a thing like this. Never before had he not weighed the pros and cons and seen that danger was absent from an undertaking. The thought of it all made him sweat. He saw in the future further deeds: worse deeds, crimes and irresponsibilities.

Mrs. da Tanka laughed again. But she was thinking of something else.

"You have never slept with a woman, is that it? Ah, you old poor thing! What a lot you have not had the courage for!" The bed heaved with the raucous noise that was her laughter, and the bright spark of her cigarette bobbed about in the air.

She laughed, quietly now and silently, hating him as she hated da Tanka and had hated Horace Spire. Why could he not be some young man, beautiful and nicely mannered and gay? Surely a young man would have come with her? Surely there was one amongst all the millions who would have done the chore with relish, or at least with charm?

"You are as God made you," said Mr. Mileson. "You cannot help your shortcomings, though one would think you might by now have recognized them. To others you may be all sorts of things. To me you are a frightful woman."

"Would you not stretch out a hand to the frightful woman? Is there no temptation for the woman's flesh? Are you a eunuch, Mr. Mileson?"

"I have had the women I wanted. I am doing you a favor. Hearing of your predicament and pressed to help you, I agreed in a moment of generosity. Stranger though you were I did not say no."

"That does not make you a gentleman."

"And I do not claim it does. I am gentleman enough without it."

"You are nothing without it. This is your sole experience. In all your clerky subservience you have not paused to live. You know I am right, and as for being a gentleman — well, you are of the lower middle classes. There has never been an English gentleman born of the lower middle classes."

She was trying to remember what she looked like; what her face was like, how the wrinkles were spread, how old she looked and what she might pass for in a crowd. Would men not be cagey now and think that she must be difficult in her ways to have parted twice from husbands? Was there a third time coming up? Third time lucky, she thought. Who would have her, though, except some loveless Mileson?

"You have had no better life than I," said Mr. Mileson. "You are no more happy now. You have failed, and it is cruel to laugh at you."

They talked and the hatred grew between them.

"In my childhood young men flocked about me, at dances in Shropshire that my father gave to celebrate my beauty. Had the fashion been duels, duels there would have been. Men killed and maimed for life, carrying a lock of my hair on their breast."

"You are a creature now, with your face and your fingernails. Mutton dressed as lamb, Mrs. da Tanka!"

Beyond the curtained windows the light of dawn broke into the night. A glimpse of it crept into the room, noticed and welcomed by its occupants.

"You should write your memoirs, Mr. Mileson. To have seen the changes in your time and never to know a thing about them! You are like an occasional table. Or a coat-rack in the hall of a boardinghouse. Who shall mourn at your grave, Mr. Mileson?"

He felt her eyes upon him; and the mockery of the words sank into his heart with intended precision. He turned to her and touched her, his hands groping about her shoulders. He had meant to grasp her neck, to feel the muscles struggle beneath his fingers, to terrify the life out of her. But she, thinking the gesture was the beginning of an embrace, pushed him away, swearing at him and laughing. Surprised by the misunderstanding, he left her alone.

The train was slow. The stations crawled by, similar and ugly. She fixed her glance on him, her eyes sharpened; cold and powerful.

She had won the battle, though technically the victory was his. Long before the time arranged for their breakfast. Mr. Mileson had leaped from bed. He dressed and breakfasted alone in the dining room. Shortly afterward, sending to the bedroom for his suitcase, he left the hotel, informing the receptionist that the lady would pay the bill. Which in time she had done, and afterward pursued him to the train, where now, to disconcert him, she sat in the facing seat of an empty compartment.

"Well," said Mrs. da Tanka, "you have shot your bolt. You have taken the only miserable action you could. You have put the frightful woman in her place. Have we a right," she added, "to expect anything better of the English lower classes?"

Mr. Mileson had foolishly left his weekly magazines and the daily paper at the hotel. He was obliged to sit barefaced before her, pretending to observe the drifting landscape. In spite of everything, guilt gnawed him a bit. When he was back in his room he would borrow the vacuum cleaner and give it a good going over: the exercise would calm him. A glass of beer in the pub before lunch. Lunch in the ABC; perhaps an afternoon cinema. It was Saturday today: this, more or less, was how he usually spent Saturday. Probably from lack of sleep he would doze off in the cinema. People would nudge him to draw attention to his snoring; that had happened before, and was not pleasant.

"To give you birth," she said, "your mother had long hours of pain. Have you thought of that, Mr. Mileson? Have you thought of that poor woman crying out, clenching her hands and twisting the sheets? Was it worth it, Mr. Mileson? You tell me now, was it worth it?"

He could leave the compartment and sit with other people. But that would be too great a satisfaction for Mrs. da Tanka. She would laugh loudly at his going, might even pursue him to mock in public.

"What you say about me, Mrs. da Tanka, can equally be said of you."

"Are we two peas in a pod? It is an explosive pod in that case."

"I did not imply that. I would not wish to find myself sharing a pod with you."

"Yet you shared a bed. And were not man enough to stick to your word. You are a worthless coward, Mr. Mileson. I expect you know it."

"I know myself, which is more than can be said in your case. Do you not think occasionally to see yourself as others see you? An aging woman, faded and ugly, dubious in morals and personal habits? What misery you must have caused those husbands!"

"They married me, and got good value. You know that, yet dare not admit it."

"I will scarcely lose sleep worrying the matter out."

It was a cold morning, sunny with a clear sky. Passengers stepping from the train at the intermediate stations muffled up against the temperature, finding it too much after the warm fug within. Women with baskets. Youths. Men with children, with dogs collected from the guard's van.

Da Tanka, she had heard, was living with another woman. Yet he refused to admit to being the guilty party. It would not do for someone like da Tanka to be a public adulterer. So he had said. Pompously. Crossly. Horace Spire, to give him his due, hadn't given a damn one way or the other.

"When you die, Mr. Mileson, have you a preference for the flowers on your coffin? It is a question I ask because I might send you off a wreath. That lonely wreath. From ugly, frightful Mrs. da Tanka."

"What?" said Mr. Mileson, and she repeated the question.

"Oh well—cow parsley, I suppose." He said it, taken off his guard by the image she created; because it was an image he often saw and thought about. Hearse and coffin and he within. It would not be like that probably. Anticipation was not in Mr. Mileson's life. Remembering, looking back, considering events and emotions that had been at the time mundane perhaps—this kind of thing was more to his liking. For by hindsight there was pleasure in the stream of time. He could not establish his funeral in his mind; he tried often but ended up always with a funeral he had known: a repetition of his parents' passing and the accompanying convention.

"Cow parsley?" said Mrs. da Tanka. Why did the man say cow parsley? Why not roses or lilies or something in a pot? There had been cow parsley in Shropshire; cow parsley on the verges of dusty lanes; cow parsley in hot fields buzzing with bees; great white swards rolling down to the river. She had sat among it on a picnic with dolls. She had lain on it, laughing at the beautiful anemic blue of the sky. She had walked through it by night, loving it.

"Why did you say cow parsley?"

He did not know, except that once on a rare family outing to the country he had seen it and remembered it. Yet in his garden he had grown delphiniums and wallflowers and asters and sweet-pea.

She could smell it again: a smell that was almost nothing: fields and the heat of the sun on her face, laziness and summer. There was a red door somewhere, faded and blistered, and she sat against it, crouched on a warm step, a child dressed in the fashion of the time.

"Why did you say cow parsley?"

He remembered, that day, asking the name of the white powdery growth. He had picked some and carried it home; and had often since thought of it, though he had not come across a field of cow parsley for years.

She tried to speak again, but after the night there were no words she could find that would fit. The silence stuck between them, and Mr. Mileson knew by instinct all that it contained. She saw an image of herself and him, strolling together from the hotel, in this same sunshine, at this very moment, lingering on the pavement to decide their direction and agreeing to walk to the promenade. She mouthed and grimaced and the sweat broke on her body, and she looked at him once and saw words die on his lips, lost in his suspicion of her.

The train stopped for the last time. Doors banged; the throng of people passed them by on the platform outside. They collected their belongings and left the train together. A porter, interested in her legs, watched them walk down the platform. They passed through the barrier and parted, moving in their particular directions. She to her new flat where milk and mail, she hoped, awaited her. He to his room; to the two unwashed plates on the draining board and the forks with egg on the prongs; and the little fee propped up on the mantelpiece, a pink check for five pounds, peeping out from behind a china cat.

Irvin Faust

The World's Fastest Human

The European tour of the cream of the cream was to be my first international competition, for I had never before capitalized on what the sportswriters called my unlimited physical reach. Most of them described me as mental (partly true) and the Telly man, a college grad, called me the Hamlet of the cinder paths, which I liked even if it was stupid. No, the simple, unglamorous truth, which the most basic legwork would have revealed was that although I was the twelfth mouth in a zoo of fourteen, I was just not *hungry* enough—competitively speaking—that lovely under-bellied drive the writers love so to pin on Willie Mays or the young Sugar Ray. In the early days, when college was a word for town kids, I just loved to *run*, not to race. To stretch it out and float where nobody could reach me. Here is a catchy bit for my future pocket book biographer (gratis): My earliest memory, boys and girls, was sprinting out of the old shack when the arguing started and leaving the boozy old man and all the yappers behind; hell, boys and girls, I'd shout up to the sky just for the joy of it, and I'd chase the little jackrabbits and catch up and match them stride for stride, then leave them in the dust, which was plenty victory for me, see, I was all of fifteen before I learned you were supposed to beat *people*. And then I took every kid around Wildon easily. Every white kid. The black ones could stay with me; we ran the same way, happy and freewheeling, so I buddied with kids like Obediah Jason and Otis Carp and we raced alongside each other around that town like frisking railroad trains. That was when their heroes became mine: silky Jesse Owens, Eddie Tolan, Long John Woodruff. (End of item.)

This ingrained tan, which still fools people, I worked on just to belong, and my scholarship to Brevard was swung by Choo Johnson, track coach

G

in the colored school (hated by my old man for filling the paternal void)
who sent me up there with Obediah and twelve dollars. But big time
athletics were still a lark, not kill or be killed, which about choked Big Jack
Jackson, the Brevard wonder coach, who had to protect the school's invest-
ment, and I think he had decided to chuck me as his all-time monument,
when I caught fire. It happened just in time, in Denver, for the Nationals.
They simply dangled that overseas ticket before me and *slam,* like a hungry
greyhound dog, I achieved full, crosscut integration and was a no-waste
machine at last. Big J was ecstatic; a grump of a man, he was screaming
with joy as I breezed through three heats, a semi and the final. Victory man,
I learned then, is the only true Gestalt, and I awoke the next morning to
find I was the World's Fastest Human. The old jungo build-up, of course,
but I honestly *did* believe in my gastrocnemii, where you have to know it,
for integration—as I learned early on—is a gut commodity. (Jesse found it
in a rush in '36, you'll discover, if you watch the Olympic films.) I won in
Denver, going away, finally shaking Chester Hallahan, a gutsy little priest-
to-be from Saint Joe, who always exploited my conflicts by crossing himself
so much at the start I felt it was a sin to beat him, but then they announced
the grand tour for win and place and the upper half (natural) of a Follies
girl suddenly loomed over the tape and when I looked back Chester was still
uncrossing.

"Deleware has arrived," bleated the *Times;* "He is unleashed," blatted
the *Trib*; "Poised and ruthless," blabbed the *News*; "In charge of the
exquisite components of his power," blobbed *Newsweek* . . . Hell, I was,
in simple reality, just eager, hungry for the scene the great Jess had made
twenty-five years before. All I need do to secure this month of perfection, in
which I would be groomed, curried and turned loose like a Black Beauty,
was perform the basic act of racing the other savage for the coconut, a
picture which always gives me a direct, atavistic charge and seemed small
price for such pleasures.

With my imminent future in mind, I checked into the Empire Hotel,
the first week in August, and began to fit into the picture. The greatest
athletes in America, we were a motley, Bermuda-shorted collection of
thirty-two men and eighteen women, serviced by six managers and officials,
a doctor and a rubber, all of whom in three days would weld into an instrument of single-minded invincibility and international good will. The connection, we were assured, was there.

I consider the Empire and New York and those three days as the first
phase of the tour, even as Mack my big brother tells me that Fort Dix was
an essential part of his overseas duty. My *true* indoctrination began that
first evening. It began, as in every period of confinement, such as vacations
at home, because I turned itchy as soon as I had time to think. Long and
careful study has revealed the cams and gears of my metabolism and I knew
that uncoiling was far more important to the parts of my poised and trig-
gered machine than winding it tighter, and as soon as Lou Zipser, the AAU
man, delivered his evening orientation lecture, I took off for the kind of

preparation my body and I, both of whom understand each other, demanded. (Also I knew the *real* New York, having examined it for three winters on the indoor circuit. After Wildon, Manhattan is pure daylight and I thank my legs regularly for their coefficient of revolution, which shot me over the horizon.)

I had by this time impressed my training philosophy on two open-minded boys from nearby State U: Lister Lee, a baby mountain shot putter from Kansas, and Gray Ginzberg, a beautiful Jewish albino from Texas, who is the perfectly balanced Decathlon man. The three of us, I might add modestly, were about the highest-priced amateurs in the business.

So, as *Laramie* came on the screens in every room, I walked down the backstairs, which are in the same relative position in all hotels, and circled around the block to the junction of Broadway, Amsterdam and 72nd Street, a sociopsych concept in itself, that had already served for three term papers . . .

The crystal neon twilight that outlines benches, stores and theatres splashes over me as I converge with Lister and Gray and the early evening lookers at the subway kiosk. My accomplices stand out in bold relief, even on this Broadway treadmill:

Lister triangulates neatly to a small, lightweight head, which is clean shaven. His face is composed and neutral, his neck, the thickness of a dollar pancake, is a collar for his chin. Around his legs, his pleatless pants swell like Lastex trunks pulled to the ankle. He has with him, of course, his sixteen-pound shot and is slipping it from hand to hand, fondling it like the sleek head of a puppy.

Gray worries about ten events, so favors none. When he screen tests for Tarzan, his destiny since the age of eight, he will need all the skills, and he would as soon break into a javelin run-up as stand fast and quietly flexes his latissimus, the giant shale of muscle beneath his shoulder wings, while he squints into the brightness. He is a pure white, with no hangdoggedness for what he is, the perfect foil (which, frankly, I exploit) for my coffee tan, a negative to my positive. He rarely talks, nor needs to, and will be better than Weissmuller if they have sense enough to use Technicolor.

The Kansas Whale, The Texarkana Milk Baby and Calvin Coolidge Delaware, the World's Fastest (and most unified) Human, promptly turn west on 73rd and walk toward the Hotel Riverside Crescent, which three years ago, Gaylord Cohen, the erratic left-footed hurdler, introduced me to. Gay, also a soc major from Emory Henry, demonstrated that for an inclusive, all-out shot, such as we needed right after the meet, the choice had to be the Dansant of the Riverside for Folks 28 and Over, Refined and in Good Taste, No Jitterbugging Permitted. I liked its style, the sparring was clean and honest and for some reason they always passed me through, although I am only 22 and have that suspicious chocolate color. (Impressionable coeds say a thin Sugar Ray, without the moustache, or so much of the screw the world look, which will, I fear, come in time. I have also been Minnie Minoso's half-brother, Ibn Saud's nephew and young chief Laughing

Cloud educated in the white man's school, and if a chick will go under all these conditions, who am I, as a potential social scientist, to be intolerant?)

We pass at the ticket window and are wriststamped so we can go to the john and walk safely back through the electric eye. We push through the milling in the lobby and into the bare, giant ballroom, with only revolving chandeliers for atmosphere; it is hot and sweetly damp and deadpan serious, the New York I know and love. I know, too, what I will find and I'm not disappointed: in the middle layer, the OPERATORS, dancing and working their points; weaving in and out of the sidelines, the CHECKERS, seeking, never finding; and the STIFFS, never moving, with hands locked behind backs, leaning in at forty-five, neither smoking, talking or flicking faces. It is rat race night, and despite personal tragedy they must be there.

I move Ginz and Lister, who still caresses his steel ball, to the bar in the near corner, order sherry (for the blood) and check the POSSIBLES lined up in the mirror, also my unclasped tie, carefully mussed hair and dansant expression, which is not quite stiff and not quite eager. Already, in the cross from the door, Ginz has a variety of styles looking all around the room in the embarrassed hope of fingering him. Our first problem, therefore, is solved, for leaning delicately together down the bar are three quiet DESPERATES, façading skillfully, but with exquisite taste, drinking vodka martinis with lemon peel, so their breathing will not tell, dropping the self-conscious signals I have deciphered in all the big, no nonsense cities. (Small towns are much too complex for me.) Silently we lock plans and without a word, which conforms strictly to the code, I move back and steer mine away from the bar, through CHECKERS and STIFFS, onto the swaying island, and maintaining casual silence for two numbers, spin her through a pachanga and a peabody, while I absorb the essence of the girl—Maidenform, whalebone, garter belt, fatty dorsals, flaring behind and introversion. Then as if fuses have been snapped, we flash faces—hers, once firm, slightly crushed around the edges and over the mouth; mine warm, accepting and barely amused. We exchange lives during the foxtrot and just as the band bloop de bleeps and breaks, I am neatly into the present and Muriel Hillwitz has not loosed her hand, so promise is in the air. On return, it is clear that Ginz' congenital charm has bemused the friends, for they are talking too much and not listening. My Muriel, the leader, is brisk.

"Girls," she says, "I would like you to meet Pone Kingpetch. Pone is a Veetnam athlete here on a Fulbright."

"Hello Pone," says Florence, husky and stable.

"How do you do, Mr. Kingpetch," says Bernice. She is third, the necessary conscience.

"Well," Muriel decides, "why stand around when we can just as easy sit and be comfortable." A tide bears us backward to the table and we all unlax, in a way the charming part of the evening, for now comes the tensing and sniffing and all the endless possibilities. We are therefore completely, unscrupulously honest, except, of course, on names, origin, orientation and purpose. Lister is Paavo Nurmi tonight, Ginz Elmo Lincoln. It is obvious the girls believe everything, but that we are champions, and that is understandable. Only undernourished wise guys, like myself or albinos or pinheaded giants become champs. (Who would peg Yogi Berra, except as a put down shipping clerk?)

"Why does Paavo carry that heavy iron ball," Florence, who wears the Magdeburg spheres for armor, says, making conversation, like what do you think of Mickey Maris.

"Because," Ginz explains, "he must learn its every groove so they can become one for maximum efficiency." It is the way he will someday say, If I am Tarzan you must be Jane.

"Oh stop it," Flo blushes, her intuition saying he is already onto every secret, including her detachable crotch, and he has never missed yet.

"Sombitch, sombitch," Lister, whose world is an internal one, mutters.

"What did he say?" Bernice says nervously.

"He is psyching himself," I explain quickly. "Working on his inner self so he can hate his opponent, whoever he is. So when his time comes, he will be ready."

"Goddam lousy finkin cruddy bastid."

"He is peaking early tonight," Ginz says mildly.

"It is his key concept," I reply. "As a child he was chicken runty."

"My, you fellas got some routine," Muriel says admiringly. "Certny diffrent."

I tune to the sad, life-cycle flash and see the eldest daughter, the solid secretary, the two weeks in the mountains. And yet, yet, after three hours and six sherries (for the blood) the gray in her head glints with a soft maturity and I see the Widow Rutkin, down the road a piece, stacking the garbage in her flopping housecoat. Magnetically we couple hands under the table; her fingers are ten busy mouths.

We dance. Lister is deft with the shot and Bernice; Ginz steps impeccably through the underbrush, Florence clinging heavily, overjoyed with her fortune. We are truly helping I say to myself, gauging the heat under Muriel's corset. The tinny combo soars around us, enhancing her mystery, enhancing mine, until at last it is midnight and the mean body heat soared past the acting point. The CHECKERS have begun their thermostatic run through the LEFTOVERS, the STIFFS are leaning at forty-five. All around us little books are flashing against subway travel time. The moment has come for the questioning; have we come this far for nothing, or do they appreciate . . . Better yet, our luck holds, we are entitled; they have a car. You know that coming this far is like a life-expectancy chart; the farther you get, the better your chances.

We walk with tense confidence through the STANDEES and out to the sidewalk. We turn west for Tenth Avenue, Hell's old kitchen. How I would love to keep going and make it on a yacht in the marina after a swim in the Hudson, but these girls are not, I know, *that* classic. And I must not push for it is still the semis and I can still tie up. Yet the new Dodge is wide and deep and Muriel's, and I am supple while she is out of shape; as the others climb in back, I double over and slide her far enough to squeeze in and wedge us together. I have the wheel and the transverse of hip, thigh, calf and foot, giving me the edge. I know it is hardly sporting when you are 22 and run the hundred in nine four and Europe is ahead, but I still remember shanty town and the feeling that I will never be safe.

I head for 96th and the West Side Drive and run along a black stretch that had to lure Hendrik happily to his end. We are adjusting to the seventh presence, the car, and its message. The breakthrough is sudden but clean. There, between 125 and 135th, where the river is a hundred feet deep and the neons are hidden, in the rear view mirror Florence unfolds and like a giant pitcher plant ingests Ginzberg in a feat of breathtaking skill and timing. Thus making *her* the World's Fastest Human.

A hot swamp fills the car, gagging me; the breached dam is flooding us; I turn on the defroster. "Pone," Muriel, the good friend, says, "talk to me in Veetnam."

As I wrestle the wheel, the car sways drunkenly. It is obvious that Flo has never had a Decathlon man before, but good luck for all—Lister, his ball and Bernice are huddled ballast in their corner. "Well," I say, gaining control, "my folks spoke mainly English and French and Tagalog for my benefit, but let me see. Denbeeyenfoo."

"Oh, what does it mean," she shivers.

That cold, indifferent river has made me reckless, I swear, or the swaying is unhinging me. I say to myself don't tie up. But it's too late. "Tongue me, baby."

Silence.

"I'm not sure I like that." The high pressure is released.

"Hah hah I was only joshing."

"Some things one does not josh about."

"Goodness it is hot." Defeat is looming, but I must gamble. "Say hey, I know a place where the wild time grows, that is very refreshing in mind and spirit. I go there often for inspiration. It reminds me of Bangkok."

"Oh?"

"Yes. The Cloisters, the highest, most inspirational point in this wonderful town."

"Yes, I've been . . ."

"Not on a night like this I will wager. Now they are a midsummer mid-dyevil dream come true. When there is a candlemoon like now you can see Richard Core de Leon on the highest tower. And Rebecca fighting off Briandeebwahgillbair. And Ivanhoe climbing up Riverside Drive to the rescue. See?"

She goes molten beside me. "That is nice," she whispers. "You're a crazy." I smile into the agreeable shapes along the road.

At 181st I turn off and circle slowly up to the monastery and park on the edge of a cliff, beneath a parapet, where already the nuns and jolly friars are getting set to gambol.

"Hot damn, let's catch air," Ginz says, which is part of the arrangement, depending on who is up front. Lister has suddenly come to.

"This is a pretty stretch of lawn," he says. "Come on."

And so Muriel and I are alone at last. I turn to QXR and half close my eyes; she slides down and rests her head against the seat. A sensitive, gathering moment.

"It's peaceful here, Pone. A person can relax and be herself."

"I told you. Look."

"Where?"

"There. See, the moat. That expanse of water curving around the shore, protecting us. The Hudson moat. See?"

"Oh Pone, you certny do have some imagination."

"Do I . . . Rebecca?"

"Yes you do . . . Prince Val . . ."

I somehow am touched; I know she has never played this way before and in her corked up way she is really trying. What if I am a comic strip, at least the era is right . . .

"Pone . . . You are a strange one."

Ahhh. There it is, the intrigue at last. I thought it might get sidetracked and my impatience was building, for like all good sprinters I have a very short fuse. Hunched over the wheel, I reply (and I am sincere), "I know dammit, I cannot help myself." The lump in my throat is for my miserable childhood, which I have forged into a top weapon. It does not fail me now; the hand on the nape of my neck has started, as on signal, up the grain of the bristle and at *that* signal, so gently that it is barely happening (but is), my hand is climbing, climbing, and kneading the fat ball behind her knee, where the stocking crinkles and flares out to the softly swelling hamstrings. All the while the competitor in me is watching the action, thinking around the periphery. I find myself wondering if these knees—as big brother Mack says all mature knees do—resemble Herbert Hoover? Funny. Very funny. A chicken in every pot. A car in every garage. Hah hah. The chuckle starts in my belly and gurgles up and out. Oh God, Herbie Hoover. Hoobert Heever. And again that miserable inversion that has me wondering if the finish tape is made of steel and will decapitate me, killing victory in the last stride, snaps the moment. Clang! The nylon gates, so soft and yielding a finger ago, have swung shut.

"Please don't spoil it."

Oh how sick these walls must be of that. Who first said it a thousand years ago, "Prithee donte spoille itte, Arthur. Or Robin. Or Quent."

Yet I was so close that the bitter reflex rises before my good sportsmanship can take over. "It really isn't uranium you know."

"Will I see you again?"

Oh God, did Rowena ask Ivanhoe, Isabella Columbus? Please Muriel, I have marred our rhythm, probably laddered your stocking. Come on already, when I butcher a big one, Jack will not reprieve me for a week. For your own good don't be so good.

But even so, in defeat I am thinking, one last big drive, what's to lose?

"Look doll, I am going to level with you all the way. I am not Pone Kingpetch. I am Cal Delaware, from South Carolina, where basically I was white trash, although I have managed through superhuman effort to rise above my socio-economic level. Now doll, I am leaving for Europe in two days to represent you and all the Muriel Hillwitzes in the USA. Now it is like I am going overseas you know and planes can crash and boats collide or you can get the bubonic plague, I mean it is all possible. But I and all I stand for am here. Right NOW."

"You're not Pone Kingpetch?"

OK, I tried. I should have known, for I am just miserable with the truth, I simply cannot handle it.

"No doll."

With an endless, pushing sigh, she sinks deep into a depression, leans against the window and stares out. The shoulders stiffen. Well, I have done what I can; frankly I feel exonerated if you get my meaning. It's purely organic, for my weak span of attention, which is a fact and you can look it up on Big Jack's charts or ask a Brevard coed, has run down. But instead of a sporting handshake and a nice race fella, there will be tense profiles all the way home. Oh why, you thousand years of mama's proverbs, must you crystallize on poor Cal Deleware's innocent head, here, now, at this moment in history? Such a waste, a deprivation. Worst of all a bore. A *serious* bore . . . But wait, that great, splatting thud outside the window. Lister Lee to the rescue, contracting and exploding in a last second reprieve. Yelling, "Top that, goddam sombitch." Putting the shot sixty-one feet easy, for a new Cloister's record. Great follow-through. I feel better already. This I know, this is me. The adrenalin pours into the small of my back . . . Another thud and Bernice is skipping after the shot, pouncing and swinging it under the hiked-up dress. "Give it to the bastids good," she yells, a brand new Bernice. That is a very nice little gluteus she is posing against the yellow background. My muscles start to twitch. Again Lister hangs in space and the arm flashes. "Lousy lousy lousy." She picks it up and scoots off, a little bird dog. I sit entranced. Muriel is forgotten; she does not grasp the perfection of one night anyway . . . Across the Palisade screen glides Gary, with his imaginary spear—step, cross; step, cross—launching himself and his weapon into space. And launching beside him is Flo, sailing like a huge navy blimp. Behind her on the ground is her molded armor, piled in a heap . . .

I am up to here with cerebrating, with wheeling and dealing. I shuck it as a gun goes off in my head. I flick out of the car and crouch, and then the grass is unreeling beneath me and I am flowing forward. My insides fill with motion like a parched sponge. I soar up the brick wall that runs along the cliff. Colonel Deleware reporting, sir. "Mountcalm, cheese it, here comes the Wolfman!" I look about for support. "All right Bunker Bill, you may fire when you see the whites of their eggs." This is the old jackrabbit chaser again! . . . On the highest parapet, a white gargoyle hangs. Beowulf, the first Tarzan, was pure, an albino perhaps? Beau cups hands and yodels upriver and Roland sings back, *"Frigit Mac."* And now we are joined. Elves, trolls, knaves, friars and squires, holding their robes and visors, wraithing and falling. We are met and moonmad. I sprint off the wall and head for the car with a magnificently formed image in my guts. I am impala at last (the broadjump is my weakest event). I thrust off the right leg and soar over the roof of the car, feet churning, arms levering. I hang up there, a spy in the moonlight. Miles up valley I can see Newburgh and Albany and Paris Falls and Montreal, the Arctic Circle, the Northern Lights, a shivering little white rabbit. I can see yellow windows, steeples, hushed streets, woods and paper pulp plants. It's a wild historic ride and for a glorious moment I think I may never come down. Then I am arcing, thrusting forward. I land softly fifteen feet beyond the car. I scramble to my feet, power-packed and quivery, and I look up to the moon like a crazy hound dog. Is the old guy watching? Hot damn, *there* is Herb Hoover. "Hey you, Herbie," I bay, "you busted my old man, you broke his mean little heart, but I don't begrudge. Did you catch me just now?" Herb winks.

Finally I have shot my bolt, with no help from anyone and the hell with them all. The lactic acid is shooting through like novocain and I sink to the ground. Gary and Lister too, have burned off the overfat, and the history I have made is crawled back into the woodwork and the Cloisters are breathless.

It is then, in the dark, that I see a ghost of the present. The all but forgotten, practically written off Muriel. She is running at me with arms outstretched and a wild, sainted look on her face, which is suddenly, smoothly young. SHE DOES NOT HAVE A GODDAMN THING ON.

In that moment I realize I have found the big second effort, the secret of all the great ones, from Saladin to Archie Moore. Miraculously my reflexes rise to the challenge. As she streams toward me, her virginal shell gleaming, I know a history of behavior is being overturned, a whole lifetime reversed, and I am properly respectful for the gift we have wrought. For she is saying in a breathless, shiny, little voice, "Oh please, *let* me play, too." And I brace for one of the great gestalts in the thousand-year history of these jaded towers. Somehow in this charming moment, I know I can be counted on to exploit the knowledge I have fallen into. I am *ready* for the stiffest competition Europe can offer. From the *Place Pigalle* to the *Via Veneto*.

Sol Yurick

The Siege

After twenty-seven years and two hours of Departmental contact, it came down to just this moment . . . the three of them, Kalisher, the Social Worker from Friends of the Community, Miller the Relief Investigator, and Mrs. Diamond, the client, were immured in a stasis. She refused to show them the fourth room.

They had contended with her for two hours. Her head was kept turning from Kalisher to Miller; they pressed, wanting to know; they ranged from kindness to brutality. Now they sat resting in the cluttered kitchen. They could hear the constant gurgling of water in the decayed pipes. They inhaled the thick smell of chicken or fish. Miller kept cataloguing. For the third time he made a neatly printed list: piled food cans; boxes of dried cereal on the washtub cover; two kinds of Kosher soap; grease-spattered pictures of her long-deserted husband and her runaway son hung over the stained sink; a pot of soup—enough for two—was being heated over a low flame. Mrs. D.'s wary little eyes watched him out of a mask of wrinkles. Miller held his pen poised above his case-book. He sat stiffly.

Mrs. D. sighed again; Miller knew what he had known before: they were never going to get into the room beyond the bedroom. How. had it escaped notice so long? Neglect. Past Investigators had come in, questioned briefly . . . she met the bare essentials of Eligibility: her case was hopeless. She was alone: deserted: too old and sick to work now. They had made their inspections quickly, noted nothing except her statement that it was a closet, perhaps wanting to get away from the stench and from having to listen to a long, old lady's complaint. Or if they suspected, did they really want to fight this old woman? Leave well-enough alone. That was the trouble, Miller thought: everyone left well-enough alone.

Mr. Miller had gone to see Mr. K., her social worker at Friends of the Community: did he know about the room? After all, Mr. K. had worked with her for three years. Mr. K. knew nothing . . . he had been concerned with her psychic welfare, helping her, an old, disturbed woman, adjust. Miller had expected Mr. K. to be angry at the deception, but Mr. K. had broken into a wide smile and said that it explained so many things.

"She gave me a weekly cup of tea, Mr. Miller, but that was all. I begin to see it, how much she hasn't ventilated. I thought we were relating well . . . My God, Mr. Miller, aren't people wonderful?"

"Wonderful?" Mr. Miller had asked. "But didn't you investigate?"

"It isn't the business of Friends of the Community to investigate in the same sense the Relief Department investigates, Mr. Miller," Mr. K. had said.

"All right, I'll close the case."

"But you can't do that. She'll starve. She has no resources . . ."

"She probably has a boarder."

"It isn't as simple as that. Have you . . ."

"She has a boarder and therefore, extra income."

"But Mr. Miller; please. It might be more than a boarder," Mr. K. had said. "Why don't we go over her case completely?"

Now Miller didn't care anymore. After two hours of questioning, the required veneer of polite, investigative procedure they had agreed on was about to peel away. He had spoiled six sheets of his case-book with elaborate doodles. Mr. K. was more patient, Miller saw, but that was because Mr. K. accepted. Miller thought Mr. K. was ridiculous; he simply didn't know. Sly Mrs. D., in spite of her years, poverty, swollen ankles, pipette legs, was faster on her feet than Mr. K. Her hands were crumpled into grasping roots by arthritis. Miller looked away from those gnarled, calcified bones. He wanted to go. She made him feel uncomfortable. He was afraid she might reach out, touch, and infect him. She sighed. Her lips wrinkled into fleshy rays and her righteous mouth pressed tightly against the three or four teeth she had left. Miller knew they were beaten unless one of them —and it would have to be him—was direct about it. Miller's leg shook up and down on the ball of his foot; he lost count of the shakes. He had no patience for the long, unprofitable silences necessary to proper social work atmospheres.

Kalisher pointed to a picture: "Your husband?"

"Don't touch," she told him.

"Mrs. Diamond, we're only trying to help you," Kalisher told her while his eyes tried to look past her.

She sniffed. She had learned. In the past she had been betrayed. "To the grave you'd help," she said. She was sharpened by those tricky years of contact with Investigators sent to deprive her; her cunning must beat them. Kalisher, dripping honey, talking "adjustment" and "rehabilitation," soft words, had come before. The Millers too; without pretense, hard, uncaring: their looks said "you're cheating." Did they know or care how it was to live like she lived? She fought them all. She held on. "How much longer am I going to be able to stand it?" she asked matter-of-factly. Torture and martyrdom were something she imbibed with the thin, white farina she ate every morning. To remind them they had done this to her, her hands picked and clutched at the frayed rope that pulled her brightly flowered housecoat together.

Kalisher saw a soft, gray wisp of frail hair float out against the loud colors of the detergent boxes. His heart went out to her. He knew what psychic martyrdom moved mothers. He was reminded of those art-photographs of old people's hands; wonderful, abiding roots. He heeded the plea of those hands. If poor Mrs. Diamond could only know his feeling . . . warm, empathetic community flooding through his veins. His face shone. He could barely see through his glasses. He knew and understood the pain and anguish of withstanding them, the provisors, the father-figures. She wanted freedom and resented needing them. It was why she fought. It was why she rejected. He smiled.

Miller was afraid her housecoat was going to fall open. He saw that K. was about to tell Mrs. D. again how long she would be able to stand it. But Miller was tired after the two-hour siege. He was tired of sitting in the kitchen in his coat; he was sweating in the steamy atmosphere. He was tired of having to divide his time between Mrs. D. and Mr. K. A splotch of grease seemed to expand, slowly seeping up through the checker tablecloth; he moved his sleeve away. He was sitting on crumbs. Mrs. D.'s clock said three: he didn't trust it. He was hungry. He was tired of making lists and neatly narrowing spirals in his case-book. It was the grabbing motion of her hand that decided him.

"Mrs. D., we've been here for two hours. You realize that. We haven't got all day. You're not our only case. Are you going to show us that room?"

Kalisher shook his head imperceptibly, disapproving. Smiling apologetically, he hastened to undo the harm. He talked Yiddish to Mrs. Diamond to show her he was really on her side. The long discussion hadn't begun to faze him; does one unravel a complex or pierce through to a pre-psychotic personality in a mere two hours? Kalisher interpreted Departmental policy. His voice droned soothingly through the kitchen as he tried to re-establish contact with her. He asked her to help *them* . . . as people. He thrust blame on a vast impersonal machine that ground down the lives of clients, investigators, and social workers impartially: the three of them were pawns; really allies. *He* was here to protect her interests. He hinted they could make some kind of arrangement. "It isn't him," he told her; "it's the Department. Mr. Miller doesn't like prying. But he has to see every room in the apartment. It's his job. You understand."

"If he doesn't want to do it, then why do it? I never heard of such a thing," she sniffed.

Twenty-seven years of getting Relief and she never heard of such a thing, Miller thought. He saw a sly roach follow a cupboard crack. She could quote the manual, chapter and verse; she knew her rights better than the both of them. He couldn't see signs of a boarder: no man's shoe, no sock, no half-smoked cigarette or cigar was left; she was careful.

"The *Department*, Mrs. Diamond, the *Department* wants him to look around. It's the law. But . . ."

"So why are *you* here?" she asked.

She saw Kalisher's greedy look. She had been fooled by sneaks before. They had worked it out together. They were the enemy. They came around saying, "Listen to us; we're on your side; tell us everything; we can do something for you." Once she had a little job; a few extra pennies; how else could you live? She had listened to them. They had closed her case. She now knew better. Back to the Relief Office she had gone and made a scene, screaming for two hours till, to get rid of her, they gave her help. For them it was some kind of game; to see if they could deprive her. She knew. If she passed their tests, she was safe for another few months. But this time . . . two of them . . . they knew . . . she was choking . . . circles in Miller's notebook . . . what did those mean? Tight strings quivered under the flesh of her neck. Why did they sit there, playing, laughing at her? Her hands felt weak. Did she have much left? She was worn down. Her hands held tightly to the rope around her waist.

Miller saw she didn't have anything on underneath the housecoat. He watched her spit into her sink and wash it down. His pen tore a little hole through his case-book. She was old, diseased, dirty, possibly senile. If they could put her in a home . . .

"The way to stop it," he had told Mr. K., "is to take her and put her in a home."

"She wouldn't go. After all, she's lived there for thirty years."

"It's the answer."

"You can't do that. She wants to be independent."

"Don't they all?" Miller asked sarcastically. "Who's stopping her, Kalisher?" and they sat down and read the two-inch thick case record . . . twenty-seven years of contact.

"This is a waste of time," Miller had said.

"You wouldn't think everything had been covered. But yet . . ." Mr. K. said.

"Look at that." Miller had held up some sheets. "That's three times she's cheated the Department. Why do we bother? We'll ask to see the room. If she refuses, we close the case."

"You can't do that. She's an old woman. She's disturbed. You can't treat a human being like that."

"She's got a boarder there. She's probably got more than enough money saved by now."

"It's not the material things; it's that she gets support from the Welfare situation."

"Support is right," Miller had said.

"I don't mean in that sense," Mr. K. had said, being obviously patient with Miller. "And I don't think she has a boarder there. I think . . . it's pretty clear, isn't it? Don't you see it? Look at all these social work contacts."

"I see that she's a miser."

"That's a sickness too."

"She's got mattresses stuffed with money . . ."

"Miller, everyone has a treasure house . . . but it's a hiding place, of psychic possibility."

"For God's sake, what . . ."

"That room is an extension of her . . . a part of her psyche." Mr. K. had smiled at him.

"She's laughing at you, Kalisher. She's a miser."

"She's a miser, but not in the sense you mean it."

"I won't argue the point," Miller said, "but Department rulings on added income are clear."

"Listen, she's a sweet old woman, a free soul. She needs to bring forth her problem. She wants love and understanding. She's been left by her husband, deserted. She's been brutalized. She's been kept on a substandard existence."

"The budget allows . . ."

"Mr. Miller, you can't break psychic needs into grams, calories, municipal food reports, or monetary allotments. Such treatment demeans . . ."

Miller thought that Mr. K. could never admit she might be intrinsically brutal, only that she was sick.

". . . and she blocks, represses, she can't relate, she's compulsive, antisocial, she conceals. It's a form of hoarding, yes, but why, Mr. Miller; why?"

"Mr. Kalisher, who cares?" Miller had said.

Life would be more organized for her in a home, Miller thought, and this couldn't have happened. Going by the psychological book was well and good, but could you rehabilitate those arthritic, withered hands? Could she be sent to work? Years of support had made her parasitic. Don't starve her, but let her at least follow the rules. She was doomed. If she didn't show him the fourth room very soon, he would cut her off. She knew her duty. His pen jabbed through the sheet again. He saw her cunning eyes dance mockingly in her decayed face. A little smile showed the tip of one black tooth. He tried to breathe calmly: the reek, like fish, of the bubbling pot, was too much for him. He began another careful curve on a fresh sheet of paper. Of course Mr. K. would fight a case-closing; not until he tried every trick of pleading with her; whining, ingratiating himself, all of it. Miller slid his chair back a little. He saw Mr. K.'s soft, loose-lipped look, his indefatigable smile. Mr. K. missed the point, Miller thought. Mr. K. was trying to get into the fourth room with Mrs. D.'s good will, as if he owed something to her. She owed *them*—if she got ten dollars a week rent, the usual rate—and it had been going on for—he would be liberal—only ten years, then . . . No, her goodwill didn't matter; it was an unnecessary handicap. If they simply went away, left her alone, didn't bother her, sent her checks twice a month, *then* they would have her goodwill. If they left her the hidden resources of that room, *then* they would have Mrs. D.'s endless goodwill. He started to loosen his tie and stopped.

"You just want to take away; out of spite; I never heard such a thing. To come in, to tear me apart," she was muttering, convincing herself that

they didn't have the right. They were playing with her. They were going
to take everything away from her.

But Kalisher was lovingly patient; it didn't bother him that his under-
shirt, and now his shirt, was drenched. He permitted her to act out her
aggressions. He talked to her as he might to his own mother, striving to rest
those neurotic terrors. "Of course he doesn't mean *you* Mrs. Diamond, but
some clients are cheats. Some clients have television sets, washing machines,
telephones, cars, all sorts of things they try to hide. You understand."

"So what has this to do with me? What could I have to hide? On relief
for twenty-seven years; what could I buy? A twenty-seven inch television
set on what they give me? I can hardly afford what to eat."

"No. No, Mrs. Diamond. I don't mean *you*. Heaven forbid," Kalisher
told her; "but that means that Mr. Miller will be able to record in the case
that he saw and checked everything. You see?"

"So? Let him put it down."

"But that wouldn't be honest; just to put it down, I mean . . . Now
what could be in that room?"

"Nothing. Before, I told you; nothing."

"Then what do you have to be afraid of?"

Miller saw that Mr. K. would have gone through it all a fourth time;
a fifth time; a sixth time if necessary, probing, using that soft, that silly,
that sympathetic approach. Miller moved violently; the table jarred. A cup
clattered. He looked up. Her hands clutched at her chest. He saw that she
had never stopped looking at him. "So we have to look into the fourth room
and see what's there. Who knows," Miller forced his lips to grin; "maybe
you have diamonds there, Mrs. D."

But Kalisher laughed quickly to show her the idea was beyond the
realm of the conceivable. He saw Miller's twisted lips tensed over his teeth.
He had worked so hard to win her, and every time he almost had her on his
side, Miller compulsively spoiled it.

"Now supposing," Kalisher had said, "we work it out that you play the
villain and I her hero. You attack; she comes to me, you see. My relation
with her is a little different, warmer, than . . ."

"Why bother?" Miller had asked again. "I ask. She shows. Why cater
to her whims?"

And Kalisher wondered why Miller was blinding himself. He was
rationalizing his hostility to Mrs. D. into a fetish for carrying out rules.
Didn't he see what was perfectly clear in the case record? Kalisher had
almost been tempted to see how long Miller might go on without seeing it
. . . what . . . who was in the fourth room. "Because she's a human being."

"She's almost a cheat. The boarder . . ."

"Does that make her less a human being?"

Mrs. Diamond didn't think Mr. Miller's quip was funny. "Drain my
blood," she told them. "Make me suffer. Go ahead. What does a human
being mean to you? Do you know pity? Take everything from an old
woman. Are you human beings?"

Being human had nothing to do with it, Miller thought. Pity? he had none left. He had seen too many clients. He knew them. Animals, he thought, just animals. No amount of readings in social case-work would give them dignity. Leave "humanity" to the K.'s. She was alien; a constant drain on public funds; she could bring no returns. What would happen later? She would die alone, like an animal. Her body would lie there for days in the gloom. Someone would smell rotting flesh and call the police. They would exhume her. Her burial would cost the city. Unless, of course—and he could sense it—the secret boarder found her. Miller intersected circles with squares, enclosing equal areas.

Watching her, Kalisher felt something inside of him wrench to see her suffering. He felt sure that she was appealing to him to save her; to save her secret. For he had said to Miller, in the office, "The husband deserted; the son, Paul, sixteen at the time, ran away from home twenty-one years ago."

"What has that to do with it?"

"There it is." And Kalisher had felt the glee again.

"What? I don't understand."

"The missing son. He disappeared without much explanation. She never complained. She never called the Missing Persons Bureau," Kalisher told Mr. Miller. "Isn't it obvious?" And left it unsaid.

"Don't be silly; things like that don't happen. She has a paying boarder. Don't be romantic. My God, what wishful thinking." Miller had almost shouted.

"Wishful?" Mr. Kalisher had said and wondered why Mr. Miller fought it so hard. "I know of cases like that; they're not as rare as you think. It's what any mother really wants to do."

"It's all stupid nonsense."

"He'd be thirty-seven now."

Mr. Miller had refused to credit it.

But suppose, Mr. Kalisher had insisted, the missing son had been living in the little room for the last twenty-one years? He felt it. It was right. He knew it. He had the insight. "Think of that kid in the warm room, like a womb, really, secured to her forever. Think of her feeding two people on the allowance for one."

"Or think of her as getting extra funds," Mr. Miller had said. They had argued it out. In the end Mr. Kalisher had agreed reluctantly to go along with it. What she hid in the fourth room represented the core of her existence. He nodded knowingly at Mr. Miller. But Mr. Miller was looking into his case-book, rejecting the situation. Her face's old nobility, the wrinkles that time, privation, yet dignity had engraved there, were spoiled only by the fearing eyes and the neurotic denying quiver of the lips; she couldn't bring it out; she wouldn't deliver herself of the guilt. "You have no idea, Mrs. Diamond," he told her, his voice trembling in a rich, inaccurate Yiddish, "how much it hurts me to have to do this. Believe me. I'm on your side. I understand." His smile should have told her he had seen deeply.

"I know you. I know you all. Watching me all the time for something.

You want me to starve. Look at me. Look at the way I live." Her twisted arm, waving, took in for Kalisher, all of the suffering, the poor, the sick, all the lonely, old, and deserted in the slums.

Miller noted: the tablecloth was fairly new; the kitchen chairs were not too old; the dish-towels were serviceable; and through the cupboard glass he saw that she had two sets of dishes, one light blue, the other white. She burned two candles in glasses; she was rich enough to afford that nonsense, Miller thought. She wasn't starving. It was a question of what the boarder earned and contributed. The signs were hidden, but he knew. "Lady, you've managed to live, somehow or other, for twenty-seven years and never once did you admit you had an extra room. If I hadn't happened to recheck the registration of this apartment, I wouldn't have known either. *You* wouldn't have told me, would you? What about that, Mrs. D.? What about that?"

"No one asked me . . ."

"I'm asking now . . ."

She stood, hunched over a little, pulled in on herself, waiting for them to make their move. "There's nothing in there; I told you."

"Why haven't you ever shown that fourth room to any investigator, Mrs. D.?" Miller asked, pointing his pen at her.

She sniffed. There was nothing Kalisher could do for her either. He sat there, smiled, and felt his hands strain and tremble.

"No one asked. There's nothing there. It's none of your business," she told them.

"I've been reasonable for two hours; it *is* our business. *Everything* about you is our business. We give you money. *We keep you alive.* It has to be our business." And Miller saw she understood now. She had him alone to contend with. Kalisher was out of it; *his* agency didn't dispense funds; Miller's did. He sat before her, fuming because of her stubbornness. He crossed out a figure; he could compute it when he returned to the office. He made it very clear to her, stressing it, lingering on it, "Sooner or later we find out, lady. If you have nothing to hide . . . You know, you wouldn't be the first person to cheat the Department. You won't be the first to be caught either."

Kalisher's wounded sigh sounded helplessly in the room; and then he realized . . . Miller was jealous of his relationship with Mrs. Diamond . . .

Miller couldn't wait any more. "We know you have someone in that room."

They were caught in the thick smoke of Miller's cigarette: it hung in soft eddies. A thin plume of steam spurted from the pot. Did he detect a gleam under the tears, Miller wondered. He began to boil. "Who's in that room?"

"I can't show it to you."

"You won't . . ."

"Let me starve. Tear me apart. Kill me. Take everything away. Throw me into the streets. My life . . ."

"Don't be foolish. Who's . . ."

"Don't talk like that."

"A boarder?"

"Twenty men in a closet. A dormitory," she said. Their voices were growing louder.

"Or . . ." Miller smiled at Mr. K. ". . . your son?"

She screamed, Kalisher leaned forward, looking at her face; his mouth was open and moist. "My son! My son should only be there." Her face was twisted. The black teeth showed. Her hand clawed toward Miller. He slid back; the chair-feet screeched on the floor. "Who ever heard of such a thing? Where do they dream up such things to torture me? You got nothing better to do with your time than to torture an old, sick woman? It gives you fun?"

Kalisher's mouth kept opening and closing. After that inhuman violation of case-work principles, that sadistic wrenching-out, what could he possibly have said? A little while longer, another ten minutes, and it would have come out easily; she would have shown them the room. Each sob that shook Mrs. Diamond's body shook him too.

"What have you got to hide then? What are you making such a fuss about?" Miller asked loudly.

"I'm not making a fuss. There's nothing there. Dirt. I'm ashamed. The door has things laying in front of it. You're trying to make me look a fool. You're not ashamed?"

Miller looked at her and shrugged his shoulders.

"An old woman . . . I'm so tired . . . Only rags. Why don't you just kill me?"

Miller nodded.

Kalisher was horrified at the both of them . . . hating. He was appalled to find that reason had failed in the face of primitive emotion. Mrs. Diamond and Miller's hostility was steaming and overpowering in the small kitchen. "Kill you? Kill you? What kind of nonsense are you talking, Mrs. Diamond? Who talks of killing you? Kill my own mother, you should say."

She knit together, for the last time, a fragility of bone and meagerness of flesh. She clutched at the flowers on her breast. She clenched her toothless mouth and shook her head. She wouldn't listen. She would starve first. She fought her own weariness. She fought them. She had outwitted them, outfought them, outscreamed them in the past. It would pass. She gathered herself to start screaming.

Miller looked at her and rose. He capped his pen. It was pointless, undignified, to have to fight her. Calming himself, Miller thought it wasn't a matter of anger; could the Department be angry? It was a matter of balances and perspectives. They had given too much to this old woman. That was it. "Mrs. D., there's nothing more I can do for you. We've been patient," Miller told her. "Let's go, Kalisher."

"Now wait a minute, Mr. Miller; surely . . ." Pale, anxious, Kalisher pleaded.

"No."

"But look . . ."

"Look, nothing. There's nothing to look at. Two hours . . . She won't cooperate. She won't show us the room. She's simply not Eligible. Let *your* agency give her funds."

"Don't be hostile."

"Don't give me that jargon."

"For God's sake, be a little objective."

"Not eligible; simply; he says," she said bitterly.

Kalisher tried . . . "You have no idea, Mrs. Diamond, how all this pains me. You have disappointed me. You have hurt me."

She looked at plump Kalisher's face and saw all that professional Social Worker's pain, that charitable sorrow. His breathless eagerness she also saw. She didn't believe his sorrow or his hurt; she believed his greed. There was nothing left. She would starve to death. They stood up, towering over her. She was between them and the kitchen door, standing in their way. "What are you going to do?" her dead voice asked them.

"Close your case, Mrs. D.," Miller told her.

"I'll die," she said.

Kalisher's lips were round and he shook his head. Miller looked over her head.

She had fought too long; she understood; it was final. "Don't go."

Kalisher tried to look out the window into the gray, drab yard, but had to look into the living room. He felt a soft tick in his mouth-muscles. Miller uncapped his pen. They waited.

"All right," she screamed. "All right. Look. Do what you want with me. Make a fool of me. Look." The last wailing shriek, the sum, that final sum of the years of humiliation and deprivation came pouring out of her. "Look!" The word hung, wailing in the stillness. Her hands hung by her side. She turned and went out. They followed her.

They went through the living room. The room was spotless, clean, and unused. On the floor, flowers faded into an old Persian rug. Stained wood shelves nailed to the walls held cheap little porcelains. The rose-colored wallpaint had long yellowed into sallow orange. A bronzed chandelier holding fake, pasteboard candles with flame-colored bulbs canted a little loose from the cracked, white ceiling. The flowered brocade covering the couch was unworn at the handrests. Old group-photographs hung on the walls in black frames; stiff, family figures, long lost, stood still, paled, as if the sunlight's fading fused figure and background into one. There was no dust anywhere. Miller tallied the hundred gimcrack vases, the glazed figurines, and saw that she had been able to afford these. Kalisher noted her compulsive neatness and knew she entombed some dead, traumatic moment here too.

The bedroom was dirtier; she lived here. A cheap chest of drawers stood against the wall. She showed them a closet holding a few frayed dresses. A gold-faced clock ticked. Another row of pictures, faded relatives, were lined up in front of the mirror on the chest. Kalisher picked up one of the pictures showing a young Mrs. Diamond standing next to a boy who towered over her. "Is this your son?" Kalisher asked. "My, how big . . ."

She snatched the picture out of his hand, wiped its glass on her house-coat and put it into a pocket. "Torturing me isn't enough?" she screamed at him.

A double bed was against the door which, she had always maintained, led to a closet. A blue, chenille spread covered the bed. A pair of cracked shoes stood underneath. Miller pushed the bed aside. It rolled, bumping on the uneven floor. The shoes were turned over and swept aside. He looked at the floor, trying to detect permanent scrape-marks which indicated Mrs. D. moved the bed back and forth frequently. There were no scrape-marks, but Miller couldn't be sure. They listened carefully, but only heard Mrs. D.'s sobbing. Kalisher could feel a little tightening of his throat. Miller thought of the computation . . .

She looked at them, standing, waiting for her. "So? Go ahead. Go," she told them. "Tear away my skin. Open my body." Kalisher watched Mrs. Diamond carefully to see how she was taking it. Politely, Miller stepped back, seemed to bow a little, and waved his hand, arcing his pen, almost courtly in his concern now, giving her a victor's magnanimous courtesy, restraining himself. Kalisher's rimless glasses were misted, hiding his eyes. But she folded her arms over her stomach. One hand was forever crooked into a clutch that plucked spastically at her elbow. She looked away, petulant, stubborn; her lower lip overlapped the unsupported upper lip.

"Go ahead, Mrs. D.," Miller told her.

She refused to answer. They could see a tear roll, break apart, and proliferate in the seams and wrinkles of her cheek, making one side of her face gleam. "Maybe we should come back tomorrow? I mean maybe you want time to think about it?" Kalisher stumbled. "I mean, she should have time," he almost shouted at Miller. "Well, I mean somehow it isn't right!" Miller pushed the door in. He looked. Kalisher's breath was at his ear.

"See," said she. "Treasures," she said.

The endless maw of her existence she filled by grasping. Against the day when she would be deprived, utterly, she collected. The little Depart-mental pittance was on loan to her by a capricious God. She knew; because here they were, two messengers of that vengeful God, ready to snatch back everything from her. She delivered up the pains of accumulation: threads; scraps; ribbons. The room had never been lived in; it was reduced to a passageway between two banks. Old, frayed chinos, now washed and shin-ing; damasks, double and single, she had piled to one side of the room and the other. Faded pants and chintzes, all neatly scrubbed, and of rare value, were carefully folded. A bright swatch of flowered cloth, picked out in pinks, blues, and reds, was spread next to a meandering green nylon ribbon bubbling cool, like a tongue of liquid, shining brighter than the light that filtered in. Strips of material, carefully ripped from brocaded chairs and couches, she saved from rot. Cloths of gold, she had, and secret bolts of Eastern silks. No. There had never been any point to anything any of them had told her. They didn't understand. She knew better.

Miller recoiled and turned his back on the tumbled mess of cloths, cartons, the thick, choking welter of rags, the old smell of musk and entombment, the fast dust-motes that danced in the heat-wavering sunlight, streaky from crusted windows half-blocked. He wrinkled his nose at the fetid stench that fumed up from the shards of her diseased mind. He shuddered, smelling it, hearing the thick stillness; he tried to turn away from it quickly before he was contaminated. But he felt the perspiration break loose again and pour down his chest. He looked away from that sickening sight of her soul, looked away from the pulsing festoons of dust hanging in the gloom. No Welfare manual could account for it, no amount of planning and regimentation could straighten it out. The dust-rats stirred and came for him and his skin itched unbearably. He felt, for one second, as though something had been opened inside of him; warped fingers warped his mind; her sickness, for one terrible second, was his sickness. He tried to make a notation in his notebook, but closed it.

Looking past him eagerly, Kalisher's face clouded over as he craned to see, stretching till he almost fell into the room. He tried to see if there could have been a burrow under the piles. He saw dirt; he had labored in vain. "Is that what you've been fighting us for two hours? Really, Mrs. D." She had merely acquired. She had saved. Where he had expected warmth, he felt the chill from all the little items that, no doubt, she translated into funds. All the hours he had spent with her were meaningless. She had made him look stupid in Miller's eyes. She had fought for the leavings of strangers. He added two more hours to the debris. He turned and glared at the cold tear that silvered Mrs. D.'s avaricious cheek; she was laughing at him. He scolded, "You should clean up this mess. What if a fire breaks out?" Kalisher saw that her eyes were hard, bright, glittering dryly.

Past them she scrambled and closed the door. "You satisfied?" she asked them. "You satisfied you made a fool out of an old woman?"

"Just our duty, Mrs. Diamond," Miller tried to answer coolly. He made a notation in his case-book; a drop of sweat blotted the entry. Her distorted and demented face leered at him.

"Some duty, to torture a dying woman."

"We weren't torturing you, Mrs. Diamond," Miller sighed, "don't be dramatic."

"That stuff is a fire hazard. Get rid of it. Mrs. D.," Kalisher told her again.

She made a gnarled club out of her hands and waved them at Kalisher and Miller, laying blame on their heads. Her housecoat flapped open. "So who cares? I'm alone. There's nothing for me. There never was. What do you care? Let me burn." Her hard shrill voice rang out and she began to weep tears of joy and deliverance.

Kalisher and Miller looked at each other, embarrassed. "Mrs. D. . ." Kalisher began.

"Oh, come on," Miller said, plucking Kalisher by the sleeve and leading him out.

On the stairs, Kalisher told Miller, "She's probably got money hidden there."

"You want to look for it?" Miller asked, walking down. "You still want to pick through that sickness? Go ahead," he said. He was half a flight ahead of Kalisher.

Bruce Jay Friedman

The Enemy

For as long as Samuel could remember, Aunt Emma had been the enemy. She always looked pretty much the same to him, a large woman with an enormous but vaguely defined bosom, much white powder on her face, and skin that did a great deal of hanging, especially in the neck area and along her arms. As the years went by, all that happened to her was that her powder got a little thicker, and her skin hung some more. It was as though she were some kind of exotic tree whose age could be determined by the amount of hang added each year. She was a concert violinist, spoke with a thick Viennese accent and had great, darkening teeth which seemed a little decayed and Viennese to him; the few times she hugged Samuel he was horror-struck and held his breath so that he would not have to smell her powder, clenched his fists so that he would not somehow disappear into her great hanging folds of skin.

She was married to Uncle Rex, and presumably, before Samuel was born, she had not been the enemy at all. She and Uncle Rex lived modestly in a small Newark apartment filled with musical instruments—antique violins, lutes and strange, slender, gracefully curved, reedy things that were on the tops of lumbering, ruined pianos. Later on, when Samuel came to visit, he remembered that the walls were crowded with darkened, brooding oil paintings, each one with a little light switch above it. When he turned the little lights on, the paintings would remain dark and brooding, the only difference being that the darkness glistened a little. He remembered thick, musty Oriental rugs and music stands and things that seemed to be remnants of old, rotting Viennese fortunes. In the days before Aunt Emma became the enemy, she went out on concert tours while Uncle Rex did mysterious things involving the trading of one large batch of fabric for another.

One evening, Uncle Rex attended a concert given by Aunt Emma, and after five minutes of hearing her perform, stood up in his seat and tore at his collar, saying he couldn't breathe and that there was gas in the concert hall. He got out to the aisle and then fell down and began to roll around, gasping for breath and tearing at his clothes. Someone sat on him while the police were called, and he was taken to Bellevue where attendants found bankbooks on his person totalling half a million dollars. Samuel was two years old at this time. It was about then that Aunt Emma became the enemy.

There began a twenty-year war between Uncle Rex's family on the one side and Aunt Emma and her two daughters on the other. The money, in a court transaction, had been taken from Uncle Rex and put into a trust fund, with small, regular payments being made to Aunt Emma on which she and her two daughters were to live. The war involved Aunt Emma's efforts to get the money in a few great chunks rather than to receive it in meager allotments. Uncle Rex's family, with Samuel's mother as commanding general, stood for keeping the payments modest so that Uncle Rex, once he was cured, would have a financial backlog. During the twenty-year period, he was trundled in and out of rest homes and mental institutions, both public and private. Another issue in the war involved Aunt Emma's side trying to keep him in these places and Uncle Rex's family, hence Samuel's team, getting him out of them.

Samuel's mother, as the leader of what Samuel came to know as the "good side," was a slender woman with slightly bowed legs, who never got over her bewilderment at Uncle Rex turning up with quite so much money. Uncle Rex was her oldest brother and had always been her favorite. She told Samuel that when she used to visit him before his collapse, they would sit together in his apartment watching fast new cars pass in the street below. "I told him which ones I liked," she said to Samuel. "Little did I know he could have bought the whole fleet of them." She told Samuel what a bad person Aunt Emma was; her main charge was that she was a "phoney" and that she had misrepresented herself as coming from an important Viennese family. When Samuel asked where Uncle Rex had met her, his mother said, "God only knows. God only knows where he found her." Samuel's mother and Uncle Rex had been brought up in New York's Harlem section; she would say to Samuel, "There weren't enough girls in the neighborhood for him. He had to go to twenty neighborhoods away to dig up that queen of his."

Second in command on the good side, and chief lieutenant to Samuel's mother, was her sister, Aunt Ramona, a tiny, saintlike person who ran a hardware store. She was very nervous and was always rolling up things, pieces of napkin, matchbook covers, edges of menus, and sticking them in her ear for a quick shake. When she used up one ear sticker, she immediately got to work on another. Much less strident in her criticism of Aunt Emma, she would occasionally take Samuel's wrist, lead him aside and say to him, "Shall I tell you something, Samuel? Your Aunt Emma is not a nice person." The third member of the general staff was Samuel's grandmother, whose main function was the taking of suitcases of things to Uncle Rex during his stays in institutions. Samuel remembered her as always getting up very early in the morning, earlier than anyone he had ever heard of. He was quite boastful of this fact and would tell his friends, "I've got a grandmother who gets up earlier than anyone in the world." Old when the war began, she hung on for many years, her role growing smaller until senility reduced her to rising before dawn and then sitting in a rocking chair to spend the day rocking away and heaping ancient Hebraic oaths upon Aunt Emma's head. Each of the three general staffers had slightly bowed legs, although Samuel's grandmother considered hers straight and would often point at other old ladies and insult them for having crooked feet. In any case, Samuel always carried with him an image of these three frail ladies, graduated in height, marching bowlegged but unafraid—Spirit of '76 style—to do battle with giant, heavily powdered Viennese Aunt Emma of the frightening, hanging folds of flesh.

Most of the battle reports came to Samuel via frenzied, shouting telephone conversations between his mother and her two lieutenants that ate up entire evenings. It seemed to Samuel that the calls could always have been condensed if the parties had made an agreement to have first one talk and then the other. But sentences were rarely finished; almost never did either side get to string two of them together. Samuel's mother would say, "Now wait a minute . . . now let me finish . . . I want to tell you something. Wait, Ramona . . . You know what the trouble is? . . ." And at the other end (Samuel knew this because he visited his saintlike aunt on numerous occasions) Aunt Ramona would say to his mother, "Just a second . . . Shall I tell you something . . . You've got to understand one thing . . . Now hold on there . . ." The Uncle Rex calls seemed to yawn forth endlessly, taking up great sections of Samuel's youth. He lived with his parents in a small apartment, and was often hard-pressed, because of the calls, to get his homework done. When the phone rang in the evening, he would go into the bedroom he shared with his mother and father, close the door, press his hands tight over his ears and try to concentrate on his lessons. Sometimes, when he was really annoyed, he would stand in his father's bedroom closet, his head among the ties. Samuel's father, not a terribly loyal soldier in the battle, would station himself opposite Samuel's mother, and begin to make disgusted faces, crossing and uncrossing his legs, getting up and down, and occasionally, as the hours wore on, hollering out, "When in hell are you getting off the goddamned phone."

Among the phone phrases in frequent use by Samuel's mother were "The son of a bitch . . . Let her (1) Drop dead (2) Burn in hell . . . What she's done to that poor boy . . . What she's turned him into . . . There weren't enough girls in the neighborhood . . ." and Samuel always knew these could only have to do with Aunt Emma. "The two little beauties" and "the two bargains" made reference to Aunt Emma's daughters and "that prince" and "the angel" were synonymous with Henry

Howell, the family attorney, who had for twenty years gone before state mental health boards and neurological commissions to get Uncle Rex out of bad institutions and into good ones, out of *all* institutions and back to his apartment in Newark. Whenever he succeeded in the latter task, and Uncle Rex was carted back to his Jersey apartment, a new species of phone call would get under way at Samuel's house. Though equal to the other in length, they were a gentler, less frenzied variety; in these, Samuel's mother would try, and totally fail, to convince Uncle Rex that there was no gas leak in his apartment, that his fish was *not* being poisoned and that Aunt Emma hadn't bought a special kind of smothering pillow for him so that when he put his face in it, he would wake up dead one morning. "I'll come over and sleep in the pillow," she would say to him. "Is that what you want?" Or "I'll eat the fish and show you that it's all right. Would that convince you?" And then, "There's no gas leak. I'll come over to breathe in your kitchen to show you." These calls were not exactly pleasurable to Samuel, but he looked forward to them nonetheless as a form of respite. He was able to concentrate on his homework while they were being carried on and felt no need to go among the ties. But then back Uncle Rex would go to a home, and once again, the violent, warlike conferences would get under way, driving Samuel into the locked bedroom and impelling his father to take up a muttering, leg-crossing sentry duty opposite the phone.

Each time Uncle Rex checked into a new institution, Samuel would accompany his mother (and often her two lieutenants) on a visit to see that Uncle Rex was well situated and happy in his new headquarters. Most of the places Samuel could remember were sunny, flowered terraced ones that seemed just like ordinary resorts, the one difference being the people all wore bathrobes and pajamas in midday and out on the grounds. He remembered one in particular that was especially fragrant and colorful. The summer garden perfume was so balmy and unbalancing he thought it would rise up and tear his head from his body. Samuel wanted to stay at that place and just parade around in the flower beds. There was another dark one that frightened him from the start. It had tall, ominous gates and the reception rooms inside seemed too bare and high-ceilinged. Uncle Rex came out wearing a bathrobe, but this time it was the same kind as everyone else wore. His head was shaved and he looked much thinner, but it was his adam's apple that really got Samuel. It protruded much more than it should have and Samuel thought how easy it would be for someone to just snap it off. He ran to Uncle Rex and dug his head into his waist, crying into his bathrobe and wanting to get him right out of there. For the first time he realized he had an uncle in a mental institution who couldn't just walk out and live in an apartment if he wanted to. "Can't we take him home?" he cried to the three bowlegged ladies. "I want to take him home. He can live with us. He's my uncle." Who would stop them if they just stuck him in a car and were brave enough to drive right out of there.

There was another place that seemed to be made up of a series of large empty yards where women, many of them surprisingly young, with hair cut either boyishly or allowed to flow deep down their backs, walked slowly in the sunlight, occasionally breaking into joyous dances; but his memories here were vague and most of the homes he remembered clearly were fragrant, sunny ones, where Uncle Rex would be waiting for them on a bench. Samuel always brought along a box of pralines, Uncle Rex's favorites, and for the first few minutes his troubled uncle would make a fuss over him, saying "How big you've gotten" just as though he were any of Samuel's uncles outside. Samuel's mother would then ask Uncle Rex a question and, before he was able to answer, say to Samuel, "We should all have his brain. Even with all he's been through. I'd like to know what he's forgotten. His mind? Don't ever sell him short." But then, after a few minutes more, a cloud would pass over Uncle Rex's face and he would begin to air small grievances, then increasingly larger ones. "They give you itchy clothes," he would say, squirming around in his bathrobe. "You want to pull your skin off." He would then ask Samuel's mother if she could have food sent in for him. "I don't like what this new doctor's having them give me. I don't like what he's having them put in my food." And then his head would tilt at a strange angle and he would say, "You smell something?" and Samuel would know it was time for the visit to end. At those head-tilting times, Samuel saw a connection between his Uncle Rex and the long-haired ladies who broke into dances.

It was only when his uncle was between institutions that Samuel got to see the perfidious Aunt Emma. Uncle Rex stayed, during these intervals, at his old, gloomy apartment in Newark and Samuel would accompany the three bowlegged warriors there, his grandmother hobbling along at the formation's rear; she carried a suitcase bulging with fine shirts that didn't itch and untainted fish. It was a strange war in that most of the guns were fired harmlessly in the air and when the opposing enemies met in the field there would be nothing but hugs and conciliation. The princelike attorney, Henry Howell, had advised Samuel's team that Uncle Rex, despite Aunt Emma's dark nature, was still better off with his family than without them; as a result, the visits would commence with the three warriors lining up to kiss and hug Aunt Emma whose name they had damned in a thousand phone calls. Samuel's mother would say, "How have you been, darling?" and the saintlike Aunt Ramona would take the villainous woman by her fleshy wrists and say, "You know what, Emma? I still think you're a sweet person." Samuel's old grandmother herself would clasp Aunt Emma's great hands and say, "We should all live and be well, that's all," and then look swiftly at the ceiling as though asking heaven forgiveness for what she really felt in her heart. Samuel wasn't fooled by all the light atmosphere, however. He hated his Aunt Emma with a purple rage. She was bad. He hated her hanging arms and her teeth. He hated her for being foreign. He couldn't stand her smell. Whenever he ran into someone or something disgusting in his life, he would say, "Ugh, reminds me of Aunt Emma." Even the violin became a sickening instrument to him, and at concerts, he kept his eyes glued to the woodwind section. When she hugged him during these visits, he felt as though he were being embraced by a great powdery Viennese dead woman. On some of these rare visits, Aunt Emma's two daughters would be present. He considered them the enemy, too. One had black, tangled hair and a perpetual storm on her face; she did some of the brooding paintings with the little lights on top of them and Samuel had never seen her smile. Her name was Mary, but he gave her the private nickname of "Muddy." She stayed in a small, darkened half-room filled with stacks of old sheet music, painting equipment and piano stools; she always had charcoal smudges on her beclouded face. Aunt Emma, in a gushing Viennese voice, would call her in to play a lute selection and she would always refuse, slamming the door. The other, younger daughter was fresh and sunny with features so lovely and a mouth so saintlike it seemed to Samuel to be some sort of mistake. Each time he saw her he hoped to find he had been wrong, that she had some outrageous facial flaw he'd somehow never noticed before, but she became lovelier as the years passed. Because she was the enemy, her beauty, of course, did not count, and it seemed such a waste to Samuel. Her disposition was golden and cheerful, too, and this added to Samuel's discomfort; it took a powerful effort of will, but he managed to spread the blanket of his hatred out far enough so that it enveloped her too, perfect features, golden smile and all.

These visits were short. After the opening hugs and kisses, Aunt Emma would ask Samuel if he wanted something to eat, an invitation he always considered preposterous. He would giggle and swiftly decline. Then, after a while, she would excuse herself and take the two girls out for a walk, beckoning them in some harsh, middle European tongue, another sign of evildoing, Samuel always felt. As soon as Aunt Emma had left the room, Samuel's grandmother would pop open the suitcase while his mother and Aunt Ramona went inside and began testing the food in the refrigerator and smelling for gas leaks, assuring Uncle Rex finally that everything was in order. Samuel would prowl the two daughters' bedrooms then, looking in bureau drawers and always coming up with at least one book of nude sculpture, final evidence that the girls were nasty and twisted.

His last visit to the Newark apartment came when he was 17 and about to go off to college. It was a visit totally different from the others in that Aunt Emma's living room, instead of being musty and darkened, was all aglow with floodlights. The brooding pictures had been taken down and in their place were bright, vividly colored canvases, most of them depicting religious scenes. The people in them were stiff and squarish and great-eyed as though an eight-year-old child had drawn them. In each of the paintings there stood at least one person whose hands were raised spread-fingered and gleeful as though he were singing out in exultation. It seemed to be a kind of artist's signature. There were some people standing around looking at the pictures, taking notes, and Aunt Emma explained to Samuel and the three warriors, each of them a little tired at this stage of the campaign, that when violin-playing had grown too strenuous for her weighty arms, she had taken up painting, which she found less physically exerting. She did 25 canvases and had been encouraged by a professor friend to exhibit them. This was a preview for some art magazine people. It was a little awkward to do any tasting and gas-sniffing this trip. Uncle Rex seemed remarkably placid, and so after a quick visit with him, Samuel's grandmother dropped off the suitcase and the bowlegged trio backed out of the door, calling it a day.

Samuel went off to college the following year, liberated finally from the endless nightly calls, and only via letters and visits home during intersession was he kept apprised of the war's progress. It dragged on for years, reaching no climactic moments and finally petering out uncertainly with no clear-cut victors. Uncle Rex began to spend more and more time at home in the Newark apartment and almost no time in institutions. The trust fund became depleted and reached the point where there really wasn't enough money left to fuss about; Henry Howell, the attorney, saw fit to drop all dealings with it and let it fend for itself. Samuel's grandmother died, getting up before dawn one morning and then dropping off in the middle of a rocking and oath-making session. This left only two key warriors, who didn't really seem to know where they stood, what goals to press for. Uncle Rex finally began to spend all his time in Newark, apparently liberated permanently from homes. He was 77 now and seemed rather hearty, although he still craned his head around now and then and sniffed at the air. His three younger brothers had all passed away, and he admitted to Samuel's mother that he took occasional trips downtown to "see about some fabric."

"I wouldn't be surprised if they found another half-million on him," Samuel's mother wrote to him at college. "Don't ever sell his head short."

Aunt Emma spent little time at the Newark apartment, finally disappearing altogether. There was a brief renewal of extended phone call attacks. The wires again began to sizzle, the main charge against Aunt Emma now being switched to licentiousness, "fooling around." The "professor friend" came in for some heavy criticism, too. But it must have seemed a little silly, even to the two hardened old veterans. They had always accused the Viennese lady of being "years older than Rex," and if this were at all true, she would have been comfortably in her eighties, certainly entitled to a little dalliance by any moral standard. Whatever the case, Aunt Emma showed up for the last time at her younger daughter's wedding. The two increasingly bowlegged warriors attended this one, but stayed away from the second daughter's wedding months later, as though unable to arrive at a clear-cut policy.

Samuel got married in his senior year of college. He did not know exactly what he was doing married. All he knew is that he had grown attached to a dark and quiet, wintry sort of girl with whom he felt terribly comfortable. Someone had pointed her out as having lots of money and that had been in the back of his mind. But it was more a case of losing his balance and saying the hell with it and turning up married six years ahead of a date he'd once jotted down on some crazy schedule he'd always planned to adhere to. He called his mother and said, "I'm coming home with a girl I'm married to."

He took her to see his mother and father and all his relatives, and she was as quiet and shy with them as she was with Samuel, sitting with her legs crossed, and for the most part, just listening to people. He felt very good with her when she did that. He took her to see saintlike Aunt Ramona who locked onto her wrist, led her off and said, "Shall I tell you something. You've got yourself a darling boy."

He went with her to visit Uncle Rex, not exactly at the Newark apartment, but to a windy hill nearby that overlooked some water; there Uncle Rex spent his afternoons, sitting on a bench and watching boats. "This is my wife," Samuel said to Uncle Rex who held out a weak hand to her and said, "Oh you're married. Good." The three sat silently then for a few minutes and when Uncle Rex shrugged a little and said, "I can't get a decent overcoat. This one itches me," Samuel rose and said good-by, going off with his new wife.

The next day, Samuel went to his mother's house for dinner while his wife spent the evening with some college girl friends. Tired after the dinner, he took a nap in the bedroom and then seemed to trip in his dream, waking up suddenly, shaking his head. He heard his mother's phone voice then, lower than the old days, but still audible. "That's what you get," she was saying. "What do you expect . . . That's when they're very rich . . . That's when they've got money . . ."

He flicked on the lamp and cleared the sleep out of his eyes, taking a picture of his wife from his wallet. You'd never know it to look at her, he thought, but he had the damndest feeling he'd married himself an Aunt Emma.

Virginia Moriconi

Simple Arithmetic

Geneva, January 15

Dear Father:

Well, I am back in School, as you can see, and the place is just as miserable as ever. My only friend, the one I talked to you about, Ronald Fletcher, is not coming back any more because someone persuaded his mother that she was letting him go to waste, since he was extremely photogenic, so now he is going to become a child actor. I was very surprised to hear this, as the one thing Ronnie liked to do was play basketball. He was very shy.

The flight wasn't too bad. I mean nobody had to be carried off the plane. The only thing was, we were six hours late and they forgot to give us anything to eat, so for fourteen hours we had a chance to get quite hungry but, as you say, for the money you save going tourist class, you should be prepared to make a few little sacrifices.

I did what you told me, and when we got to Idlewild I paid the taxi driver his fare and gave him a fifty-cent tip. He was very dissatisfied. In fact he wouldn't give me my suitcase. In fact I don't know what would have happened if a man hadn't come up just while the argument was going on and when he heard what it was all about he gave the taxi driver a dollar and I took my suitcase and got to the plane on time.

During the trip I thought the whole thing over. I did not come to any conclusion. I know I have been very extravagant and unreasonable about money and you have done the best you can to explain this to me. Still, while I was thinking about it, it seemed to me that there were only three possibilities. I could just have given up and let the taxi driver have the suitcase, but when you realize that if we had to buy everything over again that was in the suitcase we would probably have had to spend at least five hundred dollars, it does not seem very economical. Or I could have gone on arguing with him and missed the plane, but then we would have had to pay something like three hundred dollars for another ticket. Or else I could have given him an extra twenty-five cents which, as you say, is just throwing money around to create an impression. What would you have done?

Anyway I got here, with the suitcase, which was the main thing. They took two weekend privileges away from me because I was late for the opening of School. I tried to explain to M. Frisch that it had nothing to do with me if the weather was so bad that the plane was delayed for six hours, but he said that prudent persons allow for continjensies of this kind and make earlier reservations. I don't care about this because the next two weekends are skiing weekends and I have never seen any point in waking up at six o'clock in the morning just to get frozen stiff and endure terrible pain even if sports are a part of growing up, as you say. Besides, we will save twenty-seven dollars by having me stay in my room.

In closing I want to say that I had a very nice Christmas and I appreciate everything you tried to do for me and I hope I wasn't too much of a bother. (Martha explained to me that you had had to take time off from your honeymoon in order to make Christmas for me and I am very sorry even though I do not think I am to blame if Christmas falls on the twenty-fifth of December, especially since everybody knows that it does. What I mean is, if you had wanted to have a long honeymoon you and Martha could have gotten married earlier, or you could have waited until Christmas was over, or you could just have told me not to come and I would have understood.)

I will try not to spend so much money in the future and I will keep accounts and send them to you. I will also try to remember to do the eye exercises and the exercises for fallen arches that the doctors in New York prescribed. Love, Stephen.

New York, January 19

Dear Stephen:

Thank you very much for the long letter of January fifteenth. I was very glad to know that you had gotten back safely, even though the flight was late. (I do not agree with M. Frisch that prudent persons allow for "continjensies" of this kind, now that air travel is as standard as it is, and the service usually so good, but we must remember that Swiss people are, by and large, the most meticulous in the world and nothing offends them more than other people who are not punctual.)

In the affair of the suitcase, I'm afraid that we were both at fault. I had forgotten that there would be an extra charge for luggage when I suggested that you should tip the driver fifty cents. You, on the other hand, might have inferred from his argument that he was simply asking that the tariff—i.e., the fare, plus overcharge for the suitcase—should be paid in full, and regulated yourself accordingly. In any event you arrived, and I am only sorry that obviously you had no time to learn the name and address of your benefactor so that we might have paid him back for his kindness.

I will look forward to going over your accounting and I am sure you will find that in keeping a clear record of what you spend you will be able to cut your cloth according to the bolt and that, in turn, will help you to develop a real regard for yourself. It is a common failing, as I told you, to spend too much money in order to compensate oneself for a lack of inner security, but you can easily see that a foolish purchase does not insure stability, and if you are chronically insolvent you can hardly hope for peace of mind. Your allowance is more than adequate and when you learn to make both ends meet you will have taken a decisive step ahead. I have great faith in you and I know you will find your anchor to windward in your studies, in your sports, and in your companions.

As to what you say about Christmas, you are not obliged to "apreciate" what we did for you. The important thing was that you should have had a good time, and I think we had some wonderful fun together, the three of us, don't you? Until your mother decides where she wants to live and settles down, this is your *home* and you must always think of it that way. Even though I have remarried, I am still your father, first and last, and Martha is very fond of you too, and very understanding about your problems. You may not be aware of it but in fact she is one of the best friends you have. New ideas and new stepmothers take a little getting used to, of course.

Please write me as regularly as you can, since your letters mean a great deal to me. Please try too, at all times, to keep your marks up to scratch, as college entrance is getting harder and harder in this country, and there are thousands of candidates each year for the good universities. Concentrate particularly on spelling. "Contingency" is difficult, I know, but there is no excuse for only one "p" in "appreciate"! And *do* the exercises. Love, Father.

Geneva, January 22

Dear Mummy:

Last Sunday I had to write to Father to thank him for my Christmas vacation and to tell him that I got back all right. This Sunday I thought I would write to you even though you are on a cruze so perhaps you will never get my letter. I must say that if they didn't make us write home once a week I don't believe that I would ever write any letters at all. What I mean is that once you get to a point like this, in a place like this, you see that you are supposed to have your life and your parents are supposed to have their lives, and you have lost the connection.

Anyway I have to tell you that Father was wonderful to me and Martha was very nice too. They had thought it all out, what a child of my age might like to do in his vacation and sometimes it was pretty strenuous, as you can imagine. At the end the School sent the bill for the first term, where they charge you for the extras which they let you have here and it seems that I had gone way over my allowance and besides I had signed for a whole lot of things I did not deserve. So there was a terrible scene and Father was very angry and Martha cried and said that if Father always made such an effort to consider me as a person I should make an effort to consider him as a person too and wake up to the fact that he was not Rockefeller and that even if he was sacrificing himself so that I could go to one of the most expensive schools in the world it did not mean that I should drag everybody down in the mud by my reckless spending. So now I have to turn over a new leaf and keep accounts of every penny and not buy anything which is out of proportion to our scale of living.

Except for that one time they were very affectionate to me and did everything they could for my happiness. Of course it was awful without you. It was the first time we hadn't been together and I couldn't really believe it was Christmas.

I hope you are having a wonderful time and getting the rest you need and please write me when you can. All my love, Stephen.

Geneva, January 29

Dear Father:

Well it is your turn for a letter this week because I wrote to Mummy last Sunday. (I am sure I can say this to you without hurting your feelings because you always said that the one thing you and Mummy wanted was a civilized divorce so we could all be friends.) Anyway Mummy hasn't answered my letter so probably she doesn't aprove of my spelling any more than you do. I am beginning to wonder if maybe it wouldn't be much simpler and much cheaper too if I didn't go to college after all. I really don't know what this education is for in the first place.

There is a terrible scandal here at School which has been very interesting for the rest of us. One of the girls, who is only sixteen, has gotten pregnant and everyone knows that it is all on account of the science instructer, who is a drip. We are waiting to see if he will marry her, but in the meantime she is terrifically upset and she has been expelled from the School. She is going away on Friday.

I always liked her very much and I had a long talk with her last night. I wanted to tell her that maybe it was not the end of the world, that my stepmother was going to have a baby in May, although she never got married until December, and the sky didn't fall in or anything. I thought it might have comforted her to think that grownups make the same mistakes that children do (if you can call her a child) but then I was afraid that it might be disloyal to drag you and Martha into the conversation, so I just let it go.

I'm fine and things are just the same. Love, Stephen.

New York, February 2

Dear Stephen:

It would be a great relief to think that your mother did not "aprove" of your spelling either, but I'm sure that it's not for that reason that you haven't heard from her. She was never any good as a correspondent, and now it is probably more difficult for her than ever. We did indeed try for what you call a "civilized divorce" for all our sakes, but divorce is not any easy thing for any of the persons involved, as you well know, and if you try to put yourself in your mother's place for a moment, you will see that she is in need of time and solitude to work things out for herself. She will certainly write to you as soon as she has found herself again, and meanwhile you must continue to believe in her affection for you and not let impatience get the better of you.

Again, in case you are really in doubt about it, the purpose of your education is to enable you to stand on your own feet when you are a man and make something of yourself. Inaccuracies in spelling will not *simplify* anything.

I can easily see how you might have made a parallel between your friend who has gotten into trouble, and Martha who is expecting the baby in May, but there is only a superficial similarity in the two cases.

Your friend is, or was, still a child, and would have done better to have accepted the limitations of the world of childhood—as you can clearly see for yourself, now that she is in this predicament. Martha, on the other hand, was hardly a child. She was a mature human being, responsible for her own

H

actions and prepared to be responsible for the baby when it came. Moreover I, unlike the science "instructer" am not a drip, I too am responsible for *my* actions, and so Martha and I are married and I will do my best to live up to her and the baby.

Speaking of which, we have just found a new apartment because this one will be too small for us in May. It is right across the street from your old school and we have a kitchen, a dining alcove, a living room, two bedrooms—one for me and Martha, and one for the new baby—and another room which will be for you. Martha felt that it was very important for you to feel that you had a place of your own when you came home to us, and so it is largely thanks to her that we have taken such a big place. The room will double as a study for me when you are not with us, but we will move all my books and papers and paraphernalia whenever you come, and Martha is planning to hang the Japanese silk screen you liked at the foot of the bed.

Please keep in touch, and *please* don't forget the exercises. Love Father.

Geneva, February 5

Dear Father:

There is one thing which I would like to say to you which is that if it hadn't been for you I would never have heard of a "civilized divorce," but that is the way you explained it to me. I always thought it was crazy. What I mean is, wouldn't it have been better if you had said, "I don't like your mother any more and I would rather live with Martha," instead of insisting that you and Mummy were always going to be the greatest friends? Because the way things are now Mummy probably thinks that you still like her very much, and it must be hard for Martha to believe that she was chosen, and I'm pretty much confused myself, although it is really none of my business.

You will be sorry to hear that I am not able to do any of the exercises any longer. I cannot do the eye exercises because my roommate got so fassinated by the stereo gadget that he broke it. (But the School Nurse says she thinks it may be just as well to let the whole thing go since in her opinion there was a good chance that I might have gotten more crosseyed than ever, fidgeting with the viewer.) And I cannot do the exercises for fallen arches, at least for one foot, because when I was decorating the Assembly Hall for the dance last Saturday, I fell off the stepladder and broke my ankle. So now I am in the Infirmary and the School wants to know whether to send the doctor's bill to you or to Mummy, because they had to call in a specialist from outside, since the regular School Doctor only knows how to do a very limited number of things. So I have cost a lot of money again and I am very very sorry, but if they were half-way decent in this School they would pay to have proper equipment and not let the students risk their lives on broken stepladders, which is something you could write to the Book-Keeping Department, if you felt like it, because I can't, but you could, and it might do some good in the end.

The girl who got into so much trouble took too many sleeping pills and died. I felt terrible about it, in fact I cried when I heard it. Life is very crewel, isn't it?

I agree with what you said, that she was a child, but I think she knew that, from her point of view. I think she did what she did because she thought of the science instructer as a grownup, so she imagined that she was perfectly safe with him. You may think she was just bad, because she was a child and should have known better, but I think that it was not entirely her fault since here at School we are all encouraged to take the teachers seriously.

I am very glad you have found a new apartment and I hope you won't move all your books and papers when I come home, because that would only make me feel that I was more of a nuisance than ever. Love, Stephen.

New York, February 8

Dear Stephen:

This will have to be a very short letter because we are to move into the new apartment tomorrow and Martha needs my help with the packing.

We were exceedingly shocked by the tragic death of your friend, and very sorry that you should have had such a sad experience. Life can be "crewel" indeed to the people who do not learn how to live it.

When I was exactly your age I broke my ankle too—I wasn't on a defective stepladder, I was playing hockey—and it hurt like the devil. I still remember it and you have all my sympathy. (I have written to the School Physician to ask how long you will have to be immobilized, and to urge him to get you back into the athletic program as fast as possible. The specialist's bill should be sent to me.)

I have also ordered another stereo viewer because, in spite of the opinion of the School Nurse, the exercises are most important and you are to do them *religiously*. Please be more careful with this one no matter how much it may "fassinate" your roommate.

Martha sends love and wants to know what you would like for your birthday. Let us know how the ankle is mending. Love, Father.

Geneva, February 12

Dear Father:

I was very surprised by your letter. I was surprised that you said you were helping Martha to pack because when you and Mummy were married I do not ever remember you packing or anything like that so I guess Martha is reforming your charactor. I was also surprised by what you said about the girl who died. What I mean is, if anyone had told me a story like that I think I would have just let myself get a little worked up about the science instructer because it seems to me that he was a villan too. Of course you are much more riserved than I am.

I am out of the Infirmary and they have given me a pair of crutches, but I'm afraid it will be a long time before I can do sports again.

I hope the new apartment is nice and I do not want anything for my birthday because it will seem very funny having a birthday in School so I would rather not be reminded of it. Love, Stephen.

New York, February 15

Dear Stephen:

This is not an answer to your letter of February twelfth, but an attempt to have a serious discussion with you, as if we were face to face.

You are almost fifteen years old. Shortly you will be up against the stiffest competition of your life when you apply for college entrance. No examiner is going to find himself favorably impressed by "charactor" or "instructer" or "villan" or "riserved" or similar errors. You will have to face the fact that in this world we succeed on our merits, and if we are unsuccessful, on account of sloppy habits of mind, we suffer for it. You are still too young to understand me entirely, but you are not too young to recognize the importance of effort. People who do not make the grade are desperately unhappy all their lives because they have no place in society. If you do not pass the college entrance examinations simply because you are unable to spell, it will be nobody's fault but your own, and you will be gravely handicapped for the rest of your life.

Every time you are in doubt about a word you are to look it up in the dictionary and *memorize* the spelling. This is the least you can do to help yourself.

We are still at sixes and sevens in the new apartment but when Martha accomplishes all she has planned it should be very nice indeed and I think you will like it. Love, Father.

Geneva, February 19

Dear Father:

I guess we do not understand each other at all. If you immagine for one minute that just by making a little effort I could imaggine how to spell immaggine without looking it up and finding that actually it is "imagine," then you are all wrong. In other words, if you get a letter from me and there are only two or three mistakes well you just have to take my word for it that I have had to look up practically every single word in the dictionary and that is one reason I hate having to write you these letters because they take so long and in the end they are not at all spontainious, no, just wait a second, here it is, "spontaneous," and believe me only two or three mistakes in a letter from me is one of the seven wonders of the world. What I'm saying is that I am doing the best I can as you would aggree if you could see my dictionary which is falling apart and when you say I should *memmorize* the spelling I can't because it doesn't make any sence to me and never did. Love, Stephen.

New York, February 23

Dear Stephen:

It is probably just as well that you have gotten everything off your chest. We all need to blow up once in a while. It clears the air.

Please don't ever forget that I am aware that spelling is difficult for you. I know you are making a great effort and I am very proud of you. I just want to be sure that you *keep trying.*

I am enclosing a small check for your birthday because even if you do not want to be reminded of it I wouldn't want to forget it and you must know that we are thinking of you. Love, Father.

Geneva, February 26

Dear Father:

We are not allowed to cash personal checks here in the School, but thank you anyway for the money.

I am not able to write any more because we are going to have the exams and I have to study. Love, Stephen.

New York, March 2

Night Letter

Best of luck, stop, keep me posted exam results—love, Father.

Geneva, March 12

Dear Father:

Well, the exams are over. I got a C in English because aparently I do not know how to spell, which should not come as too much of a surprise to you. In Science, Mathematics, and Latin I got A, and in French and History I got a B plus. This makes me first in the class, which doesn't mean very much since none of the children here have any life of the mind, as you would say. I mean they are all jerks, more or less. What am I supposed to do in the Easter vacation? Do you want me to come to New York, or shall I just stay here and get a rest, which I could use? Love, Stephen.

New York, March 16

Dear Stephen:

I am *immensely* pleased with the examination results. Congratulations. Pull up the spelling and our worries are over.

Just yesterday I had a letter from your mother. She has taken a little house in Majorca, which is an island off the Spanish coast, as you probably know, and she suggests that you should come to her for the Easter holidays. Of course you are always welcome here—and you could rest as much as you wanted—but Majorca is very beautiful and would certainly appeal to the artistic side of your nature. I have written to your mother, urging her to write to you immediately, and I enclose her address in case you should want to write yourself. Let me know what you would like to do. Love, Father.

Geneva, March 19

Dear Mummy:

Father says that you have invited me to come to you in Majorca for the Easter vacation. Is that true? I would be very very happy if it were. It has been very hard to be away from you for all this time and if you wanted to see me it would mean a great deal to me. I mean if you are feeling well enough. I could do a lot of things for you so you would not get too tired.

I wonder if you will think that I have changed when you see me. As a matter of fact I have changed a lot because I have become quite bitter. I have become quite bitter on account of this School.

I know that you and Father wanted me to have some expearience of what the world was like outside of America but what you didn't know is that Geneva is not the world at all. I mean, if you were born here then perhaps you would have a real life, but I do not know anyone who was born here so all the people I see are just like myself, we are just waiting not to be lost any more. I think it would have been better to have left me in some place where I belonged even if Americans are getting very loud and money conscious. Because actually most children here are Americans, if you come right down to it, only it seems their parents didn't know what to do with them any longer.

Mummy I have written all this because I'm afraid that I have spent too much money all over again and M. Frisch says that Father will have a crise des nerfs when he sees what I have done, and I thought that maybe you would understand that I only bought these things because there didn't seem to be anything else to do, and that you could help me somehow or other. Anyway, according to the School, we will have to pay for all these things.

Concert, Segovia	(Worth it)	16.00 (Swiss Francs)
School Dance		5.00
English Drama (What do they mean?)		10.00
Controle de l'habitant	(?)	9.10
Co-op purchases		65.90
Ballets Russes	(Disappointing)	47.00
Librairie Prior		59.30
Concert piano	(For practising)	61.00
Teinturie (They ruined everything)		56.50
Toilet and Medicine		35.00
Escalade Ball		7.00
Pocket Money		160.00
77 Yoghurts	(Doctor's advice)	42.40
Book account		295.70
	Total:	869.90 (Swiss Francs)

Now you see the trouble is that Father told me I was to spend about fifty dollars a month, because that was my allowance, and that I was not to spend anything more. Anyway, fifty dollars a month would be about two hundred and ten Swiss Francs, and then I had fifteen dollars for Christmas from Granny, and when I got back to School I found four Francs in the pocket of my leather jacket and then I had seventy-nine cents left over from New York, but that doesn't help much, and then Father sent me twenty-five dollars for my birthday but I couldn't cash the check because they do not allow that here in School, so what shall I do?

It is a serious situation as you can see, and it is going to get a lot more serious when Father sees the bill. But whatever you do, I imploar you not to write to Father because the trouble seems to be that I never had a balance foreward and I am afraid that it is impossible to keep accounts without a balance foreward, and even more afraid that by this time the accounts have gone a little bizerk.

Do you want me to take a plane when I come to Majorca? Who shall I say is going to pay for the ticket?

Please do write me as soon as you can, because the holidays begin on March 30 and if you don't tell me what to do I will be way out on a lim. Lots and lots of love, Stephen.

Geneva, March 26

Dear Father:

I wrote to Mummy a week ago to say that I would like very much to spend my Easter vacation in Majorca. So far she has not answered my letter, but I guess she will pretty soon. I hope she will because the holidays begin on Thursday.

I am afraid you are going to be upset about the bill all over again, but in the Spring term I will start anew and keep you in touch with what is going on. Love, Stephen.

P.S. If Mummy doesn't write what shall I do?

Paul Bowles

The Hyena

A stork was passing over desert country on his way north. He was thirsty, and he began to look for water. When he came to the mountains of Khang el Ghar, he saw a pool at the bottom of a ravine. He flew down between the rocks and lighted at the edge of the water. Then he walked in and drank.

At that moment a hyena limped up and, seeing the stork standing in the water, said: "Have you come a long way?" The stork had never seen a hyena before. "So this is what a hyena is like," he thought. And he stood looking at the hyena because he had been told that if the hyena can put a little of his urine on someone, that one will have to walk after the hyena to whatever place the hyena wants him to go.

"It will be summer soon," said the stork. "I am on my way north." At the same time, he walked further out into the pool, so as not to be so near the hyena. The water here was deeper and he almost lost his balance and had to flap his wings to keep upright. The hyena walked to the other side of the pool and looked at him from there.

"I know what is in your head," said the hyena. "You believe the story about me. You think I have that power? Perhaps long ago hyenas were like that. But now they are the same as everyone else. I could wet you from here if I wanted to. But what for? If you want to be unfriendly, go to the middle of the pool and stay there."

The stork looked around at the pool and saw that there was no spot in it where he could stand and be out of reach of the hyena.

"I have finished drinking," said the stork. He spread his wings and flapped out of the pool. At the edge he ran quickly ahead and rose into the air. He circled above the pool, looking down at the hyena.

"So you are the one they call the ogre," he said. "The world is full of strange things."

The hyena looked up. His eyes were narrow and crooked. "Allah brought us all here," he said. "You know that. You are the one who knows about Allah."

The stork flew a little lower. "That is true," he said. "But I am surprised to hear you say it. You have a very bad name, as you yourself just said. Magic is against the will of Allah."

The hyena tilted his head. "So you still believe the lies!" he cried.

"I have not seen the inside of your bladder," said the stork. "But why does everyone say you can make magic with it?"

"Why did Allah give you a head, I wonder? You have not learned how to use it." But the hyena spoke in so low a voice that the stork could not hear him.

"Your words got lost," said the stork, and he let himself drop lower.

The hyena looked up again. "I said: Don't come too near me. I might lift my leg and cover you with magic!" He laughed, and the stork was near enough to him to see that his teeth were brown.

"Still, there must be some reason," the stork began. Then he looked for a rock high above the hyena, and settled himself on it. The hyena sat and stared up at him. "Why does everyone hate you?" the stork went on. "Why do they call you an ogre? What have you done?"

The hyena squinted. "You are very lucky," he told the stork. "Men never try to kill you, because they think you are holy. They call you a saint and a sage. And yet you seem like neither a saint nor a sage."

"What do you mean?" said the stork quickly.

"If you really understood, you would know that magic is a grain of dust in the wind, and that Allah has power over everything. You would not be afraid."

The stork stood for a long time, thinking. He lifted one leg and held it bent in front of him. The ravine grew red as the sun went lower. And the hyena sat quietly looking up at the stork, waiting for him to speak.

Finally the stork put his leg down, opened his bill, and said: "You mean that if there is no magic, the one who sins is the one who believes there is."

The hyena laughed. "I said nothing about sin. But you did, and you are the sage. I am not in the world to tell anyone what is right or wrong. Living from night to night is enough. Everyone hopes to see me dead."

The stork lifted his leg again and stood thinking. The last daylight rose into the sky and was gone. The cliffs at the sides of the ravine were lost in the darkness.

At length the stork said: "You have given me something to think about. That is good. But now night has come. I must go on my way." He raised his wings and started to fly straight out from the boulder where he had stood. The hyena listened. He heard the stork's wings beating the air slowly, and then he heard the sound of the stork's body as it hit the cliff on the other side of the ravine. He climbed up over the rocks and found the stork. "Your wing is broken," he said. "It would have been better for you to go while there was still daylight."

"Yes," said the stork. He was unhappy and afraid.

H*

"Come home with me," the hyena told him. "Can you walk?"

"Yes," said the stork. Together they made their way down the valley. Soon they came to a cave in the side of the mountain. The hyena went in first and called out: "Bend your head." When they were well inside, he said: "Now you can put your head up. The cave is high here."

There was only darkness inside. The stork stood still. "Where are you?" he said.

"I am here," the hyena answered, and he laughed.

"Why are you laughing?" asked the stork.

"I was thinking that the world is strange," the hyena told him. "The saint has come into my cave because he believes in magic."

"I don't understand," said the stork.

"You are confused. But at least now you can believe that I have no magic. I am like anyone else in the world."

The stork did not answer right away. He smelled the stench of the hyena very near him. Then he said, with a sigh: "You are right, of course. There is no power beyond the power of Allah."

"I am happy," said the hyena, breathing into his face. "At last you understand." Quickly he seized the stork's neck and tore it open. The stork flapped and fell on his side.

"Allah gave me something better than magic," the hyena said under his breath. "He gave me a brain."

The stork lay still. He tried to say once more: "There is no power beyond the power of Allah." But his bill merely opened very wide in the dark.

The hyena turned away. "You will be dead in a minute," he said over his shoulder. "In ten days I shall come back. By then you will be ready."

Ten days later the hyena went to the cave and found the stork where he had left him. The ants had not been there. "Good," he said. He devoured what he wanted and went outside to a large flat rock above the entrance to the cave. There in the moonlight he stood a while, vomiting.

He ate some of his vomit and rolled for a long time in the rest of it, rubbing it deep into his coat. Then he thanked Allah for eyes that could see the valley in the moonlight, and for a nose that could smell the carrion on the wind. He rolled some more and licked the rock under him. For a while he lay there panting. Soon he got up and limped on his way.

John McPhee

The Fair of San Gennaro

Jenner came out of the BMT at Delancey Street and walked a few blocks south and west, heading toward the glow of light. She couldn't see the fellow very well. She first heard his footsteps, running up behind her. The street, Broome between Elizabeth and the Bowery, was dark and she was alone in the block. She didn't look around but kept on walking.

"Lady," he said. She turned and before anything else saw the knife, its fixed blade nervously rocking so that it caught light and lost it, caught it again. "Don't yell. Help me," he said. "Please don't yell."

"What do you want?"

"I want you to walk with me, in the fair. Not for long."

"All right."

They walked on into the edge of the crowd. Tables had been set out on the sidewalk; old Italians were sitting at them, arguing, laughing and drinking burnt coffees. Waiters in small white aprons squeezed in and out among the chairs. Everyone liked to think that it might have been Naples.

The old people made close watch on all who passed. Some nodded with pleasure when they saw Jenner and her escort. If they were not Italian, they were at least a young man and woman holding each other's hand and walking out for an evening of pleasure. All the Italians approved. "Remember, don't try anything," the young man said to Jenner. "I don't want to hurt you, but I will."

"I said all right," said Jenner. "Put that knife away. It bulges too much." He had the knife blade up under his jacket sleeve and the handle in his hand. "Go ahead," she went on. "Move it. That's a terrible way to carry a knife."

"Shut up."

"I'm only telling you for your own good. Leave it there if you like. You'll just be picked up sooner, that's all."

He moved the knife to his inside breast pocket. They went on into the light that blazed down from uncovered hundred-watt bulbs spaced along metal piping and arched over the streets. In the brightness she glanced up at him. He wore a cap and under it he had handsome dark hair, but he needed a haircut. His nose was straight and his mouth strong;

he had dark eyes and was much younger than she had thought, maybe twenty-one or twenty-two, younger than she by half a dozen years.

She took a firmer grip on his hand and led him into the mainstream of the Mulberry Street crowd. Along the curbs, concession followed concession. People were trying to pitch nickles onto dinner plates, break balloons with three darts, knock over cloth cats with soft baseballs. Huge numbered wheels were spinning. The lucky one-in-ten-thousand shot could win a portable TV. Every fifth or sixth stall sold food, mostly sausage heroes packed in a bed of red and green peppers and onions. Men and women stood shoulder to shoulder at counters eating cherrystone clams, shrimp, lobsters. Children had cotton candy, candied apples, and Italian ices, orange and raspberry, at fifteen cents a cup. There was beer in barrels, cartons, beer stacked in garbage cans full of cracked ice; and the city air was full of the smell of charcoal broiled sausage and the sound of aria, Puccini, Leoncavallo, Verdi, Verdi, Verdi.

"We'll go through here to the next block then I'll go down that street," he said. But at the corner they looked toward the edge of the fair and saw the flashing red dome light of a police car. He hurried her on to the next corner. Up the side street was another squad car.

"What did you do?" said Jenner.

"Let's get back," he said, pushing her toward the center of the crowd. Two streams of people pressed into one another in the middle of Mulberry Street, going in opposite directions. Jenner and the fugitive let themselves be caught first in one flow, then the other, moving north, then south, with no aim.

"What did you do?"

"Shut up," he said again, not looking at her but turning his head this way and that as if he were hunting someone he had lost in the crowd or perhaps looking for a way to get clear of Jenner as well as the police.

"Whatever you did, if you don't want to be caught you'd better throw away that hat," she said. "Who ever heard of a man wearing a hat like that on an evening out with a girl?"

It was a khaki fatigue cap, the sort the Cuban rebels wore. He ignored her and went on looking over the heads of the people, watching for blue uniforms.

Jenner kept on talking. "You're going to be picked up in about two minutes," she said. "I would give very little for your chances." His eyes stopped scanning the crowd and looked directly at her. "Why did you stop me?" she continued. "What could you possibly have wanted with me? Did you think that having me with you would make you look like just another guy out at the fair with his girl?"

"That's right," he said.

"Then play the part yourself."

"What did you say?" He nearly shouted because of the barkers, the violinists, the aria singers and the thousands of noisy people.

"Play the part. You stick out like a sore thumb. Understand. Play the roulette game. Laugh. You look like someone who's wanted by the police."

"What?" he said, leaning down.

"You look like someone who's wanted by the police," Jenner shouted. He took her by the arm and squeezed the muscle hard, dragging her between two concession booths and back to the narrow passage of sidewalk remaining between the backs of the booths and the store fronts. In the relative quiet, they could hear each other easily; he whispered loudly and angrily.

"Do you know what's good for you?" he said. She looked at him steadily and didn't answer. "One more stupid act like that . . ." He showed his knife again.

Large tears welled up in her eyes and rolled down her cheeks. She looked on, steadily, into his eyes and said nothing.

"Jesus Christ," he said, and turned away.

She took a handkerchief from her purse and carefully patted each eye, trying to smear her mascara as little as possible; nonetheless two streaks of blue did come off. She returned the handkerchief to the purse and snapped it shut. "If you want to blend into the crowd," she said, "you have to be like them. These are happy people out for an annual fling. They're spending money, taking chances, listening to their favorite music. They're all smiling. You don't fit in. You're frightened . . ."

"I'm not afraid of a goddamned thing."

"You're preoccupied. Your eyes are too shifty. Come on, take the cap off, I'll take your arm and we'll pretend we're enjoying ourselves. You can buy me a hero."

"I have no money."

"Here then." She handed him five dollars. "I brought that to spend tonight anyway."

He stood motionless and speechless for a moment, then reached out and took the bill.

"What's your name?" she said.

"Rock Kennedy."

"What's your real name, Rock Kennedy?"

"Ferenc Zsuzsi."

"My name is Jenner."

She moved through the narrow space between concessions and he followed. Halfway through, he ducked down and pitched his cap under a wooden platform. On the street she took his arm and smiled up at him like a bride of twenty-four hours. They walked without speaking. "This place all right?" he said eventually, and stopped at a food stand to buy two sausage heroes, wadded with onions and peppers.

"Come on, Frank, try the darts," said Jenner, pulling him along to a booth where he paid twenty-five cents for three tries at any of a hundred balloons. His first two darts missed, but the third hit a balloon and it popped. He won no prize but he did smile. "You're getting the idea," Jenner told him.

She let her hand slide down his arm to grip his hand. He began to forget himself and look for more games to try. He fired rifles, threw baseballs, took a basketball shot, and won on the odd numbers in roulette. Watching him, Jenner was pleased with herself. She had turned him into the most typical twenty-one-year-old on the street. What could a boy with such a gentle face have done to be a fugitive from the police? It didn't matter very much; he could have robbed, or broken out of somewhere, or even murdered or raped for all of her. Jenner was a little mad. She didn't care, so long as he had picked her for his partner in getting away.

Two young policemen came up the thoroughfare from the direction of Canal Street. They stopped by a stall where a fat woman with wispy gray hair was rolling mozzarella, cottage cheese, and sliced ham into thick dough and frying it in deep oil. They seemed to be looking carefully through the crowd. The fat woman tried to sell them a couple of her *calzoni* but they paid no attention to her.

Jenner discreetly pulled Ferenc away from the rail of a nickel pitch. "We'd better head back up the street," she said; but they turned and another pair of policemen were coming that way, too. Jenner felt the boy's muscles tighten as if he were about to break into a run. "Don't be foolish," she told him. "Here."

Across the street in a vacant lot was a ferris wheel, cramped between two buildings, with its top rising far above the rooftops. Jenner and the fugitive crossed to the ticket booth, where a handpainted sign said, "Ferris Wheel, 15¢."

"Buy six," she said.

Ferenc handed the woman in the booth a dollar, took the six tickets and started away. The woman called after him and he went back to get his ten cents change.

They had to wait in line. "Put your arm around me," Jenner said. He hung an arm over her. "Put your arm *around* me," she said again. Ferenc drew her in beside him.

"That's the idea. Look at the others." Almost every young fellow in sight was slouching against a girl, one arm dangling around her. The man took their tickets; they sat in the pendulous seat and he clamped down the safety bar; he pulled the big lever and they rose through a short arc before the wheel stopped at the next chair to unload and load again. Thus they went toward the top in small stages. After the second stop, they sat swaying twenty-five feet above the watching crowd. The police were there, of course; and when they turned toward the ferris wheel Jenner turned to the fugitive and pulled unobtrusively at his shirt until he understood and kissed her. "Don't stop," she told him. "Not until we're up above and out of sight."

When the rising seat stopped one stage below the top of the great wheel, it swayed unsteadily and they looked far down at the scene beneath them. The Fair of San Gennaro was going at full current. Near one end of the main Mulberry Street midway a politician was flailing his fist against the wooden railing of an elevated platform, shouting into a microphone that amplified his excited Italian across the babble of the streets. Toward the other end a plump soprano on a bandstand was singing *"Caro Nome."* Small, old men circled her, accompanying her voice with violins, and the people in the street nearby were not moving and grinding one another as they were everywhere else. "La Scala is a juke box," Jenner suddenly cried out. "Don't you think so, Frank?" Ferenc merely stared at her.

"Look at the coals," Jenner said, leaning forward and pointing down into the red fires everywhere on the grid of lighted streets. The smell of burning charcoal and cooking meat was all through the air even at that height. The fair was whole from up there. They could see it all, watch the mechanical toys bobbing around on the pavement by a vendor's stall, the jammed people sliding by one another, the sparkling reflection of light in the liqueur glasses of the old people at the sidewalk tables. The ferris wheel jolted up another stage and they were suspended on the top, looking out across the rooftops to the midtown skyline, rising out of the baking city, an immeasurable distance from Italy, afire in its own light.

"I broke into a store over on Canal Street near the Manhattan Bridge," Ferenc said. "The alarm went off. I didn't get much."

"Too bad," said Jenner.

"Yeah, I wish like hell I hadn't done it."

"What did you take?"

He put a hand in a coat pocket and pulled out three rings. Two were fat carnelians, like wellings of blood, in ornate settings of gold. The third was a small diamond, less than half a carat, also set in gold. They shone in the palm of his hand. Jenner picked up the diamond and slid it onto her finger.

"One for me, and one for you, and one for the mayor of Kalamazoo."

"Would you like it," he said quickly. Jenner looked aside. "Take it," he hurried on. "Take it. I want you to keep it."

"Some other time," she said, dropping the ring back into his palm. "Who saw you at the store?"

"I don't know. I ran. There were some people on the sidewalk shouting behind me. I think they got a look at me. I saw the lights over here and came this way."

"Easy, then. You're probably o.k. They won't know who they're looking for, and if you play the part right, you've got nothing to worry about."

"I've been in trouble before," he said. "Not around here. Around home. I'm from Avenue D. But I've been told. One more time for anything and I get at least five years."

"Well, this isn't the time," said Jenner. "I live near you, on Avenue B as a matter of fact, on the corner of Eleventh Street over the dry cleaner's. You'll have to come see me. We'll bake a Birdseye pizza to remember the fair."

"Why do you act so good to me?" he asked her.

"Why did you break into that jewelry shop?" she said. "You don't really need the money. Or do you?"

"Everybody needs money."

"You broke in just for money? Didn't you get just a little kick out of it?"

"I said I wish I hadn't done it."

The ferris wheel was finally spinning and they swooped down the far, back side past the brick wall of a warehouse and a sign put up by "The Seven Brothers" that showed a heavy moving van. She tugged his shirt as their seat buzzed the loading platform and he responded willingly, kissing her as they were pulled up again to the aerial view of the city.

"Are you an actress?" he said.

"What makes you ask?"

"You make me think of one, know what I mean?"

"Lot of people say that. I'm on TV every once in a while; nothing anyone would notice."

He was satisfied about his guess. "I *thought* you were an actress," he said proudly.

"To tell you the truth I would never pass up the smallest chance to act," said Jenner. "It's all I've cared about, ever. But I'm not good-looking enough to get very far. The casting directors all shake their heads about me. 'Too bad about that one,' they say. 'She has it, but we have to have more than talent.' So I work in an office."

"You're no movie star," he said, "but you're a good-looking girl. Haven't you got no husband?"

"I haven't even got no man," said Jenner.

The ride was short because a longer line had formed below. When their seat stopped at the platform, Ferenc tried to give two more tickets to the operator but he wouldn't accept them. "There's a big line here, Mac, sorry," the man said. "You have to wait again if you want another ride."

"The lady didn't tell me that when she sold me the extra tickets," Ferenc said.

"Too bad. I'm sorry," said the man. "Nothing I can do about it."

Jenner pulled Ferenc's arm. "Don't argue," she said. "Do you want to collect a crowd? Give the tickets away. Here. Give them to me."

They walked away from the ferris wheel, Ferenc still looking over his shoulder at the man who worked the lever. Jenner saw an old woman, at least eighty-five, in a black shawl, begging. "Here," she said to her. "Here's four tickets for you. Enjoy yourself and stop working for a while." The old woman took the tickets automatically, pinched them in her hand like a string of sausages and, with the same hand, crossed herself as she bowed twice in gratitude.

The police had moved on. Jenner and the boy let themselves be shoved along toward the principal intersection at Mulberry and Hester. They tripped over a baby stroller caught in the jam of people, the foolish mother looking helpless behind it, the helpless one-year-old looking up at the passing faces with an open mouth. Fathers had children on their shoulders, high school boys walked behind their girls with both arms around their waists. Fat women laughed at themselves as they tried to squeeze along between other people's hips. A little boy cried when a cigarette popped his balloon. The expectable odd beings were at the Fair of San Gennaro, too, the young men with Penguin Classics in their pockets who had beards to show but no accomplishments, other men in pairs, and three women together, one with close-cropped caramel hair and dressed in a riding habit, another a tall, smart-looking colored girl in a light trench coat, the third a prematurely gray woman in her upper thirties who might have been the mother of two children at Rye Country Day, wearing a dark blue blouse with three buttons open, showing a good part of her large and freckled breasts.

Ferenc had begun to look around again, watching for the police.

"You shouldn't do that," Jenner told him. "The only way they'll find you from now on is if *you* look for *them*."

"I still have to get out of here."

"We'll manage that."

"How?"

"We'll have to think. Look here; it's San Gennaro himself." They were passing the shrine of the saint who owed his exaltation to the wild beasts that refused to eat him in a public amphitheater. The saint was made of gold-painted wood and to Jenner he looked a little like Buddha, housed in a huge porcelain frame that stood twenty feet tall and was covered with patterned sticks of fluorescent light. At the top was a coldly glowing fluorescent cross. "Beautiful, beautiful," said the people going by. More people kept coming up and humbly praising the lighted setting of the wooden saint. "Have you ever seen anything so beautiful?"

Dollar bills, and fives, even some tens and twenties, hung down in long chains, paper-clipped together and suspended from San Gennaro's feet, cascading into pools of coins. August gentlemen in shining tuxedos stood at the idol's feet accepting the paper money and coins. For the coins they said, "Thank you, thank you," and for the bills they said, "God bless you."

Jenner saw a patrolman, half out of sight behind the men in tuxedos, there to guard San Gennaro and the cash. Gently pushing Ferenc, who was rooted to the sight of the money, she said, "Come on over here, here's a game for you. I'll bet you can win at this one."

Catty-cornered from the shrine of the saint, a concession charged twenty-five cents to test anyone's skill with a hammer and nail. Across the front of the stall, a rough heavy beam, eight by eight inches and made of dark, treated ash, bristled with nails, all standing ready with tips a quarter-inch into the wood. The concession was popular. While their wives looked on and laughed and joked, men with rolled up shirtsleeves drove the nails. Jenner and Ferenc stood at one end of the beam and looked along the line at the pounding hammers and the nails going down into the wood.

The woman in the stall came over to them. She was middle-aged and wore rimless glasses and a money apron. "One quarter," she said. "Want to try it? Get the nail all the way in up to the head in three hits and you win a horseshoe magnet. If you get it in two hits you get a rabbit's foot for your girl there; want to try?"

"What if I hit it once and it goes all the way?" said Ferenc.

The woman in the stall pointed at the upper center of a set of shelves behind her, decked with the prizes. In a tilted, open cardboard box on a backing of purple felt was a crucifix and chain. "Genuine gold plate," said the woman. "Worth maybe twenty, twenty-five dollars. You look like a strong boy. Want to try?"

Ferenc gave the woman a quarter, picked up a hammer and came down quickly and without all the preliminary sizing up, all the joking and sleeve-rolling preparation that was going on along the rest of the beam. The nail went in about half way. He hit it again, and the nailhead went down flush with the surface. "Strong boy," said the woman smiling at Jenner. She handed Ferenc a rabbit's foot with a chrome cap and chain.

Ferenc put down another quarter and the woman picked it up. He raised the hammer higher than before and smashed it down. It missed the nail altogether, leaving a smooth crater in the wood as if a coin had been pounded into it, flat side to, then taken away. Jenner didn't seem to notice. She had withdrawn a few steps and was staring silently at the nails with a sudden brooding look in her eyes. The stall woman laughed at Ferenc and said, "You try too hard, a little easier next time."

He gave her another quarter. The hammer went up and came down just as viciously as before, but this time the nail went into the wood all the way to the head. "Ai," said the woman. There was a murmur up and down the beam from the other men with hammers and the women beside them.

"A perfect one, a perfect one," the woman called out loudly to all around, making the most of the publicity of awarding the highest prize. She climed on an overturned wooden tub and reached for the golden crucifix, brought it down and handed it to Ferenc. He turned to give it to Jenner, but she was not beside him and had backed even further away. He walked over to her, took the crucifix out of its container and handed it to her, with the rabbit's foot.

"It's for you," he said.

She smiled just a little. "Thank you, Frank. You're really good. They should keep you away from here or you'd clean them out." Then she kissed him and walked around to the back of the booth. "Stay there, Frank," she said. "When things start happening, you go."

Before he could follow, she walked into the booth, around the shelves of prizes, past the woman concessionaire in the money-pocketed apron, and climbed up onto the wooden beam itself. She gave the crowd a broad, professional smile and stepped carefully among the stands of nails. She began to twirl her prizes on their chains, the crucifix in one hand, the rabbit's foot in the other. Jenner had beautiful slim legs and some men whistled. She took on the slouch of a street-corner whore, slid her skirt up above one knee, and spoke out of the side of her mouth. "Twenty-five cents," she called. "Come on, ladies and gentlemen, just two bits. Step up and crucify the Lord. Play it. Play it. It's the crucifixion game." Jenner's bluish eyelids fluttered and she laughed, shifting the rabbit's foot to her other hand and twirling it there with the crucifix.

"Police, police," called the stall woman. "Are you crazy girl? Get off of there." The woman tried to push Jenner off the plank but Jenner danced aside, knocking down about fifty nails as she went. The crowd only stared in awe.

"Step up," said Jenner. "One quarter. Drive the nail in two blows and you win all the luck in the world, a genuine, imported rabbit's foot. See, here's one. Come right along and try. All the way in one blow and you get a crucifix plated in pure gold." She had to dance away from the woman again. An enormous surge of the curious pressed in toward the stall and with them the patrolman from across the intersection who was guarding San Gennaro. More police came.

Looking for her fugitive friend, Jenner saw him moving backward through the people, away from her. Because he was so tall, she could keep track of his head among the throng. Up Hester Street, she could see, too, the red light spraying out from the bubble on the top of a squad car, and the police who had been stationed there now shoving their way into the center of the crowd to see what was causing the disturbance.

"Cast your robes aside," she called to the crowd and winked her eyes. "Take off your robes, peel off your seamless stockings, come crucify the Lord Jesus."

The police were almost at the stall. Ferenc had made his way through the crowd to the far edge.

"Get her, get her," cried the concession woman, who had seen a policeman at last. Three other patrolmen reached the wooden beam at the same time. "What's the idea, sister?"

"Crucify the Lord!" Jenner shouted with a bright smile, looking out over the heads of the crowd. The smile went away all at once. Her eyes had continued to follow Ferenc. Over by San Gennaro, the men in the tuxedos had left their positions at the saint's feet to stand on the curb on their toes and try to see what was going on. Jenner saw Ferenc step into the fluorescent glow by the wooden image and pluck the chains of paper-clipped one, five, ten, and twenty dollar bills. He stuffed the money into his jacket and bolted away, running up Hester Street, toward the empty squad car with the flashing red light. Some people saw him and seemed to cry out; the noise of the crowd was too great for Jenner to hear their shouts.

"I said what's the idea, sister?"

Jenner looked down at the policeman at her feet. "Idea, officer?" she said in a smooth, secretarial voice. "That's one for the book." She kicked away some nails, sat down on the beam and dropped easily onto the street.

"It sure is," said the patrolman, "come on." And they walked away together.

The stall woman rattled the coins in her apron pockets and picked up the fallen nails. Trying to smile at the people standing near her wooden beam, she shook her head and made circles with a finger by her ear. "Twenty-five cents," she called out. "Who wants to try?"

But word had by now spread all the way through the crowd and the people were ebbing from the nail-and-beam stall, pressing toward the opposite corner of the intersection to see for themselves where the thief had stripped the folding money from the treasury of San Gennaro.

Alfred Chester

Ismael

(Being a fairy tale extracted from a writer's diary and concerning the two meetings, twin matings and tormentings of the Queen of Light and the Queen of Darkness.)

Saturday dawn; July 25

Last night about eleven he was standing in a doorway on Mercer Street, a Puerto Rican boy wearing white ducks and red shirt, lovely he was, and it seemed to me he smiled to me but being me I thought no and walked on for two blocks before thinking yes. So I went back and there he still was only a woman was with him this time. Yet when I passed he gave me a smile, such a smile, unmistakably a smile full of "here you are come back again to love me as I love you myself" and I burst into laughter at the pleasures of life, but walked on. At Houston Street I bethought myself, perhaps he will follow, so I stopped and LO! he cometh lazily-but passed me right by without a glance and I swore at myself, a vain unworthy creature. And I walked back to Prince Street then thought again and again returned and now there he was, now both of us smiling, both laughing and finally speaking at the same time, he saying merely, "Hello" while I: "Isn't it about time we said Hello?" We talked and his name is Ismael and we went for a drink at Tommy's Bar and then came home to make it as it was never made before, as surely God in His Glory made it to be made, and he is lovely, 22, hung like a horse with a little body of steel, and laughs he laughs and loves himself and perhaps me with a joy that is foreign. My hands now smell of him. And we sneaked up after on the roof here only in our shirts to catch the breeze and his body against me always his body for he knows the truth about the soul, and his white teeth glare and glitter and laugh when he smiles or talks. My body's known a miracle. Ismael, imagine! My blood exults, my skin joyous from lips to groin. When I walk him back home to his mother's he said to come see him when I pleased and he said he would come to me and he put his dark fingers to my lips and said *hasta mañana*. Then I danced down the streets and into the park to lie dizzy under the stars and the trees until the cops chased me.

Saturday noon

Sobriety and reality, after some sleep. In my haste to get my pants off last night all the dollar bills fell out of my pocket—about five singles. Only one of them is still there. It is true he told me he was out of work —when we were going up Bleecker Street to Tommy's Bar, he said: "Why we don go home to you house? I ain got money for a drink. I had pneumonia and now don work one month." (I paid for his Schenley's-and-Seven-Up but felt a twitch of mistrust even as our legs touched and our eyes wrestled—after all, I've never had a Puerto Rican before.) And he is no Puritan, as my flesh will testify, and it is probably somehow better to take money lying around than to ask for it. But it alters the ecstasy, reminds me of the mind toiling and the mind toiling. And makes me feel like the foolish sentimental fagola.

Sunday; July 26

As no word from Ismael, kept my appointment with the Bergs last night. A dinner party on the terrace of their penthouse. Cool starry evening, delicious food, much to drink, charming guests. Ugh to it all. Smart young moderns—the women use obscenities, though of course only among their own set. One can even talk in mixed company of one's ho-mo-secks-you-all adventures; no, not adventures. This is the world where people have experiences not adventures. Publishing people. Advertising people. Oh I am dying, Egypt, dying! I sit mainly in silence, feeling as I felt at sixteen when I was in love with Bernie Schwartz—the beautiful anguish; how tedious and tawdry everyone else's life has suddenly become. There is only one possible place, one passable person in all the world. A wind came up and Sally suggested having cognac indoors. Peter, however, asked me to stay with him on the terrace while he smoked his cigar. I knew this meant a man-to-man and a conversation I have been sure we would one day have. We lean over the flowerpots and look across Manhattan, avoiding each other's eyes. "I'm numb," he keeps saying. "I used to be a great talker, but I was always talking clichés. But when I stop talking clichés, I'm all muddled and I have nothing to say." He is bored with Sally, longs for new love and passion, pleasure and pain, keeps repeating: "I'm going to go—maybe in a week, a year, five years . . . One day I'll leave." But he is too rich, too successful now to abandon anything but his dreams, or rather the fulfillment of them. We talk of love, and I torture him a little: "Ah, the taste of a stranger's mouth! . . . Love is the only ecstasy we can know! . . . To go off for a short fling on the side is empty, meaningless; when there is someone waiting at home, however awful to return to, we aren't giving our all to the new love. When to lose this love is to lose everything—ah then, there is the exquisiteness and horror . . . Tonight almost for the first time in my life I knew why poets have spent so many words on love . . . Yes, it is unmanly to live a life of love, and yet when you feel compelled toward it, there can be no other." And Peter says: "I will go. You'll see."

Though it was still early, I left soon after, pleading a headache. But didn't want to go home, so stopped for a while in one of the few queer bars still open here in the Village. A Saturday night, and naturally Madison Avenue was represented in force. Mobs of dacron suits crowned by vacant, stupid, unlived faces, cute as buttons most of them, like an army of Tom Sawyers. Where are the screaming queens, the gigolos, the outrageous Harlem faggots—where is Ismael?

I stand at the bar for an hour or so, eavesdropping. The conversations are refined, witty, slightly bitchy like those up in Peter Berg's penthouse. I stand, enduring the unsuffered, the wholesome, the unwise. All-American boys who at thirty or forty or fifty are still All-American boys. Fresh-faced, clean-cut; who dares apply words like sodomy, pederasty to them? Who would want to apply the acts? If Tom Sawyer's desires are unnatural, illegal, surely Aunt Polly and the rest of America must agree that nature and the laws are wrong.

My neat gins taste, under the circumstances, like ice cream soda. I begin to feel like a hood, a pervert, an impostor. But wait! This army of Tom Sawyers is as perverted as I am, and our perversion isn't merely a question of physical detail. Like Peter Berg, we are perverted deeply, in our dreams, suffering out the doom of the butt-end of romance—destined never to profoundly have whom we love nor to profoundly love whom we have. We are creatures living in despite of ourselves, contemptuous of those who are foolish enough to love us, adoring of those who find us unworthy.

I want Ismael—perhaps outside the traditional doom. I want him for the pleasure of his laughter, for his joy, his vanity, his narcissism, for his arms like a vice, for his so-serious no-nonsense philosopher's love-making face. But my mind works out a series of trickeries, such as that he made me say goodnight in a doorway that wasn't his, lest I realize about the money and come hunting him out. I look at the bed and think love was made here, created here, exhausted here—but for him there may have been nothing extraordinary; another American, a quick drink, a meeting of eyes then arms then hips, some talk and good-by or *hasta mañana* in some other life, plus a pocketful of silver.

Left the queer bar at midnight and went home by way of Washington

Square. On the railing round the park—the Meat Rack, so called—sat the eternal hosts of black and white angels in skintight pants, waiting to fly toward love or money. Somber and joyless. Ashes. I pitied them no Ismael.

Monday; July 27

So with the help of a few drinks, I gathered up my courage and went to see him last night. The doorway was no deception.

He was wearing only shorts and Japanese sandals; seemed pleased to see me. His body even more beautiful than on Friday—so too his face, especially the long dark eyes. His charm extravagant. A white uncle and a black aunt, sitting stiff as playing cards, were visiting the television in the parlor. ("They don unnerstan English," says Ismael, raising an eyebrow, and to them in Spanish he brags of me shamelessly, saying I am a very famous writer.) The apartment excessively, sterilely clean, all in bad taste or tasteless, without character; ugly printed wallpaper, ugly printed seat covers. And Ismael.

He sits me down opposite the relatives and gives me beer and heavily begins to entertain me. Photograph albums. I steal glances at his chest or back or legs or crotch; our eyes don't meet. Scores of photos of Ismael; none of them please me. "Don you like even this one . . . or this one . . . or this . . .?" He is distressed and whines childishly, "Oh you don like me. Nobody likes me." Inexorably, I rise to the bait: "Yes, Ismael, I like you."

He shakes his head gravely. "Don like me. I don like nobody, only Frankie."

My heart sinks, and I remember that at Tommy's Bar he (unnecessarily, I then thought) mentioned a friend, an advertising man, who was spending the summer in Europe. Ismael brings another album, opens it to the back and shows me numerous pictures of Frankie—Tom Sawyer. "Frankie is the only person in this world I love."

"Does he love you?"

"Frankie says: Ismael, I love you But."

"But what?"

He hesitates, then shrugs, smiles sourly. "I am a Puerto Rican. I don blame him. I don like my people either."

I stare hard at the pictures and ask Ismael how it is he goes with other men; I am fishing, but it's a dragon that I pull out of the waters: "It don mean nothing. I gotta lotta love inside me but it ain for everybody."

I feel strangled, quickly look through the album. Elegant East Side queens. Ismael too is surrounded by an army of Tom Sawyers but—though he's fairer than mulatto—his spirit is Nigger Jim.

After the photos, the souvenirs. He has been in New York for eight years, so has a diploma from junior high, report cards. I look through the cards. He was not a good student, but in that section called Character Rating he has all A's. He Respects the Rights of Others; he Works Well

With Others; he Shows Great Effort. This is obviously not the boy who would take money off the floor of another's bedroom. A teacher would surely know who covets the purse even if she can't tell which of her students will break a heart, will destroy a soul.

The television show is over. The aunt and uncle stand up. Ismael takes them to the door. Returns. Stands in the middle of the room. Takes my eyes with his. Holds them. Kicks off his sandals. Drops his shorts and my breath like boulders.

But it isn't like the first time. We have lost our innocence, our anonymities. We aren't bashing selfishly toward our own pleasures. We (I) seek to please. Not only does my body want his, but my heart wants his, and his wants Frankie's, and Frankie's wants—whose? How many men are here with us in bed, flailing and laboring with us, locked with us not only in the body's terrific heat but in the heart's terrible romance? I come after he does, wake to find him stroking me. Am overwhelmed with gratitude, despise myself for it.

I want to spend the night there, but he says his mother will soon be back. I ask him to come with me. "We go out now," is his vague reply. As we dress, he takes a bit of paper from his pocket. "Look what the grocer gave me." It is the slip with my name and phone number. "Why didn't you call me yesterday?" I ask.

"You say to phone when I feel like it."

"But you said *hasta mañana.*"

We leave his house, go up to the park, pass the Meat Rack. Three or four of the boys call, "Hi, Ismael!" My lips tighten. He teases me: "How you like to take one home? We do it all together?" I say nothing. We walk up Fifth Avenue.

He: Did you drink a lot before you come to me?

I: Why?

He: Just tell me.

I: I had a drink, yes.

He: *One* drink I smell already on your breath. All the others I see from how you walk. Walk straight! It don look nice if people see you go zig-zag.

I paused to take some deep breaths and he goes ahead. I would have to run to catch up with him, but my pride won't let me. I call. He stops, turns and waits. But my joy of him is strangling.

We go as far as Fourteenth Street, then around and down Sixth Avenue, back toward the Village. This, he tells me, is a walk he takes every night. I don't have to ask if he ever reaches home alone. I see the way men look at him, and I am not flattered, but jealous. And I see the look he returns to most of them. Like the first look he gave me: eyes loaded.

We exchange funny stories from our adventures. He becomes annoyed that I am talking too loud, that I say "him" when I *mean* "him" and not, as he says, "a person" or some other euphemism. "If you don

take care when you talk I will go home." Outraged at being made to feel
vulgar, uncouth, I bellow: "I wasn't taught my manners by your Madison
Avenue closet queens. I'm a writer, Ismael, like you told your aunt and
uncle."

He softens and smiles. "Put my name in a story."

"No. Someone already has."

"Melville," he says to my surprise.

Back in the Village. He wants to go to Tommy's Bar because we have
already been there, and he is not fond of new places. On the way I speak
of a Yoga exercise. My impulse is to lie down on the pavement and do it,
in spite of my clothes, as I would with any of my friends. But I am afraid
of Ismael's disapproval. I say: "I'll show it to you when we get home."

"What home?"

"My home."

"Why you so sure I go back with you?"

I do not speak until we reach Tommy's. My bitterness makes me
petty. When I ask what he wants to drink, he says, "the same thing"—
meaning of course Schenley's-and-Seven-Up (it might as well be ice cream
soda). I tell him I cannot remember what the same thing is. So he reminds
me and adds: "And you will take neat gin." We drink; he talks of his job as
an operator in a hat factory. We leave and do the Village—ending up in a
little bar on Sixth Avenue. His eyes have begun again to look for mine. But
I know my pride would not allow me to take him home, and it would not
even allow me to admit it had been wounded. Even my pride has pride. It
cannot say: you have hurt me, and I want to go home alone.

We leave. Both fairly drunk. I stare at people sitting on the terrace of
O. Henry's. Ismael, irritated and impatient, calls to me. I turn, grab
him and hold him tight. "Will you cut out that crap!" he cries. We're
crossing Sixth Avenue. I beg of him the *coup de grâce* by shouting for
all the world to hear: "Ismael, Ismael, you're such a silly little girl."

He goes ahead rapidly and silently, like a sword. I keep up with him.
"Ismael, are you angry?" Silence. "Are you?" Silence. I don't know what
to do. I am not frightened or anxious really, but mainly concerned with
my pride. "Ismael, say something, for God's sake." Silence. We reach
the park and stop in full sight and hearing of the boys on the Meat Rack.

"I'm sorry," I say wearily.

He gives me a rather friendly swat on the belly and says: "You better
go home now. Thank you for everything."

The sword plunges ahead. The moment of truth and love—the
instant of separation.

And I lose sight of the beautiful silhouette in the shadows of the
Judson Church. I go home dizzy, fall asleep at once. A restless night.
Horrible dreams. I keep waking, but don't want to wake for fear of
the feelings that await me. I pull sleep over my head like a fortress. At
seven o'clock I wake in profoundest misery and remember that he told
me he wakes every morning at seven, just as if he were still going to

work. There are sobs inside me. I fly back to sleep. I sleep. I wake at nine and decide to masturbate though my senses are blank. It is not sexual but purgative. This is to be the first in a lifetime of orgasms that will not belong to Ismael, and it is to be arrived at for literary reasons, so to speak. To punctuate my love affair. The phone rings. Marty. He asks me how I am. Automatically I say terrible, gloomy, sunk in sadness and woe. But as we talk I realize that I am not sad, perhaps hurt—but how should I be sad when there are a million anonymous and innocent Puerto Ricans in New York and a whole island full of them in the Caribbean?

Jean-Claude van Itallie

François Yattend

"Who am I here?" François Yattend often asked himself. Sometimes he asked with a deep concern but usually it was from habit; he liked the sound of the words.

He had a hotel room in Paris. "The Hotel Adelphi," he wrote on a postal card to his mother, "is near the Bois de Boulogne. My room has two large windows on the street." He didn't write this only to impress her; he liked the windows. Not that he enjoyed sunshine—he didn't—but he liked being near the rhythm of things without himself being seen. The noise of the cars was a comfort to him. If there were an accident he might witness it and be asked to court to testify; he was in order with the police. With his *carte de residence* there was nothing to fear, and he admired the fierce gendarmes who made their business of everyone else's. Once a blonde girl with short-cropped hair—she might have been an American— had looked up for nearly a whole minute toward François's windows. He had watched her from his usual place behind the curtain. Whenever he thought of her it made him content all over again to have windows on the street. Why, simply on a whim she might have come up and knocked on his door, perhaps she was lonely too and she would tell about herself and cry; she would come live with him in his room. The room was large, one of the best in the cheap hotel, with worn crimson furniture placed just so, replaced just so even if François decided to move anything himself (he didn't do that anymore because it was no use). The worst thing there, or one of the three worst things, was the cold from which François suffered more than a Parisian because he came from the south, from Tarascon.

In Tarascon he had achieved some small fame for receiving, upon graduation, the lycée's *premier prix de mathématiques* as well as the *premier prix des sciences pratiques* and the *prix de biologie.* He used the prizes to convince his parents to allow him to leave for Paris to make his fortune. No one in the family would ever get anywhere, he grumbled daily, if even he, François, who had won the *premier prix,* were to remain working in the enameling factory like all the rest of them. He had two sisters and three brothers—"Like Napoleon," he had once remarked to his mother—and all of them worked at the enameling factory. His insistence on leaving was based on inner certainty that his parents wouldn't listen; it became merely a habit for him to urge them. And then, as François played in his mind with teary farewells and a triumphal return, each equally unreal, his mother came over to his side. The old priest, half out of his senses and inordinately proud of François, argued with François's father for him. When Monsieur Yattend finally had a rage and cursed out his consent it was too late for François to back down if he wanted to.

Until his money ran out he looked for work only halfheartedly, spending his time walking about Paris. Then for two weeks he was substitute ticket-puncher in the metro. That was about the time he grew his moustache; it made him look much older, about thirty he thought. Finally he got a job as a clerk in the accounting department of Ivoire Laboratories, pharmaceutical manufacturers. Sitting at a high desk he calculated columns of figures. As soon as he finished one batch he had it stamped by the assistant manager and received another one; usually he did about six per day with the aid of a small calculator next to his desk. He was allowed three quarters of an hour for lunch, and he ate always at the Café du Sud. The waiter knew him there, smiled when he arrived and automatically served him his usual menu, steak and fried potatoes with some red wine, unless François asked for coffee which was rarely. After he had come there two weeks the waiter offered him a weekly rate, sometimes charging extra for the coffee and sometimes not. On the second day at work he had asked a timid-looking laboratory worker to accompany him, but the man had just shaken his head and scurried off.

The second worst thing about the hotel room was the bed which was bumpy and valleyed and had a pillow arrangement François didn't like. Instead of a real pillow which one could beat or cry into (François never cried) it was a hard sausage-like thing sewn onto the mattress. Going to bed was an added, and an acute, discomfort.

The third worst thing was the impossibility of taking a bath in the hotel. At home what he had enjoyed the most was sitting in the metal tub; he bathed luxuriously, first sitting quietly, soaping himself gently, and then rinsing with a soft sponge. The heating of the water, which took him an hour in the kitchen, was a work of love. And now in Paris he couldn't afford a room with a bath.

So his first Sundays were spent in search of a bathhouse. He was not content with the public one near the hotel, the one with a dingy sign:

Bains Municipaux, but indeed explored several areas of the city before finding one to his liking. It was tile outside too, with large blue lilies and half-naked mermaids beckoning. In the damp courtyard, just inside from the shaded street, was a tiny fountain spurting courageously and around it an unplanted garden with not even weeds growing. Indoors was a ticket office like a railroad station's and a tacked price list which François studied closely. He would have liked a massage but felt it was above his income and station. The woman behind the counter, who had first smiled encouragingly but now ignored him, would undoubtedly disapprove such a request. But he finally asked for a bath and the woman, again all a smile, pushed a bell-button which produced a serious little girl to conduct him to a whitewashed cell where there was a clean bath, a fat cake of soap, and a large white towel.

François came here now every Sunday, like church (he hadn't actually been to Mass since leaving Tarascon, and he felt guilty about it). It was the culmination of his week. And it was here, on a certain Sunday, that he made a discovery. It was before stepping into the tub, at the very most voluptuous moment before letting his foot slip into the water when already practically comatosed in anticipation of the water's maternal warmth, that he saw when he looked down a red sore on both feet. He had not noticed his shoes rubbing. He found, on looking closer and getting a little away from the steam from the bath, that there were two small red dots on the back of his hands as well. Strange, he thought as he sat on a chair, that it should be he, François Yattend, out of all the people who frequent the bathhouse (he hadn't actually seen any other clients), out of all the people in Paris, out of all his large family, out of all others it should be he who was so marked. "Who am I here?": the phrase was now more revelation than question. For he knew immediately what the marks were: the stigmata. This unexpected communiqué from God was disturbing. He looked down again to make sure he wasn't mistaken, but no, right there, too precisely marked to be anything else were the marks of the suffering of Our Lord Jesus Christ on the Cross where He died so that other men might live. François made a slow sign of the cross.

There was nothing else. No vision appeared although the walls of the cell seemed propitious for it, white and clean as a movie screen. He got dressed without having taken his bath—that would be undignified now—and modestly avoided looking at the spots.

He felt quite sure that he would never return to the bathhouse. He felt that either it, or his coming here, was the indirect cause of his marks. Nothing else in his life would merit the heavenly attention unless of course he had always been destined for it. He was not so much surprised (François never got excited) as uneasy. He smiled a small smile of relief, feeling somehow he had finally come into his own, that his period of waiting was up. Once outside, however, he merely retained solemnity.

He followed his usual post-bath route to the Tuileries and there walked slowly through the park with its brightly colored formal flower beds, repeating again and again, making a game of it: "Who am I here? Who am I here? Who am I here?" Keeping his hands behind his back he accentuated the "I," giving the phrase a forced rhythm. He tried smiling at a small boy jumping rope. The child stuck its tongue out and ran away. François was pleased with the sun this once; he did not suffer from the contrast of the seclusion of the bathhouse to the expanses of the public park. He walked around and around the pond, "Who am *I* here? Who am *I* here?" carefully placing one foot in front of the next. Here was an event imposed on him, perhaps an opportunity or perhaps a duty, in any case it could not be ignored.

The children around the pond were so occupied with launching and greeting again their toy boats that no one at all noticed François's sudden strange action. He stopped pacing, stared at the high ejaculation of the fountain in the center, and stepped into the pond.

The cold water was like one of his mother's unexpected slaps on the face. He took his foot out quickly and went gingerly to one of the metal chairs. He had not been completely certain he would be able to walk on the water but hazily he had considered it possible. He took off his wet shoe and sock and saw that the red spot had washed away. The cold water drops, tiny blinding reflectors, got on his hands as well, and the spots there too had disappeared.

No one noticed the small moustached boy, shoulders slightly hunched, walking away from the park, eyes down, muttering to himself, nor did they see his limp caused by the inconvenience of a wet trouser leg. He left behind him a trail of water that the violent sun soon evaporated from the pavement.

Shirley Schoonover

The Star Blanket

They had walked miles that day. They walked miles every day that they changed grazing land. The man and woman followed the sheep silently, the only conversation was that of the sheep as they flowed down the hills. The dogs were merely extensions of the man's will, moving to his short whistles, guiding the woolly mass down from the summer grazing lands to the winter flatlands. The man raised his right hand and the dogs fell to the ground, allowing the sheep to stop and graze.

The man threw his pack to the ground and sat next to it.

"Ought to be good grazing farther on down." He pulled tobacco from his shirt and bit off a corner.

The woman remained standing, looking up the side of the mountain they had descended and down the foothills.

"All the steps it took for us to get down here. All the steps it'll take for us to reach winter pasture. Who'd think there were that many steps to a mountain?" She shook her head and eased one booted foot against the other.

"You sure waste your time thinking about steps in mountains. If you want to get from one place to another it always takes steps." He rolled the tobacco around his tongue, savoring the fresh flavor, the bite on his tongue.

"And when we go back up the mountain again, what a waste of steps. We don't even leave marks to remember from one spring to another. Or even spring to fall."

"Don't worry about it, we don't need marks, we find the best grass, that's enough." He stood up and whistled the dogs into action.

The rest of the day they spent following the sheep down the shallow hills, down to a valley that would hold them all the California winter.

As they went the man kept his eyes to the ground remarking the grass and the dryness. "It's going to be a hard winter in the mountains." From time to time he would spit brown juice onto the gray grass.

The woman walked behind him, carrying her pack, looking at the sky and the progress of the sun and clouds. She watched the man ahead of her, thinking, He never looks at the sky unless it's going to rain or snow. He doesn't notice the sheep-clouds or the feather-clouds, just the rain clouds. She stumbled over a hummock of grass and the man turned and laughed at her.

"Get your nose out of the clouds, they won't save you any steps."

"I was just watching the sky, and the clouds running down it."

"No use watching the sky, it'll be there tonight and tomorrow. It's not good for anything except weather."

"Sometimes I think a thing doesn't always have to be used to be good. The sky is good to look at." She spoke softly to herself, not seeing the land around her; rather seeing into the land and sky in dimensions she could not explain, but merely sense.

"What?" The man called back, then, watching her unseeing progress down the hillside. He turned, grinned, and walked on, head down.

That night they bedded the sheep down in an outcropping of gray boulders and sandy ledges. The dogs gathered the sheep like needles gathering beads, and scolded them into a bumping, blatting, woolly scuffle of bodies.

The man and woman sat beside their fire, drinking black sour coffee from tin cups. The man threw small shards of wood into the fire, and thought about the sheep and the dogs, and his need for another dog.

The woman lay on her back, half dozing, lying against the earth, feeling its outward thrust against her back.

"Do you suppose the mountains are growing?" she asked her husband.

"I don't suppose anything so crazy. These mountains have been here all my life, never grew an inch that I saw." He squinted at her through the fire. His pale eyes took on a white cast from the flames; and as he looked, his face changed, becoming cunning and sensual. He arose and went to her. He lay beside her, taking her body with his hard hands, gripping her rather than caressing her. She lay passive, looking at him with mildly wondering eyes. When he was through he left her and rolled up in his blanket to sleep. She continued to stare up into the sky, past the stars.

She had come to him from her father in exchange for three pregnant ewes. She had been thirteen then, and a plain, quiet girl. Her father had been a sheep rancher who had fallen into difficulty, and with a large family of girls, it was expedient to bestow his middle daughter upon a wandering sheepherder who promised to keep her. She had been a good wife to the shepherd, having a quiet gentleness with the lambing ewes, and a quickness of foot when needed to herd the sheep. She had lived these two years with him in the mountains and the flat lands, wearing levis and flannel shirts, cropping her hair once a year like the sheep, and had pleased him in the secret moments of their life together. He had taken her with him into the small town that was their outside world every spring during the shearing time, until a vagrant cowboy had noticed her feminine form under the heavy shirt.

"I'd sure like to take your daughter into the dance tonight." His eyes had spoken more than the words, and understanding flashed between the men.

"My wife ain't free to go dancing. We're going back to the sheep tonight."

"Sheepherder!" The cowboy narrowed his eyes at them. He mounted his horse and, looking tall and arrogant, he said, "Maybe we could wash the smell off your woman, but right now it would be like bedding a lousy sheep."

The man never took her into town again; instead he left her to tend the sheep when he made trading trips. She was no more lonely during these trips than when he was with her.

The next day they reached their small cabin which was their winter shelter. It was adequate for shelter and no more. The man had built it ten years before, and owned the acres that surrounded it. They established themselves in it, the sheep in a large pen, the woman cooked supper in the iron stove. The man dozed while the woman folded blankets into the bed and pushed the table and chairs into a new design against the wall. She heated water and bathed herself, washing her hair and body over and over with yellow soap until she felt clean of the sheep dust and grit of the trail.

"You going into town tomorrow?" she asked.

"Yeah. I'm taking some of the lambs for selling. We need stock for the winter, so clear out the shelves for whatever I can pick up." He turned noisily onto his side.

"Bring me something from town," she spoke softly to his back; hands brushing through her hair, drying it, twisting it into a knot at the back of her neck.

"What like? I can't spend money on foolishness."

"Just something little for me to look at. I saw a picture card when we were at the cowboy's camp. That was pretty. I could look at that and think of what other places there are."

"You want that card? I'll bring you a new shirt and pants, they're pretty when they're new."

"No, something for me to look at and hold. I don't want to use everything. Remember that fair we saw that first trip? They had cards and pretty boxes with shells. Bring me a pretty box with shells. I could look at it and touch the shells . . ."

"I'll see what there is to bring that doesn't cost too dear. Come to bed now so we can sleep."

When he had gone into town with the lambs she shook out the blankets and swept the floor.

All the day long and night that he was gone she thought about the town and the rushing cattle in the stockyard, the lighted cafés, and the pretty goods in the store and the town women who wore colorful dresses.

If he brings me the box I'll keep it on the table all winter. I can see the watermarks on the shells and think of all the miles they've come to be here. She hummed to herself and tended the sheep.

When he came home she waited, breathless, while he unpacked the borrowed mule. He unloaded a package of wadded shirts and denim pants, wool socks, and a pair of boots for her. She watched him, and put away the sacked flour, coffee, sugar, tobacco, and tins of food. She dug through the sacks looking for the thing she had asked for.

"Did you bring me something pretty?" She hugged her arms to her chest.

"I spent all I could on things we need. I can't see what you needed that box for." He unwrapped a dozen tins of snuff and stacked them on the table. "Here's something you like, lump sugar for your coffee." He handed her a box of sugar.

She took the sugar from him and put it on the shelf.

"No thanks, hey? Well, I can get my thanks in bed." He touched her shirt front with a hard, accustomed hand.

"Look outside in the sheep pen. There's something else I got in town."

She went slowly outside. In the gray mass of sheep stood a large, dark shape. It was a horse, standing solemnly in the half dark, looking toward her with mysterious black eyes. A fringe of forelock covered

its eyes so that it seemed to look at her from a shadow. She entered the
pen and pushed the sheep aside to walk to the horse. It stood unmoving
when she touched its nose. She ran her hand up between its ears and
stroked its neck. Its head drooped and it sighed. It neither welcomed her
nor rejected her, but stood accepting her attention without resistance.

The man buffeted his way through the sheep and stood before her.
"I got him free from that cowboy we saw last spring. He was going to
shoot the horse because it's wind broke and can't keep up with the cattle."

The woman looked at them both. He put his arm possessively around
the horse's neck. "I can use him for packing our stuff up mountain next
spring. One thing's sure, he won't be running away from us, he's too
windbroken."

"He's a pretty thing," she said.

"Well, see, I brought you something to look at. He isn't much good
for anything but looking at right now, but come spring he can be used."
He slapped the horse's shoulder and turned away. The horse looked at
the woman and closed its eyes.

During the winter the dogs herded the sheep into nearby valleys for
pasture. The horse grazed with the sheep, following them listlessly from
spot to spot. The dogs nipped its heels and made it trot, causing it to
breathe heavily in a wheezing, whuffling shortness of breath. The woman,
seeing this, would call the dogs to stop; but they, listening to the man,
would loll their tongues at her and dart at the horse until the man whistled
them down.

At night, when the sheep were penned, the horse would stand at the
fence looking off into the mountains. The man would sit beside the stove
oiling his rifle, splicing tanned hides into a rope. The woman would sit on
the floor staring into the grated opening of the stove, listening to the
nightsounds. It was during one of these nights that she said: "I think I'm
starting a baby."

"Well, that's good." He stopped his work to touch her hair. "When did
this happen?"

"I think three months ago. I haven't had any woman signs for that
long, and my belt's too tight."

She stood while he felt her belly and sides.

"A baby, hey?" He thrust his hand within her shirt to her breasts.
"You are fattening up and filling out. Next time I go into town, I'll bring
you some more sugar and some canned fruit. You feel all right?"

"Oh, yes. I think it'll be born in the summer. Could you bring me
some cloth to make it some clothes?"

"Yeah, I guess I could. Flannel, I expect, and some pins and thread.
You'll have to pack it with you when we go up mountain." He held her
to him and kissed her head. "Give me a boy. He'd be a big help and we
could keep more sheep."

That night when they were in bed and he lay against her he repeated,
"Give me a boy. Give me a boy."

When he slept she rose to one elbow and watched him. In sleep his

I

face was the tender version of the day face, the pale eyes were hidden beneath a short run of lashes, the animal cunning mouth was relaxed into softer lines, tinted by tobacco juice and perpetual windburn. In sleep his face allowed no more knowledge of him than did his day face, it was so utterly expressionless. Whatever imagination or feeling he might have had was covered by the continuous need for material satisfaction. He had been orphaned at six years and had herded sheep for other men until he had begun his own flock. Since he had lost his parents, he had lost all identity except as a shepherd in the mountains. His dreams were of wool and sheep and the steadily increasing roll of money in a tin container under the floor. Some nights he panted like a dog in his sleep, dreaming of the heights and slow unwinding of the pasture lands up into the emptiness of the sky.

He had first seen his wife while she was tending her father's sheep on a winter pasture, sitting in the scrubby grass bent over some knitting. She was thirteen, just budding from a youth into womanliness. Her small, round head bent so seriously over woman's work touched some memory of his dead mother; her brown boyish hands knitting steadily and her yet unformed, unmarred face struck him in the groin with a kind of sad desire both to possess her and father her. In his late thirties, he had had few dealings with women, and so instead of courting her, he spoke with her father.

"She's a little bit strange," said the father. "She reads books and wanders off alone into the hills and we never know when she'll come back. But if you want her and figure you can put up with her ways, take her."

The girl had stood silently watching from the doorway of her father's house. For the exchange of three sheep she was given to the man. Her mother had spoken to her, bidding: "I never had time to tell you what to expect from a man. I can't tell you now except to be good to him. When he comes to you at night, take him." The girl had looked at her mother with mute eyes. "There's no way to find out about men and their ways except by doing. In ten years you'll not remember what it was like not to know a man. It seems to have been going on forever, and it will go on that way until he's too old." The mother held her daughter for the last time. "If you can take joy from his man's ways, that's good. If you can't, try to give him what you can, there's some joy in that too." She kissed her daughter's round forehead. "Now go to him, he seems to be kind, and you'd have to marry someone someday."

The man had taken her away with him into the cabin he had built. He watched her arrange her small store of clothing on the high shelf. She walked about the room, touching the table and the chairs. She looked into the cupboard at the supplies, patted the dogs and touched the window ledge. Her presence in the room made it a less lonely place for the man and he smiled at her hands when they touched the dogs.

The room was a new and lonely place for the girl. The smells of the man and dogs, wet fur and wool, the low flickering fire in the stove,

the absence of her mother made her aware of being pitched out into an
alien world. The presence of the man, his physical urge toward her, made
her feel shut in and apprehensive. She had some knowledge of what her
mother had meant, but only enough to keep her nerves tense. She remembered the rams in mating season, their arrogant, almost cruel way of
commanding the ewes; the ewes falling to their knees under the onslaught
of the rams, the heavy odors of life regenerating itself. She tried to think
if her father had ever looked at her mother that way, and the patience of
her mother's eyes when night came.

"Come now, you've seen all the things I have." The man took her arm
and held her close against his chest, stroking her hair and back gently.
He took her to the bed and watched her undress to the pale baby skin.
She lay beneath the wool blanket, eyes closed.

If I must learn man's ways, let it be now. Don't let it hurt. Don't let
him hurt me.

When the man touched her shoulder she flinched and opened her
eyes. She stared at him and clasped her hands over her breasts, hiding
them and herself from his maleness.

"Ah, now, I won't hurt you," he said. "Let me hold your hand and
we'll talk a bit."

She gave her hand to him and pulled the cover up to her chin.

"You're still afraid, hey? I won't hurt you." He leaned over her and
touched her face with his. "You're so small, more like my child than
my wife." He touched her body under the blanket, gently, as if plucking
a fragile plant. She turned her face to his shoulder and closed her eyes.
He stroked her body carefully, she sensing the rushing of his passion,
he building his desire slowly so as not to frighten her.

"Will you let me?" he asked her. She had fallen into a musing state.
She nodded.

When he was through he turned her head and looked at her.

"Well, now, it didn't hurt, did it?" She looked at him with patient
eyes and shook her head. He took her hand and rested with her until
they both fell asleep.

During the years before she became pregnant her figure filled out
into feminine contours. Her waist lengthened and diminished to a fitting
slimness, her breasts lost the baby roundness and drooped slightly, her
hips and buttocks rounded to firm, earth-round lines. Her walk changed
from a girl's gait to a purposeful stride, although she still walked as if
paying no attention to the earth, but walked slightly above it.

She and the man spoke little, they shared all their activities, but his
mind rested on the sheep while hers mused over the eternally silent
mountains and the dimension of sound and color.

In the spring of her pregnancy and after the lambing, they made their
way back over the foothills and into the mountain pasturelands.

The woman had become fond of the horse, feeling that it and she
shared the same state of uselessness. The horse had recovered some of its

broken wind and moved more alertly. Daily it was packed with their supplies and carried them silently after the sheep. The man walked ahead, whistling the dogs into the familiar patterns of action, watching the new grasses come up before them. The woman stepped behind him watching the rain mists climb higher up the mountain each day, seeing the horse move ahead of her, flicking its tail against the constant flies, reaching for the short grasses along the way. She drew pleasure from the horse's grace and its increasing strength and wildness. At night when the horse was unpacked, it would roll on the earth, rubbing its skin against the sharp strength of the mountain side, rising and kicking itself into the air. At these times she would clasp her hands and laugh while the horse nickered to her and coaxed her for the secret lumps of sugar she kept for it. The time came when she would ride the horse around the camp, calling the dogs to romp with her and the horse. She and the horse would pick their way from the camp to sudden ledges of the mountain and look down through the ground fog to the foothills, catching glimpses of occasional rivers and lights from other campfires. She would always return with the horse running and snorting, both looking wild and fresh from mysterious journeys in the night. The man would wait for her return and she would prepare the supper.

"What do you find in the night to look so happy about?"

"Oh, we look for the different stars. We saw camplights down east of us. We smelled the pines up mountain. It's all so different from the day. The stars are different up here from downland."

"The stars are always the same. No matter where you are." He drank his coffee and sat back. "You're getting as strange now as you were when I first brought you home."

"Strange? No, I'm not." She looked at him anxiously.

"It's that horse. You ride him too much, and you're away from me too much. You need to settle down to thinking about regular things like the sheep and the camp. You're going to have a baby soon, you should think about that."

"I do. Everytime he moves, I think about him. I made up a song to him." She began humming to herself.

"Songs." The man grunted. "I mean the sewing of clothes, that thread and cloth cost too dear to be wasted."

She looked at him and smiled. "I have been sewing. But my mind keeps straying to the other things he'll need."

"What else will he need? Plenty of flannel there."

"Oh, I meant the sun to shine on him, the stars to sparkle at him at night. I hear little voices in the wind singing for him. I want him to have flowers to look at and pull apart."

The man looked at her and shook his head. He settled into his blankets for the night.

The woman continued sewing straight white seams up and down squares of flannel. She threaded and rethreaded the needle, dreaming of her child.

That night while she was sewing she saw stars falling, running down the hill of the skies and disappearing behind the mountain. She wondered to herself, If the stars never change, why do some fall out of the sky? She watched hard for some minutes to see if certain stars would lose their place and fall. But they didn't. Rather, as if from some place beyond the familiar stars, the falling stars appeared and then began their descent. The idea of familiar and new stars held her breathless, and she spoke to the child within her.

Did you know that there are old stars and new ones? Or maybe the old ones are those that fall out of the sky, and we just see their ending. She fell asleep and dreamed of the falling stars.

The next morning she was struck with the idea of making a blanket for the baby with stars on it. "I remember when I was little, ma had a blanket with patches and designs on it. I want to make the same kind of blanket, but with stars on it."

The man looked at her and jostled her arm. "Stars on a blanket, hey? Well, if you've got any of that cloth left you could make it, I suppose. But what's the use of it?"

She smiled, "There doesn't have to be a use for it except for me to look at. I look at the stars at night, and this way, I can carry the baby in them when he's born. And he can look at them when it's cloudy."

They walked many strenuous miles that day and came to a camp of cowboys and cattle. They settled near it and walked to the campfire. The cowboys greeted them with jokes and glances at her burdened figure. They sat around the campfire and shared supper and coffee.

"Yeah, this is as high as we'll take the cattle. You're welcome to the rest of this mountain," the foreman said.

"We'll go up to the broken pass and summer graze there," the man said, offering the cowboys his tobacco, and accepting a handrolled cigarette.

"Your wife going to have that baby soon?" the foreman asked.

"In about two months, she figures."

"You'd better send her down the mountain then. She'll need help with it." The foreman was father to seven children, and knew of the difficulties of childbirth.

"Oh, could I go down to a ranch?" she asked.

"You figure she'll need help? I'll be with her when the baby comes." Her husband exhaled cigarette smoke and glanced at his wife.

"Bringing babies is woman's work. You never know what might happen. Bring her down to our ranch, we have an old woman there who brings lots of babies."

"Well, I guess I can spare her for a couple of weeks." He took his wife's hand and held it on his knee.

"Why don't you let her stay at the ranch until you come back down mountain? She can pay her way by helping the cook. And she'll need the rest. You don't want her bringing the baby back up mountain."

"Oh, I'd like that." The woman sat back thinking about the society of other women, the talk she missed, and the help she'd have when the baby came. "I could make the star blanket then, if somebody would help me."

"Star blanket?" The foreman looked at her and then at her husband.

"Yeah. She got a notion the other night she wants to make a blanket for the baby with stars on it. No use in it, though."

"What kind of blanket is that, Missus?" the foreman spoke kindly.

"I thought I'd make a white blanket with blue stars on it. The baby could look at them when it's cloudy, and it could know what stars are right off."

"I have an old blanket like that." He stood and went to his pack, pulling out a small saddle blanket of some Indian design. He held it out to her. "You can have it if you want."

She took it in her hands and smiled at him. The blanket was white bordered with bands of black and blue and with blue stars and lightning shapes. It was heavy, coarsely woven wool. "That's pretty. I take it with many thanks." She smiled again at him and stroked the stars.

"You don't have to give my wife anything like that." Her husband frowned in gratitude.

"No, no, take it. You can keep it for the baby, and it will be warm for him in the winter."

The foreman turned to the husband, "I mean what I say about sending her down mountain when her time comes. You've got that horse, it'll carry her down in a couple of days."

"I'll have to think about it."

"Mister, don't take this unkindly. I've watched the two of you go up and down the mountain these years, and I know you're tight with a dollar. But don't be tight with your wife or your baby. You can't ever get them back when they're dead. So just risk the sheep for that last month and send her down to the ranch." He turned to the woman. "When you feel your time coming, ma'am, you just start down the mountain. If you need help down, I'll be glad to ride down with you."

"Thank you. I'll try to come down without help." She touched her stomach and sighed. "But how will I know when it's time?"

"My wife says when the baby moves down so you can breathe again, that's the time to get ready. So you just get on that horse and start down."

That night the cowboys talked and told stories about their lives with the cattle. The man and woman watched and listened. As it is with all lonely men they sang the melancholy songs and played handmade guitars. The woman saw them as beautiful and kindly strangers who shared her loneliness on the mountain. She saw the glint of their saddle decorations in the night light and watched their dark figures slump in the darkening, star-filled night. They spoke of towns she had never seen; one spoke of the ocean and its strangeness. He showed her some shells he had brought from the ocean shore. She held them and touched the water-etched designs. The cowboy had linked the shells together on a hand-braided cord. The shells tinkled together and shone blue and white under the stars.

"See, ma'am, the inside is shiny and smooth. The outside is rougher and dull." He turned the shells over and over. "Folks say that they've found shells like this up here in the mountains."

"What? Shells in the mountains?" She looked at him for the joke.

"Ma'am, I'm not fooling you. When I was down on the coast last year, I ran into a fellow who told me so. He said if we keep our eyes open in the raw parts of the mountain, sometime we might spot marks of shells and plants that live under the water. I've been looking ever since then. But I haven't seen any." He poured the last of the coffee into her cup. "If you get up higher you might just keep your eyes open. You might find some. This fellow told me these mountains are still young. And that they've hardly finished growing."

"I never heard of such a thing." She looked at him sharply to see if he was making fun of her.

"The way he tells it, the mountains grew up out of ocean water, pushing and shoving each other, and carrying the shells and plants with them." He looked at her earnestly.

"I've heard some tall stories in my day, but this takes them all." Her husband rolled into his blanket and eyed the cowboy. "Don't fill her head up with any stranger ideas than she already has."

"Tell me the rest. How young are these mountains?" She leaned forward to hear every word.

"Ma'am, they're way older than we are. They've been here before white men or Indians ever came, but this fellow said that they are babies compared to mountains in other parts of the world."

She looked away from him to the mountain looming over them. "Could we tell if they were still growing?"

"I figure if this mountain ever starts to grow again, we can forget about getting off. I don't think a mountain's growing pains would be easy to take. This man said that when mountains grow they grow from the inside out, and parts break off." He smiled at her and said, "He didn't think they'd be growing any more for years, so don't you worry about it, ma'am."

"Thank you for telling me about it. My husband thinks I'm strange for thinking such things." She looked apprehensively at her sleeping husband.

"No, ma'am, you're not strange. There's a lot to be known about this world, and the only way I figure you can find out anything is to wonder about it and ask somebody. I've got some books back at the ranch, you're welcome to read them and look at the pictures."

"Thank you, I look forward to reading them. How did you get them?"

"Every winter when we're in slow times I go out to the towns and look around. There's ways to find books and ways to learn things. All you have to do is go out and hunt for them."

"Why do you look for books?"

"Ma'am, I guess I'm just part cat. When I see something I've got to know all I can about it. That star blanket you wanted. I think you're smart to give it to your baby. He'll grow up looking at the stars and maybe be a better or smarter man than his dad. I don't mean disrespect toward your husband, but every little shove we can give to another person, means they'll go a lot farther than we did."

He stood up and moved away from her. "I'd better let you get some sleep now. You listen to Jake and go down mountain when your time comes. And you read all the books you want. When winter comes, if you want, I'll bring you some more."

She lay rolled up in her blanket looking into the darkness where the cowboy had disappeared. Her mind hummed and murmured with the things he had told her. And he hadn't thought her strange for her thought and questions. She hugged the star blanket to her and fell into a deep sleep.

The sounds of men moving and the barking of dogs woke her. She lay for minutes watching the men in the dawnlight squatting over their coffee cups and tin plates. When her husband leaned over her, she smiled and struggled to her feet. They shared breakfast with the cowboys and left the camp. They had walked a mile when they heard a horse coming behind. They stopped and saw the cowboy riding up the slope. When he reached them, he stopped his horse and handed the woman the string of shells.

"I thought you might like these for the baby, ma'am. I'll be going down to the ocean again in a couple of years, and I'll get more." He saluted her with his hat and turned his horse.

"Thank you! Thank you!" she called after him.

"Well, he's a strange one. You forget all that fooling with shells and books." Her husband turned up the mountain and whistled at the dogs. She followed him, holding the string of shells and wondering at the cowboy's goodness.

That summer as they followed the sheep higher into the mountain she looked for marks in the raw sections of the ledges. She wandered from the sheep trail onto ledges and shelves, scratching into the sliding shale for the shell marks. But she found none.

She gazed into the side of the mountain as if willing it to disclose its hidden shells. As her size and awkwardness increased she was forced to ride the horse for the major part of the day, or stay in camp while her husband took the sheep to new grazing. When she was left alone she sewed more garments for the child or took slow walks with the horse, talking to it about the cowboy and what he had said to her. The horse had become doglike in its devotion to her and followed her, nuzzling her pockets for the sugar. She sat long hours on the mountainside, making bouquets of the spring flowers, garlanding the horse's mane with them, and laughing when he ate them indiscriminately.

The man changed with the summer, growing more irritable. He would watch her while she turned the shells over in her hands, or take out the star blanket and count the stars on it. He watched her find things on the mountain and rejoice over them, things that he had seen, unseeing, for years. What new dimensions she found and lived in were not of his liking, and he grew to dislike and then hate the mountain and her pre-occupation with it.

"Next spring," he said, "we're going up another mountain. This one's been overgrazed, and it's too crowded."

She glanced at him and then up at the ledged peak.

"We'll find new places on the next mountain. Maybe it will have shells like the cowboy said."

"You're wasting time looking for shells on a mountain. That kind of talk is for kids and old folks, we're looking for grazing land." He frowned at her and held her arm tightly. "You forget that kind of talk. And forget that cowboy."

"I won't. You always think I'm strange. But I'm not. I can wonder about anything I want to." She pulled away from him.

"You're thinking about that cowboy. I heard you talking to him, and looking at him." He raged at her, suddenly jealous, suddenly aware that she was more than a convenience.

He took her by the shoulders and shook her. She glared at him and ground her teeth. He released her and went to the fire. They had supper and lay down to sleep. After a few minutes he went to her and took her body fiercely to his. She lay passive, looking at him with a fresh aware-ness of his body. She felt the coarse hairs of his body and the perspiration running down his face. At once she remembered his kindness to her on that first night. What had made him change over the years? She felt the thrusting of his body and a quick discomfort about the child. She tried to push him away, saying, "Stop. The baby. You're hurting me."

He continued to thrust against her, determined to reclaim her from the mountain, to bring her back to the docile wife she had been. Through the haze of desire and his own loneliness he finally heard her words and their meaning. He stopped, resting heavily against her, looking into her eyes. She resisted him now not only with her body, but with her will. He turned away from her body and lay beside her. They lay side by side on the mountain slope, he gazing at her with a lonely despair, she lying silent, no longer resisting him, but mute and aloof, part of the mountain, removed utterly from his grasp, eyes turned inward to the remote workings of her own mind and body.

She lay resting softly against the mountain, listening somehow to the silent workings of the child within her, feeling the kicking and stretching of the unborn, sensing a rebellious anger in its movements. She touched her stomach, marvelling at the fruitful fullness that jutted imperiously against the black night sky.

"Mountains grow from the inside out." It was that way with her. The vigorous, active wonder within her was pushing her body out of shape to accommodate its own demands, lying heavily against her spine. She stretched a hand out against the peaceful tilting mountain slope, feeling

I*

the roundness of it, imagining the massed bones and structure beneath. She nestled against the curve of the mountain and slept.

The next day they reached the summer grazing land. The mountain here was open for miles to flats of grassland and small ponds filled with ice water from underground springs. The sheep would graze for weeks before exhausting the ground cover. The man and woman set up a tent against a windfall of trees, gathered the broken, sun-dried wood into stacks for their small summer fire, and prepared for the weeks of wandering after the sheep during the day and returning at night to the same spot.

The woman continued her search for shells, although aware that none would be found in the grass-grown flats. She walked with the sheep and the horse, disappearing into the alleys that led up and into the mountain. From time to time she saw deer and rabbits staring out from the mountain's secret avenues, heard birds calling above her and felt the silence of the mountain. She walked daily higher through the trees and ledges, following dead stream beds into echoing chambers of the mountain's interior. As she picked her way deeper into the mountain she lost track of what she was looking for, listening to the stillness of the mountain and the creak of trees. She followed the mysterious silent voice of the mountain as it led her farther from her husband and his sheep to some invisible, lost, unspeaking essence that beckoned her and charmed her senses with a provocative, almost sensual desire. When night fell on the mountain she would drift down through the ground mists to the camp, lost in the wanderings of her mind, to prepare supper.

Her nights were filled with the campfire, her husband and his talk of the sheep, the alien duties of cooking and eating. She cooked and ate in silence, looking at the pots and plates, trying to recognize some familiar quality about them. Her husband's face, once so involved with herself as to be her own identity, now was foreign and harsh.

He would look at her over his plate, wondering at her silence. He spoke to her and received no answer.

"I shot a deer today," he'd say. "We'll have meat every day now and dry the rest." He'd pause and wait for her reply. None came.

"How's your sewing? You finish all that flannel?" He stoked his mouth with tobacco and closed the tin.

"Hey! Answer me!" He threw a stick at her.

She turned her head in his direction, inquiringly.

"Talk to me!" He threw another stick at her.

"Yes." She smiled in his direction, her eyes looking through him into the dark beyond.

"You are queerer now than you used to be." He rolled the tobacco in his mouth. "Is it the baby?"

"The baby is fine. We walked into the mountain today. There's something up there." She took out the star blanket and unrolled it over her knees.

"What's up there? I suppose there's deer and a few bear. You be careful when you go alone." He peered at her, watching her hands stroking the stars on the blanket.

"No, there's something up there that I can't find. I can almost hear it. Sometimes when I come around the corner of a ravine I think it will be standing there. But it never is."

"You take a dog with you tomorrow. And take the rifle."

"No. The dogs might frighten it away. And I don't want to shoot it. I want to find it and see what it is."

Her husband stood up, throwing the remaining coffee into the fire. "Well, you better stay close to camp. Your time is almost here and you don't figure that thing in the mountain is going to help you any, do you?"

"No, I just want to find it." She opened her blankets for the night. "I feel like the baby is moving down. When can I start for the ranch?"

"I don't figure on letting you go. You talk so strange they might not let you come back." He lay next to her, holding her head in his hands. "You going crazy on me?"

She shook her head. "No, can't you tell there's something waiting in the mountain?"

"There isn't anything in that mountain but deer and bear." He pulled her down to his chest. "Now you just forget that crazy talk and think about how you're going to have that baby here in camp."

"You promised I could go to the ranch and have a woman help me."

She huddled beside him, her distended abdomen pushing him away from her as his arms tightened about her.

"No, I've been thinking. You go down mountain to that ranch and read those books about shells and growing mountains and you'll get so crazy you won't come back."

"I will come back. Oh, let me go down. I'm afraid of being alone when the baby comes."

"What help you need, I'll give you. If I can bring sheep, I can bring a baby." He looked at her cunningly, "If you stay here you can hunt for that thing."

She looked levelly at him. "You are breaking your promise."

"Promises are for people who can use them. This promise is better used broken. I'll take care of you and the boy when he comes."

Her eyes flickered and she looked away toward the horse.

"I'll be taking the horse with me every day from now on, so you won't be trying to sneak out on him." He spoke with his eyes closed.

"I don't like you for this," she said. "If the baby is hurt by your keeping me here, it's all your blame."

"No blame will be coming. I'll take care of that." He slept leaning against her, holding her body as if to keep her with him even in sleep.

During the rest of her time, the woman walked restlessly through the mountain's interiors. She spoke to the mountain and the thing that haunted her. "Let me have the baby easily and quickly, don't let the baby be hurt." The listening air around her echoed upon the mountain walls: *Hurt*.

Early in the morning her labor began. She went into the tent and lay on the blankets. Her husband watched her face and said, "I'll just take the sheep out to the grazing and come right back." She nodded and he left.

When he didn't return when she expected him, she crept out of the tent to watch for him. She lay on her side against the yielding slope, resting between pains, holding the star blanket to her, twisting it between her hands when the pains reached their peak, relaxing when the pains subsided.

She watched the sun climb the hill of the sky and descend. At times it seemed as if she must fall off the shoulder of the earth and down into the sky. Moments went by that she clung to the side of the mountain, feeling a pulsebeat under her, hearing a beating in the air as if the mountain were heaving with her and falling out from under her. She was sweating heavily, her body sliding within her clothes, her hands were slippery in the grass and on the blanket. The pains increased in rapidity and strength until she was constantly knotted with them, breathing harshly through her mouth. She was swept from the side of the mountain at one second, and pushed back into it at the next. Then, suddenly, the child was forced from her body into the air, and the mountain stopped twisting beneath her. She lay spent, watching the mountain fall back into place above her. Then she sat up and reached for the child. Its face turned up to hers, utterly lifeless. The cord between the child and the afterbirth had strangled it, choking off its first cry. She looked down at it dumbly, hearing a forlorn wail from beyond her ken. She held the dead child to her, rocking it. She twisted the cord from its neck, and covered the child and all in the star blanket.

When the man returned he found her sitting on the slope, holding the dead child wrapped in its bloodied star blanket.

"I lost my way in those ravines. How's the boy?"

"He's dead. He choked on the cord." She smoothed the blanket over the child.

"Let me see. Huh. He never got his breath." The man turned the child about in the blanket, touching the round, puckered face, the blunt features, the scruff of hair.

"Well, you rest. I'll bury him in the trees." He walked away with the child.

"No, don't bury him up here. Let me take him down so he can have a mark on his grave." She went after the man, reaching for the child.

"No need in that. He died here and he can stay here." He laid the baby under a tree and dug a shallow grave. She stood, leaning against the tree, eyes averted. He buried the child and covered the small enclosure with branches and stones. "This tree can be his mark. He never needed more than that."

The woman sat beside the grave and dropped leaves gently on it, seeming to hear a heartbeat from the buried child. She laid her head down on the branches and closed her eyes. "I'll stay here with him until morning. He might be lonely and afraid all alone."

The man nodded and walked to the camp.

That night, lying next to her child's grave she listened to the sounds of the mountain and dreamed about the child.

In the morning the man prepared to take the sheep away to the grazing. The woman went to the fire and cleaned herself. When the man spoke to her she said: "You take the sheep today. I want the horse."

The man looked at her. She found her string of shells and put them into a pocket. "I'm going down mountain."

"What for, you don't need help any more."

"I'm going down mountain," she said stubbornly. "I let you strangle my baby with your ideas of keeping and using."

"I didn't strangle the baby." He stepped toward her, hands out.

"No, not likely, but it's the same." She called the horse and turned down the mountain.

"You figure you're going to find some shells?" He called at her, running after the horse. "You won't find any. Ever. There's no use looking!"

"I want to look. I want to see what it's like to look."

"You'll be back. You'll see. There's no use in it at all!"

"No, no use at all." She looked at him for the last time and rode down the mountain.

George Garrett
A Game of Catch

On the way to the beach the two brothers began to argue. Naomi sat between them in the front seat of the convertible, Tee Jay's car, and ate candy bars. Naomi didn't drink or smoke, but when she was away from it all on a day like this, going to the beach without a worry in the world, she would stuff candy. Sometimes she ate so much she got sick. Tee Jay knew all about it. He was the one who brought a whole box of Baby Ruth's along for the trip. Courtney, the crazy one, brought her a flower. When they tooted the horn for her in the alley behind the gymnasium and she came running out of the back door smiling at them, it was Tee Jay who handed her a box of Baby Ruth's. He knew about her sweet tooth. Courtney got out of the car to let her in and gave her the gardenia, one fifty-cent gardenia.

"What's this for?" Naomi said. "Are we going to a dance or something?"

"I don't know," Courtney said to Tee Jay. "Are we?"

Tee Jay ignored him. He kept staring into Naomi's eyes, half-smiling, until she looked down at her flat shoes.

"Don't look at me," Tee Jay said. "It's *his* idea."

"I'll tell you what," Courtney said. "Why don't you eat it? For dessert, after you finish the candy, I mean."

Naomi laughed and clapped him on the back, hearty, comradely. What else could she do? That Courtney was something, you never knew what he might think of next. You never knew how to take anything he said. Besides, he was just out of the State Asylum. He had been in and out a couple of times. They said he was cured now, but you wouldn't know it. You couldn't be sure about a thing like that.

They drove along the highway to the east coast, and the brothers were arguing as usual. Naomi chewed candy and let the warm air trouble her hair. It was dark and cut close, but with the breeze fingering it, combing it, she imagined it was long and blowing in a dark cloud like smoke behind her, long and mysterious as Lady Godiva's. Floating on her skirt between the firm bulge of her thighs, the gardenia was already turning brown at the edges, but it was sweet.

"I don't care where you read it," Tee Jay was saying. "It sounds like crap to me."

"I'm telling you that something like that, a murder, is just love in disguise. He might have just kissed them. It would be the same thing."

"Books! Books! That's all I get from you. Do you believe everything you read in a book?"

"He's got a thing about books, you know," Courtney said to Naomi. "Do you know the only book Tee Jay ever read? I mean *read*, all the way, every word from the beginning to the end."

"Don't try and involve me in the discussion," Naomi said, her mouth rich with chocolate.

She had been listening vaguely to their words, but it was all so morbid. They were arguing about some old man who had gathered his whole family together for a photograph, sat them down in a tight group on his front steps, his wife, his grown children, even his grandchildren. When he had them all ready and posed for the picture, he excused himself for just one moment and went back in the house. He returned with a shotgun, and before any of them could even move, he fired both barrels into them point blank. He was reloading the gun to shoot himself when the next door neighbor came running over and knocked him out with a shovel. The papers were full of it. They were always full of things like that. And Naomi couldn't care less. Trust old Courtney to bring up the subject. Trust him, too, to try and get her in the argument.

"I'll tell you the only book Tee Jay ever read all the way through. It was called *The Bitter Tea of General Yen*."

"So what," Tee Jay said. "It wasn't a bad book."

"How would *you* know? What have you got to compare it with?"

"Look," Tee Jay said. "You're the one with the college education. I'm the one that went to work. I don't have time to read a lot of books. All I do is pay for the books you read."

"It doesn't take a lot of time to read a book," Courtney said.

"It takes too much time for me."

Naomi licked the candy off her fingers and reached forward and turned on the radio. When it warmed up, she twisted the dial until she found some music playing, then she turned it up as loud as it would go. It roared over and around them like a storm, scattering music to the four winds. She saw their mouths still moving furiously, but *they* couldn't hear each other if *she* couldn't, sitting between them. Courtney leaned close and whispered in her ear.

"Flaming Youth," he said.

"What?" she mouthed.

"Flaming Youth," he whispered again. "It's a sort of a joke."

Then he stuck out his wet tongue and fluttered it in her ear, and she jerked away from him. If it had been anyone else in the world but poor Courtney, she would have slapped his fresh face. Tee Jay, who was turning down the radio, missed the whole thing.

"Reach in the glove compartment," he said. "Hand me my cigarettes."

"I'd prefer if you didn't smoke," Naomi said. "You know how I feel about it."

"Who cares how you feel?" Tee Jay snapped at her, taking the pack from Courtney. "Maybe *I* don't like candy. Maybe it makes me sick to watch people who eat candy. I don't have the right to object, do I?"

"Candy is altogether different," Naomi said. "If God had intended for you to smoke, He would have made you a chimney."

"Yeah? Yeah?" Tee Jay said, lighting his cigarette. "Maybe you'd like to walk to the beach. If God had intended for you to ride, He would have put wheels on your ass."

Naomi glared straight ahead.

"It makes me sad to be the only one who isn't indulging in something, some lonely, stupid, solitary, ineffable private vice."

And with that curious remark Courtney simply put his hand in her lap and took the gardenia. He held it under his nose, sniffed it, and then began to chew the white bitter petals.

"Don't *swallow* it!" Naomi cried. "What's the matter, are you crazy?"

She blushed then, realizing that it had just slipped out like that.

"Oh, no," Courtney said, his mouth white and full of flower. "I *used* to be, but I'm not any more. I'm just as sane as everyone."

Inexplicably, Tee Jay laughed.

"How does it taste, boy?" he said.

"Not too bad," Courtney said. "On the other hand, don't feel that you're missing out on anything."

"You better be careful," Naomi said. "I've heard tell they're poison."

"You'll never know for sure until somebody tries one," Courtney said. "That's science for you."

After that they rode without talking, just listening to the music on the radio. Naomi felt a lot better now that they had stopped arguing. The only trouble was still Courtney. He kept putting his hand on her leg. That would be all right, just resting there, but he wouldn't leave well enough alone. After a while, all of a sudden, he'd stiffen all his fingers at once and start edging up her thigh like a spider, sort of on tiptoes or tip-fingers. When his hand got too close for comfort, sneaking toward the ultimate destination which Naomi, in spite of all, to her dying day, would call her privates, plural, she would have to firmly take his hand in hers and remove it. Then the whole process would begin all over again. Courtney kept looking straight up the road, and so did she. She didn't want to make a scene, and she knew if Tee Jay noticed anything, he'd stop the car and beat Courtney up.

When they got to the beach it seemed like a perfect day. The sun was bright, the water was blue and scaled with the whitecaps of a brisk east wind. The tide was down, but rising, so they could still drive up and down the beach in Tee Jay's good-looking car. Far out along the horizon clouds like dark bruises were massing and swelling, but they were a long way away. They drove up and down the beach a few times, slowly, just looking at the people, the children running and jumping and splashing and throwing sand, as shrill and swift as gulls, the muscular young men, bronzed and cocky, the girls in their bright bathing suits, and, too, the old people, the fat and the thin, misshapen and grotesque, sprawled under beach umbrellas, or burning lurid shades of pink in the sun. The men with mountainous stomachs and the little jiggly breasts like girls at puberty, and bandy, veined legs, and the women, thin and wrinkled as old, cracked leather, or enormous, all rippling, shaking bellies and buttocks, and great breasts sagging like overripe fruit, disgusted Naomi. She could not stand to look at them. *They* had a nerve, exposing themselves like that! Still, she was irresistibly fascinated; she couldn't help studying them and wondering, with an inner chill as if her blood had turned to quicksilver, if she would ever be like that.

After they had driven up and down a while, Tee Jay turned south and drove past the last of the cottages, clinging precariously to the dunes like driftwood on the swelling sea, past the last of the swimmers, the last lifeguard, dozing and golden on his stilted perch, to the open beach.

"Where are we going now?" Naomi asked.

"Swimming," Tee Jay said.

"Well," she said, "I'd like to go to the Bath House and put on my bathing suit."

"The Bath House? Christ, what *for*?"

"Turn the car around, please," she said.

"That's the craziest thing I ever heard of," Tee Jay said. "The Bath House costs fifty cents apiece. We can dress in the dunes for free."

"I'd *prefer* to dress in the Bath House."

"What's the *matter* with you? Courtney won't mind."

"Can't you see the girl is moved by natural modesty?" Courtney said. "Take her to the Bath House."

"Natural modesty, my ass! Fifty cents is a whole lot of money to fork over all of a sudden just because for the first time in her life Naomi decides she's modest."

"Women are that way," Courtney said. "Full of little surprises."

He only said that, Naomi knew, because of the way his own wife had done him. After three years of married life and two children, she simply left one day, drove off with Billy Towne who was a salesman of fishing tackle up and down both coasts, from Fernandina to Coral Gables, from Pensacola to Key West. Yes, Billy Towne could take Maxine all over the whole state. She could go to the beaches while he was working, and at night they could go to all the bars and nightclubs. It was a good life for her. The thing was how hard it hit Courtney. He worshiped Maxine, like a fool, because anybody could have told him how she was born a bitch and would die a bitch, no matter how pretty she was. So, away went Maxine, *with* the two little girls, living in open unashamed sin with that Billy Towne. And *poof*, Courtney was in the State Asylum. Then *she* could divorce him because he was legally crazy. Oh yes, he would make all of those nasty cracks about women in general, but the world knew that if Maxine crooked her little finger at him, he'd go back to her on his hands and knees. Tee Jay, of course, had never married anybody. He hadn't mentioned marriage in all this time. Still, there was always the chance that he would.

"I'm sorry," Naomi said, "but I really would rather dress at the Bath House. I'll pay for it myself."

"In *that* case . . ." Tee Jay said.

And he turned the car around in a wild, wide, sand-scattering circle and sped back toward the main beach. He hunched over the wheel, close to the windshield like a racing driver, and put the gas pedal to the floor. That was Tee Jay for you!

Once inside the small unpainted cubicle in the Bath House, standing on the wet, strutted slats, Naomi undressed and hung her clothes on a nail. She was a tall ungainly girl. Her face, though cast in large, coarse features, had a uniformity that made her seem conventionally pretty. But her body was oddly proportioned. Her thick, heavy-muscled legs, her hard high large buttocks and flat stomach, seemed to belong to someone much larger, perhaps even, except for the curve of her hips, to a powerful man. ("My fullback," Tee Jay called her.) Her upper body was slight and frailboned, flatchested like a young girl's. In her clothes, wearing full skirts, loose peasant blouses, and flat shoes, she achieved a kind of equilibrium, but at moments like this, alone and naked, she felt a shame and self-revulsion that nearly brought her to tears. She struggled into her black, one-piece suit, too tight at the hips, padded at the breasts, put on her white bathing cap, and placed the elastic-banded key around her wrist. She pulled the door of the cubicle to, sharply, behind her.

The two of them were waiting for her in the car. They turned their heads together and stared at her as she came across the boardwalk and down the wooden steps and across the powdery sand near the dunes. She began running toward them.

"Look," Courtney cried, "a female Centaur. Whatever that may be."

"Let's get the show on the road," Tee Jay said.

Then, still staring at her as she got into the car, Courtney said, "Cough drops."

When Tee Jay found a place that suited him, out of sight of the main beach, the two of them took their swimming trunks and went up into the dunes to change. Naomi spread out a beach blanket and covered her exposed skin with suntan oil. She had a little plaid beach basket from which she took a pair of dark glasses and a confession magazine. Just then, settling comfortably in the sunlight, she heard the thunder and felt the breeze coming stronger and cooler off the ocean, saw lightning far off in the clouds and whitecaps flickering across the whole expanse of the visible sea.

"It's going to squall," she called.

"So what?" Tee Jay replied from the dunes.

And she looked and saw the two of them, the twins, standing side by side on top of a dune, perfectly identical except that Courtney was pale and soft beside Tee Jay. They came charging down in a little whirlwind of sand and legs, leapt right over her and past with flashing heels and flanks, raced into the water. Soon they were splashing each other and shouting, but she couldn't hear what they were saying to each other. She went back to the car and got the box of Baby Ruth's. She returned and, opening her magazine, began to read the sad thrilling tale of an innocent girl who was seduced by a State Policeman.

By the time the two came back from their swim, they were arguing again, and about the same old thing. Tee Jay opened the glove compartment and produced a pint of whiskey. They both had a drink. A lot they cared about her approval! Then Tee Jay went around and opened the trunk. He fumbled around until he found a softball and two gloves. It was a brand new softball, white, hard and shiny.

"You want to play catch?"

"No," she said. "I don't feel much like it right now."

"*Well*, how do you like that?"

"I'll throw a few with you," Courtney said.

They moved out in front of the car and began to lob the ball easily back and forth. Tee Jay was the athlete. He played third base for Morrison's Department Store Softball Team. Naomi loved to go and watch him play on a spring or summer evening under the lights, in his red and green and gold uniform. He was so quick, so deft, so dandy around the bag. He was the only man she had ever seen, except in newsreels and such, that she could really *admire* when he was playing a game. The others, even the good ones, were so sloppy and careless, like they didn't care, like it was so easy for them, running and throwing and just being men, like they didn't give two hoots what anybody thought. She hated them. Tee Jay was nervous and quick and delicate; every move he made seemed to have its reason. Naomi's heart leapt for him when she saw him move swiftly to snag a hardhit ball, or when he came running full speed, but like a dancer on points, to scoop up a bunt, whirl, and in the same motion burn it down to second or to first base. Courtney, on the other hand, had never been much at sports. That was a funny thing. The first time he was at the State Asylum he got the notion somehow that he was going to play shortstop for the New York Yankees. It was terrible. Tee Jay would have to drive up there and spend whole weekends batting him flies and grounders, and playing catch with him. At least, Naomi noticed, he had improved from the practice. She returned to her magazine story.

The storm moved in on them. Drops of rain began to fall, and, looking up, Naomi saw that the black clouds were overhead and all around them. They seemed to be shaggy and running like buffaloes in the movies. The waves were much bigger now and broke on the sand with huge crashes and bursts of foam like breaking glass. She bundled her things together and ran to the car. She pulled the lever that controlled the mechanism, and the gray top began to creak forward into place.

"Who told you to do that?" Tee Jay yelled at her.

He ran over, his face pinched and flushed with anger, and let the top down again. The rain was falling harder now, in thick drops. The trouble was that they had started the argument again.

"Cut off your nose to spite your face," she said. But a lance of lightning and a barrage of thunder drowned out her voice.

"What was that? What did you say?"

"Never mind," she replied.

She crouched in the front seat and the cold rain fell on her. The two of them, heedless of rain, thunder and lightning, stood there shouting at each other and throwing the ball as hard as they could. They had thrown their gloves aside. They shouted and threw the ball so hard she didn't see how they could catch it barehanded. It was very dangerous for all of them, she knew. She'd heard stories about people being struck by lightning on the beach. Besides the tide was rising; pretty soon they wouldn't be able to drive back along the beach. She got out of the car and ran to Tee Jay.

"Let's go," she said. "Let's go home."

Tee Jay threw the ball to Courtney. He threw it gently.

"Let's quit," Tee Jay said. "This is crazy."

"Are you *afraid*?" Courtney yelled.

The full strength of the squall was on them now. With the rain pelting, the high wind and the lightning and thunder, they had to scream to each other. Courtney fired the ball back to Tee Jay and he threw it back just as hard. Naomi could see the red round shape of the ball printed on Tee Jay's palm and fingers.

"*You* catch it," Courtney screamed at her. "You're the coach."

She caught it and threw it to Tee Jay. Then it was a three-cornered game. For a few minutes she was glad to be shielding Tee Jay, catching that wet, hot, skin-wincing ball and throwing it, easy, to him. But it hurt and Tee Jay seemed impatient to throw again. He didn't seem to appreciate what she was doing at all. So she threw it to him as hard as she could.

"Damn you!" he said.

Her hands were bruised and aching, and she was afraid of the thunder and lightning, but still they kept throwing the ball so fast that she didn't know what to do. Finally Courtney dropped one and it rolled away down the beach. He chased after it, and she was running behind him. When he seized it and spun around, wild-eyed, to throw it to her, she was close enough to kiss him if she had wanted to. Surprised, he began back. The tears started streaming from her eyes.

"Please, please, let's stop now and go home."

"No," he said. "No, we aren't going to stop."

"Please," she said. "Please."

He squeezed the ball in both hands.

"All right," he said. "I'll tell you what. You take off your bathing suit, and we'll go home."

"Throw the godamn ball!" Tee Jay yelled.

Courtney waved at him to wait a minute. Tee Jay stamped his feet angrily, but waited.

"Go on, take it off," Courtney said to her.

"Will we go home then?"

He nodded.

She undid her shoulder straps and slipped and wriggled out of the rain-soaked suit. It lay like a small shadow at her feet.

"Now dance."

"What?"

"When I brought you the flower, you made a joke about going to a dance. Well, this is it. Dance for me."

Clumsily, cold, shivering in the wind, and still crying, she began to dance. Courtney laughed at her. He reached out and touched her small, brown, shrunk nipples with his fingers.

"See what I meant about cough drops?" he said. Then he cupped his hands and yelled into the wind to Tee Jay. "See what I mean? See what I mean about love? I *love* her."

"Never mind all that crap," Tee Jay replied. "Just keep throwing the godamn ball and we'll see who's afraid around here."

Naomi knelt down then, beside her bathing suit, and hid her face. She huddled on herself like a child asleep, and the two men continued to throw the ball back and forth with unrelenting fury.

V. S. Pritchett

The Educated Girl

July. There was a new waitress at Bianchi's.

"Justine!" Mrs. Bianchi called, from her desk at the doorway of the little restaurant. "Number four."

The new waitress slipped her sandals back on and walked very slowly, her head lowered and a handful of straight fair hair hanging forward over her face, exposing one large, still, strong gray eye to the customer at table number four.

"We got her from the Art School," Mrs. Bianchi comfortably explained to an old customer.

"Yes," said Mr. Bianchi, making a despairing distinction. "Mrs. Bianchi got her. Staff is the big headache."

"It's pocket money for them," said Mrs. Bianchi wistfully, her eyes going very small.

"She's an educated girl," said Mr. Bianchi suicidally.

"You can't pay the wages," said Mrs. Bianchi. "They come out of the slums of Naples," Mrs. Bianchi opened up sharply on Mr. Bianchi, "and they want the earth."

"She's got her shoes off again," said Mr. Bianchi.

"She's British," said Mrs. Bianchi who was enormously British.

The new waitress stood by the table waiting for the customer to give her order. The customer was wearing a wide-brimmed red straw hat.

"Good morning," the customer said, "I think I will have—"

"My sister has a hat like that," the waitress said. "She got it at Bourne's. Did you get yours at Bourne's? I want to get one. Hers is yellow, pale yellow. She can't wear strong colors."

The woman took off her glasses.

"I should like to have an omelette," the woman said.

"She wears hers with gray," the waitress said. Her voice was slow, clear and low like a funeral march.

"I tell her to try putting a band round it, nothing fancy, just a plain silk band round it and tie it under her chin—well one could do that, couldn't one? Or let it fall back on your shoulders—it wouldn't suit me but *you* could do it. You have got to be the type. Cheese or ham?"

"A mushroom omelette," said the woman coldly.

"I can't eat them," said the waitress, speaking with one foot in the grave. "It must be an allergy. I love picking them, but I can't eat them. I was reading a book where it said that four hundred people have died in France in the last three years from eating them."

Her single eye gazed at the woman's hat.

"False Blushers, I expect," said the waitress. "Many people confuse the real Blusher with the False."

The woman did not answer.

Slowly the new waitress walked to Mrs. Bianchi's desk.

"A plain omelette," she said to Mrs. Bianchi. "She was wearing a green cloche yesterday. She doesn't speak."

Mr. Bianchi, whose job it was to stand near Mrs. Bianchi and welcome the customers, closed his eyes with pain. Mrs. Bianchi caught this and took a full, carnivorous look at Mr. Bianchi. He was a green-faced man; a chicken bone with not much left on it that she might have picked up and had a chew at from time to time. She resumed the usual expression of satisfied consternation that was set between her thick black brows and her black moustache. In getting the kind of girl Mr. Bianchi would never run after, Mrs. Bianchi had frightened herself.

At number seven, Mr. Rougemont from the Museum had just sat down and was unloading his pockets. He propped a book against the water jug.

"Soup," he said to the new waitress.

"Soup?" she said.

"Yes, soup," said Mr. Rougemont.

She was trying to read the title of his book. He closed it and stared at her.

"On a hot day like this?" said the new waitress.

Heavily made and with a scholarly readiness for controversy, he asked: "Does soup have to be hot? Isn't there such a thing as cold soup?"

"Yes," said the girl. "But it is not good for ulcers."

Mr. Rougemont put his book aside and with a fighter's grin of pleasure looked around to see what the audience was like. There were few customers, the nearest was the woman in the red hat.

"Who put that nonsense into your head?" said Mr. Rougemont.

"Lettuce, as well," said the girl. "The doctor will not allow my father to eat lettuce."

"Ho!" exclaimed Mr. Rougemont with a glance at the red hat. "I should think not. We are not rabbits."

The red hat lowered its face.

"Or salads," said the girl. "Americans are always eating salads and they have ulcers."

"Yes, but I am not an American," said Mr. Rougemont.

"You have thick white hair," said the unsmiling girl.

"Bring me some cold soup and stop generalizing, girl—now don't go away, wait for the rest of the order."

"There is not cold consommé," said the melancholy girl. "There is salami. Or *pâté de foie*, if you're not afraid of rich things. My father—"

"Do I look ill?"

"Egg mayonnaise . . ."

"Would your father mind if I had a sardine? I don't want a sardine, but let us say your father is about to have a sardine—what would that do to him?"

"Give him gout," said the girl. "Like tomatoes and spinach. But he could eat herring."

"Ulcers, gout," called Mr. Rougemont loudly to the woman in the red hat. "Is this a restaurant or a hospital? Now, don't go away. Veal—what is the matter with the veal?"

"It's done with mushrooms."

The woman in the red hat spoke across two tables to Mr. Rougemont. "The young lady tells me," the woman said in a polished way, "that four hundred people died in France last month . . ."

"In the last three years," the waitress corrected.

". . . from eating mushrooms."

"That is what I will have," called out the robust Mr. Rougemont. "And I'll have the potatoes boiled and peas."

"*Petits pois*," said the girl in a docile voice.

"I said peas," said Mr. Rougemont.

"I said," said the girl.

"You didn't," said Mr. Rougemont. "You said *petits pois*. Peas are one thing, *petits pois* another."

"Yes," said the girl. "The only peas we have are *petits pois*."

The girl's one eye stared at Mr. Rougemont. His eyes stared at her and went very blue. He had a very white forehead and a large vein began to swell in the middle of it.

"Send Mr. Bianchi to me!" he shouted.

Mr. Bianchi came down from the desk to the table.

"Is there anything wrong, Mr. Rougemont?" said Mr. Bianchi, snapping his fingers at the girl who went back to the desk.

"Where did you get that Cyclops?" said Mr. Rougemont.

"Cyclops?" said Mr. Bianchi, picking up the menu and looking at it.

"No, no, not on there, Bianchi—the girl. With one eye."

Mr. Bianchi turned and stood with his back to Mrs. Bianchi, moved his hands a little, wagged his shoulders a little, rolled his eyeballs in Mrs. Bianchi's direction.

"She talks like a hearse," said Mr. Rougemont.

"Five days and she kicks her sandals off. Customers do not like it," Mr. Bianchi whispered. "Give me your order. I will see to it."

The girl now came with a plain omelette and put it on the table before the woman with the red hat. Mr. Rougemont saw it.

"No!" he shouted getting to his feet. "No, madam, refuse to eat it. You ordered a mushroom omelette. Make her take it back. Waitress, take it back."

The woman hesitated. Mr. Rougemont looked around at the two or three customers.

"Are you eating what you ordered?" he cried.

There was no answer.

"Cowards," muttered Mr. Rougemont.

"Mr. Rougemont," pleaded Mr. Bianchi, touching his arm.

"No," said Mr. Rougemont, going to the woman's table and taking away the omelette.

"You will drop it," said the waitress in a sad voice.

"Give it to me," said Mr. Bianchi, taking it from him.

"I'm in a hurry," said the woman. "It doesn't matter."

The waitress took the omelette and went away with it.

"Bring it back," called the woman and stood up herself and got the omelette back.

"They owe you an apology, madam," said Mr. Rougemont, quietening and sitting down at his table once more.

"Now give me your order, Mr. Rougemont. I am very sorry. We have a very nice egg mayonnaise, or the *pâté de foie*. A little *pâté* . . ."

"I said soup," said Mr. Rougemont, sulking.

"Or tomato salad."

"Don't you start, Bianchi, for God's sake," said Mr. Rougemont, getting his breath.

"Shouting is bad for his digestion," said the girl in a low sorrowful voice, from a distance.

"Soup," hissed Bianchi at the girl. "Quick."

"Roast veal, potatoes and peas," said Mr. Rougemont, exhausted. Then he said: "Where is Rosa, Bianchi?"

"She left," sighed Mr. Bianchi.

"And Maria?"

"They both left," said Mr. Bianchi.

"Why did they leave?"

Mr. Bianchi shrugged and sighed.

"And the big one, with the golden hair? She was heading for trouble."

"Lucia," said Mr. Bianchi in a low voice, with a glance back at Mrs. Bianchi. "She's still around." He nodded to the street.

"Ah," nodded Mr. Rougemont knowingly.

"Yes," admitted Mr. Bianchi, "Mrs. Bianchi does not like Italian girls. So—we carry on."

"Not with that one, you don't, Bianchi," said Mr. Rougemont. "I will tell you something about her. People say witchcraft has died out. It hasn't. She's a witch—you be careful, the northern type. I know them. They haunt you."

"Ha! ha!" said Mr. Bianchi feebly, looking happier. "How is Mrs. Rougemont? Well, I hope?"

"Of course not," said Mr. Rougemont. "I say, they haunt you."

Soon Mr. Rougemont's food was brought to him. He buttered a roll and nodded cheerfully to the woman with the red hat.

"Still alive?" he said.

The woman smiled with contentment.

"I've been coming here for years," he said.

"So have I," she said.

"I'm afraid this one will finish Bianchi," he said. "She has a voice like a crypt."

Presently he saw the girl standing near and watching him eat.

"You get in a temper. It heats the blood, it's bad for the heart," said the girl gazing at him. "An income tax collector shouted at my father because he wouldn't pay his taxes. I don't know what he was going to do to him, have him arrested—"

"No," said Mr. Rougemont equably, with his mouth full. "They don't arrest. They distrain."

"And my father said, 'If you go on shouting and banging the table like that you'll drop dead.'"

"And I suppose he did," said Mr. Rougemont genially.

"Not then," said the girl. "Later."

Mr. Rougemont put down his knife and fork and gazed at her.

"You have an unusual interest in death in your family," said Mr. Rougemont, frowning.

"Yes," said the girl. "My brother—"

"No," said Mr. Rougemont, holding up his hand. "Bring me a fish knife and fork."

"Are you having fish now?" said the girl.

"No," said Mr. Rougemont. "But I like to eat at a table that is properly laid. How do you know I mightn't have wanted fish?"

The girl brought the fish knife and fork.

"Thank you," he said. "And another wine glass. Not for me. I already have one." He nodded at the vacant place on the other side of the table.

"For my friend," he said.

"You are expecting a friend?"

"Now, do as I tell you. He will want knives, forks, a side plate, dessert spoon."

The girl got them and waited. Mr. Rougemont went on eating.

"Good. Now, take his order," he said.

"Is he coming soon?" asked the girl.

"He is there *now*," said Mr. Rougemont, still eating. "Take it. He is impatient and hungry."

The new waitress brushed her hair back from her face and two gray eyes looked like stones at Mr. Rougemont.

"Look after him well," said Mr. Rougemont. "Because I shall bring him again tomorrow."

A very thin smile came to the lips of the girl. She took her pad and wrote a few lines on it. It was Mr. Rougemont's bill.

Mr. Rougemont did not come to Bianchi's for a week or more. But when he did the new waitress came to his table.

"I liked your friend very much," she said to him. "He's been in several times."

"What?" said Mr. Rougemont.

"He's taking me out on Thursday," she said. "What are you having today? There is cold soup—but the weather's changed, hasn't it?"

Harry D. Miller

Johnny Dio and the Sugar Plum Burglars

Several days ago one of the two people who broke into my apartment last year dropped by to ask me how I was feeling and to retrieve a shoe—a small, black Capezio I had been keeping in a Brooks Brothers box in my closet. It fit her foot wonderfully well, and she was pleased, I think, that crime hadn't particularly altered her, though she was still rather worried about me. I was, she said, probably the silliest American she's ever known. Why I left my window open on the fifth of May, 1959, and in a neighborhood—the lower East Side—where burglary is almost as commonplace as the morning mail, she still finds hard to explain. She thinks, I suppose, that I was lonely and knew that someone was going to crawl through it.

Perhaps I should mention that what follows is an accurate account of what took place last spring. Rather than precipitating family quarrels, it might be wise for me to substitute the names of the lawyer and the detective, but otherwise the only fancy in the case was introduced by the burglars themselves. It was, as Detective Derry later said—and the only judgment ever given the crime—all very strange.

On the morning of that day in May, I had painted the floor in the second room of my eleven-dollars-and-ninety-cents-a-month apartment. It was a good, substantial black deck paint, and I was assured that it would wear well. When, however, I left the apartment at four in the afternoon, it was still tacky, and I erected a chair barrier in order to keep my beagle from sitting in it. Twenty minutes later when I returned, the chair had been carefully placed against the wall, and my beagle was resting in the middle of the light gray carpet; around him, in a floral, Victorian way, were both his footprints and another's. The other's led to an open window where the Capezio sat (I learned later that the shoes were taken off not to promote stealth, but because the burglars were more comfortable barefoot), and arranged on my bed were most of the few things that I own. They, with the shoe and the black footprints, waited by the window and a still shivering fire escape.

On the roof no one could be seen, but the abandoned building next to mine is the kind that Alfred Hitchcock advertises for now and then but never finds, and it seemed a likely place for criminals. Its door was open; its windows were not—were, in fact, boarded-up. It was quite dark, and I would have hesitated had I not then heard footsteps. Certainly they sounded just the way the black prints on my rug *looked*.

I won't trouble you with the details of capturing my burglars except for mentioning that two of the young men in my neighborhood, having heard the noise from the street, broke through a second-story window and held them at bay with razors—as much a part of pockets on the lower East Side as Clorets are in the East Seventies—until the police arrived.

"Man!" one of them said when he saw what he had found.

"You're not going to hit me?" the first and prettier of the girls said. She was tropical looking and rich-skinned, and she stood on one leg in the corner of the room. She was disarmingly composed. She pointed to the second girl whose eyes were closed and who was whimpering. "Gloria is very nervous," she said. "Don't make her crazy."

"All I want," I began to say, as I was to say often during the next two days, "all I want you to do is clean my rug and my dog."

She looked up surprised, and Gloria, for the first time, opened her eyes. "I don't know what you mean," the first girl said. Then, as if it had just occurred to her, "What are you doing here?"

I told her that I was chasing her, and she laughed; she nudged Gloria, spoke a few words in Spanish, and Gloria too began to laugh, a little nervously. "What a joke," the pretty one said.

The door to the street was then broken through, and the police arrived, followed by several shopkeepers. More people came in, and my two razor-carrying friends—who were, I like to believe, probably burglars themselves—managed to walk away. The police, who had a kind of calm about them, asked me why I was causing such a nuisance. I explained, and they began to work on the criminals.

"Florence," the pretty one answered when she was asked her name. "This is Gloria. That man," she pointed at me, "is bothering us."

"I speak much little English," Gloria said.

"Man!" Florence said. "Can't you ever shut up!" Gloria retreated into silence again while Florence explained to the police that the two of them had become lost, looking for Hester Street.

"Sure, Sugar," the policeman said. "You always wear one shoe?"

She had been standing on her naked foot and had perhaps forgotten that it was shoeless. She looked at it carefully. "Sometimes," she answered.

"We'll go someplace and talk about it, OK?" the policeman said. No, it wasn't OK. Florence was going to meet a friend at five o'clock, and she couldn't imagine why everyone was making such a fuss over nothing at all.

Once in the squad car, she settled down and began to look afraid.

"Are we going to jail now?" she asked the driver. He didn't answer, and we sped down Canal Street.

"*Man!*" Gloria said.

The next morning, equipped with more evidence than Detective Derry, who had been assigned to the case, could hold in his arms for more than a few minutes (not only had Florence left her shoe in my apartment, but her friend had left her coat, her wallet—containing a good bit more money than I had—and a grocery bag with a screwdriver, a small crowbar, and some Kleenex), we appeared in the Court of Special Sessions. Detective Derry, whom I had met the night before, motioned for me to follow him into the hall.

"You sure you don't know these broads?" he asked me. I told him that I had met them rather unexpectedly the day before, that they seemed quite nice, and couldn't we forget the whole thing? He then reported that Florence and Gloria had probably committed fifteen or twenty burglaries in the neighborhood during the last month, and he was glad that someone with an open-window disposition had finally caught them. At that moment, we could see the burglars being led into the courtroom. Florence was still wearing one shoe.

"It's a real pity," Detective Derry said. He looked at her foot, stained along the edges like a barefoot country girl's on a newly oiled road. "But this'll be quick," he continued. "They'll have to get themselves a lawyer." He then added, with a kind of remorse, "Today's my day off. Second time this month something comes up on my day off." I told him that I was sorry. "That's alright, kid," he said, looking at Florence.

On the morning of their trial, the first of many, a worried, disheveled looking man named Mr. Arbuckle, their lawyer, asked for a postponement; it was early, and Gloria wasn't there. No one seemed to know or, for that matter, care where she was. Mr. Arbuckle came up to me afterward, introduced himself, and invited me to have coffee in the lunchroom with him, with his one client, and with Detective Derry. "Sorry about Miss —————," he said. "She's a little nervous. We'll get this thing out of the way next week. You know Florence, of course." Florence smiled.

In the lunchroom, Mr. Arbuckle and Florence got along very nicely. Detective Derry and Florence got along nicely too. We talked about Cuba (Florence said that she had come to New York without papers, but we weren't to mention it to *any*one), about how hard it was to be a policeman and how soft the firemen had it, and about Mr. Arbuckle's real estate in Manhattan. "Where are *you* living, Sugar?" he said to Florence.

"A terrible, terrible place on Eldridge Street," she answered. "There's no gas and someone turned off all the lights."

"I know a place," Mr. Arbuckle said, "matter of fact, *own* it—up on First Street. You can get a room up there for fifteen a week or so. Nice place, too. You interested?"

Florence was. After we talked a bit more, Florence and I left, and I walked her to the subway. I told her how kind I thought Mr. Arbuckle was, but that it was unfortunate that she had to spend what little money she had on a lawyer.

"Oh, but he's not charging anything," she said.

"He's Legal Aid?"

"No," she said, "he just wants to help." Had she known him for some time? No, she had met him on her first morning in court. "That's amazing," I said.

"He's very old, isn't he?" she then said, and it seemed to me that she didn't expect an answer. I was to understand that she pitied Mr. Arbuckle.

That night I met several of Florence's family. At six o'clock, the first one, a young lad of nineteen or so, presented himself at my door and said, "You the one with the typewriter?" Apparently Florence had forgotten my name, but recalled that she had carried my typewriter to the open window on the day of the burglary. I said that I was. He then asked that I forget what Florence had done and not appear in court the following week. I explained that I would probably be fined, since I had been sub-poenaed, and he was kind enough to offer to pay it for me. He was her husband, he said, and she was also a mother. He left, after having had a drink and after suggesting that he send me a bottle of his favorite Tennessee whiskey. Perhaps two hours later, another young man appeared. Yes, he said, Florence was now and then a little crazy, but she was a good kid. He was, after all, in a position to know, since he was her husband. Common law, he added. Did they have children? "No," he told me, "but you never know."

On the following week, never having received my whiskey, I arrived at the Municipal Building in Centre Street to find Gloria waiting for me. She was sitting with Detective Derry. It seemed foolish, at this late date, for me to play the claimant, so I sat with them. Detective Derry leaned over to tell me that Florence couldn't make it. "You know she's getting married, I suppose?" he said. Of course, I said, I knew the man—a pleasant, soft-spoken Italian Boy? "No, some guy from Cuba," he went on. "They have all the luck. Hell of a place to be—*here*. I mean, before you get married." I told him that it was; a courtroom was no place to plan a trousseau. And I wondered who had been talking to *him*.

Mr. Arbuckle then interrrupted us long enough to lead us before the Judge where he again requested a postponement. Detective Derry made no objections. Afterward in the hall he said, "Say, Arbuckle, she still living at the same place?" Mr. Arbuckle said, "Sure." Derry thanked him and walked down the steps to the first floor, still carrying the shoe, the coat, and the sack.

Three weeks later both Florence and Gloria stood before the by-this-time rather impatient magistrate, but Detective Derry wasn't there. "Where *is* the detective?" the Judge asked the room, and several attendants began to hum, "Detective Der—ry?"

The man from the District Attorney's staff leaned a little forlornly against the table. "We can't proceed," he said. "This is the second time this case has been delayed."

The Judge looked at us not too kindly. "Are *you* the defendant?" he said to me.

"*I* represent the defendants, your honor," Mr. Arbuckle said, waving his arm at Florence and Gloria.

"The Court would like you to account for these," the Judge searched for the word, "frivolous delays."

"My clients have a case in General Sessions, your honor," Mr. Arbuckle answered. "The Johnny Dio case, you know, has—"

"The Court asked a simple question, and the Court expects an answer. What does Johnny Dio have to do with the defendants?"

"My clients have a case pending in General Sessions, your honor, and the outcome could be prejudicial to *this* case. Everything's going slow upstairs because of the Johnny Dio trial." He looked pleased with himself, younger, I thought, than when I first met him. "I request a postponement, your honor, until the 13th of September."

"Why didn't you say that? Does the District Attorney have any objections?" The D.A. looked at me helplessly and said that he had none.

Going out, I said to Mr. Arbuckle, "I didn't know Florence was on trial upstairs."

He took me by the arm. "Florence? A marvelous girl like Florence? What put that into your head?" He walked sprightly. "That judge is a terror, isn't he?"

The night before the trial, and four months after the crime, there was a knock on my door, and when I opened it Florence was standing there. I was surprised to learn that she wasn't married yet.

"I changed my mind," she said. "Can I sit down? Or are you still mad at me?" I said that I wasn't. "Well that's a relief," she said. "Timothy is."

"Timothy?"

"Detective Derry."

"That's too bad," I said. "Do you think he's going to make trouble tomorrow?"

"Tomorrow?"

"The trial."

"*That!*" she said. She sat down and stroked my beagle whose underbelly still had remnants of black paint on it. "I don't think so. He has the day off. And Gloria's sick. She's learning English now."

"*Well!*" Apparently there was a future for English-speaking burglars, but studying English was still a nervous occupation.

She picked up my beagle. "Mr. Arbuckle says you don't have to go tomorrow. He says that Johnny Dio . . ."

I looked at her, and it seemed to me that Detective Derry was quite right. It was all very strange, and there was nowhere to go. "Yes, I know," I said.

Much later I learned from Mr. Arbuckle that he alone appeared in Court, and only, it seemed, because someone had to apologize to the State. The case was dismissed before the Judge—a grandfatherly looking man, but certainly vulnerable—became involved. Since then, I've seen Detective Derry on the streets one or two times, and on one occasion he dropped by to give me the shoe. As a *recuerdo*, I suppose. We always asked after Florence, but neither of us saw her again until the other day. She was thinking of getting a job, she said, and she thanked me—with economy, I thought—for preserving the Capezio.

Frank Tuohy

At Home with the Colonel

When a train entered the cutting, smoke welled up between some beech trees and died out on the lawn in front of the house. From a window a girl watched it fade. Then she moved back into the room, where she put her arms round another girl, who was sewing attentively, and pressed her cheek on the shoulders and rubbed herself like a cat. Anna, the girl who was sewing, gently pushed her away.

The first girl returned to the window. She yawned.

Downstairs an old man, Colonel Starcross, was sitting before an unlit fire of paper and sticks, on to which people had thrown cigarette ash, sweet-wrappings and tufts of wool. He was thinking: "Those girls up there all day. Don't seem to want to do anything. Only an hour from London. Lots of friends." He stirred uneasily from indigestion. "I'd invite the young men myself, but it's difficult, they mightn't like it." The occupant of an isolated house, he could imagine nobody coming up the drive unless he had lured them there.

"All this dreaminess, introspection! Yes, I'll invite the young men myself, kill a chicken, make up the spare beds," he thought, with the testy effeminacy of an old man who, alone now, his lifework over, enters the world of food and comfort assigned to women, finds himself forced into gossip and women's ways.

The Colonel stood up; he fastened the buttons below his waist that he always undid when alone after luncheon. He shuffled to the stairs and called.

Bridget Starcross came out on to the landing and leant over.

"Yes, what is it?"

He had been lonely and he had nothing to say. The hall clock ticked. His house smelt stale in the dead afternoon.

"What's all this about?" His throat was stretched tight with looking up, and his voice became thin and hoarse. "What's going on? What are you doing all this time?" He was making himself angry because he had been left alone.

Her eyes were sleepily egocentric. "Nothing's going on," she remarked. "Anna is making a dress."

"Dresses!" he said wildly, not meaning to criticize the guest in his house.

"No, a dress," Bridget said, unamiably watching her father at the foot of the stairs. "For me."

He turned away in bewildered anger.

She went back to her room. Passing the back of the chair, she stroked one finger along the clipped nape of Anna's neck. Anna caught the crimson-nailed rather dirty finger and with mock cruelty began to twist it. Both girls giggled.

Bridget lay back on the counterpane of her bed. She rubbed her bare arms together, staring at cracks on the ceiling. She wriggled her feet until the shoes fell off. "A-ah!" she said.

She appeared to go to sleep, but she could hear her father rattling the buckets of hens' food downstairs.

The big house threw a darker twilight onto its shrubberies, where the Colonel, carrying a bucket, made his way into the wind toward the railway line. He was early today: the four o'clock train, thundering through the cutting, found him still at the henrun. He hid from the smoke behind the henhouse, his eyes shut. But the smoke made him cough and then his chest started hurting again. Drops of water fell on him—they might have been rain or spray from the engine—and he shivered with cold.

While the Colonel was coughing, the smoke died away. But his eyes still watered; the young man approaching between the vegetable beds was just a vague blur to him.

"You looking for me?" he shouted. Then he wiped his eyes and recognized the visitor, who was wearing a shoddy demobilization overcoat and black army shoes. He was bareheaded, his fair hair still rawly clipped. But the Colonel registered him as a friend, connected in some way with his dead wife and the summers before the war. When they shook hands, the Colonel realized that he had forgotten the young man's name.

"Glad to see you again. Just back, what? We'll go back to the house—Bridget's at home." The Colonel felt very shy. He opened the door of the henhouse and groped round for eggs, although he already knew that there were none. He had felt obliged to ask the young man something about his military service; he needed time to beat his fuddled memory until the facts would drop out of it.

The young man, similarly afflicted with shyness, cleared his throat and said: "Are your hens laying well, sir?"

The Colonel could look at him again. "Bloody," he said. "I feed 'em up, give 'em this balancer meal stuff, and they loaf around, scratching themselves." He stared at the hens still fussing around the trough. "I'm lucky if I get one egg a day," he said.

"D-do you give them cod-liver oil, sir?"

"Cod-liver oil!" the Colonel shouted, in such a voice that the young man was sorry for the hens, and slammed the door of the house, raising anguished shrieks and a dusty fluttering of wings. "So they give it to hens now, do they? That's all those bastards want, cod-liver oil and pap for every loafer in the street!" The Colonel was suddenly very angry; however, the young man could not feel offended, for the anger was not aimed at himself or even at the Labour Government. Colonel Starcross looked up apprehensively; his gray eyes were watery like the winter sky. He put his hand on the young man's arm. "Tell you what, come up to the house. Get you some tea."

The old man lit the gas under a kettle on the stove, and brought down two tins, one of which contained tea, the other a slab of grocer's cake. His visitor helped him set the tray. "Why four cups?" he asked.

"This friend of Bridget's," the Colonel grunted.

Carrying the tray, he went through and called "Bridget!" at the foot of the stairs. He continued into the drawingroom, while the young man waited. The bedroom door swung open, letting twilight into the landing. Bridget and Anna appeared, arm in arm.

"Hullo, Bridget," the young man said.

"Oh dear, hullo." The girl peered shortsightedly into the dark well of the hall. "It's John, isn't it?"

"Get a move on, there," the Colonel called. "I've made the tea." Nervously enthusiastic, he rubbed his hands together. "Everything's ready."

He had switched on the electric fire, but its single glowing bar could not melt very far into the cold air of the room; the empty spaces beyond the armchairs were as draughty as the woods outside.

The conversation at tea was left to his daughter and John, for Anna did not speak, though she ate a great deal of cake. The old man sat with his face drawn and exhausted by the efforts he had made. His thoughts, sour with tiredness, kept on saying: "If only I could ask him to take her away, take her away from my house. I'm fed up with her and her sulky bitches of girl friends"—though Anna was the first guest they had had since the war. "If only I could get that bitch out of the room and leave them together." But he could think of no way to do this. During the weeks she had been in his house, he had scarcely addressed a word to his daughter's friend; she herself rarely spoke in his presence, though he heard the two of them chattering and laughing behind closed doors.

Bridget sat carelessly unattractive on the sofa. She was completely ignorant of what her father thought of her. Too lazy to find a job, she secretly imagined herself saying later to a critical audience—possibly of rela-

K

tives, though she had few who would be interested: "I have nothing to blame myself for. After all, I was his only companion through those last years, and pretty dull it was too, sometimes, I can tell you. It's only fair that I should get the mon—" but at this point of her harangue, she usually became slightly ashamed of herself: if she was curled in an armchair or lying on her bed, she would jump up and pace round the room once or twice, or start hurried sentences which had no purpose except to batter down her own unruly fantasy.

"I often wonder what happened to all our friends," the young man said. "The Shaddocks, the Armitages, the Bentleys. Do you remember when you fell off Heather Shaddock's pony?"

Bridget would not let herself help him. "I can only remember how dull this place was. I know I was always bored stiff really." Her eyes moved toward her father.

She may have succeeded in hurting him. His fingers drummed on the chair, and one of his knees vibrated. "Well," he said at last, "I suppose I'd better go and shut those blasted chickens up."

When he had gone, Anna moved into the deeper recesses of the room. The young man decided to try and ignore her. Her turned back to Bridget. He told her about his job at the Estate Agents; he questioned her about the other people they had known. But he found the conversation increasingly difficult. Each of his sentences seemed to be suspended for inspection, even for mockery, in the cold air of the drawing room. Finally he knew that all his gambits would fail because he couldn't make himself interesting to her.

"It's been jolly good to come here again," he said. "I hope that you— and your friend of course—will be able to come over to our place one day. Mother's always talking about you."

"Thanks very much. But I'm afraid our plans are rather uncertain." She began to be as conscious as he was of the waiting figure behind them.

"Or—I come this way quite often. I could drop in, if you like, and we could make some plans."

He couldn't see Bridget's face; she had moved beyond the circle of light from the standard lamp. "Well, if you want to."

"But I thought . . ."

"Perhaps I've got other interests," she said sharply. "Have you read this?" She threw a book across at him. It disappeared behind cushions and he did not trouble to find it. He felt heat bursting in his cheeks.

"I'm sorry," he said. "I suppose I must be intruding."

She did not answer and he began to humiliate himself. "Perhaps I'm a frightful bore. You used—I mean, I didn't think I'd changed all that much." He gulped. "I haven't any wish to stay where I'm not welcome."

"Oh God," the girl opposite him said. But in a moment she would have relented and asked him to stay. He heard a new sound, however, from the back of the room: it was Anna, laughing at him.

The young man went out into the hallway; he was dimly conscious of the Colonel somewhere in the house, but he was too angry to say good-by. He walked down the drive between the rhododendrons. The village stretched out in front of him; the bus went every half hour through the dull empty fields to the county town where, if there wasn't another war, he would live till the day of his death.

After he had gone, the two girls slipped down on to the floor in front of the electric fire. Bridget, who had a guilty conscience, held her friend tightly by the arm.

"But he was so funny, my dear," Anna said. Her short black hair was coarse, her face shiny in the strong light. Then Bridget laughed too.

When the Colonel came in, neither of them looked up at him.

"Where's that young fellow? Nice young chap, isn't he?"

"He's gone."

"Gone where?"

"How should I know? Just gone."

The Colonel bewilderedly contemplated the young man's bad manners. He was lost and hurt.

Bridget turned away and he began to tidy up the tea-things. They heard him fumble and curse his way into the dark kitchen with the laden tray.

Bridget put her arm around the friend's shoulders. She could feel the firm padding in the jacket.

"How dull it all is," she murmured sleepily. "But we'll have our cottage one day, won't we?"

Walter Clemons

A Different Thing

Betty felt people eyeing her right cheek whenever they looked at her. And they were, since they didn't get a chance to see much else: as soon as she was looked at, Betty lowered her eyelids, or at least made her eyes non-committal and flat, and presented her bad cheek. It was an ugly strawberry blotch, from her eye to the corner of her mouth, and she'd thought about it so much that her very expression made it seem to spread and deepen, like a permanent blush of mortification. The men who came into the place mostly talked to Dixie.

The funny thing was, Dixie was nothing herself to write home about, with her rimless glasses and Shirley Temple curls, her big jaw. But she acted good-looking, was the difference. When she carried beers to a table and a breeze through the screen door ballooned her skirt and flashed her fat thighs, Dixie would truck around and sass right back, whatever the men said. A man knew where he was at with Dixie.

When they first teamed up, Betty had envied Dixie, who was so free and easy. Dixie had one fellow after another, and Betty didn't have any. But the truth came out when Dixie's bird got killed, a parakeet she'd taught to talk and let out of its cage to drink beer with her. The bird would perch on Dixie's shoulder, Dixie would take a swallow, and then the bird would hop on the rim and drink his share. "Sweet?" said Dixie. "Sweet," the bird allowed.

The day the bird disappeared, Dixie got drunk out of her mind, the first time Betty ever saw her like that. She even called the Port Arthur police, who told her to go to hell. "A cat got my bird," Dixie kept insisting. "Okay, lady, so we'll arrest the first cat we see," said the cop. Dixie sank down in a chair by the phone and told Betty how the parakeet got the flu one time and she gave it penicillin shots. "I wouldn't let the doctor touch him. I gave him the shots my own self. He looked up at me so pitiful with his little eyes, but when he got well, he knew I'd done it for his own good. That bird understood me, Betty, and that's the God's truth. Nobody ever meant that much to me."

Truly, Betty had never seen Dixie like this over a man, and it made her think. One of the ways Dixie was such a good friend, she never gave Betty any cheap cheer about fixing herself up and getting a boyfriend, and now Betty saw why. Betty was blue because the man who'd see past her face and understand her hadn't showed up yet, but all those men that liked Dixie, Dixie didn't even *hope* they'd understand. Finally Dixie said straight out, she'd rather have that bird back then all the slobs who came into the place in a year. Dixie stopped to consider and mended her speech: "Oh, men are all right. It's a different thing. But I miss my bird worse than anything."

So Betty didn't feel so bad after that when Dixie kidded around with the men or made a face to Betty to keep an eye on things while she went out back with somebody. Betty felt she had hope, at least, a way Dixie didn't. She began to perk up and smile at the customers a little, not trying too hard, just minding her business and being nice.

They did a fair business for an out-of-town spot. Dixie's Place was located on the pass from Port Arthur out to the Gulf, where the snappers and shrimpers sailed back and forth all day. Colored people with cane poles fished along the jetty, and Dixie sold them beer and bait out the side door. A lot of fishermen came in, who got a laugh out of the biblical thing Dixie had written up behind the bar, above the empty birdcage—"He riseth early in the morning and disturbeth the whole household, mighty are his preparations. He goeth forth and returneth when the day is spent, smelling of strong waters and the truth is not in him." They got some truckers and travelling men from the highway too.

Every Thursday at dusk, a seismograph crew put in at Dixie's pier, since they weren't allowed to load explosives on the Port Arthur dock. The Nitroman was brought out here in trucks, and when it was aboard, the twenty men drank beer for an hour before setting out for another week on the Gulf. Dixie did her blown-skirt routine, the jukebox played "Shake, Rattle, and Roll" while the country boys off the boat jigged around and snapped their fingers; and in this hubbub, Betty particularly noticed a fat man who came in all by himself, only on Thursdays, and didn't give anybody any trouble. He just sat with a friendly look through his pink-rimmed glasses at the goings-on. He had two beers and left without a word.

He was a short fellow with very pink cheeks, and though his sport shirt was practically transparent with perspiration, he still looked dressed up and proper beside the loose-legged boat boys. They didn't bother with him any more than he bothered them, till one Thursday one of the seamen spoke to him from the next table—another fat man, with piggy blue eyes right close together, practically two in one, the boat engineer. They were riding this engineer he shouldn't have another beer, he'd be such a butterball he wouldn't be able to get down the ladder to the engine room. He turned to the man sitting alone: "Well, it keeps us warm in the winter, don't it?"

The pink-cheeked man rolled his eyes behind his glasses, and his ears and forehead shifted. "I guess so," he said with a grateful smile.

The engineer said to him, "It's like that joke, feller goes to a doctor. Says, 'Hey, doc, how can I lose weight?' and the doc says, 'Tell you what you do, you put your hands on the edge of the table and get up after the first helping.'"

The engineer looked joyfully around at everybody and died laughing. Betty frowned, mystified, and the man in glasses smiled as if he'd just opened a present and didn't like to ask what it was. Now at the engineer's table, a sour, skinny man, the boat cook, screwed up his face. "Aa, you meathead, I never heard anybody could gum up a joke to compare with you." He smoothed his apron and leaned forward with a demonstration of getting a grip on his patience. He spoke very slowly. "I'll *tell* you how that one goes. Feller says, 'Doc. What kind of *exercise*, see, can I do to lose weight?' Doctor says, 'Put your hands on the edge of a table, see, three times a day, and push back.'" The cook shrugged. "It was probly funnier in the original Greek."

"Well, some can tell em and some caint."

"True," said the cook, grimly.

The engineer's close blue eyes blinked rapidly, and he was inspired to try again. "Like that story, new convict comes into this prison, he goes in to lunch his first day. Pretty soon some guy stands up and says, 'Forty-four!' and everybody busts out laughin. So another guy stands up and says, 'Fifty-seven!' and everybody laughs again. So this new convict he don't know what's comin off. Pretty soon another guy stands up and says—"

The cook, watching him like a hawk, snarled, "Okay, okay, don't go through the whole goddam penitentiary. We got it."

"So——" said the engineer. His memory folded on him, and he pondered for a time. The man at the next table leaned forward encouragingly. Then the engineer's face lit up with happiness. "Oh, yeah! So this new convict asks his roomie, 'What's all this forty-four kick?' The old convict says, 'Well, you see, them's jokes. We heard em all so many times, now we just call em out by number.' So that night he tells the new convict all the stories, see. The next day this new convict thinks he'll give it a whirl. So he remembers this joke he liked, and he stands up—this is at lunch, the same as yesterday, I shoulda told you—anyway, he yells out, 'Sixty-eight!' Well, nobody laughs. This new convict sits back down and says, 'Gee, what'd I do wrong?' He's all mortified, see. 'Well, son, that's the way it goes,' this old convict says. 'Some can tell em and some caint.' "

When the engineer coughed from laughing, the cook patted him on the back and gave him a curt nod. "That's better, fat boy. I could pretty near recognize that one."

The table of seamen now took swigs of beer and huddled together. The man at the next table, leaning forward smiling, was caught out on a limb. Only the stooge of the group had spoken to him, and now he'd disappeared back into his own circle. The outsider leaned very slowly back in his chair and tried to look easy, as if he hadn't cared whether anybody talked to him. Only Betty caught it—she knew that gesture well. She rubbed the bar with a damp gray rag, and when she glanced up again she found the fat man staring at her.

Betty instinctively turned the purple side of her face to him, to warn him off, and rubbed the bar some more. She felt him still looking. She couldn't help but look back, and this time the little man smiled at her across the noise, no kind of a leering look, and not just casual either. He seemed to put her in cahoots with him. Betty smiled back, and when one of the seamen yelled for another beer she was relieved to turn away and dig down in the ice.

A couple of Thursdays passed. The man in glasses came in just the same, but he sat at his table without paying Betty any mind, until one Thursday a thing happened. The boat whistle blew, and the seamen scraped their chairs back and marched out. On the pier, Dixie cast the rope off and called to the men not to do anything she wouldn't do. Then Dixie went inside, and Betty stayed to watch the boat ease out of sight. It was just about dark. The gulls were coasting around—so free and easy—and faintly squalling, the mosquitoes were thick. Betty didn't hear the screen door open, but she came out of dreamily following the gulls to find the fat man standing near her.

He said, "It's a nice cool night."

"Awful mosquitoes, though," said Betty. It came out too sharply, and to show she didn't mean to be contrary, she said, "You make trips around this way? I notice you usually come in on Thursdays."

"I'm a title-man for an oil company out of Lake Charles," he said. "It's usually Thursdays I come this way."

"I noticed it's usually Thursdays," Betty agreed.

"This is a nice place here."

"*We* like it," said Betty.

"Could get pretty lonesome, I guess, though."

"Oh no, there's plenty of people come in and out, all the time." Everything he said, she seemed to contradict him. She didn't mean to.

"I guess so," he said, sounding put-in-his-place.

Betty faced around to him, and she hardly knew what happened. He had his hand in the air, and he touched her, right on the marked cheek. Betty was too shocked to think anything at all, and it surprised her more when he didn't flinch away. He just felt her cheek and moved two thick, gentle fingers down her face as if he'd meant to all along. His eyes looked scared. Betty stepped back and said, "What'd you do that for?"

"I don't know." His voice shook like hers. "I didn't mean any harm."

"I figured you didn't," Betty said. "But—"

"You're pretty," said this man.

Now it was thoroughly dark on the pier. Betty slapped at the mosquitoes on her arms and said, "Well, I better get back inside. Dixie'll be wondering what in the world."

"You are," he said, soft, insisting. He stood very close, without touching her. "You don't think so, but you are. I swear I didn't mean anything out-of-line."

"Well, let's just go back inside," said Betty. He followed her in silence. Inside, the rude ceiling light stung her eyes as if she'd been asleep. Dixie said, another day another dollar, and the fat man said he guessed he'd be shoving off.

"Name's Harry Blech," he said. "Betty, isn't it?" She nodded, still rather dazed, and looked down to see he'd stuck out his hand. Betty's thin hand was swallowed up in his: soft, but bigger than she expected; somehow it didn't go with his glasses and mild pink cheeks. When he left, Betty was careful not to stand listening, with Dixie watching. She banged chairs in place; Dixie didn't say anything.

All the next week, it was like after a quarrel, when you couldn't think, you just went over a thing, I said, he said, then I said. Just as if she'd had a fight, Betty got weak and irritated. By the time Thursday came around again, she was embarrassed to face him. She had half a mind to tell Dixie some story and get away till Thursday evening was past. But she stayed.

Then he didn't come in that Thursday, after all her stewing. Betty felt relieved—and let down. She was all right again, though. When she let herself try to think how he looked, all she got was the pair of glasses. It was just a thing that had happened.

One afternoon, when her lunch beer had sent Dixie off to sleep, Betty went out for a walk, with an old fishing hat to keep the sun off, humming to herself to fill out the empty afternoon. On her left, across the sulky water, the oil refinery waste-flames licked up against the sky. She felt very low down in the world, by the water, hardly anybody fishing along the wall in the terrible heat, a few gulls reeling around overhead. She felt she could just sink into the marsh grass and let the sun burn her.

Pretty soon she came to a place on the jetty, nobody in sight fishing in either direction. Her tune dried up in her mouth. Dreaming out toward the Gulf, she gently touched her bad cheek as if it were somebody else doing it and found it scarcely rough at all, only a little tougher than the rest of her face. When she shut her eyes and very slowly raised her other hand, both cheeks felt practically alike; she could imagine there wasn't any red place at all. But the touch stirred her cruelly. She opened her eyes and let the tears that had collected run down her face. She turned and stumbled back the way she'd come, crying, with the stiff grass tickling her bare legs, though by the time she came in sight of Dixie's red-and-white sign she was able to get hold of herself.

The next day it rained from morning till night, and all day the next day too. By Thursday the water had risen over the wall nearly to the door of Dixie's Place. It got dark early. The seamen loaded their supplies in the rain and crowded into the bar shiny and noisy from their soaking. About eight o'clock Harry walked in and took a stool at the bar. Just as if he'd stood her up for a date, he said, "I'm sorry I didn't make it last Thursday," and Betty said, as if she'd thought the same way, "Oh, that's all right. I figured you's held up somewhere."

"My old lady was sick," he said. He hadn't looked married. Betty took the news inside and showed nothing on her narrow face. "My mother, I'm talking about," said Harry. "She's better now."

His crinkly yellow hair was wet from the rain. Instead of serving him, Betty watched him take off his glasses and wipe them. "Don't you have any hat to wear in this weather?"

He shook his head and grinned. "Naw, I like this weather. Just let it pour! It sure feels cozy in here."

Dixie, down the bar, heard him. "You'll laugh out the other side of your face, brother, when the roof caves in." She gave a public wink at Betty. "Give your sweetie a beer on the house, honey. What the hell, we may be floatin in the Gulf tomorrow."

Several faces along the bar wheeled around at Betty. Too rattled to look at Harry, she bent her head and dug around in the ice. The fat engineer from the boat lurched up to the bar and pulled Dixie out to dance. While Betty poured Harry's beer in silence, they both paid enormous attention to the other two dancing. Under cover of the rain and jukebox noise Harry asked if Betty liked to dance. She said, "No, I never was any count at it."

"Me either."

He took a gulp of beer and his eyes wobbled nervously. "Tell you what we ought to do, we ought to go dancing some Thursday somewhere nobody'd know us, all by ourself. We'd be a pair."

"You wouldn't kid a cripple, would you?" said Betty, using one of Dixie's comebacks, and dumbfounded how easy and flirty she felt.

It didn't go right. Harry's face turned pasty and found-out. She'd said something wrong. Then he threw back his head and laughed. "Naw, I mean it. You stomp on my feet and I'll stomp on yours." He stuck out his hand and Betty shook it. She looked in confusion at Dixie flashing to a finish while the engineer, who didn't get it, stood and blinked at her feet, intrigued. Harry didn't let go of her hand. "How about it? Could you get off next Thursday?"

"Oh, no. I couldn't. I couldn't leave Dixie like that."

Her face burned. Harry looked sideways down the bar and then leaned close to her ear. "I don't care who hears me or not, Betty. I'm crazy about you. I think about you all week. Help me."

Betty went white as a sheet. "Help you?"

"Help me."

Betty just looked at him with wide eyes. His face flickered, as if he might cry. A seaman was rapping a quarter on the other end of the bar, and she pulled her hand free. "I've got to—" She gave Harry a pleading look, whether to leave her alone or wait till she'd served her customer she didn't know herself. But when she turned away, Harry slid down off his stool and walked straight out the door into the rain. A glass slithered through Betty's fingers into a million pieces on the floor.

She looked where Harry had been sitting and saw his Zippo lighter. She just snatched it up, left the seaman waiting, and ran to the door. She couldn't see anything through the sheet of rain off the roof until a pair of headlights flashed up at her, out in the dark. She ran to the car over the loose shells, crying as the cold rain hit her neck. Inside, when he reached for her, she grabbed for his wet, surprising hair and felt of his small ears, crying out loud. Their faces came together. When she hunted with her open mouth for his, Harry planted his lips on her cheek. She sank back with a moan, and the lighter tumbled from her fingers into his lap. "I thought you were gone. I missed you all week." She groped for his mouth again, but his lips didn't leave her cheek. She let him hold her.

Harry leaned forward to start the car. Betty sat up and said she couldn't go. At that, he forced her head back against the seat till her neck ached. "Don't tease me, Betty, I don't go for that. You wouldn't tease me?"

She gave a weak cry. "No, Harry, I like you." Then he was suddenly nice again, and she sat up and touched her neck with her fingers. She promised to get off and meet him in Port Arthur next Thursday. Betty got out and just let the rain drench her while she watched him drive off.

Then when they met after a week apart, they found it hard to talk. Nobody could say Harry wasn't polite, though. In the cafeteria in Port Arthur he insisted on carrying both trays. He fussed around her chair and then took his place opposite, leaning so far across the table she wondered if he was going to cut her smothered-steak for her. She wasn't used to a person making such a to-do. It really was like she was crippled.

She wanted to hear all about him. Well, he had been raised in Lake Charles, his daddy was a railroad man, killed when Harry was little. His

K*

mother made a living out of pies and special salads for a cafeteria until Harry was old enough to support her. And that was all he had to say. "That's plenty about me. Let's hear about you."

She didn't have much to tell either. She described growing up in Beaumont until her parents died, then working as a waitress and joining up with Dixie. But during her brief story, she seemed to feel Harry's attention seeping away. It disheartened her a little. There were all kinds of things she wanted to talk about. What she said the first night they talked, on the pier, about Dixie's Place not being lonesome, she'd thought about that since. All those people that come in and out, she just got to know pieces and outsides of them, and that was all they saw of her either. Until now, she'd had hopes, but she hadn't really felt what it might be like, a kind of life different from the screen door banging and hello and men just taking in her face and looking away again in a hurry. She wished she and Harry would get on to how strange it was they'd met; how he first noticed her; whether he got blue the way she often did—things like that. Instead: "Do you want some more to eat?" "I don't believe so, thank you." "Sure?" "Oh, I couldn't eat a single other thing really." "Positive?" Smiles. "Positive." That was how they talked. Well, he was shy, and she was probably not much of a help.

When they walked out of the air-conditioned cafeteria, the sun hadn't quite gone down. The street was a furnace. Harry hovered in silence while they looked blindly into store windows and Betty made little mewing complaints against the heat. "Too early for a dancing place yet," said Harry faintly. His forehead and upper lip were clustered with sweat. "Would you like to take in a movie?"

"If you'd like to."

"I don't mind. Why don't you say."

"It doesn't make me any difference." Well, this was awful. Betty perked up and laughed. "I don't believe either of us wants to see a movie."

Harry laughed too and reached out awkwardly to grab her hand and squeeze it hard. That wasn't what she'd meant, but she bowed her head and studied the pavement while they walked to the car.

The flat main street slid past. When Harry turned right at the railroad station Betty watched the town thin out into olive-green open country. Harry put his arm around her; she moved near him. She did think to herself things were happening too quick, she was too easy, maybe Harry would just get what he wanted and ditch her afterward. But she had already consented inside. She promised herself she wouldn't complain. When Harry stopped the car on a dirt side-road, she put her hand on his damp shirt and turned to him. And after a while, when Harry reached behind her for the door handle on her side, she got out without a murmur. While Harry cleared some rolled-up maps off the back seat she lifted his portable typewriter and put it out of the way in front. He took her in his arms. When she felt his fingers having trouble, she helped him with her dress.

Later, when they lay still, neither one said a word. Betty looked at the dusky square of sky in the car window and slowly reached out for something, a bird whistling coolly way off in the dry grass. She'd been hearing it all along, but she just now waked up to it. She listened, and stroked Harry's fat shoulders tenderly and touched his wiry hair. He was hunched up in their cramped space with his face on her neck. When he reached up blindly to her mouth and moved his fingers onward to her cheek, Betty waked up to something else, that all the while they'd made love Harry had kissed and bitten her cheek. It seemed so strange that he didn't mind it. Betty said, "You don't mind even a little bit about my face, Harry?"

He lifted his head and said in a voice new to her, "Naw, honey, it gives me a charge, honest."

She lay still. Then the monotonous stroking began to chafe her, and she turned her face restlessly to kiss Harry on the mouth. His other hand suddenly tightened on the back of her neck, so she couldn't move. He kissed her on the cheek again, but she had seen his eyes without his glasses, white and wide.

Betty lay there, cold as ice, while his tongue licked at her cheek. "Harry."

Her voice stopped him short. "What, honey?"

"Give me a kiss, Harry . . . No. The right way." He did, and he couldn't disguise. He jerked his mouth away and burrowed in her neck.

"I love you, Betty," his voice said against her skin.

She just stroked his head. Then she said softly, "But I didn't want to be loved just because of—because I'm ugly, Harry." As if he didn't hear her, Harry went on kissing her, more purposefully now. When she realized he was wanting to again, Betty stiffened. "No, Harry. I don't want to be, I don't want to be . . . I'm not like that, ugly . . ." She began to cry, "Ugly ugly ugly ugly . . ." and when he was finished she pushed him off and abruptly sat up straight, with an intent, listening look: it was that she was trying not to get sick. Harry watched her.

"What do you expect?" he said with a cold cheeriness, now the desire was over. "I said I loved you."

She said nothing. Harry leaned close to her. "I'll treat you sweet, Betty. I'm crazy about you." Soft as flies on her arms, fingers. "Don't be mean to me. Lonesome people don't have any right to be choosy, you know that? Ask for the moon, you wind up with nothin."

"I'm not asking for any moon." She felt too upset to talk, and she gave it up and reached for her things draped over the front seat. When she'd dressed, Betty got out and looked around the silent, darkening fields. She lifted the typewriter off the front seat and put it in back; then she sat quiet while Harry climbed behind the wheel.

Harry said, "I'll still take you dancing, like I said."

"I better just get on back, Harry."

He seemed relieved. But with a return to his cafeteria style, he said, "You *sure*, now. Because I said I'd take you dancing and I want to do the right thing."

"No, Harry."

"Positive?"

"Positive," she said with a friendly smile, instead of screaming.

As they drove back the way they'd come, Betty sat frozen. Once Harry chuckled. Startled, she looked at him out of the corner of her eye, and he said, "I was just thinking about my old lady, what she'd say if she could see me now. She thinks I'm such a good boy." Betty just turned empty eyes toward the road in front of the headlights.

When they reached the turn-off where the arrow pointed to Dixie's Place, Betty said, "Let me out here. I want to get a breath of air before I go in just yet."

He pulled up obediently. "Maybe we'll try out that dance floor another time."

"I never was much for dancing."

He leaned over to grab her hand, but she was too fast for him. "Remember I love you, Betty. Maybe you'll appreciate that another time." As she got out, Betty looked back at him curiously in the eerie light from the dashboard. He had melted down to two eyes pleading, she couldn't put him together again. "I'm not one of these guys that'll love you and leave you," his voice said out the car window.

She turned and started up the shell road with his voice coming after her. "You just gonna get what you want and ditch me? I'm offering myself to you, Betty?" She ran. When she was within reach of home she turned and watched his headlights move off toward the highway.

Betty stood outside an orange square of light on the shells and listened to the hoarse laughs above the jukebox music. She couldn't face it. She wandered off along the water and sat down in the dark to listen to the gulls. For a long time she just sat holding herself together. Then Harry's voice began to eat into her, how she didn't have any right to be choosy, how he loved her. She felt mean and in the wrong. But if he was all there was, there wasn't anybody. She just couldn't. She wasn't all that lonesome; her life wasn't so bad.

But oh, yes, it was pretty bad. A wave of hopelessness smote her. Inside her, her heart broke open and ran like a sore. Betty put her hands on her cheeks and shook all over and cried. Lousy, it is just lousy and unfair. Then, down the water from her, she heard the wheelhouse whistle blow. She raised her head and listened to the screen door banging and voices calling things she couldn't make out. She could see the mast light over the top of the grass. In a few minutes it began to move against the black sky, and she started matter-of-factly home to help Dixie.

When Betty got to the porch, though, she heard voices in the bar. She hesitated. One was Dixie's, the other some man's. "Well, you got a heart, I can see that," Dixie said. "It ain't everyday I meet somebody that gets what I mean."

The man's voice murmured something Betty didn't catch.

Dixie's voice rose. "That's just how it was. Oh, I shouldna drunk those beers, it always makes me sad to think of that cat. I'm tellin you, that bird was a sorrow to me."

The man's voice came out to Betty in the dark. "I know how you feel, sugar." It was the engineer from the boat. "It was the same way with me the time Alec the midget died. I liked to never got over that."

Dixie blew her nose. "Who's that?"

"Just the best pal a guy ever had, that's all. You seen one of us, you seen the other. We went everywheres. To show you how I felt, one time we's at a party, and I couldn't find my girl. I went to look in the car, and there she was with Alec, this midget, all over her. And I didn't say a word, I just tiptoed off like I hadn't seen nothin. He was such a nice little guy! The only time I ever seen him mad, he was dancin with an old tall gal and she got to feelin jazzy and kicked her leg out in the air, clean over Alec's head. He just walked off the dance floor and said, 'Show-off smart-alecky bitch!' He was sensitive about that one thing. Most of the time he was just laughin to beat the band. When he got run over by a police car—I'm tellin *you* —I thought I'd never care what happened after that. So I mean, I know how you feel."

There was a long silence. Betty turned to go. Then Dixie's voice, muzzy but stern: "What d'you think you're pulling? Take your hands off."

"What's wrong, sugar?"

"Don't sugar me. You and your damn midget. What's that got to do with my bird? Nothing, that's what."

"Why, Alec the midget meant more to me than some moth-eaten parrykeet anyday."

"It's a different thing entirely," Dixie said coldly. "A lot you understand how a woman feels."

"Aw, sugar."

"Turn loose of me, I said."

Another silence. Then Betty heard the engineer's I-give-up snicker. "Well, some can tell em and some caint, I guess."

"You said a mouthful, brother. Now blow, before I lose my poise."

When she heard him scuffing toward the door, Betty ran down the steps, around the corner of the inn, and waited while he slammed into his car and drove off. Dixie was banging chairs around inside. Then it was still. The light in the bar went out, then the single light on the pier.

The sky was thick with stars, the water lapped close to where Betty stood. In a dream, she moved slowly down to the black edge, under the shadow of the pier. She was tired in her very bones. She couldn't do anything about the thoughts that now began to lap against her in the dark, on the quiet. She was wondering how it would be, to see Harry again. It was somebody. It wasn't good for a person to be alone. Maybe she wouldn't feel ugly and dirty another time. He might be different. Maybe if she had a little something to drink first . . . A deep boat whistle groaned over the water. Somewhere, some gulls were still drifting around in the dark, she could hear their thin voices pointlessly complaining.

William Goldman

The Ice Cream Eat

They walked into Slattery's place at the usual time, ten in the evening, Flynn first, Presky right behind him. Flynn went immediately to the bar and put his foot on the rail, his chin cupped in his small hands. Presky stopped in the middle of the room. "Champagne," he bellowed. "Champagne."

Slattery moved to the beer spigot and began drawing two draughts. "Imported or domestic?" he asked.

"Give me the imported," Presky answered, advancing toward the bar. "And give some to my little friend here too, while you're at it." He slapped Flynn on the back.

"Why do you always have to slap people?" Flynn muttered. "Don't you know it stings? Don't you have any sense at all?" He was an angry looking little man with a pockmarked red face and blazing red hair that was forever falling down over his eyes.

"I'm sorry," Presky said.

"You're always sorry," Flynn told him. "Why don't you just stop slapping people?" He turned abruptly and headed for the "free lunch" counter.

"What's the matter with Artie?" Slattery asked.

"He had a bad night," Presky answered. "Got caught in a traffic jam for close to an hour without a fare. That's all."

"Oh," Slattery nodded. "How about you?"

"Good." Presky grinned. "I picked up this Park Avenoo babe about three hours ago. 'Drive,' she says, 'Just drive. I feel in the mood.' So I drove through the park for awhile and then she tells me to stop, so I stop, and then she starts making with the . . ."

"The food stinks tonight," Flynn interrupted, coming back to the bar. "All you ever have is that lousy rancid cheese. I hate rancid cheese. Sometimes I can hardly get it down."

"You can't beat the prices," Slattery said. "Isn't that right?"

"I keep hoping," Flynn mused. "Someday I figure I'll come in here and there'll be some decent stuff on the counter. Then I'd show you how to eat."

"How much could you eat?" Presky laughed. He picked Flynn up easily and set him on the bar.

Flynn reddened. "Wise guy," he said, climbing·down.

Presky laughed again. "Go on. Tell me. How much could you eat?"

Flynn blew some hair out of his eyes. "It all depends," he began. "I could put away four cube steaks easy."

"I could eat twice that," Presky said.

Flynn went on. "I don't figure half a cherry pie would be any trouble."

Presky roared. "A fine meal for a midget."

Flynn whirled on the larger man. "Boy . . . boy," he stuttered. "You're such a goddamn wise guy."

"That's right," Presky told him. "I'm pretty smart."

"Now fellas," Slattery cut in. "Let's take it easy. Go on, Flynn. Tell me. So I'll know what you like."

Flynn looked straight at Slattery. "O.K.," he said. "I'm talking to you. Just you. We're holding a private conversation."

"Absolutely," Slattery agreed.

Flynn leaned forward on his elbows, staring down at his beer. "My favorite food in all the world is shrimps," he said softly. "That's how I want to die. Eating shrimps. I could eat thirty shrimps and walk away smiling."

"I could eat sixty," Presky interrupted.

"Sixty shrimps is five pounds," Flynn said, his voice suddenly high and thin. "You think you can eat five pounds of shrimps?"

"If you can eat thirty," Presky told him. "I can eat sixty."

"You're crazy!" Flynn yelled.

"I'm a big boy," Presky laughed. "I got a big appetite."

Flynn clenched his fists and threw a punch at Presky. Presky caught it easily and held on to Flynn's hand. "Artie," he said. "Don't get mad. I'm only kidding."

Flynn jerked free. "Talk, talk, talk. All you can do is talk. Hell, my dog can eat more than you can."

"It's a bet," Presky said, holding out his hand.

"You're damn right it is," Flynn echoed. He held out his hand, then tried to pull it back, but Presky grabbed it.

"Ten bucks?" Presky asked.

"Now boys," Slattery said. "Let's take it easy."

"Ten bucks?" Presky repeated.

Finally Flynn nodded. "O.K.," he muttered. "Ten bucks. Ten bucks says Harlow can outeat you. It's a deal."

"Correct," Presky said. He stopped, looking at Flynn. "Hey, hold the phone. First we got to have some rules."

"Such as?"

"Such as what kind of food. I insist on human food." He pounded his fist on the bar. "I will not eat kibble."

"Reasonable," Flynn nodded.

"Well, what kind of human food?"

"I have to take that up with Harlow," Flynn answered.

"Fair enough," Presky said. "Whatever Harlow wants is fine with me. I'll give you the break on that."

292 STORIES FROM THE TRANSATLANTIC REVIEW

"Fine," Flynn said. "Where and when?"

"Well boys," Slattery began. "If you're bound and determined to have this thing, how about right here. Saturday night. I'll judge and supply the food."

"Why?" Flynn asked.

"Advertising. Free publicity. I'll have people here from all the bars in the neighborhood. I'll make a killing."

"Then it's settled," Flynn said. "I'll call you in an hour. After my talk with Harlow."

"Shake." Presky put out his hand.

"A man of honor don't have to shake," Flynn replied, and head held high, he turned and left the bar . . .

But once outside, alone in the cool evening, Flynn's shoulders sagged. Shaking his head slowly, talking softly to himself, he walked home, scuffing his shoes on the sidewalk as he went, stopping only once, at the corner delicatessen, for a loaf of bread, some eggs, and a pint of ice cream.

When he reached his building he paused and peered up four flights to the open window. "Pssst, Harlow," he whispered. "I'm home."

Instantly, Harlow's head appeared in the window. "You have a good day?" Flynn asked. Harlow growled softly. "You glad to see me?" Harlow barked. "I'll be right up," Flynn said, hurrying inside. He checked his mail box quickly, found it empty, inserted his key in the front door, pushed it open, and started the long walk up to his room.

Harlow was scratching on the door when he got there. "No, Harlow," Flynn said. "Mustn't do." Opening the door he laughed out loud as Harlow came leaping at him, growling, licking his face.

Setting his groceries in the sink, Flynn closed the door and picked Harlow up. "We got to have us a serious talk," he said. "Very important. Harlow, what do you like to eat? What can you eat the most of?" Flynn opened the icebox door and took out a carrot. "Here, boy," he urged. "Eat this." Harlow sniffed and turned away. Throwing the carrot back, Flynn took out a head of lettuce. Again Harlow sniffed and turned away. Sadly, Flynn shook his head. "Harlow," he said, "I guess you're just not a vegetable man. And that's a shame. 'Cause Presky ain't too happy with vegetables either." He sighed. "Oh baby. He'll murder you on meat."

The telephone rang. Putting Harlow down, Flynn went to answer it. "Artie Flynn here," he said.

"Hello, Artie? This is Slattery."

"I ain't decided on the food yet, Slattery. But you can tell that tub Presky that he better stock up on rhubarb, because my man just ate a pound of it like it was nothing."

"I didn't call about that, Artie. It's just that Presky says he feels kind of low about tricking you into this and he says for me to tell you that if you want to call it off, it's O.K. with him."

"Haw," Flynn said. "You tell him nothing doing."

"You sure?"

"After watching my man put away a whole pound of rhubarb, you can say I'm completely confident. My man cannot lose."

There was a long pause on the other end of the line. Flynn waited nervously. Then Slattery started talking again. "Sorry, Artie, but I had to get pencil and paper. I need some information."

"For what?"

"Publicity. Now, how old is Harlow?"

"Nine years," Flynn admitted.

"Isn't that kind of old?"

"He's nine years old but full of fight. Put that in."

"What kind of dog?"

"All kinds."

"Weight?"

"How do I know? Thirty. Maybe forty pounds."

"Height?"

"Slattery, you writing a book? I don't know. He's short but well built. Maybe eighteen inches. Always in perfect condition."

"O.K., Artie. We're waiting for your call."

"You go tell Presky that rhubarb looks like a winner."

"I did. He says he loves rhubarb."

"Oh." Slowly, Flynn hung up. "That pig Presky," he moaned. "He's probably eating kibble right now, trying to trick me. Harlow," he called.

Harlow did not come. Going to the kitchen, Flynn saw Harlow perched on the sink. The bag of groceries was ripped open. The bread and the eggs were untouched. Harlow was wagging his tail furiously, bouncing up and down.

And the ice cream was gone . . .

At 9:30 on Saturday evening Flynn approached Slattery's place, Harlow walking obediently a few paces behind. Stopping outside, Flynn gaped. For there, taped against the inside of Slattery's window, was an enormous, hand-painted sign.

"BIG ICE CREAM EAT" it proclaimed. And, in letters equally as large, "HERE, SATURDAY NIGHT, 9:30 P.M." Eagerly, Flynn read the rest of it:

Felix Presky, 37 years old, 6 foot 5, 240 pounds
VS
Harlow, 9 years old, 1 foot 6, 40 pounds

Nodding, Flynn picked Harlow up and walked in.

A roar went up from the mob waiting inside and Flynn stopped by the door, staring. The room was jammed. More than 100 men stood packed tight together, forming a close semicircle around the bar. Flynn was turning for the door when he felt a hand on his shoulder.

"What a night, what a night," Slattery said. Flynn looked at him. Slattery was wearing a top hat, a fight referee's shirt and tuxedo pants. "You ever see such a crowd?" he yelled. "Huh, Artie, huh?"

Flynn shook his head.

"Hell," Slattery went on. "There's been more than two hundred bucks bet already. Some of the boys figured you wouldn't show."

Flynn snorted. "Let 'em worry about Presky. Is he here?"

Slattery nodded and took Flynn by the arm, leading him toward the bar. "C'mon," he said. "Everyone wants a look at your man. Honest to God, Artie. They're here from every bar on the block. All the other places are empty. Isn't that something?"

Flynn set Harlow on the bar and an appreciative murmur went up from the crowd. "He's kind of small," somebody said.

"But a bear in competition," Slattery answered.

"I don't know," a voice said, and everybody stopped talking and looked to the end of the bar. It was Pop Nomelini's voice, and they all waited. Pop Nomelini was a mainstay at the Red Horse Inn two doors down, and, at the age of 76, had the reputation of being the finest weight for age drinker in the city. "I seen a St. Bernard in French Morocco once that eat half a cow." Again there was murmuring. "Course, he was bigger than this one." Pop Nomelini indicated Harlow. "But I say this one's got a damn good chance."

"Betting is officially open," Slattery shouted over the noise. "Both parties showed."

Another roar went up as Presky suddenly appeared at the very back of the bar and began making his way through the crowd. Presky was wearing a red sweatshirt, faded khaki pants and an old pair of army boots. Flynn watched him as he approached, towering over the others. Then he looked at Harlow, standing nervously on the bar. For a moment, he closed his eyes.

Slattery scrambled up atop the bar, frantically waving for silence. "A few rules," he shouted. "Just so everything's clear." The crowd quieted. "As you all know," Slattery went on, "this here is an ice cream eat. The ice cream is vanilla. Sauce is optional."

Flynn spoke up. "We're going plain."

"Same here," Presky said.

Slattery set a plate and a spoon in front of Presky. "You bring your own?" he asked Flynn. Flynn nodded and set an oblong tin dish beside the plate. "The one who eats the most wins," Slattery finished. "Are there any questions?"

"One," Pop Nomelini said. "Just one thing I want to know. Is this a speed eat or an endurance eat?"

"The ice cream will be brought out in pints," Slattery answered. "Five minutes allowed for each pint, with a two minute rest period in between, after which a new pint will be brought out. Both contestants must finish in five minutes. That way the dog will not be able to let it melt and then lick it up. Is that clear?" Presky and Flynn nodded.

"That dog looks better and better to me," Pop Nomelini cried. "Five on the dog."

"We're almost ready to start," Slattery announced, looking at the clock high on one wall. His words were the signal for near pandemonium as money suddenly began appearing all over the room. Pop Nomelini was screaming about the St. Bernard and French Morocco. A fight almost started over in one corner. The noise was tremendous.

Then it stopped. Suddenly.

Big Greco and Little Greco shouldered their way into the room and everyone stood quietly, watching them as they pushed and shoved until they stood in the front row, right next to the contestants.

Big Greco and Little Greco were identical twins, the same in every way, except that Big Greco had been born first. Large, muscular men with jet black hair, they almost never left Gulkins Saloon, where they alternated as bouncer and bartender.

"I hear there's an eat going on," Big Greco said.

"Yes, yes, that's right," Slattery said nervously. "There certainly is. Right now. You're just in time."

"That the dog?" Little Greco asked. Slattery nodded. "What's its name?"

"Harlow," Flynn answered.

"Dumb name for a dog," Little Greco said.

"Once it was Jean Harlow," Presky explained. "Until Artie found out it wasn't a girl."

With that, the bar exploded into raucous laughter, and Flynn, redder than ever, turned away. Presky grabbed him. "Shouldn't I have said that, Artie?"

"You go to hell, you dumb tub," Flynn muttered.

"Oh, Artie," Presky said over the laughter. "I'm sorry."

Finally, the bar quieted and the ice cream was brought out. Presky raised his spoon. Flynn patted Harlow and spoke to him soothingly.

"I like the dog," Big Greco said.

"You got him." Little Greco said.

Slattery pushed the ice cream out of the white pint containers. Then he glanced at the clock. "Go!" he shouted. "And may the best man win."

Presky dug immediately, taking large spoonfuls in a smooth even rhythm. "Lookit that motion," Little Greco roared. "I got me a winner."

Harlow began slowly, first sniffing the ice cream, walking slowly around his tin dish. Then he started, taking small bites around the perimeter before attacking the center. "That dog is part St. Bernard," Pop Nomelini shouted. "Five more on the dog." Betting continued heavy, with Presky the decided favorite, sometimes by as much as four to one. He justified the odds by finishing the first pint a full minute before Harlow.

During the rest period, Presky jumped up and down, smiling confidently. "Attago Presky," somebody shouted. Flynn pulled a towel from his belt and gently rubbed Harlow. "You're my dog," he whispered. "Yes you are." Harlow licked him once, then took a short stroll along the bar.

Slattery put the second pints in the dishes and they began to eat. Presky, obviously enjoying himself, showed no signs of slowing up. Then, halfway through, a roar went up from the crowd as Harlow stopped eating. But Flynn pointed his nose back toward the dish, and Harlow finished the second pint.

At the two pint rest period, the betting grew heavier. The odds on Presky went way up, and one old man over in a corner was giving nine to one. Flynn gently put his hands on Harlow's stomach. It was bulging. "You got to do it," he whispered. "You just got to."

The third pint had the fastest time of all. Presky, his motion working flawlessly, appeared almost to have increased his speed as he gulped the ice cream down, a smile fixed on his face. But Harlow also seemed stronger than ever, having gained a second wind, and he finished the pint without a pause.

"That dog is a winner," Pop Nomelini shouted. "You can take my word. That dog can go all night."

"He better," Big Greco warned. "If he knows what's good for him."

The odds on Presky suddenly dipped, and it was obvious that his pride was hurt. Grimacing once, he pounded his spoon on the bar, awaiting the fourth pint. Flynn massaged Harlow's stomach, which was now bigger than ever. "You got him worried," he whispered. "Yes you do. He's caving in."

Halfway through the fourth pint, the crowd groaned. Presky had faltered; there was no denying it. A huge mound of ice cream rested in midair on his spoon, and Presky could only stare at it, shaking his head.

"Finish it up, you slob," Little Greco said.

Presky turned and faced him. "Keep your advice," he said. "I'm pacing myself." But it was obvious to the crowd that Presky was tiring.

But so was Harlow. Once, he tried sitting down on the bar and it took all of Flynn's urging to keep him on his feet. "Keep going," Flynn pleaded. "You just got to."

After the fourth pint, a small Italian man began taking bets that neither would be able to finish the fifth. "It looks bad," Pop Nomelini admitted. "My man looks all washed up."

The fifth pint was agony. Presky, his face almost the color of the ice cream, had to strain each time he lifted his spoon. Where before he had chewed the ice cream and swallowed it, now he was content merely to let it sit inside his mouth, where it melted and slid down.

But Harlow was in worse shape. His eyes closed, he could barely nibble at the white mound before him. Sometimes he only licked it with his tongue.

Presky, in a sudden frenzy, managed two quick spoonfuls, and his plate was empty. A sickly smile on his face, he turned and looked at Harlow. Harlow was dreadfully weak, hardly able to stand. Flynn, tears in his eyes, stood proudly beside him, his hands clenched together, the knuckles white.

It was obvious to everyone in the room that Harlow was going on heart alone.

"Slap that mutt," Big Greco roared. "Get him moving."

After four minutes and forty-two seconds, Harlow managed to lick the last particle of ice cream from the dish. Wearily, he tried to lie down.

As Slattery slid the sixth pints out of their containers the tension was tremendous. Everyone was yelling, jumping up and down, clapping hands in a wild rhythm.

Presky, feebly trying to smile, lifted his spoon and dug out a huge mound of ice cream. Raising it to eye level, he stared at it. The weight was too much and he dropped the spoon on the bar. "I'm done," Presky muttered, and he stretched out full length on the floor, groaning audibly.

"We got him!" Big Greco yelled. "Go you mutt! Go!"

Flynn looked down at his dog. "You done beautifully," he whispered. "You're my dog. Yes you are."

Game to the core, Harlow approached his tin dish and studied the enormous mound of ice cream. Then, with a grunt, he lay down and rolled over on his back, his feet sticking up in the air.

Slattery fought his way atop the bar and shouted for silence. He pointed to Presky, lying on the floor. He pointed to Harlow, lying on the bar. "Could anything be more obvious?" he said. "The match is a draw."

Disappointed, the crowd buzzed softly. "It was a good fight," Pop Nomelini sighed. "Fair and square."

Then Big Greco stepped clear of the others. He scowled at Harlow and at Flynn, bent over his dog, whispering. "That dog got no guts," Big Greco said.

Flynn straightened. "You better take that back," he said. "He almost killed himself."

"That dog," Big Greco laughed. "He got no guts."

With a cry, Flynn ran at him. Stepping aside, Big Greco caught him in a bear hug and squeezed. Then, with a push, he sent Flynn flying backward against the bar. Flynn landed with a crash, the air knocked out of him. Slowly, he sank to his knees, helpless. There was no noise in the bar.

Then Felix Presky was on his feet, roaring. "That dog got more guts that anyone in this room." With that, he swung.

His giant fist crashed down on the side of Big Greco's jaw. Big Greco half pivoted, stopped, and crumpled to the floor.

"Hey," Little Greco said. "Nobody does that."

"My mistake," Presky told him. He slashed Little Greco in the stomach with the edge of his hand. As Little Greco bent over, Presky met him with a tremendous punch on the cheek, and suddenly Little Greco lay beside his brother.

Bending down, Presky grabbed them by their belts and dragged them to the door, dropping them on the sidewalk outside. "O.K.," he announced. "Any other comments about the dog?" There were none. The bar was emptying rapidly.

Presky ran over and lifted Flynn to his feet. "You O.K., Artie?"

"In a little," Flynn said softly.

Presky looked down at Harlow. "You're a good dog," he whispered. "Yes you are."

"Ah," Slattery said, coming up from under the bar. "But it was a fine night. The till is full. My pockets are bulging. Can I buy you a beer?"

Presky picked Flynn up and set him on the bar. "For me and my little friend here," he said. Flynn nodded happily. "And maybe I'll have a little something to go with it," Presky went on, walking toward the "free lunch" counter. "Just to help wash it down."

"Oh that Presky," Flynn said, full of admiration, cradling Harlow in his arms. "That is a man who can eat."

"Some rancid cheese, Artie?" Presky called to him.

Flynn smiled. "Don't mind if I do," he said.

Biographical Notes

ASA BABER JR. was born in Chicago and educated at Princeton University. He has taught in Illinois and spent three years on the staff of Robert College, Istanbul. He has recently published a novel, *The Land of a Million Elephants.*

JOHN BANVILLE is a young Irish writer who makes his home in Dublin. His work has appeared in various Irish publications. "Summer Voices", his first story to appear outside Ireland, is included in *Long Lankin,* a collection of his stories recently published in England.

PAUL BOWLES is the author of three novels, *The Sheltering Sky, Let It Come Down, The Spider's House* and a collection of short stories, *The Delicate Prey.* Mr. Bowles has lived abroad for many years, in Latin America, on an island off the coast of Ceylon, and in Morocco. He is also a well-known composer and has garnered for the Library of Congress one of the largest collections of recordings of native North African music. Mr. Bowles was born in New York City in 1911.

MALCOLM BRADBURY's "The Adult Education Class" is an excerpt from his first novel, *Eating People Is Wrong.* Other works include a novel, *Stepping Westward,* two collections of humorous articles from *Punch* and *The New Yorker,* and various critical books. He presently teaches English and American literature at the University of East Anglia in Norwich, England. Mr. Bradbury was born in Sheffield, England in 1932, is married and is the father of two boys.

PAUL BRESLOW makes his home in New York City. He was once a movie critic and has recently completed a film about *Incwala* (kingship ceremony) in Swaziland. Mr. Breslow has a law degree from Columbia University, has contributed to many publications and is presently completing a novel about mongooses.

THOMAS BRIDGES, a native New Yorker, was educated in Texas and has lived in San Francisco's Haight-Ashbury. The young writer's work has appeared in various little magazines and underground newspapers. The opening line of the novel he is completing: "I am a guerrilla."

JEROME CHARYN's four novels are *American Scrapbook, Going to Jerusalem, On the Darkening Green* and *Once Upon a Droshky*. "Sing, Shaindele, Sing" is included in a collection of his stories, *The Man Who Grew Younger*. Mr. Charyn is founding editor of the *Dutton Review* and teaches contemporary literature at Lehman College of the City University of New York, the city in which he was born in 1937.

ALFRED CHESTER, an expatriate for a number of years, was born in Brooklyn in 1928. He has published two novels, *Jamie Is My Heart's Desire* and *The Exquisite Corpse* and a collection of short stories, *Behold Goliath*. His stories, essays and reviews have appeared in a number of publications.

AUSTIN C. CLARKE's three books are *The Survivors of the Crossing, Amongst Thistles and Thorns* and *The Meeting Point*. Now a lecturer at Yale University, Mr. Clarke was born in Barbados, British West Indies, and has lived in Toronto.

WALTER CLEMONS has published a short story collection, *The Poison Tree and Other Stories*. Born in Houston, Texas in 1929, Mr. Clemons is now an editor of *The New York Times Book Review*.

IRVIN FAUST has just published a new novel, *The File on Stanley Paton Bucta*. His short stories have appeared in a number of publications; "The World's Fastest Human" is included in a book collection, *Roar, Lion Roar*. His first novel was *The Steagle*. Mr. Faust was born in Brooklyn in 1928 and educated at Columbia University.

EDWARD FRANKLIN's "Girl in a White Dress" is an extract from his new novel, *Behind the Monkey Tree*. His first novel, *It's Cold in Pongo-Ni*, was published in 1965. A native Californian, Mr. Franklin lives with his wife in Berkeley, where he produces a children's educational radio program.

BRUCE JAY FRIEDMAN has published two novels, *Stern* and *A Mother's Kisses* and two collections of short stories, *Black Angels* and *Far From the City of Class*. His first play, *Scuba Duba*, had a long New York run of 704 performances. Mr. Friedman was born in New York City in 1930.

GEORGE GARRETT, a poetry editor of the *Transatlantic Review*, has written 12 books including four collections of short stories, four volumes of poetry, three novels, and a children's play. His latest works are *A Wreath for Garibaldi* (short stories), *Do, Lord, Remember Me* (novel) and *For a Bitter Season: New & Selected Poems*. Mr. Garrett was born in Florida in 1929 and is currently Professor of English at Hollins College, Virginia. He has taught at one time or another at Rice, Princeton, Wesleyan and the University of Virginia.

PENELOPE GILLIATT has published two novels, *One by One* and *A State of Change,* and a collection of short stories, *Come Back If It Doesn't Get Better.* Born in London, Miss Gilliatt was brought up in Northumberland. A former film critic for the *London Sunday Observer,* Miss Gilliatt now makes her home in New York City and is a film critic for *The New Yorker.*

WILLIAM GOLDMAN, a former editor of the *Transatlantic Review,* lives in New York City with his wife Ilene and their two young daughters, Jenny and Susanna. He has written six novels including *The Temple of Gold* and *Boys and Girls Together,* movie scripts including *Harper* and has co-authored two plays including *Blood, Sweat, and Stanley Poole.* Mr. Goldman was born in Chicago in 1931.

HUGH ALLYN HUNT's "Acme Rooms and Sweet Marjorie Russell" was Mr. Hunt's first published story; it won *Transatlantic's* Third Annual Short Story Contest and was chosen for *The Best American Short Stories 1967.* Born in Nebraska, Mr. Hunt lives in a small Mexican village and is art editor of an English-language newspaper in Guadalajara, where he frequently exhibits his paintings. He is presently completing a novel set in Mexico, a book of poems and a series of articles on youthful revolution in Latin America.

MORRIS LURIE was born in Melbourne, Australia in 1938. He has published two novels, *Rappaport* and *The London Jungle Adventures of Charlie Hope,* and a collection of stories, *Happy Times.* His latest book is for children, *The 27th Annual African Hippopotamus Race.* Mr. Lurie lives with his wife in London.

JOHN MCPHEE's published books include *Levels of the Game, A Roomful of Hovings, The Pine Barrens, The Headmaster, Oranges, A Sense of Where You Are* and *The Crofter and the Laird.* Mr. McPhee was born in Princeton, N.J. and was educated at Princeton University and Magdalene College, Cambridge.

NORMA MEACOCK was born in Birmingham, England in 1934 and lives in London with her writer husband Peter Fryer and their three children. Miss Meacock has published a novel, *Thinking Girl,* and has had three short stories in *Transatlantic.*

LEONARD MICHAELS has recently published a collection of short stories, *Going Places.* His stories have appeared in various magazines and he was awarded the *Massachusetts Review* Quill Award twice, an O. Henry award, and a prize from the National Foundation on the Arts and Humanities. Mr. Michaels has taught at the Universities of California and Michigan.

HARRY D. MILLER's novels are *The Great Sweet Days of Old Shibui* and *Fathers and Dreamers*. Mr. Miller lives in Kingsville, Ohio in an 1815 mill house with a private waterfall as high as a four-story building. Mr. Miller, who studied at the University of Michigan, teaches English at a local high school and is completing a new novel.

VIRGINIA MORICONI is an American who makes her home in Rome. "Simple Arithmetic" was chosen for *The Best American Short Stories 1964* and has appeared in high school and college anthologies in the United States, the United Kingdom, and Sweden; the story has also been broadcast several times on Italian Radio, 3rd Program. Miss Moriconi has published a novel, *The Distant Trojans,* and a translation from the Italian, *The Deserter* by Giuseppe Dessi.

JAY NEUGEBOREN published his first short story in the *Transatlantic Review* when he was 25 years old. Since then he has had a number of stories in the magazine, has published two novels, *Big Man* and *Listen Ruben Fontanez,* a collection of short stories, *Corky's Brother and Other Stories* and has had stories chosen for *The Best American Short Stories* and *Prize Stories, The O. Henry Awards.*

JOYCE CAROL OATES is a young writer who has published seven books including *A Garden of Earthly Delights, Expensive People, Them* and *Anonymous Sins* (poems). Her numerous short stories have appeared in *The Best American Short Stories, Prize Stories, The O. Henry Awards* and magazines, large and small. Miss Oates was born in Lockport, New York in 1938. She now lives in Windsor, Ontario, where she is Associate Professor of English at the University of Windsor.

V. S. PRITCHETT, short story writer, novelist, critic and traveler, has published numerous works. He is a director of *The New Statesman* and has been a life-long contributor. *The Living Novel and Later Appreciations* is his collection of critical essays from *The New Statesman.* His novels include *Mr. Beluncle, Dead Man Leading* and *The Key to My Heart.* His travel books include *The Offensive Traveler, London Perceived* and *Dublin: A Portrait. The Sailor and the Saint* and *When My Girl Comes Home* are short story collections. Mr. Pritchett was born in England in 1900 and lives with his wife in London.

SHIRLEY SCHOONOVER's "The Star Blanket" was chosen for *Prize Stories 1962: The O. Henry Awards;* another story was chosen in 1964. Miss Schoonover's novel, *Mountain of Winter,* was nominated for a 1966 Pulitzer Prize in fiction. A recent novel, *Sam's Song,* is being made into a film. Miss Schoonover was born in a Finnish-American community in Minnesota in 1939 and now lives in Lincoln, Nebraska.

ALAN SILLITOE's published works include *Saturday Night and Sunday Morning, Key to the Door, The Ragman's Daughter, Death of William Posters, A Tree on Fire* (novels), *The Loneliness of the Long Distance Runner* and *Guzman Go Home* (short stories), and three volumes of poetry. Mr. Sillitoe was born in Nottingham, England in 1928 and now lives in Kent. He travels extensively and devotes time to his hobby of maps-topography.

DANIEL SPICEHANDLER's novels are *Let My Right Hand Wither* and *Burnt Offering.* He is completing a new novel and has had short stories and some poems published in various magazines. Mr. Spicehandler was born in New York City and at one time taught at City College. He now lives permanently in Paris.

WILLIAM TREVOR was born in County Cork, Ireland in 1928 and presently lives in London. His novels include *Standard of Behaviour, The Old Boys, The Boarding House* and *The Love Department.* He has published a short story collection, *The Day We Got Drunk on Cake* and his plays include *The Elephants Foot, The Girl, A Night with Mrs. Da Tanka* and *57th Saturday.*

FRANK TUOHY was born in Cambridge, England in 1925, and has been lecturing in English at foreign universities for a number of years. He has published three novels, *The Ice Saints, The Warm Nights of January, The Animal Game,* and any number of short stories, including a book collection called *The Admiral and the Nuns,* which includes "At Home with the Colonel." Mr. Tuohy is the recipient of the James Tait Black Memorial Prize for *The Ice Saints* and the Katherine Mansfield Menton Short Story Prize.

JOHN UPDIKE is the author of 12 books, five of which are novels, the latest one being *Couples.* His numerous short stories and poems have appeared in various collections and magazines. Mr. Updike was born in Shillington, Pa. in 1932.

JEAN-CLAUDE VAN ITALLIE was once an editor of the *Transatlantic Review.* He is a playwright whose successful off-Broadway *America Hurrah* has been produced in some 10 countries. His many plays, including *The Serpent, War* and *Almost Like Being* have been widely produced off-Broadway, off-off-Broadway and on educational television. Mr. van Itallie was born in Brussels in 1936, grew up in Great Neck, N.Y. and graduated from Harvard. He lives in New York City and Charlemont, Mass.

SOL YURICK's novels include *The Warriors, Fertig* and *The Bag.* He has had six stories in *Transatlantic* and has published in other little magazines. "The Siege" is included in a new collection of his stories,

Someone Just Like You. Mr. Yurick was born in New York City in 1925 and presently lives in Brooklyn where he "works with a network of people and an information-retrieval system which proves that the computers are in the wrong hands."